PRAISE FOR THE AUTHOR

Lethal Code

"Taut, tense, and provocative, this frighteningly knowing cyber-thriller will keep you turning pages—not only to devour the fast-paced fiction, but to worry about how much is terrifyingly true."

—Hank Phillippi Ryan, author of *Truth Be Told*, and winner of the Agatha, Anthony, and Mary Higgins Clark Awards

"*Lethal Code* is not just an outstanding, harrowing thriller about a massive cyberattack against the United States, it is based on the very real cyber threats we face today and should serve as a wake-up call to all Americans. As the president and CEO of a cybersecurity firm, I can tell you that Waite has done his homework."

—Corey Thomas, President and CEO of Rapid7

"*Lethal Code* is a compelling and well-researched thriller about a major cyberattack against America. Waite's characters bring to life the very real cyber vulnerabilities we face every day and demonstrate that America's cyber insecurity is a serious national security issue."

—Melissa Hathaway, President of Hathaway Global Strategies, and former cyber advisor to Presidents George W. Bush and Barack H. Obama

"No matter what you do or where you live, a massive cyberattack against the United States will impact your life. That's what Waite demonstrates so convincingly in *Lethal Code*. He shows us the effect a hit to the country's solar plexus would have with a tale that will leave you gasping for days, whether you're a business person or a private citizen concerned about our nation's defense vulnerabilities."

—David DeWalt, Chairma   n FireEye

Terminal Value

"I believe with time he will be called the John Grisham of the murderous technology novels. This is an excellent beginning to, what I hope is, a long writing career for Mr. Waite."

—*Literary R & R*

"Thomas Waite opens a window into the world of technology that even a technophobe can appreciate. Filled with tension, romance, humor, mystery, and avarice, *Terminal Value* is a captivating tale that holds your interest right through to its surprising conclusion."

—David Updike, author of *Old Girlfriends: Stories* and *Out on the Marsh*

"*Terminal Value* is to the corporate world what John Grisham's *The Firm* is to lawyering: a taut, fast, relentless thriller. A most impressive debut novel."

—Jim Champy, co-author of *Reengineering the Corporation* and author of *Outsmart!*

"*Terminal Value* is a sizzling thriller convincingly set in the world of emerging technologies that even industry insiders will appreciate. Thomas Waite has earned the right to belly up to the bar with the likes of Brad Meltzer, Scott Turow, and David Baldacci. A great read!"

—Paul Carroll, author and Pulitzer Prize–nominated *Wall Street Journal* editor and journalist

TRIDENT CODE

BY THOMAS WAITE

Lana Elkins Thrillers
Lethal Code
Trident Code

Terminal Value

TRIDENT CODE

THOMAS WAITE

47NORTH

Published by 47North, Seattle

www.apub.com

Amazon, the Amazon logo, and 47North are trademarks of Amazon.com, Inc., or its affiliates.

ISBN-13: 9781477828403
ISBN-10: 1477828400

Cover design by Stewart Williams

Library of Congress Control Number: 2014957278

Printed in the United States of America

*To the men and women whose unstinting efforts
to defend citizens against potentially devastating
cyberattacks should be applauded every day.*

IN 2014, THE PENTAGON RELEASED A REPORT ASSERTING DECISIVELY THAT CLIMATE CHANGE POSES AN IMMEDIATE THREAT TO NATIONAL SECURITY, WITH INCREASED RISKS FROM TERRORISM, INFECTIOUS DISEASE, GLOBAL POVERTY, AND FOOD SHORTAGES.

Former U.S. Defense Secretary Chuck Hagel: "Defense leaders must be part of this global discussion. We must be clear-eyed about the security threats presented by climate change, and we must be proactive in addressing them."

We ignore this report—and the former defense secretary's warning—at our peril.

AUTHOR'S NOTE

Since the writing of *Lethal Code*, the world has witnessed an ever-increasing number of cyberattacks aimed at governments, corporations, and individuals. While the books in my Lana Elkins series are works of fiction, most of the cyberattack vulnerabilities and cyberwar scenarios are based on facts.

PROLOGUE

DR. BRIAN AHEARN PULLED into his four-door garage, taking the spacious slot reserved for his Beemer between his wife's silver Mercedes SUV and his summer car, a yellow Porsche 911 Carrera Cabriolet. The perks, he reminded himself, of a job well done.

He cut his headlights and moved to click the big door shut, but stopped to look in his rearview mirror at the sunset's startling rose tint, the color of blood on a microscope slide. Years ago, in his undergraduate days at Brown, Brian had looked at many of those red splotches before deciding that pre-med wasn't for him.

And a fine move that had proved to be. He'd switched to computer engineering and found a job with a lot more challenge—and considerably less gore.

Until today.

But what did the chisel-chinned, sandy-haired Harvard professor know of grisliness as he watched the door roll down behind him? Nothing, in short.

At that very instant his ears began to ring. He paid no mind till it occurred to him—a very odd thought, he realized at once—that it might be the body's own alarm system. A feral instinct trying to protect him, like the hairs on one's neck coming alive under the insistent gaze of a stranger.

He was too much of a scientist to believe in a sixth sense, but too much of a husband and father to ignore it. He had to go into his house. Marla would be there. So would his four-year-old twin girls, the little loves of his life. It was pizza night, his daughters' favorite. His, too, he pretended.

Right then he told himself to pretend that he was not afraid. *Open the damn door.*

As he entered his access code into the garage's security panel, he caught the comforting scent of roasting mozzarella and pizza dough.

"Hello, I'm home," he called.

He hung up his coat, listening intently. He heard nothing, just the strange ringing in his ears. But four-year-olds are not silent. It's not in their nature. Certainly not Eva or Erica, unless they were sleeping. And they wouldn't be napping at 5:15 on a Friday afternoon. If they weren't racing around, they would be watching the sixty-inch screen, or playing computer games, or imploring their mother to read to them. *Something.* Not this . . . absence.

The first cold drip of perspiration streaked down his spine. It was the only one he would notice.

"Marla," he called out. "Eva, Erica?"

He rushed into their spacious kitchen, finding immediate relief in the custom pizza oven at work, offering its glassy view of the treat within.

Brian took a breath, freed now of his irrational fear, finding normalcy in pizza night proceeding apace. He hadn't been that spooked since he was old enough to stop checking for a bogeyman under his bed.

Marla must have been giving them a bath. He looked at his watch again. *Of course she is.*

And on any other evening, she would have been.

He cracked the oven, sniffing the cheese and tomato sauce, oregano and basil, green peppers and mushrooms, and for the first few seconds the scents pleased him, making him feel as warm as the crust gently browning before his eyes.

Truth be told, Brian would have liked it even better if there were pepperoni on his pizza, even the vegan variety, although the latter would have been at odds with everything Marla had held dear about the family's diet. She had always been firmly opposed to "priming" the girls for meat eating by offering them soy in any of its carnivorous impersonations.

He had to sneak his meat. He and a professor in MIT's math department scooted off together for "Hamburger Wednesdays" at Tasty Burger in Harvard Square. Both their spouses would have considered their clandestine affairs with hamburgers to be culinary slumming. His midweek lunch was only one of many secrets Brian kept from Marla. He kept even more from his colleagues.

He turned from the oven and saw the chopping block wiped clean, just the way the fastidious Marla always left it . . . except for the cleaver with its thick dark handle. It lay a foot away with fresh red smears—worse, far worse, than anything he'd ever seen on a slide. Then he noticed the spatters on the counter and cabinets, so vivid he could not help imagining the red spray, as if the cleaver were at work *right now.* And there was Marla's engagement diamond, in its exquisite setting, gleaming on the tile counter. Her gold band stood on its side inches away, as if awaiting her finger to slip inside.

Finger?

"Oh, no," he murmured, for his eyes were roaming past the chopping block to the tile where Marla's ring finger lay in a pool of blood.

His Adam's apple moved. Only then did he realize he was fighting an eruption of bile. His hand slipped a Wüsthof chef knife from its polished wooden perch on the counter.

He wanted to back away, retreat through the door he'd just entered and run down the street. But he couldn't: *Marla, Eva, Erica.*

Shamed by his own fright, Brian had to force himself to take the first step; already he felt sentenced to death.

Before reaching the living room, he spotted a tall bulky man in black overalls and a black ski mask standing on the inside of the wide passageway, and realized that he must have been watching him the entire time. Startled, Brian raised the knife.

The man shook his head patiently. Didn't even point his black pistol at him. Didn't need to. Brian simply dropped the blade. He was no match. He knew it even then. The point stuck in the floor and the handle shuddered, as if a sudden chill had swept through the house.

"Keep coming," the gunman said.

Two more men, also masked and fully attired in black, sat forward on a long cinnamon-colored couch as Brian made his way past original oils by renowned contemporaries and over hand-loomed carpets that he and Marla had purchased on vacations in the Middle East and Asia.

He found his wife sitting between the pair of masked men. Her mouth was duct-taped, eyes wet and red. So was one of her bloody, gauze-covered hands. Brian realized she was in shock, pained beyond any bounds she had ever known.

He tried to rush to her side. The behemoth with the gun— trailing silently behind him—grabbed Brian's arm. His strength was enormous.

"The girls?" Brian asked, terrified. He realized he was begging. The fear he'd known in the garage had returned—with good reason. "Where are they?"

No one answered. Not with words. Not yet.

The shorter of the two men on the couch rose, telling Brian to sit next to his wife. "Hold her hand." It sounded like he was smiling. Brian couldn't tell through the ski mask.

He walked over to Marla, who did not raise her eyes to him. Her long hair had fallen forward, crowding her fine features, blocking most of her eyes and the corners of her mouth. Red streaks tinged the left side of her handsome blonde cut, as though she'd tried to push it out of her face and failed.

She fell against him, sobbing behind the gag of gray tape.

"Are the girls all right?" Brian asked the short man, who appeared to be in charge. Despite his height, he looked strong: thick in the legs, torso, and neck, like a hard-core bodybuilder.

"They're fine," he told him. "Tied up at the moment."

"Promise?" Brian asked from what he recognized was a position of complete weakness. But he was wrong.

"They are right now, but they won't be if you don't cooperate with us."

Brian didn't need to ask. He knew they wanted his work on Ambient Air Capture, AAC, the Holy Grail of geoengineering, which used technology to fight climate change. AAC extracted carbon dioxide directly from the atmosphere. But unlike previous AAC efforts—puny in their impact—Brian's prototype, built in his home lab, removed massive amounts of CO2 efficiently.

But he'd had to go rogue to do it. The American Oil Producers Association, AOPA, had insisted that he work for them in secret. The race to perfect AAC was so fierce among so many scientists and engineers that they'd wanted only a tight handful of men at the very top tier of their association to know where they'd placed most of their research money.

AOPA, along with the rest of the fossil-fuel industry, stood to make trillions from Brian's work, for it would permit carbon fuels to be burned forever—and the industry's massive profits to continue—because the heat-absorbing CO2 molecules spinning wildly into the atmosphere could be reclaimed by Brian's invention, along with the carbon dioxide that had been up there several hundreds of thousands of years.

In malevolent hands, AAC could create an ice age or turn the earth into an oven. More responsible parties could use AAC to reduce global temperatures to what they had been at the dawn of the Industrial Revolution, when massive amounts of carbon started getting pumped out of smokestacks. Regardless, whatever CO2 was removed could be turned into carbon monoxide, CO, and combined with hydrogen to produce hydrocarbons, including gas and jet fuels.

Work on AAC had begun in earnest with the development of artificial trees that could be placed anywhere; they did not have to be at the end of a factory exhaust pipe for Direct Air Capture, DAC. In fact, with the lower concentration of carbon dioxide in cleaner air, the "trees" were not overburdened with all the other noxious gases coming from factories or power plants. That made their most important task—capturing CO2—easier. AAC also addressed the nettlesome challenge of collecting carbon dioxide from widely dispersed sources, most notably from the transportation industry.

Dr. Ahearn's great achievement was to invent highly engineered catalysts that turned CO2 into carbon monoxide at much faster rates than ever before, and much more cheaply. Because CO and hydrogen formed the chief components of petroleum and natural gas, Dr. Ahearn was making possible the recycling of CO2 into the very fuels that produced the greenhouse gas in the first place.

From the waste that now threatened to toast the planet would come wonder. AAC in Brian's hands would become a perpetual money machine for the fossil-fuel industry. And that would make him a billionaire many times over.

So Brian had agreed to AOPA's insistence on secrecy, even coming to behave as if the idea had been his all along, lording it over them by saying that capturing carbon dioxide from the air was strictly his until he said he was ready. He'd felt like Superman. But now it seemed that the oil producers were exerting their power in the cruelest way imaginable.

Brian was so wrong, so simplistic in his understanding of what was actually happening right before his eyes.

"We've stolen your hard drive," the short muscular man said. "Now we want your external hard drive." He pointed to a framed bright-green finger painting by Eva, the firstborn twin. It hung on a wall less than ten feet away. "Take that down and open the safe behind it. You were no better at protecting your files than you were at protecting your family. If you want your little girls to live, you'll open that safe."

But what about Marla? And me?

"You're an intelligent man, Dr. Ahearn," the short man went on. "You must see that we really won't stop at anything. We thought you should know that from the start. Bad as that is," he glanced at Marla's hand, "it will get much worse for your little girls if you don't do what I say."

Brian nodded. "I'll do it."

"Of course you will."

"I want to see my girls first," Brian insisted. "I'm not doing anything if I don't see them."

"Fine."

He and the gunman who'd grabbed Brian's arm walked the professor into the girls' wing, past a playroom and their study with twin desks, stopping only when they came to the large bedroom the twins shared. The girls lay blindfolded on their king-size bed, mouths taped like their mother's, along with their wrists and ankles. Their ears were plugged and taped, too. Brian noticed the home security light beaming on the wall. But he knew if the men had the wherewithal to take apart his computer, they would have already disabled the alarm for private security service.

He reached for his girls. He was kicked away by a fourth man in a ski mask, who sat beside the twins on the bed.

"For God's sakes, I just—"

"When does their nanny come home?" interrupted the short man.

"She has Friday nights off," Brian said bitterly. "And Sundays."

"It's good to see you're answering honestly. We know her schedule, name, nationality, place and date of birth. We know everything about her. We even know your 'Hamburger Wednesdays' professor friend has been having sex with her since your big summer barbecue."

The man seemed to wait for a response, but Brian was speechless.

"All you have to do is open the safe and give us the external drive that you better have locked in there, and these two little girls will have long lives."

By now Brian knew there was little hope for him or Marla. There couldn't be for him, not if they wanted sole ownership of all that he'd developed. And they'd made clear that Marla was no more than a demonstration model for what they would do to his daughters if he didn't cooperate.

"Ready to open that safe?" the short man asked.

Brian walked with them back down the hall toward the living room, noticing his open office door. He slowed when he saw his AAC prototype missing, no doubt disassembled, packed up, and on its way to an oil company's laboratory.

Marla looked paralyzed with pain on the couch, still gripping her savaged hand.

Brian turned from her, removed Eva's painting, and opened the safe.

"Take it out," the short man said.

Brian handed him the external hard drive.

Then the leader told the tall bulky man to bring out the pizza. He set it on a table in front of the couch.

"Do you want a slice?" he asked Brian, who shook his head.

"How about you?" he asked Marla, ripping the duct tape from her mouth.

"No." She shook her head feverishly. Tears spilled down her cheeks. "Brian, what's going on? What have you done?"

"What have I *done*?" he pleaded to her.

"No spats, you two," the short man said. "Let's eat," he said to the others.

And they did. Each polished off a slice. Then the short man stood and took out his gun.

"Looks like your dinner got rudely interrupted," he said to Brian.

When he pointed a semiautomatic pistol at her face, Marla screamed and tried to flee. She managed only to stand before the fourth man slammed her back down on the couch. Her next scream was cut off by a bullet.

"Sit down," he now ordered Brian, "next to your wife."

Marla lay on her side, hair redder than before.

Brian shook his head. The ringing in his ears returned, louder than in the garage. He wished he'd listened to the warning. He wished he'd run for help. He wished—

"Your girls, the little loves of your life? Shall we bring them out here?"

Resigned and roiling with fear, Brian couldn't move. He looked frozen.

"Let him hear one of them," the short man yelled down the hall.

The door to the twins' room opened. Eva screamed, "Daddy!"

It was the last word he ever heard.

PART I

CHAPTER 1

LANA ELKINS SETTLED BACK in her office chair, basking in the scent of the narcissus that she'd just arranged in a crystal vase. The fragrance was so penetrating it felt narcotic. The narcissus had been waiting for her when she walked in the door of CyberFortress, her cybersecurity firm. They were the flower of the week. NSA Deputy Director Robert Holmes had sent her a bouquet every Monday since she returned to work four months ago. He'd vowed to start her week in similar fashion for as long as he lived. His first card had explained why: "Just a small token of my deep gratitude for all the exemplary work you performed during the greatest crisis of the modern age." Signed simply, "Bob."

Such an elegant term, "modern age." Who talked that way anymore? No one but Holmes, and while others in the intelligence community viewed him as a dinosaur from the dark days of the Cold War for his attitudes, if not his expertise, Lana felt certain he was precisely the kind of cybergeneral you wanted in place when a crisis threatened to become a catastrophe.

So while she'd made a perfunctory effort to stop his weekly offering—cut flowers often carried large carbon footprints, depending on their point of origin—she'd relaxed and accepted his gifts, knowing "Thank you" was as much a part of his moral code as never flinching in the face of adversity. Even as Lana suspected her own principles were grayer—more tinged by the times—she appreciated the man's spine, and, of course, the intoxicating scent of those elegant flowers with their white petals and yellow pistils.

She indulged herself with the aroma for a few seconds, thinking how much her fifteen-year-old daughter Emma would love a few of the flowers for her bedroom, before Holmes's first encrypted communication of the week arrived. He wanted to draw her attention to a pair of Russian icebreakers and a cable-laying ship in the Arctic, and provided a link to satellite surveillance of the vessels. "If possible," he wanted "CF" to intercept and relay to him all communications between the ships and their "masters in Moscow."

If possible. In Holmes-speak, that was a command, and one Lana would do her utmost to fulfill. Her success at obtaining these sorts of intercepts had kept her company at the forefront of the intelligence world since she had left the NSA more than a decade ago to start her own firm.

Still, Holmes's "masters in Moscow" line reminded her that he was a great fan of John le Carré, and always on the alert for moles and sleeper agents. Once a Cold War warrior always one, she figured of the deputy director. During the crisis last year that had all but brought the U.S. to its knees—and from which the country, indeed, the world was still recovering—Russian hackers, along with their devious counterparts in China, North Korea, Iran, and a host of other countries, had been immediate suspects in the massive cyberwar launched against the United States.

Remembering the real "masters" of all that mayhem still made her teeth grind, as did flashbacks of the harrowing events that finally led to their defeat. Well, it wasn't the Russians, in any case. And despite the missive from Holmes on her screen, she doubted the great irascible bear of the north was up to anything more than its usual posturing over the Arctic. But then she immediately reminded herself that Russia's aggressive actions in the Ukraine made any of its blustering deeply worrisome these days.

Climatologists were constantly noting that the northern region was heating up two to three times faster than the average rate for the rest of the world. Five fossil-fuel powers bordered the Arctic: the U.S.; Canada; Russia; Denmark, which included Greenland in its kingdom; and Norway. All were looking hungrily at what geologists said might be the last of the world's great untapped reserves of natural gas and oil. In theory, those five countries were peaceably negotiating over mineral rights. In reality, most were also busy building icebreakers and other naval hardware in case words proved weak in ensuring both national sovereignty and prosperity.

Already an increasing number of commercial tankers were carrying gas and oil from Siberia through Russia's Northern Sea Route, a more direct voyage for that nation and the vessels of other countries than the Northwest Passage through Canadian-claimed waters. In either case, the supertankers and container ships now plying those seas each saved many days and upwards of hundreds of thousands of dollars *per trip* over the longer runs through the Panama or Suez Canals. And on those northern routes the captains needn't concern themselves with desperate Somali pirates. Or hijackers of any stripe, though it was amusing for Lana to conceive of a Canadian pirate party seizing a Russian ship ("Beauty, eh?").

In actuality, the Canucks were assembling Arctic-worthy warships at an unprecedented pace. But if they were really smart, she thought they'd also be building ports capable of catering to the needs of those massive boats—as the Russians were already doing along their portion of the route.

At least the Canadians were moving ahead forcefully. The U.S. maintained little more than the homely presence of the Coast Guard in the Arctic with two—*Count 'em*—icebreaking ships in its entire fleet. The U.S. Navy was stretched so thin elsewhere that it didn't expect to have much of a presence up there until the middle of the next decade, and that would happen only if Congress ever got around to approving the navy's budget requests for more polar-class icebreakers.

The Russians, meanwhile, were running nuclear-powered Arctic icebreakers, while building the largest and most powerful vessel of that type in the world. So a great deal of responsibility for tracing Russian and other nations' activities in the region had been left to U.S.-based intelligence agents using satellite and other technology. Notwithstanding the U.S., at times the entire region appeared to be a free-for-all of competing interests, while the very accuracy of its icy borders—upon which so much negotiating depended—was abused not so much by the threat of war or lesser aggressions, but by the increasing impact of the warming.

Lana summoned Jeff Jensen, her carefully attired VP in charge of CF's internal security, though he was also drawn inevitably into naval affairs because the tightly wound thirty-eight-year-old Mormon was an Annapolis grad and veteran navy cryptographer. He had also served with distinction in Afghanistan and Iraq.

Jensen hurried into her office within moments, working what appeared to be a new digital device that likely came from a friend in the tech field. He kept those contacts current, which kept CF on top of all the advances in the soft and hard "wares" of the business.

"I know about the Russian ships," he said, looking up as he pocketed the device. "I was getting ready to send you a report when you texted. We've already got a satellite photo of one of them. It's leading a polar-rated ship that's laying more cable on the seabed," Jensen went on. "It's very shallow there." As it was along most of the Siberian shelf.

"Nice work, Jeff. So how long before all of that is operational for them?"

"I'll bet we'll know before our counterparts in the Kremlin."

She thanked Jeff, expecting him to leave. Instead he sat in the office's guest chair.

"There's something else you should know."

His tone set off alarm bells for Lana. "What is it?"

"We had a double murder in Cambridge Friday night. Our friends at the FBI have been busy all weekend because the presumed target was a Dr. Brian Ahearn, who worked in Harvard's Computer Science Department. I should also note that the murders have our colleagues at the Strategic Studies Institute sniffing the air."

"What's SSI's interest?"

"Apparently, Ahearn was working on a means of extracting carbon dioxide directly from the atmosphere."

Lana swiveled to her keyboard and immediately created a new file. "You're right," she told Jeff, "I should know this." And she would have learned it, sooner than later, being a member of a new, top secret task force examining the international security concerns facing the U.S. because of climate change. "What do we know so far?"

"More than Harvard does, that's for sure. They're just getting clued in now. They didn't know anything about his research."

"How do we know about it then?"

"The FBI had an asset who had lunch with him every Wednesday. A math professor at MIT. I guess they shared a taste for hamburgers, and Professor Ahearn's wife didn't approve of his eating meat. The mathematician's wife didn't care, but he pretended to be under similar constraints at home as a means of bonding."

"Over burgers?" Lana asked.

"I know, mind-boggling, but there you go. During one of their secret forays to a joint in Harvard Square—this was about two years ago—Ahearn casually alluded to his research. Nothing so precise as 'I'm working on Ambient Air Capture at home,' but enough to have piqued the interest of the mathematician and his minders, who promptly supplied him with an eight-gig fob camera."

"How did he manage to get photos of anything more than the burgers?"

"People do have to go to the bathroom," Jensen said. "And Ahearn was a creature of habit. He always used the facilities as soon as they were seated in one of the booths, and our mathematician photographed everything he could from the man's briefcase in the two minutes and forty seconds that Ahearn typically used to complete the trip."

"The computer science professor left his briefcase unlocked?" Lana sat back. "That's hard to believe."

"No, never, it was always locked. But it was a combination lock, and they hacked the code from the briefcase manufacturer."

"Did NSA do that?"

"I'm sure Ed could tell you."

Snowden. His name came up in this sort of context all the time, not always bitterly.

"Most of the time the math professor found nothing," Jensen explained. "But on four occasions he photographed notes and mathematical formulas that included algorithms applicable to AAC."

"Did Ahearn actually advance the science?" she asked.

"Considerably. The last batch of photos showed him on the verge of nearing his goal, from the reports I've received. That was two months ago. If he actually pulled it off, it would have been a world changer."

"But no final answers, I presume, for the key-fob cameraman or us?"

"None." Jensen shook his head.

"Who was the other victim? You said it was a double murder."

"His wife was killed, too, and that was bad. Her ring finger was hacked off before she was shot in the face. And their four-year-old twins were found bound in their bedroom, one still gagged. She reported that black men had been in the house. The other was just as insistent the men were dressed in black. The only thing they agree on is that the men wore black ski masks. The Bureau's forensic team has found black threads that do not match other fabrics in the house, so we think they could have been men dressed in black. A caller alerted 911 to the murders. Agents were not able to trace the call and presumed a prepaid cell had been used. Whoever did make the call spared the twins having to wait for hours for their nanny to return to the house."

"Has she been questioned?" Lana asked.

"At great length. She's from Costa Rica, a part-time student at Boston University. Speaks excellent English. She's not a suspect, just a person of interest."

Lana nodded again.

"The other interesting thing about this," Jeff continued, "is that the killers took a pizza out of the oven and helped themselves to it. No trace of it was found in the victims' stomachs, and forensics found the kind of crumbs you'd expect from people casually lounging around eating. The Bureau thinks it was the killers' way of saying, 'Hey, we're professionals. Good luck finding us.'"

"Well, the chopped finger makes sense from an intimidation point of view," Lana said. "It showed they meant business from the get-go."

"That's been leading the coverage in Beantown, but what didn't get leaked was that his hard drive was taken from his computer and his safe was left open. Agents say some of his colleagues think he might have had an external drive in there. Not unusual in their field, I guess. The Bureau has an Evidence Response Team, ERT, processing the entire crime scene now, including the safe."

"Did anything get out about AAC?"

"Not exactly, but there were reports, mostly on the Web, that the professor was involved in some rarefied research, but not the exact subject matter." Jeff started to get up, then sat back down. "One other thing. The Bureau thinks the professor might have built something in his home office, maybe the prototype. He was not a do-it-yourselfer, but they found specialized tools and instruments. Nothing definite, but the Bureau has a unit processing his work area as well. A visual observation alone suggests something else is missing."

With that, Jensen made his exit and Lana turned to the icebreakers and cable-laying ship on one of her screens, hulls and decks gray as those great northern waters. She was giving herself the freedom to simply think about the goings-on in the Arctic, how fraught such a frigid region had become, when Holmes directed her to join an urgent secure video teleconference, SCVT, with him and the chief of Naval Operations, along with two of the admiral's top-ranking Pentagon aides.

This can't be about those ships, she told herself, *not with Admiral Roger Deming on-screen.* She was right. The concerns were much deeper and closer to home: The U.S.S. *Delphin*, a nuclear-powered, nuclear-armed submarine, had been taken over thirteen minutes ago.

By hackers!

Admiral Deming leaned forward to talk, an old warrior's phantom-limb response to an absent microphone. "We didn't believe it was even possible for an enemy to do this. They must have some help onboard. A sub cannot be taken control of remotely."

"Is there any communication with the command staff?" Lana asked.

"None," Deming replied. "All contact is shut down. And they've got twenty-four Trident IIs, most with multiple warheads."

"So how is this even possible?" Lana asked.

"That," Holmes replied, "is what we need to find out."

Lana's video hookup showed not only her counterparts in Washington, but also the South Atlantic off the coast of Argentina. A crosshair indicated the sub's location.

Holmes, white hair combed straight back—looking exactly the same as when she had first met him more than fifteen years ago—said the sub was the nation's highest priority. "The President has been alerted and command posts worldwide are fully activated. We have destroyers on their way down there."

"I understand," Lana said. "Is there anything else you can tell—"

She was silenced by the abrupt appearance on-screen of the sub's interior. Now she saw why: it had surfaced and was also visible on the split screen. The hackers had taken control of the ship's cameras in the control and attack centers. Sailors were staggering, clutching their throats, and falling to the floor.

"Jesus Christ," Deming said, jumping out of his chair.

"What's going on?" Lana said, staring in horror as sailors appeared to be dying right before her eyes, just seconds after the video had come alive. They were staggering, vomiting, gasping for breath, and falling to the floor. Some were now going into convulsions.

"Poison," Deming said, still standing. "They're poisoned."

"Good God," Holmes replied. "Isn't there emergency oxygen?"

"Of course," Deming said sharply. "But this is happening so fast nobody has a chance to grab it, and it might not do them any good anyway because oxygen isn't always an antidote for poison."

Sailors kept dropping to the sub floor. All appeared to be in their death throes. It was the most ghastly sight Lana had ever seen.

And then the video ended as the sub dived back down, as if to suggest the men and women were headed to a watery grave, leaving a shadow of terror on the faces of Admiral Deming and Bob Holmes.

If she could have seen herself then, Lana would have noticed a familiar look on her own face: fear mingled with fierceness. Her jaw was tight, shiny black hair pulled behind her ears, clear blue eyes staring nakedly at the blank screen. And if she'd lowered her gaze a mite more, she would have seen her fingers flying across the keyboard, trying desperately to find her way into the deeply veiled and violent world of digital terrorism.

CHAPTER 2

YOU COULD MISS STARBUCKS if you blinked. It was so unlike Russian businesses, which screamed for attention in the post-Soviet capitalist apocalypse. Oleg Dernov had just walked past a hotel—granted, a most esteemed establishment, one his father naturally favored—with a Rolls Royce dealership in the lobby! *What, you can order Phantom with room service now?*

For so long Oleg had had such a weakness for those cars. *So beauteous.* And he would own one soon, maybe even the hotel and the block it sat upon. *Not a pipe dream. Very serious.*

So's this, he thought, swinging open the door to a more modest Moscow establishment, the Starbucks he'd been looking for. It spoke of wealth, too, but maybe not so loudly as a Rolls Royce Phantom. Though his English-speaking friends could no more read the Starbucks sign than the future, they recognized the distinctive green lettering—the color of the new one-thousand-ruble note. No wonder Muscovites loved Starbucks so much, a little bit of heaven with every sip.

For Oleg, heaven also had a name: Galina Bortnik. Where was she? The Starbucks was not so crowded, but Galina was so tiny.

Ah, there she was, her nose buried in a MacBook. *Good girl. Always working. Fast as fire.* But not online. No hacker would ever risk having their computer's Mac address captured on a public network.

So adorable in her swishy pale-blue pleated dress that fell not even halfway down her milky thighs. Such a munchkin. Five feet—maybe. Black hair cut by his own stylist, so it looked chic, as in you'd never guess Galina Bortnik was a single mom, stuck with a deadbeat dad, or a former nanny or dropout from the Moscow Institute of Physics and Technology. *Most of all, do you know what you would never guess? She is greatest hacker in all of Russian Federation. Maybe greatest in world.*

Except for me.

He rushed to her table. *Muah,* a kiss for the right cheek. *Muah,* a kiss for the left cheek. *Muah,* a kiss for her cushiony lips. She smelled like lavender. And her cheeks so red. A shy girl, a sexy girl, a girl who blushes from such a modest greeting. *How good is that?*

She already had taken her first sip of her *espresso con panna,* three shots with real whipped cream. Nothing light for her. And she had the appealing, slightly plump pulchritude of a ripe apricot, and the complexion of—what did the Brits and Americans call it?—"peaches and cream." That's it. She was the whole fruit basket. She didn't skimp on fats, but good fats. And she was slightly plump, but good plump.

True, Oleg's plutocratic father had warned him that girls like Galina turned to lard quickly, with everything "sagging and dragging" by the time they were thirty-five, but right now Galina Bortnik was twenty-six years old with full bouncy breasts and thighs so smooth and wonderfully soft when she wrapped them around his back and rocked him in the warm bath of pleasure he didn't care if she put on ten kilograms a year for ten years. They would be like candy to him. Besides, his father was a rich asshole, married six times. Still waiting for *his* Galina.

Was this love?

Not so much for Oleg. For her, yes. But for him, many girls to bed before he wed. On that he and his father could agree.

Not that his father didn't like "the rose," as he'd nicknamed Galina the first time he saw her blush. He worshipped her for nannying Dmitri after Oleg's little brother took quite a hit to the noggin. Since he was eight, Galina had taken care of him. She was the only steady female presence in Dmitri's life because Papa married three times during those tumultuous years. But now Dmitri, a hulking fifteen-year-old who towered over Galina like a polar bear, could tie his shoelaces and feed himself and take care of the business at the other end as well, which the doctors said was a miracle of no little magnitude in and of itself. Given "little" brother's enormous size, Oleg had to agree these were major accomplishments. *But miracle? No, not a miracle: Galina Bortnik.*

After ordering, paying, and insisting on a mug, not a paper cup—because this was coffee with the former regional director of Greenpeace Russia, mind you, who had to be bribed to walk through the doors of a Starbucks—Oleg sat down and opened his own MacBook. Hers was already bleeding electrons, but hers, she would remind him when necessary, used a solar cell for its juice.

"So when are you going to tell me who?" she asked softly.

He smiled but shook his head, feeling his wavy dark locks brush against his thick eyebrows. He'd split up Professor Ahearn's files to disguise his identity and give her only what she needed to break the professor's algorithms and contextual esoteric information and nothing more. So far she had been extraordinarily productive.

It was her hacking, after all, that had led him to Ahearn. To find the latest research on Ambient Air Capture, he'd hired her almost two years ago to scour the web, finding promising leads, pinpointing the most likely servers, and even identifying their network administrators.

He'd known it was out there, and the incalculable potential—and profits—to be had from the technology. Last month she'd closed in on an MIT professor. Oleg took it from there, spearfishing the administrator with a faked LinkedIn request from a beautiful academic researcher. The administrator took the bait and promptly downloaded a payload of malware, including a keylogger. Then the man logged in to the server. *Bingo!* Oleg exfiltrated the files—zipping and encoding them to avoid attention.

Oleg was doing Galina a favor by not revealing whose science she was studying, even if he could never tell her what the favor was or why he was bestowing it upon her. Galina was a peaceful person, lured into providing her hacking skills for the "benefit of all humankind." That was exactly how she put it when he told her about the AAC technology. She would not want to know about the others in the operation who got their hands very dirty. Let her think she was on the side of the angels in stealing the AAC from profit-binging pirates in the hands of U.S. oil companies.

"I think he was a man," she told him. "An academic."

"Sure narrows it down. A male academic."

"Don't make fun." She eyed him for a moment. "I'm right, aren't I? Do you know you can read gender rhythms in keystrokes?"

He shrugged. "Maybe."

She nodded, puckering, then opening her lips to mouth the word "true."

Shy, but also very sexy girl.

"I'm protecting you. I really am," he said.

She would curl up and die if she knew what they'd really done to obtain the complete files of the professor. But America had so many homicides that she would need a whole new set of algorithms just to link the Ahearns to the work she was executing so brilliantly. And why would she look for murders? This was hacking computers, not fingers, using a keyboard, not a cleaver. She wouldn't even think of such bloody business. And if she did? The consequences for her would be too gruesome to consider.

"Whoever he was, he—"

"How do you know it was a he?" Oleg jumped in. "And don't tell me gender rhythms."

"Don't dismiss them. There's a lot of research into unique biometric profiling in keystroking."

Oleg snorted. She was using fancy language that didn't fool him. All it meant was that metrics could apply to human characteristics and traits, which included keystroking. As for whether you could tell men from women working on a keyboard? Not for certain, not yet. Someday, though.

"And I have good instincts," she replied, using both hands to raise her *con panna*, elegant fingers fanning out left and right as her lips met the mug just long enough to leave a narrow creamy mustache above her inviting lips.

Oleg had an overwhelming urge to kiss it away—and would have, too, had they not called his drink order. Instead, he rose, delighted to see that the prettiest foam artist was on duty today. She had Baltic blue eyes and teeth as white as glaciers. She'd drawn Lenin's inimitable face on his latte, employing skills like that crazy Japanese artist whose foam and coffee creations— teddy bears, kittens, giraffes, and Daliesque melting clocks— had gone viral. Moscow's foam queen had a more limited range: Lenin and Trotsky mostly. Icons of the left that appealed more to tourists than Muscovites themselves. What Oleg loved most about Lenin's visage was devouring it the way the architect of the Russian revolution had devoured the motherland.

Good riddance, Vladimir.

"So now do I get to work on all of AAC?" Galina asked him as he sat back down.

"I'm betting you're trying," he said playfully.

She smiled, nodding at the remaining half of Lenin's creamy head.

"Guess what she put on mine?" Galina slid her drink around so he could see part of the face of Nadezhda Tolokonnikova, Pussy Riot supreme; Galina had already sipped away the foamy chin. Nickname: Tolokno. "She's doing her now, if you ask *nicely*."

"No way!" He marched back to the counter as she started working her keyboard again. "Hey," he said, "I want Pussy Riot, too. But the *whole* group."

Baltic Blue shrugged. "I can only do Tolokno."

Oleg plopped a one-thousand-ruble note down on the counter, about twenty-two U.S. dollars. *That's asking nicely,* he told himself.

"But there are eleven of them. In foam? I can't do that. Look, I've been working on Maria. I can try that, if you want." Maria Alyokhina. A mouthy girl just like Tolokno, always sticking it to Putin.

Oleg glanced at Galina. "Okay, give me those two."

"You're crazy," Galina said to him when he returned bearing a triumphant smile. "So you get two, and I only get one. How come that always happens?" she asked.

"I demand service. You ask for it like a nice little girl, even when we both know you can be so bad. How about if I pay you now? Before you let me see what you're doing."

Under the table, he slipped a hefty envelope filled with cash between her knees, a sex game that harkened back to her days as a nanny for Dmitri. When the boy was fully sedated—and Oleg made a sexy overture—she would tell him that she had to be paid. He would hand it over to her as he was doing right now, knowing how much it excited Galina, a girl who'd had sex with only one other man, her child's father. She was blushing once more, as she always did. Oleg loved the game for other reasons: it made him feel less emotionally indebted, so for him it was real, and close to what he did a couple times a week with far less familiar faces.

"Now show me."

"Show you what?" She reached down and took the envelope.

"Show me your screen."

She looked disappointed, but swung her laptop around so he could see the AAC schematics she'd drawn up based on the files she'd been working on.

"But there's still a problem of scale," she told him. "He made amazing advances, but unless that stuff's in the encrypted files, this isn't the game changer you might have thought it was."

Game changer. He could always tell when one of his hackers had been working American files because they started using the vernacular. But she was wrong. AAC would change everything. That was another key reason he'd held back the encrypted data— so she would not possess the means of unlimited riches, which in Russia meant her life would last about as long as it took some greedy bastards to extract the info from her. Not long, when any threat to Alexandra, her six-year-old, would have Galina giving away the worldwide "game changer."

So Oleg gave and Oleg took away—data. Which she might have suspected because she suggested they publish everything about AAC on the web. "Pull a Snowden. Give it away," she finished with a smile.

Snowden. Why did we ever let him in? Now every do-gooder— and Galina, a blushing outlaw in a short dress, was definitely a do-gooder—wanted to "pull a Snowden."

More vernacular. And no doubt the favorite phrase of a do-good hacker.

"We have to be very careful now," he told her. "You got paid and others must be paid. There were people in the States who collected the data." He would say no more about *that*. "Investments have to be monetized."

"How long will it take to pay the others?" Galina asked. "Every day is precious. We need to start extracting carbon dioxide everywhere we can. I have a list of all the solar and wind sites in Russia so we can set up carbon capture at as many as we can."

"But it's a very powerful tool, and in the wrong hands?" He smiled, for *his* hand was back under the table, thumb and pointer opening her knees again, the way you'd swell images on your screen with a track pad by spreading those fingers apart. He and Galina spoke the same sign language of sex, and had for years. Her legs opened just a little, teasingly, but enough that he could feel the velvety skin of her inner thigh right below her silky hem.

And then she took an audible breath as he reached farther and began to languorously stroke her upper thigh just below her underpants, borrowing another motion from most track pads, the one that drew three fingers toward the operator to ferry a particular document or image to the forefront of attention. Each recoil brushed his fingernails against the taut fabric at the top of her legs.

Now that he had *her* attention, Oleg took the seat next to her, leaving his jacket hanging on the back of the chair he'd just vacated to block the view. He slid his hand back under her dress, delighting in exerting a firm grasp on her thigh. Then he inched aside the delicate elastic band and felt her most intimate pleasure as Galina, eyes looking far away, whispered, "It's ready."

"I know. I can tell."

"No, I mean your latte."

"What?" He looked up. Baltic Blue was smiling, waving him over.

"I have your Pussy Riot," she called to him.

With an erection tenting his pants—and no sign of embarrassment—he picked up his latte and walked back with the likenesses of two of Russia's most notorious women sharing the circular frame of his mug.

As he sat back down next to Galina his phone went off. He had to take it—a young Ukrainian hacker who'd been working for him almost as long as Galina. Oleg thought of himself as a great conductor, offering the baton of his expertise and wealth where it could do the most good—for him. Others might have called him a venture capitalist, a *vulture* capitalist, a vulgar throwback to a greedy era, but Oleg knew better. He was fusing the techniques of terror to the Digital Age, transcending politics as he pointed his baton left and right from center stage.

"Yes?" Oleg said, boldly pulling Galina's dress all the way up and slipping his hand inside the satiny front panel of her panties. But instead of picking up where he'd left off—he froze, then gripped her pubis so tightly that she squeaked, "No!"

But he didn't hear her. How could he? His ears were filled with the kind of wonder that trumped anything Galina Bortnik could have offered.

He turned from her and spoke into his phone with great care: "Tell me again. Say it slowly."

"It is done," the voice told him. "You can see for yourself. Then we can talk."

"See for himself" meant the Ukrainian had posted an encrypted video on a YouTube channel and deliberately posted the decryption key to a Dark Web forum that the intelligence agencies monitored. That way the USIC—U.S. Intelligence Community—would find it. The Dark Web, a small portion of the Deep Web, was the part of the Internet where a lot of illegal and malicious behavior took place. It was inaccessible to conventional search engines, which meant only the most sophisticated users could access it.

Oleg already had the decryption key. He rushed out to his Maserati, away from the Starbucks's Wi-Fi and surveillance cameras, and poached an unsecured Wi-Fi signal. In seconds he was looking at the interior of a nuclear-armed submarine with dead American sailors—proof that the young Ukrainian hacker had used the guidance and funds Oleg had provided him to unprecedented advantage.

Nobody, but nobody, had ever held the reins of world power as he did right at that moment. The submarine now had a job to do—and the tools and men to do it. And so did Galina. Though neither she nor the Ukrainian knew each other, they were working hand in hand through him—the conductor, now with a nuclear-armed baton.

CHAPTER 3

"YOU MISSED IT!" EMMA glared at Lana with the disdain of a teenage daughter harboring a genuine grievance.

Despite her mother's weary appearance and late arrival home, her only child offered no greeting at the front door. Only the damning, "You missed it!" And for the life of her, Lana couldn't recall what she'd missed, but it was clear that her fifteen-year-old—going on twenty, or so she would have liked to think—thought it warranted the full arsenal of aggressive body language: arms crossed, legs crossed, so agitated, in fact, that her eyes were almost crossed.

"You don't even remember, do you?" Emma shook her head. "The big rehearsal, *Mother*. Remember? The *choir*."

Lana worked her key out of the door lock and sloughed her bag onto an entry table, trying to keep her chin up as she walked into the living room. The literal weight on her shoulders had vanished, only to be replaced by the metaphorical heft of Emma's vitriol.

Lana set down her computer case and settled into a chair that let her relax while she faced her daughter. She took a breath, fortifying herself. "Listen, dear heart, something came up. I just couldn't leave work."

She'd spare her daughter the grim particulars of watching those poor men and women die before her eyes on the encrypted video posted on YouTube. The decryption key had been found by a member of the U.S. Intelligence Community.

She couldn't share the devastating news, in any case. The whole intelligence community was in a collective lockdown: no release of any information about the events off the coast of Argentina. Also today had come the less-than-inspiring news that Admiral Wourzy, in charge of cybersecurity for the navy, had been arrested in an Indian casino in California last weekend for using counterfeit chips. *How in God's name does crap like that even happen?* That had been Lana's first thought. The admiral tried to argue that the Native American dealer had fed the phony chips into the game but casino security trumped him.

Lana knew more than she wanted to about the impulse to gamble. She'd spent countless hours gambling on virtual poker tables before finding the strength to stop throwing money away on cheap thrills that had never paid off in the long run. Even so, the desire was still inside her, recrudescing after an especially stressful period. But even at her worst, she'd never cheated like Admiral Wourzy. She'd never even thought of doing so.

Chief of Naval Operations Admiral Deming's first impulse had been to demand his underling's resignation. Which also happened to be the immediate response of the casino owner, who could scarcely believe the crook at the craps table was one of America's highest-ranking military officials.

But the Pentagon brass couldn't fire the admiral. Despite his blatant idiocy in this regard—all for measly ten-dollar chips—he was a gifted cyberwarrior largely credited with bringing the navy's old guard into the twenty-first century.

"So whatever you do," Emma went on, bringing Lana's attention back to more domestic concerns, "don't tell me you can't come to the actual performance tomorrow night because—I hope you've remembered this—it's going to be at the National Cathedral." Emma paused and performed a dramatic toe-tap. "And I want *you* to be there."

All Lana could do was shake her head. Even before the crisis with the *Delphin*, she had been slated to attend a top-level briefing at NSA headquarters at Fort Meade about a newly discovered Chinese army unit of elite hackers, code-named *Magic Dragon*. Which was why Lana had planned to attend tonight's rehearsal instead of the actual performance.

"Sweetheart, please—"

"Sweetheart, dear heart, you say all that stuff all the time, but where's *your* heart? Because it sure isn't where your home is."

If I could only tell her.

But most of the information that Lana would have liked to share would never be declassified. She'd be taking it to her grave.

A pot clattered in the kitchen, startling her. "Who's that?" she asked Emma, who only glared at her more intensely as Tanesa stepped into the room.

"I'm sorry, Lana. I was just getting us something to eat when you came home, and then it sounded like you guys needed some space."

"That was good of you, but come sit."

Mother and daughter took a pause while Tanesa, a fine calming influence on Emma, sat on the couch near her. The look on Emma's face was about as ugly as it could get for a pretty young woman who, consensus held, bore a striking resemblance to her mother. They both had shiny black hair, smooth skin, cheekbones a Russian supermodel might envy, and, in Emma's case, coltish legs that were on nearly full display under the kerchief passing for a skirt.

"Your mom has a really important job," Tanesa said to Emma. "You're not even supposed to know that, but you do."

"She couldn't exactly hide it from me after last year."

More resentment over more secrecy, even when it wasn't secret anymore.

But Emma did think the world of Tanesa, so whenever she spoke up in Lana's defense, Lana felt grateful.

Tanesa was three years older than Emma and had been the girl's nanny; odd as that might sound, it made sense in the way that life often mangled the logic of chronological age. Tanesa still watched over Emma, for which Lana paid a handsome wage, but in truth they had become close friends, much to Emma's benefit. The strikingly attractive young African American woman had also recruited Emma into the Capitol Baptist Church Choir, an award-winning ensemble. Emma's first solo was set for tomorrow night in Bach's *St Matthew's Passion*.

"Please don't do that, Tanesa," Emma said.

"Do what?"

"Sound so reasonable: 'Your mom has a really important job.'"

Emma wasn't being tart. Sadly, she was serious. As if to underscore this, she added, "This is emotional truth for me."

Another notable influence in Emma's life of late: her therapist. After enduring a harrowing abduction during last year's cyberattack, and the second-by-second threat of nuclear annihilation, Emma had suffered nightmares and anxiety. Those were classic PTSD symptoms, so Lana had gotten her daughter professional help.

And it had eased Emma's condition considerably, as well as provided her with a newly charged arsenal of emotionally laden language for skewering her mother. Which had proved painful only to the extent that Emma used her psychobabble accurately.

No denying her daughter's deadeye now. Lana was flinching internally over the truth of much of what Emma had said, but not over what she now added:

"It can't be as bad as last year, Mom, and anything short of that is a shitty excuse."

"Emma!" Tanesa, a devout Christian, had no tolerance for profanity, and—miracle of miracles!—had managed to clean up Emma's potty mouth, for the most part.

"Look, I'm sorry," Emma instantly allowed, "but I'm so sick of 'dear heart' and 'sweetheart' when I want to see my mother in the front row looking up at me in the National Cathedral!" Suddenly, she burst into tears, sobbing, "I don't have a dad. I've only got *you*."

Lana choked up and rushed to her side, holding Emma as tightly as she had in many months, feeling her daughter shake with disappointment. Yet Lana also knew that she desperately needed to get back on her computer as soon as possible. Torn, once more, by her deeply conflicting obligations.

"Mom," she said softly. "I've been tracking him down."

"Who?"

"My father."

Lana stepped back and looked closely at Emma. *You mean that good-for-nothing deadbeat who walked out on me—us—when you were two years old?*

That, of course, was what Lana wanted more than anything to say. Instead, she choked it all down before speaking: "That won't be easy. I don't know where he is."

"I do, Mom. It's not that far away."

Oh, great.

Emma peered right into her mother's eyes as she continued: "I found him through the Bureau of Prisons."

"What?" *Prison?* Even for ne'er-do-well Donald, that was shocking.

"They caught him sailing four thousand pounds of marijuana up from Colombia on his sailboat. That's two *tons* of pot, Mom."

"Please don't sound so impressed. When was this?"

"A few years ago. He's in the jail in Cumberland. It's a medium-security place. It's not like he's dangerous or anything."

Oh, yes he is. But she couldn't expect her daughter to grasp *that* truth so soon after locating him. Suddenly, a hacked and hijacked nuclear-armed submarine full of dead sailors, and the murders of a genius and his wife in Cambridge—and an admiral's gambling addiction—all seemed far away. But Lana knew none of it would remain removed for long. And as a respite from a national security crisis, Donald Fedder's imprisonment on federal drug charges left a great deal to be desired.

"Have you contacted him?" she asked.

Emma nodded. "He's actually pretty handsome, Mom."

"He's an asshole," Lana said, regretting her outburst even before she received Tanesa's censorious gaze. "And looks aren't everything."

Which is exactly why you went to bed with Donald so quickly, right?

Lana groaned out loud at the memory. Now Emma took her mother in her arms and said, "It'll be okay, Mom. He's got a furlough for good behavior. He's a model prisoner. As long as you agree, they'll let him come to the concert tomorrow night in one of those ankle bracelets . . ."

Oh, my God.

"So . . . maybe it's for the best that you're not coming."

No, it's definitely not for the best.

Minutes later, in between checking grim status reports about the *Delphin,* Lana confirmed every detail of her Google-loving girl's words. And it was all spelled out in the form that Emma had forwarded to her from the Bureau of Prisons, ready for her signature: "Request granted by daughter's mother and legal guardian."

Lana signed it electronically, groaning again when she sent it on. What choice did she have? She was in a corner. If she denied Emma's request—when she couldn't make it to the concert herself— she would appear an emotional scrooge. But what made it worse, was after attending the concert, "Doper Don," as Lana had already dubbed him, would be permitted fifteen minutes of supervised time to visit with his "long-lost" daughter.

She was never lost. He was.

Never had her profession cost her so much personally. She could see no good coming out of this, particularly after Emma had changed her life in such positive ways since meeting Tanesa.

After reviewing another status update, Lana received a call from Deputy Director Holmes.

"It's very strange," he said, eschewing all small talk, "because the hackers, whoever they are, wherever they are, aren't making any demands."

"Nothing?"

"Not a thing," Holmes said. "They just keep showing the bodies of those sailors."

"Are they surfacing to do that?"

Holmes shook his head, saying that the sub had probably deployed a radio buoy. The electronic device had small antennas that protruded just above the water line and were all but invisible on the vast reaches of ocean.

"Is there anyone alive?" Lana asked.

"Admiral Deming is certain there are. You couldn't operate a sub without some crew, but we haven't seen them yet. The video feed is still horrible to watch but you should study it, see if anything jumps out at you. Wait, get on it right now."

"Sure." She worked her keyboard. "Why?"

"There's someone in a protective suit and breathing mask in front of the camera."

Lana's screen came alive with the eerie appearance of the man, who punched numbers into a box and began to speak.

"Mayday. Mayday. Mayday. This is First Class Petty Officer Hector Gomez of the U.S.S. *Delphin*." His words were garbled with that mask on, making him sound like he was shouting from the bottom of a well. "We've been attacked with poison gas. It's killed a lot of sailors. I grabbed an anti-contamination suit and an OBA before it could get me," he said, pointing to his oxygen breathing apparatus. "I found a bottle of cyanogen chloride. It must have been put into one of the burners." Part of the sub's atmosphere control system.

"That would do it," Holmes said in Lana's ear. "You know about CK?"

"No."

"It stops your body's ability to use the oxygen carried by your hemoglobin. It's like walking through a desert with a glass of water with your mouth sewed up."

"I got the cyanogen chloride out of there," Gomez went on, "but I don't know if it's dissipated yet. If you can hear me, please respond. Over."

"But communication is cut off to the sub, right?" Lana asked Holmes.

"That was the last I heard," he replied.

"I am out of air!" Gomez shouted.

Lana could see Gomez's panic in his eyes and rigid body language. Then he started shaking and ripped off his mask. His face was covered in sweat. He took deep breaths, looking around frantically. Neither Lana nor Holmes said a word. She knew they were both waiting to see whether Gomez keeled over.

Seconds passed like hours.

Gomez nodded. "I can breathe." Then he looked at the dead bodies on the floor all around him. "Where are they? The people that did this?"

"What do we know about this guy?" Lana asked.

"I'm pulling that up right now," Holmes answered.

Lana watched Gomez, who looked shocked to be alive, still taking in the grisly evidence that surrounded him.

"A mom and dad in San Pedro in LA," Holmes reported.

"The port."

"Correct. At a glance here, everything looks right. He has two brothers and three sisters, all living in LA, all upstanding citizens. Nothing noted about them."

"So does Admiral Deming think he's in on the takeover?"

"He doesn't know yet," Holmes said. "Gomez is the only able-bodied one we've seen. But as the admiral said, no one can possibly run that sub on his own. Whoever it is has got to have at least a half dozen, maybe more, qualified officers and senior enlisted missile operators. And it's possible, not likely, mind you, but possible that Gomez isn't even guilty, that whoever's doing this isn't showing up on camera yet. Maybe they never will. Look, I think you should plan on being out here all day tomorrow." He meant NSA headquarters at Fort Meade. "I need you for a seven o'clock meeting in the morning."

"All right, I'll be there."

Lana didn't expect to sleep easily with her mind abuzz from the dire events of the day, and she was right. She dozed on and off, haunted for hours by those dead bodies.

Finally, at four thirty she arose, scrubbed her face with cold water, and logged on again.

What she saw was wrenching. Gomez, or someone, had propped the dead body of the sub's commander, Captain Hueller, against a chair in full view of the camera. Gomez, she presumed—no, *hoped*—was scouring the sub for survivors.

Keeping a cap on this "incident" would be very difficult with so many service members dead. But they had to try to maintain the silence. The hackers had yet to make their demands known.

She began to imagine what they might be, each one more dreadful than the one that proceeded it. Many harkened back to last year's horrors.

Lana told herself to stop, that no matter what she came up with, reality could turn out to be so much worse.

And she was right about that.

Unimaginably worse.

CHAPTER 4

MOSCOW, SO OLD AND so new. And so beautiful. Onion domes and brand-new skyscrapers. Gorgeous cars, like Oleg's Maserati. Purring like a pussycat as he drove from the heart of the city. Exciting like Pussy Riot punk rock. Like Galina when she took the money from him under the table.

He passed his favorite onion domes of all, the ones with so many colors they looked like frozen yogurt swirls at Creamery Dreamery. *Thank you, crazy Orthodox Church. I pray to Virgin, too. But I promise you, Vladimir, not like Pussy Riot.*

Could a country be any greater than the new Russia, with its venerable traditions and history? No, not possible. That was what most of Oleg's friends would have said. His father, Papa Plutocrat, would have shaken his head very slowly, looking very wise, or so PP would have thought, and said that it was true, he and his friends—crony capitalists all—brought Russia to its apogee. Yes, "apogee," because a wise man would use such a word, and PP had an English-language word-a-day calendar in his private bathroom so he could sound wise and say those three syllables—*ap-o-gee*—like he was blessing them under an onion dome.

But Oleg knew better. Russia was not so great as it would soon become. *In just days.* Because he would generate the greatest wealth the world had ever known. So much money his fellow citizens would have untold rubles showering down on them.

He smiled at himself in the Maserati's rearview mirror. Everything was falling into place. Engineers had reassembled the professor's prototype, and when they turned it on and saw it sucking those heat-absorbing molecules out of the air in vast quantities, their tongues hung out. And so they had to be killed. *Just a joke!* Oleg laughed to himself. No, but they did have to be properly rewarded and left in isolated wonder. *But better than death.*

The days of fossil-fuel haters would soon be over. Conservation was never much fun anyway. Burn all the fuel you want. Drive a Maserati—as fast as you want. AAC will suck out the carbon and combine it with hydrogen and we'll have—*Voilà!*—hydrocarbons. More gas. More oil. More money!

Those fossil-fuel companies would pop the bubbly when they found out. Russian ones, that is, because the others? Well, they wouldn't be drilling so much anymore. They would have other problems. Some would say crises. Especially with their offshore platforms. *Make BP in the Gulf seem like Roman candle.*

AAC would be earth's thermostat. World too hot? Okay, *whoosh,* suck out more carbon dioxide from the atmosphere. Too cold? Take out less. Auction off nice climates: "And the winner is Great Britain with a bid of 230 trillion rubles."

God save the Queen.

Think about that. Start droughts, drum up more floods, make haywire weather. Why not? Or be nice and let the world live in peace—as long as you pay proper tribute to your master.

But first the world had to be brought to its senses, especially big boys like the U.S., Europe, and China. Which meant bringing them to their knees. *Best position for learning. Ask Federal*

Security Service. And that was where the submarine came in handy. Very soon Oleg would tell those other Arctic nations to leave the gas and oil and minerals for Russia. And if they didn't— and, of course, they wouldn't—there would have to be a terrible catastrophe.

But that was so simple with a sub on your side because the world was already facing an extraordinary threat of a catastrophe of such massive proportions that nobody would even talk about it much publicly. Lots of scientists knew. Galina, good Greenpeace girl, knew, though not what Oleg was up to. The precipice was so well known it even went by an acronym in certain circles.

And when something teeters on a precipice, what does it need? A nudge. That was all. One teensy-weensy nudge. And a sub with missiles could nudge and nudge and nudge. And then everyone would hear the biggest *plop* in the history of the planet. *But* what will happen after the plop? Now *that* would be the most memorable sound of all.

Three years of planning and now he was down to less than a week, and everything that had sounded so ambitious in the beginning was falling into place. Oleg smiled over his private pun.

But he was still Papa Plutocrat's son, and PP had summoned him to cottage country outside Moscow.

In the Soviet era, they called them "dachas," special places where party officials with influence could rest and relax with one another and their mistresses—or, in Stalin's case, make fun with his pen and sign tens of thousands of death warrants and condemn hundreds of thousands to slave labor camps while he sat on his bulletproof couch. But most dachas were tiny places on tiny plots. Who wanted one anymore? Not fit for men of means.

"Why don't you just call it my country mansion?" Oleg had once needled PP.

"Not a mansion. A *cottage.*"

Okay, a cottage that was twelve thousand square feet with an indoor pool, ice-skating rink, ballroom, movie theatre, and two kitchens, one for the servants and one for the family. It looked like a French castle, complete with dungeon. Oleg wasn't sure what his papa did down there, and even as a boy he knew better than to ask. He'd been forbidden to enter the castle's north wing, under which the dungeon lay like a sleeping snake.

Still, he was a boy's boy so he'd snuck down there and looked around. Very interesting dungeon. Iron rings on the wall. And a rack, too. He had been only fifteen but thought the rack was the coolest thing he would ever see. Such big gears and a hand crank. When he turned it the rack went *clickety-click* and the table spread apart. *Clickety-click-click-click* and it spread even more. Beautiful manacles had clearly been hand forged to fit feet and wrists. Superb workmanship, which he came to admire more as he grew older. The same artist had made the iron rings for the wall, and when Oleg had seen them close-up he'd been doubly impressed.

He had led his half brother Dmitri downstairs the very day he'd discovered the dungeon and swore the mutt—born to an ex-peasant mother—to secrecy. Then he told him to lie down on the "bed."

"I'm going to make you big like Papa, stretch your bones a little. How's that sound? No more 'little' Dmitri. Make you a big boy fast."

"Big like Papa? You can do that?"

"Yes, big like Papa. Like me."

"I want to be big like *Papa*."

Whatever.

Oleg chained him up. Dmitri was not a good specimen, though. He started wailing with the first *clickety-click*. You can imagine what it was like after a couple more. So sweet Oleg had to shove one of his father's old boot socks in the boy's mouth. But he still had to threaten him with head injuries if he didn't shut the fuck up.

After a few more *clickety-click-click-clicks*, he cranked the table back together.

"Now I'm going to take out Papa's sock. But if you scream, I'm sticking it back in."

He unchained his brother and said, "Look, you're so much bigger."

Dmitri had looked down, all wet-eyed, and shook his head. "No, my pants are still in the same place."

Five years old and already an empiricist. That pissed Oleg off, so he led Dmitri toward the Iron Maiden replica, open and showing its broad array of sharpened spikes. With a cry, the peasant brother tried to run screaming from the room, but Oleg grabbed him before he could flee up the stairs.

"I will show you something else, and you can do it to me," he'd told Dmitri.

"I can hurt you?" the boy said with more vengeance than Oleg would have liked.

"Sure."

Oleg walked him over to a medieval skull crusher. Dmitri stared at it.

"What is it?" the boy asked.

He told him.

"I'm not putting my head in there," the boy said.

"I will, if you'll keep everything secret that we've done down here."

"Get in," Dmitri said.

Oleg placed his chin on the base of the torture device and told his brother to turn the wooden crank that would drive a metal cap down onto his noggin.

The child did it with abundant enthusiasm, but when Oleg felt the cap pressing down on him, he'd reached up and stopped his brother.

"No, I want to hurt you," Dmitri yelled, yanking on the crank. Then he grabbed the saliva-slick sock Oleg had used on him and tried to push it into his brother's mouth.

But he was no match for Oleg, who reached up and unscrewed the cap.

"No fair," Dmitri said.

"Someday you'll get your turn," Oleg told him.

"That's not what I mean," Dmitri yelled.

"But you *will*," Oleg had vowed.

Oleg now drove past lots of peasants on his way to cottage country. The last of the ordinary poor lived only a mile from the big green walls that surrounded the country homes of some of Moscow's richest men. Twenty-five years ago the Russian people owned everything, according to Soviet propaganda of the time, which meant, in fact, they owned nothing. There were no millionaires, much less billionaires. Now, after free-market reforms, most still owned very little but Moscow had seventy billionaires, more than any other city in the world, and those men owned a quarter of the country's entire economy. Even Oleg had to admit that his father's friends had raised the bar, but not to a truly towering height. Not for him.

At last, Oleg's red Maserati pulled up to the green wall that surrounded his father's cottage. He didn't even have to press a button. An electronic eye opened the gate. Good-bye potato-faced peasants, hello handsome happy people. Oleg didn't disdain the peasantry. Not as much as the billionaires in cottage country. They had plundered old industries—mining, petroleum, steel-making, shipbuilding—but most couldn't even work the simple computers of that era. But they all knew how to come up with fistfuls of rubles when the whole economy had come up for grabs. They'd thought that meant they were smart. They had confused greed with intelligence.

But the sharpest ones had sent their sons to school—Caltech,

MIT, University of Cambridge, and Moscow's own Institute of Physics and Technology. And the lucky offspring studied computer science, software engineering, and the emerging fields of cybersecurity and information assurance. That was what he had done. His father was always saying, "Come work for me. You can make millions." But Oleg didn't want millions. He wanted billions so his father could work for *him*.

He slowed to motor across the drawbridge at Papa's castle. Another electronic eye recognized the Maserati and the portcullis rose, revealing silver-tipped spikes on the bottom.

Oleg drove into the interior courtyard, one huge English garden with a dozen varieties of roses and pergolas and lush grass and striped canvas chairs. Like a Saturday fair every day of summer. Sometimes PP even had magicians dazzling guests, and musicians strumming and strolling, playing Russian folk tunes.

He drove into a car elevator, which lifted him to the second floor, then turned like a wheelhouse till he was pointed at his reserved place. As he parked, his phone vibrated. The Ukrainian hacker again, telling him 146 crew members were dead. "Even the captain."

Yes! Oleg pumped his fist. *Just the ones he needed alive.* Like he'd planned.

"This is very good," Oleg said. Then he affirmed that a news blackout was holding.

"So I think it's time to send a message, don't you?" the Ukrainian asked.

Oleg agreed.

"We want all—"

"Not 'we want,'" Oleg corrected. "We *demand*. They expect demands. Let's not disappoint."

"We demand that all Arctic nations renounce their claims to the region's oil, gas, and minerals and make it a non-exploitation zone."

"Yes, that sounds good. Very progressive."

"Or else?" the hacker asked.

"What do you mean, 'Or else?'" Oleg asked.

"What will we do if they don't renounce their claims?"

Oleg laughed quietly at the Ukrainian hacker. He thought the demand applied to Russia, too. That was why he was working so hard. He wants Russia to get screwed, too, the way Russia screwed the Ukraine by claiming Crimea, then backed the rubes in the eastern half of the country with guns and bombs so they might realize their dreams of separatism. Hilarious.

"We have a submarine with nuclear missiles, right?" Oleg didn't wait for an answer. "We don't have to say what we'll do. They *know*."

"When do we bomb them?"

The hacker sounded excited to get on with it. That worried Oleg, but not too much. He had him by the short hairs in so many ways. The hacker had kids. "Hostages to fortune," as some English philosopher once said. PP liked to quote him. Such a paterfamilias. But Oleg knew that kiddies kept daddies in line. Not all, but this Ukrainian daddy, definitely.

"We don't bomb them," Oleg said cryptically. "Better than that."

"What could be better than that?"

"You'll see." Oleg cut off the call. He wasn't getting into a discourse right now, not with PP on the monitor right in front of Oleg's parking place. He was wrinkling his forehead. Oleg could read his lips. "Come in. Come in." PP the Prince of Impatience. So fond of saying, "Patience is a vastly overrated virtue." But only true for plutocrats.

Oleg spotted Dmitri on the screen hovering in the background. He saw the resemblance between father and second-born son. Both handsome. PP was a "silver-haired devil" in the words of wife number six. He was seventy-six years old, but still tall and straight with shoulders that hadn't begun to slump. Clear blue eyes. He appeared twenty years younger. By all rights he should have looked like a ham hung in the smokehouse too long. He'd been puffing all his life. But he had very few lines on his face. The picture of health.

Dmitri was as well. But a skull injury had scrambled too many brain cells. The neurologist had said the accident had severely damaged the boy's brain. "It was an accident, right?" the doctor asked.

Which had made PP stare at Oleg, who'd claimed he found him at the bottom of the dungeon stairs. Oleg had nodded at the doctor and said, "I don't know what he was doing there."

In any case, Dmitri's skull had been crunched and his brain hadn't looked so good. A lot of bleeding in both hemispheres, and it had gone on for too long before he got help. Oleg knew exactly how long: four and a half hours. He'd figured that was long enough—and he'd been right.

So Dmitri looked good on the outside, but not so good where it counted. At least he didn't drool anymore, a big plus, and if he'd had any life in his eyes and didn't try to talk, just played the silent mysterious type, he could probably have gotten laid a lot—on his own. But instead, PP had to pay his "special friends" to play with him. Dmitri didn't seem to mind. Nothing wrong with the south end of the complex. PP's friends and the ten-meter waterslide for the heated indoor pool kept Dmitri very happy, except . . . he was missing Galina.

He called her "Gull," like the English word for that disgusting seabird. Oleg always told him "Gull" had flown away. "Doesn't like you anymore."

Which meant nothing to him.

"Oleg, my firstborn son," PP said when he walked into the castle. That had always been the old man's greeting. It was as if he were reminding himself of the birth order, which actually made

Oleg wonder if PP had another firstborn, the real one, still stashed away in a dacha somewhere like a lot of Party hacks had done in the old days. Of course, that would have meant that the real first-born might have been a grandfather by now. PP had been "rutting like crazed weasel" for more than six decades, which he let every-one know after a few bottles of Stoli.

He told his son to sit in a big stuffed chair in the living room that he had redone to look like the one in *Downton Abbey* after wife number six insisted that as a "lady of sorts"—an ex-stripper—she should have some gilded bookshelves, furniture, and woodwork to "grace" her eyes. So she had. Even gilded books. PP bought them by the pound. Oleg found a complete collection of Karl Marx's works beautifully bound and preserved. He never told PP. He guessed the old man would have just shrugged and said, "Let the free marketplace of ideas compete on a level playing field." Or some such platitude widely embraced by monopolists.

"Dmitri, tell your brother what you told me." As an aside to Oleg, PP said Galina had been making great strides with him.

"Galina? She was here?" News to Oleg. His lovely lady had gone behind his back? *Not good.*

"Yes. She's so helpful," PP said to him. "You remember how Dmitri was saying 'Gull, Gull, Gull' all the time? Well, Galina came over Sunday. You were busy. She's going to keep coming over. I think it's a good idea." Turning to second-born son, PP said, "Go ahead, tell him what you can say now. After just one session with Galina," PP added in a second aside to Oleg.

He watched his little brother, who was much bigger than him now, struggle to say something other than his mangled attempt at Galina's name. His lips twisted grotesquely, and all Oleg could hear at first was "Skkkk," like he was trying to say "skank," maybe. *Must have been eavesdropping by PP's big bedroom. Boy was learning.*

But then the last sound came out and it went straight to Oleg's solar plexus: "Skkkkuullll."

"What?" Oleg shook his head.

"That's what I said," PP agreed. "Why when my baby boy hasn't said a word in ten years, except for 'Gull,' does he suddenly say 'Skull'? And then baby boy dragged me to the dungeon."

Oleg reminded himself to keep a poker expression. He shrugged. *Why would he say that? That's so weird.* But the news had shaken him so that he didn't actually speak those words. When he finally said them, he had to force them out. And though he knew it was not possible, he imagined his lips twisting and his voice struggling just like baby brother's.

"So the rose is going to keep coming. See if we can make him bloom some more." PP's eyes looked clearer than ever. "Isn't this wonderful? I think Dmitri is trying to tell us something, or maybe he's remembering the names of my museum pieces. I can't wait to hear it all. Now, tell me what you've been doing, but take that device out of your ear. I'm talking to you."

Oleg removed his phone's Bluetooth earbud, but all he wanted to know was what the hell happened down in the dungeon, so he asked.

"That's the sad part of the story," said PP. "He started to cry on the bottom step and wouldn't go any farther. We'll see if Rose can get the rest out of him, yes?"

Oleg shrugged. His shoulders felt set in concrete.

PP yammered about the massive icebreaker his company was building so they could mine methane in the Arctic. The Japanese were already trying to do it in their own waters, but the Siberian shelf was so rich with methane—and the waters so relatively shallow—that the gas was bubbling up from the bottom of the sea.

Dmitri hovered over his father most of the time PP talked, but on three occasions he drifted toward Oleg, only to veer away quickly.

"So it's time you stopped playing with computers and came to work for me. Or I will have to put you on a budget," PP said.

Oleg almost laughed. Everything was playing out as he had planned for years. In no time he'd buy his father's companies and put *him* on a budget. And if he didn't want to sell? Oleg would have the clout to make him.

But for now he smiled and repeated "Yes, Papa" every few seconds before getting up to leave.

But who got the last word?

"Skkkkuullll!"

• • •

Using his Maserati like the race car it had been designed to be, Oleg made it to Galina's apartment in record time. She lived in a nice neighborhood near the Institute. Much better than student housing, but still Bohemian for someone with sweet milky thighs and big bouncy breasts. Three bedrooms, two baths, with a beautiful view of—what else? Onion domes. Enough space for little Alexandra to have her own room. And one for Oleg, too, Galina had told him many times.

Now she could tell him why she was planning to spend Sundays in cottage country.

"It's simple," she replied as she welcomed him into her immaculate foyer. "I like Dmitri and your father's paying me a small fortune to work with him."

"Let him work with someone else."

"But Dmitri wants to work with me, and he's making real progress for the first time in years, and—"

"I don't care. I pay you plenty."

"Not enough."

Together they walked into her well-lit apartment's living room.

Galina looked horrible, he realized with a start. Dark circles under red eyes, as though she'd been crying. Maybe he should stop breaking her heart. Set her free like a bird. A nice bird. Not like a dirty gull. But definitely, she should take better care of herself, not let him see her like this. She never knew when he might stop by. Not that she appeared to care what he was saying because she was still talking:

"Alexandra has—"

"You'll get millions when the AAC is running."

"But it's not yet and I need a lot of money because—"

"I will take care—"

"Stop, Oleg! You're not listening." She'd raised her voice to him. She'd never done that before. "Alexandra has leukemia."

Oleg stopped. Now Galina was crying, and he was at a loss as to what to do with her. Alexandra walked out of her bedroom in her blue bunny pajamas with the attached feet, dragging a blanket as she had done when she was a toddler.

"What's leukemia, Mommy?"

Galina rushed to take Alexandra in her arms as Oleg's phone vibrated. Ukrainian hacker again. "I *have* to take this," he said to the rose.

"I think I figured it out," the hacker said.

"Figured what out?" *What's he talking about?*

"The 'or else?'"

"Don't say another word." Oleg hung up on him even faster this time.

No telling what the Federal Security Service—or even NSA's latest-generation Echelon system—might scoop up. Oleg would take no chances with his crowning moment. Not now. Not when he was down to days.

He turned back to Galina, still holding Alexandra as if the little girl's life depended on it. He gave them both a big smile.

"Now what were *you* guys talking about?"

CHAPTER 5

THE APPEARANCE OF NORMALCY in Lana's home unnerved her. It made her feel eerie this morning. Such was the nature of cyberterrorism. The whole world could be on the very cusp of collapse, yet few, if any, palpable hints of mayhem would appear until it was too late. So while kinetic war—guns and ammo, jets and bombs, choppers and troops—made it explicit that life itself was at stake, the hackers' hijacking of the U.S.S. *Delphin* made her feel as if she had a different kind of poison seeping silently, invisibly from under the floorboards as she walked into Emma's room.

Her daughter slept on a twin bed across from the one occupied for the night by Tanesa. Their alarm was set for 7:00 a.m., when they would awaken to rowdy rock downloaded by the otherwise staid Tanesa. Despite her admirable restraint in so many respects, the young woman loved her headbanger music with the morning's first blinks. Emma also did, and Lana supposed that would hold true even on the day she would make her solo debut singing Bach at the National Cathedral.

Lana kissed Emma on the head so softly she didn't stir, then inhaled her sleepy scent in a manner not unlike the one she'd cherished fifteen years ago when her baby was a newborn and she'd cradled that dark-haired head in her hand and drawn her close enough to feel her breath. And of course Lana knew why the memory flooded through her right now and left a pang in her belly: life always felt most precious when it was under threat.

She tiptoed out of the room, knowing that by the time that rock music blasted the girls awake she'd be meeting with the nation's top cybercommand at NSA headquarters at Fort Meade. And when Emma and Tanesa stood in the National Cathedral, attired in blue satin robes along with the rest of the choir, Lana would find herself in yet another meeting—this one regarding *Magic Dragon*, the newly discovered Chinese Army hacker unit.

Lana backed her Prius out of the garage and left behind Bethesda, Maryland, a sleepy, leafy bedroom community, for DC. Most of the townspeople would rise blissfully ignorant of the crisis taking place off the Argentine coast. But a healthy number of the town's population worked for the CIA, FBI, or NSA, and would learn soon enough of the impending peril, if they hadn't been informed already. That would lead to a run on gas stations this morning; Lana had topped off last night. The more observant nongovernmental employees in town had long ago dubbed it "panic at the pumps," having learned that the sudden, otherwise inexplicable lines could foretell a national crisis.

She merged onto the Beltway, soon passing Reagan International, recalling how last year's disaster had her studying the skies as she drove to affirm that civilian airlines had been spared—and they had been, but only briefly. She winced, wondering what the latest calamity might bring.

Lana drove up to the guard station at Fort Meade's main gate at 6:45 on the dot, plenty of time to clear security and motor to the complex of fifty-plus buildings that formed the heart of the nation's intelligence complex.

At a glance, even a novice's eye would have gleaned the tough security: antitank barriers, ubiquitous guards on foot and in patrol cars, electrical fences, one-way windows, and the vast variety of antennas sprouting from the buildings. But not even the keenest eyes could have spotted NSA's copper-clad interior walls, which repulsed electromagnetic probes.

When she arrived at Deputy Director Holmes's office, his longtime assistant, Donna Warnes, stout and gray and unstinting in her loyalty to her boss and country, directed Lana—with a tight smile of welcome—to a familiar SCIF, Secure Compartmented Information Facility: a room absolutely sealed off from the hydra-headed electronic incursions that daily tried to unveil the agency's deepest secrets.

But who was the enemy this time? That was chief among the many questions plaguing Lana and, she was certain, everyone else meeting behind the windowless door still closed to her. She handed over her laptop and personal items to security personnel, black and white burr-headed men with demeanors that might have been chiseled from stone.

One of them, a former safety for Ole Miss, read her in, which meant he informed Lana that life as she had known it would end if she violated any of the security precepts to which she had long ago agreed. She acknowledged his every word, saw the slight, almost undetectable smile he bestowed upon her every time they met or passed each other since last year's attack, and signed the obligatory form.

Another security agent, fully taciturn, held the heavy door for her. No windows inside, either, unless you saw the motion detectors and cameras in the corners of the room as metaphors. They did, after all, provide a view of any unauthorized entry.

Participants were still settling in as Lana made her way to her assigned seat. They included General Clifford Sprouse, the

Commander of the U.S. Cyber Command (USCC), who sat directly to the right of Holmes. The general rose, meeting her halfway around the table for the introduction that Holmes provided with his customary briskness.

Others were more familiar to her, men such as Joshua Tenon of the NSA, a veteran cyberwarrior who'd had a salt-and-pepper beard before last year's catastrophic attack on the grid. Today, he tugged nervously on the pure white hair that framed his chin, giving Lana a lascivious stare when he thought she wasn't noticing.

Teresa McGivern was present, which came as no surprise to Lana. McGivern had been at the agency "forever," as she generally put it when queried, and had been slated to retire when the grid went down thirteen months ago. Her display of mettle throughout the ordeal made Holmes recognize, once again, how truly irreplaceable she was. "Sayonara Myrtle Beach," McGivern once joked to Lana about her postponed retirement dream.

Chief of Naval Operations Admiral Deming was seated with two senior aides across from Lana. She rose to greet him formally, having only "met" him previously in the videoconference called by Holmes yesterday. Deming looked as though he hadn't slept last night and might have nicked himself shaving this morning. Lana spied a red spot on his neck and a tiny pink smudge just below it on his starched white collar.

But for Lana's money, the shocker at the table was Admiral Wourzy, the chip counterfeiter from the California casino, who also happened to be the navy's chief of cybersecurity. He was short, squat, with hair so black and lacquered straight back that he might have dyed and shaped it with shoe polish. He also appeared unhealthily pale, as though he had, indeed, spent too many hours resting his elbows on the green felt of gaming tables. Just seeing him made her think of gambling, the way a smoker lighting up can make an ex-smoker watch in envy as the tobacco reddens and the addict draws the gray fumes deep into his lungs. She was glad she was in a SCIF with no opportunity to jump online for a quick hand of Texas Hold 'em.

When Wourzy smiled anxiously at her, she sensed his embarrassment, which she found disarming for reasons that did not register readily. She nodded at him, maintaining a pleasant enough expression, to which he responded by mouthing "Hello," as though a bond had just been formed.

Oh, great.

But Lana had always taken up for the underdog. She could easily imagine how humiliating it would be to find yourself the pariah at the table, someone so clearly tolerated only because of extreme circumstances. But it wasn't as though he'd sold state secrets. He'd been a buffoon, and would undoubtedly pay for it once his expertise was no longer part of the nation's triaged response. She'd certainly behaved foolishly at online gambling sites, where she'd watched her money disappear into cyberspace. She'd lost enough in one year to have paid for Emma's first year at the college or university of her choice. Lana winced inwardly at the memory.

"What we're seeing with the hacking and hijacking of the submarine is unprecedented," Holmes began after they were all in place. "So far, we're aware of only one survivor. He's First Class Petty Officer Hector Gomez, who's in charge of the Missile Control Center. He says he cannot take control of the *Delphin* or its missiles. But the submarine is operational and Admirals Deming and Wourzy assure us that there must be more than half a dozen men or women running the reactor plant, control room, and missile system.

"The parts of the sub in view of cameras show dozens of dead bodies. Early this morning we received their demand. They, whoever 'they' turn out to be, want all the Arctic nations making claims on the resources of the region to abandon their 'exploitive practices' and leave. That was the entire communiqué that first showed up on my *home* computer at 4:00 a.m. Of course, such abandonment is not going to happen, which they must anticipate."

Home computer? That was what resonated most for Lana, and she suspected that was true for Holmes as well. He looked profoundly disgusted over having to admit that his sophisticated cyberdefenses had also been penetrated by the hackers—plural—for surely this was a high-performance team at work. She figured a corps of the NSA's finest techies was at his house triaging and performing digital forensics on every piece of hardware he owned.

"Sounds, on the face of it, like it could be Anonymous, or an environmental offshoot," Tenon said. Anonymous, as the name would suggest, was a band of mostly unknown, decentralized hacktivists who embraced a wide spectrum of progressive and environmental causes—and had made hash of their enemies' computer systems, which included the U.S. government's on occasion.

Lana was dubious. Hacking a nuclear-armed submarine, even with inside help, went well beyond the capabilities of anything Anonymous or its affiliates had demonstrated in the past.

"We prepared a report just last month," Tenon continued, "on the increasing militancy of that sector. Although, to be frank, it feels like too easy a conclusion for my comfort, and a task too difficult for what we've seen from them in the past."

Lana nodded her agreement. The question that troubled her was: What would the hackers do *now*? Use the submarine as the weapon it was intended to be? Threaten to bomb DC and Moscow if the two most powerful Arctic nations refused to budge? Killing untold millions and spewing sickening levels of radiation over several continents seemed counterproductive from an environmental point of view. Consistency may be the hobgoblin of small minds, but in this case *inconsistency* would make absolutely no sense if it hailed from Anonymous or its cohorts.

"So that was it?" McGivern asked. "Just *leave*?"

"That's correct," Holmes said.

"How bizarre. No threats?"

"None," Holmes replied. "But with a nuclear-armed sub the threat's implied."

"But not with any specificity," McGivern countered, to which Holmes nodded.

General Sprouse asked about the hackers' TTPs: tactics, techniques, and procedures. "Do we know of any digital fingerprints that might suggest any known perpetrators? I'm thinking of APTs and the Chinese."

Beijing had made great use of Advanced Persistent Threats, which were essentially gangs so corporate in nature that many worked normal business hours to hack targets with great patience. They often spent years surveilling and doing careful reconnaissance of their targets' networks and computer systems, carefully probing a target's cybersystems. Among their favorite malware were Trojans, which provided backdoor access to a computer system, and worms, which spread their virulent code throughout the target. Sometimes their malware was even introduced during the construction of the device, which, theoretically, could include components of a nuclear-armed submarine of sufficiently recent vintage.

"It's too early for the forensics," said Admiral Wourzy. "That sub is almost a completely isolated entity. We have few trails to follow. It's not like the attack on the grid where there were defined ports of entry." Trojans and rootkits. "Our Cyber Incident Response is going to be virtually impossible with our limited remote access."

He might have been chintzy with his chips, but Wourzy lacked no confidence in his opinions. In fact, Lana would have bet that he was pleased to be back in the game.

"I find it interesting," Admiral Deming said, raking his gray hair back as he had during yesterday's videoconference, "that this attack was launched on the eve of our meeting to discuss *Magic Dragon* and the Chinese. Are we just looking at it as a coincidence that a new Chinese hacker unit has been identified and, 'Oh by the way, there's an unprecedented attack on a nuclear submarine'?"

"Are you suggesting that they know that we know and that this is payback for their exposure?" Tenon asked the admiral, with another tug on his beard.

"It's possible," the admiral said.

McGivern was their acknowledged China expert, so when she promptly placed her elbows on the table and steepled her fingers, everyone looked at her.

"The Chinese are far too invested in the status quo to make this kind of high-stakes move. What's in it for them? They're ill prepared, by all accounts, to take over Arctic drilling and shipping, if that's the end game to what we're now seeing. Nor does this seem remotely like the Chinese state's typical MO."

"I suppose," Tenon said, "they could be Chinese hackers operating without Beijing's approval, or with only the tacit approval of an arm of their intelligence service. China's suffering devastating droughts in the north and south and have millions of acres of farmland lying fallow. It's so bad they're starting to get some religion on climate change."

Unlikely, thought Lana. *To what end?*

"Are you suggesting," McGivern asked, "that the Chinese might be adopting the Russian model, letting so-called 'patriotic citizens' do the dirty business of hacking opponents? Building deniability into the plan? Because if you are, let me point out a big difference between the Chinese and the Russians. The Chinese have substantial control of Internet access in their country. They can put up their 'Great Firewall' not only to censor outbound connections, but block inbound connections and effectively isolate themselves from most of the rest of the world. The Russians would find it impossible to match that kind of control. The Internet in Russia is almost as much of a food fight as it is here. Moreover, it is still Chinese state policy to grow the economy, not stifle it. They would take a dim view of any of their citizens, or an arm of their intelligence service, hacking and commandeering a U.S. submarine to stymie oil and gas development that would benefit them." She shook her head, wrapped a wave of gray hair behind her ear, and concluded: "Not the Chinese, and not Chinese renegades. As for *Magic Dragon*," she turned her attention to Admiral Deming, "that is a Chinese Army unit, not some rogue outfit."

Lana liked McGivern; she gave no quarter to anyone, regardless of rank. Perhaps that was a perk of wanting to retire and being implored to hang around.

"I think Teresa has brought up an interesting point about the Russians," Lana said. "But it's nearly impossible to fathom that *any* government would sanction this kind of action." Tenon started to speak but she rode over him: "Yes, I know that there are cyberunits in many countries now, and a lot of them hate us, but would any of them risk life and limb to do something like *this*? Even jihadists like to pick with care their time and place to fight. Plus the Russians already control about half the oil and gas interests in the Arctic, so why would their leadership countenance such a move?"

"Only if they knew that it didn't affect them," Admiral Wourzy said. "If they were in league with the hackers from the very beginning."

"Okay," Lana said, "but whoever the hackers are they must have some consequence in mind, some punishment in store, when the Arctic nations refuse to pull up stakes. This is clearly not an academic exercise. The planning for this must have taken years. That's the only reason the Russians would play this hand. So I'd suggest we start thinking very hard about what these hackers can do with their missiles that would have minimum impact on Russia, and maximum impact on the rest of the world. Otherwise, we should start looking elsewhere."

"Noted," said Holmes. "Any ideas?" He looked around the table. "Anyone?"

When no one spoke up, Holmes resumed: "Then there's another question: Why are they quiet? Whoever they are, they're sitting on a propaganda coup of staggering proportions."

"They won't be quiet for long," McGivern replied. "First, we'll see that horrible video on every screen in the world; then we'll hear their threats."

Wourzy nodded. "You can bet on that."

"Well," Lana said, "they are hackers first and foremost. Don't be surprised if they hijack CNN and FOX and every other media outlet."

"That's what happened last year," Tenon reminded everyone unnecessarily.

"They're holding all the cards," Wourzy said. "And in a very real sense they're forcing *our* hand. If we don't come forward and announce the hijacking, especially with these deaths now, they'll do it for us. It's like we're shooting at shadows."

That phrase resonated strongly with Lana. *Shadows.* Nothing was ever as it appeared. So if that were the case, then it wasn't the Russians or Chinese or Iranians or Anonymous or any other antic actors on the cyberscene. The rogues were in the shadows. They were the Ted Kaczynskis of their time. But what alarmed Lana was the continuing recognition that the hackers in the shadows often did work hand in glove with the established war rooms of the world.

The meeting was interrupted by the sudden opening of the SCIF door. A young female aide rushed in and turned on Reuters News Online. The news channel had obtained video of the interior of the submarine, undoubtedly provided by the hackers, showing the many dead on the vessel, including Captain Hueller. Then a computer-generated voice warned against "anyone" interfering with the nuclear-armed sub, "or else."

• • •

By late afternoon Lana felt as if all the oxygen had been drained from her *own* brain. She'd made no headway in cracking the hackers' code, finding no consolation in hearing from her VP, Jeff Jensen, that he'd made no headway, either. The former navy cryptographer had been in near-constant communications with cohorts in the service, who also found themselves frustrated with every *click*.

Lana's efforts had taken her around the world through a wide assortment of servers. Though dubious, she'd finally gone to work on Anonymous, but after three arduous hours of finger-flying over their terrain she'd come to the same conclusion with which she'd started her trek: no involvement by the most notorious hacker brand.

Which did have her thinking the *Delphin*'s hackers were an entirely new crew, or one savvy and technologically sophisticated enough to have cleaned their virtual slate of every last chalk mark.

Holmes caught her sitting with her fingers sunk into her hair, clutching her head.

"*Magic Dragon*'s canceled for tonight," he announced. "The President has called an emergency meeting at the White House.

Admiral Deming and General Sprouse will be joined by the various secretaries."

She knew what that meant: Defense, Homeland Security, each of the services, plus the directors of the CIA and FBI.

"I think you should take this opportunity to go home," Holmes advised. "Get some rest and get ready for tomorrow. In fact, I'm ordering you to do it."

Her first impulse was to resist, but she felt fully depleted after last night's lousy sleep. Then, of course, she thought of Emma and the National Cathedral and knew where she was headed. But would it be fair to show up when her daughter would be meeting Don, for the first time?

Of course it would. Do you trust him with her?

The answer was a resounding no, and why should she? Delaying no longer, she headed for the District, fighting traffic all the way. She would not make a scene with Donald, but she would keep a keen, if discreet, eye on the federal prisoner in his ankle monitor.

• • •

The neo-Gothic cathedral was lit up, brilliantly displayed against the night sky as she walked toward it. Lana heard the choir even before she entered, and as she passed under the exquisite stone carving of the Last Supper over the entrance, she saw that the church was packed.

She felt fortunate to find a seat in the last pew, barely able to pick out her daughter in the broad display of blue satin up on the wide altar.

A violin solo rose to the side of the choir as she settled in. Lana hadn't realized that they would have a full orchestra to accompany them, but she'd been playing catch-up on choral music since Tanesa had led Emma down this artistic path.

Tanesa's solo came first, and Lana caught herself digging for tissues and dabbing tears as the girl's voice filled the cathedral. Tanesa sounded pure and flawless to Lana's admittedly unpracticed ear, but she looked around and saw many people nodding approvingly.

She knew little more about *St Matthew's Passion* than the name itself suggested: a demonstration of Bach's fealty for his faith. Lana lacked great devotion to any religion, but did have tremendous admiration for the art inspired by fervent spiritual belief.

That thought was interrupted when Emma began to sing her solo. Lana did not recognize her daughter's voice right away, but glimpsed enough of her to be sure that Emma was now the focus of audience admiration wherever she glanced. Her daughter had a lovely soprano voice and handled the German with aplomb.

How does this happen? she asked herself. Your child leaps from gangly childhood to exhibitions of skill and beauty that you could never have anticipated a year ago. Lana had to dig for her tissues once more.

After the choir bowed to sustained applause, Lana edged along the side of the cathedral, moving past stately stone columns, hoping to watch Emma meet her father for the first time. Mostly, she wished that she could have rushed to Emma to congratulate her right then. But she had to grant her daughter—and Emma's father, *Damn him!*—their first meeting. One more reason to resent Donald Fedder.

She caught the moment seconds later. Donald, blue suited with a crimson striped tie—looking anything but a convict— shook Emma's hand. At least he hadn't presumed to have earned a hug by showing up. Lana had to concede that much.

For her part, Emma looked curious, pleased, but also tentative as she chatted with him.

Don gestured to a pew, away from others still congregating near the altar, including the musicians packing up their instruments.

Lana checked her watch; Don was to have fifteen minutes max. She needn't have bothered; a woman from the Bureau of Prisons—that was Lana's bet, in any case—had apparently been dispatched to monitor the pair, which she did from a few rows back. Lana could pick out a spy even in a cathedral. And then she realized, naturally, that she herself was spying, which formed the first direct parallel she could think of between her professional and personal life.

The watch checking proved unnecessary, in any event; after fifteen minutes Don stood. So did Emma. He reached to shake her hand again, but Emma deftly moved it aside and took her father in her arms instead. It was such a smooth adult move that Lana choked up.

But Lana also felt a distinct pang of jealousy, followed quickly by a wholly unexpected pulse of happiness on Emma's behalf: she had found her father, and he had accorded his child the dignity she so richly deserved.

Lana slipped away quietly, knowing that Tanesa's parents would bring Emma home.

As soon as she exited the cathedral, she checked for messages. There were several, but the one from Holmes, presumably sent from the Oval Office, drew her instant attention. It provided a link to the inevitable threat from the hacker-hijackers.

Finally, she thought grimly.

Her fierce desire for them to come forward with their "or else" had been satisfied.

Standing in light bleeding from the front of the cathedral, Lana read the threat twice. It was so unthinkably dangerous to the entire world—and yet so obvious—that she knew the likelihood of an actual missile attack had escalated from the unthinkable to the probable.

And it would be far more devastating than anyone, including herself, could possibly have imagined.

CHAPTER 6

OLEG WAS SO FRUSTRATED he pounded the trident symbol in the middle of the Maserati's steering wheel to sound the horn. That earned him the temper of the long-haired blonde in front of him, who made an obscene gesture and honked her own horn. So Oleg roared past her lousy little Lada, gave her another blast, *and* the same gesture. Wanted to run her off the road.

Okay, so bad mood, Oleg. Get a grip. Don't abuse such a beautiful car.

Why was he in such a bad mood? All he'd wanted when he stopped by to see Galina was a simple apology: "I'm sorry, Oleg, for working for Papa Plutocrat and Dmitri." That was all she had to say—and then some make up sex to show that she was really sincere.

Not kiddie cancer. Who wanted to hear about *that*?

Secret for girlfriend success: Apology + Sex = NO BIG DEAL.

And then you're forgiven. Jesus.

But *she* got pissed off.

Go figure.

Bigger sturgeon to fry now. Oleg had used his own hacked channels to the White House to let them know about the threat hanging over their heads—and the rest of the world's—so it was time to make sure *Numero Uno* hacker, the Ukrainian, was fully in the loop, too.

Uno was a smart boy, so it was very possible that he'd identified the target all on his own. If not, though, Oleg needed to inform him straightaway because *Uno* had hacked the sub's communications and—with some valuable help aboard—would be aiming the Trident IIs. "Like very exciting video game," *Uno* had told him.

The target was not going to be Washington, much as Oleg hated that place, or New York, much as he loved it, or Paris, London, Hong Kong, Beijing, or Flint, Michigan, a shitty city Oleg personally would have been happy to blow up with a thermonuclear device. He had been carjacked there by big black men on a hot summer night when he was just passing through minding his own business and thought it would be a nice boost for the local economy if he bought some excellent crack cocaine for a special friend whose acquaintance he'd made on a street corner a few blocks away. Those American blacks were ingrates. They threatened to tear out his lungs for bringing his "ofay self" into their hood, which had enough problems without "fucking ofays" like him.

Ofay? Ofay? That's the best they can do when it comes to name-calling?

Maybe hard to believe, but the real target was even better than Flint. He smiled just thinking about it, so pleased at finally knowing that he could tell *Uno* where to aim those nuclear missiles. He was speeding home, prepared to bribe stupid Muscovite cops if he had to. Ripping along at one hundred fifty kilometers an hour, he checked out his mug in the rearview mirror—*What was that thump? Potato-faced peasant?*—pleased to see the handsome look of the man staring back at him. Who really needed multiple warheads when the target he'd picked out would be like hitting hundreds of cities all at once?

Leukemia? Oleg dismissed it with a flick of his hand. "Such a trifle." He'd take care of the leukemia later. Give Galina girl some money. He had a good fund-raising idea that would not cut into Ambient Air Capture profits.

No, not car wash. What, you think this is America? Need books for school kids? Car wash. Need blankets for squeegee people? Car wash.

But Oleg's fund-raising idea did have lots of liquids and—*Who knows?*—maybe some bright red spots.

And then, after taking care of the leukemia money, he would accept Galina's apology for working for Papa Plutocrat and helping Dmitri. *Little brother who's bigger than a horse does not need help. Great life. Hookers and indoor waterslide. For a man with a broken brain, doesn't get better.*

But right now Oleg needed to get up to his plush penthouse with a skylight in the living room and another one high above his bed with special heating systems to vaporize the snow so he could see the night sky burning with stars that spoke to him in ways he could never quite put into words. His poetic side that wanted to dance with the stars. The *real* stars, not those losers on bad TV for potato-faced people without satellite or even the crappy Russian version of Netflix.

When he needed ultimate encryption there was only one safe bet: *home sweet home.* He thought it and sang it as he drove into the underground garage and waited all of three seconds for the elevator before darting up to the lobby.

Argh! The cripple. Yes, it was bad to call the wheelchair-bound neighbor a "cripple," but the cripple was a nasty fuck.

And there he was, holding the hand of his crippled girlfriend, both of them wheeling around Moscow like they belonged *everywhere*. Slowing down *everyone*. Waiting for the damn elevator. Just getting them on was like loading nuclear pellets. First, she went, doing a six-point turn until she faced out. Then he got on; with even less room to maneuver, he needed a ten-point turn. By then the doors were *boing-boinging* off his chair. But each of them never seemed to notice because they were always busy flashing big toothy smiles at everyone except him.

But he didn't dare rush ahead and close the elevator doors on them. He'd done that last month and they'd filed a complaint with the co-op board, which threatened to force him to sell and leave.

"If you're not careful," he'd warned the board in his most cunning voice, "I'll buy the building and send all of you packing. Cripples first." Ha-ha-ha. That had shut them up.

But now he was paying the price of his impatience because he couldn't push past them when he really needed to. Too many witnesses getting mail, smoking, talking, watching, and waiting to see what the "Penthouse Prick" would do. That was what a crone on the co-op board had nicknamed him—and it stuck.

Oleg took the stairs, panting after two flights. Then he had a better idea. He burst through the next stairwell doorway and raced to the elevator, pushing the up button.

Ding.

And there they were, just as he figured, staring at him. No toothy smiles now. He pushed the button for the very next floor.

The doors closed.

Ding. They opened.

"Here, cripple girlfriend. You first," he said, giving her a good shove.

"And now your turn, Wheel Beast."

"No!" the cripple bellowed. "It's not our floor."

"I know, but better—no witnesses," he added as he pressed a button and closed the doors.

In seconds he rose to the top floor and stepped into his penthouse, to which only he had the key. Then he rushed to his bank of computers to bring up hacker #1.

Click-click-click. Then more clicks. Lots of clicks.

"Okay, hooked up," he said to himself. "So tell me," keyboarding to #1, "what do you think 'or else' means?"

Don't disappoint me, thought Oleg. *I want to talk to someone about this most magnificent target in all of world history.*

"WAIS," was *Numero Uno's* total answer.

But it made Oleg hug himself because *Uno* was spot-on: West Antarctic Ice Sheet.

"You are right!" he keyboarded back.

"Pure genius," *Uno* replied. "Theoretically unstable," he added.

"Theoretically?" Oleg guffawed so hard he almost fell off his Aeron.

A renowned geologist had called the massive WAIS an "awakened giant" that could reach a "tipping point"—not a metaphor, for once—and crash into the ocean. Bombing it would create the biggest *kerplunk* in history and raise sea levels by 3.3 meters (eleven feet, Americans!).

If the Arctic, with all its gas and oil, was the prize—and it most certainly was—Oleg thought Antarctica, with its deliriously unstable ice sheet at the bottom of the world, would soon provide the punishment for all those other countries that had, once again, underestimated Russian resolve.

Other than Holland, of course, the nation that would be hammered hardest would be the United States, where 40 percent of the people lived right on or near the coast. And even though the seas would rise almost everywhere, they would be 25 percent higher on America's Atlantic and Pacific coasts because as ice melted from the nuclear blast—and vast chunks were dislodged by the explosion—the planet's spin would begin to change, which would shift the focus of the earth's gravitational field farther north. That would pile up seas higher on the coasts of North America. The process was already underway. Thanks to climate change, Antarctica had one of the fastest warming rates in the world. The continent had actually shrunk by 125 cubic kilometers every year since the beginning of the decade. But a nuclear blast would make global warming's impact seem puny by comparison.

When Oleg had first learned about America taking it on the chin, he thought it was too good to be true. But what was even better was that Russia didn't have a single city in the top-fifteen list of those most in danger of sea-level rise.

All through Russian history its leaders had worried about ports. Never enough ports. All the time it was ports-ports-ports *and* the fear of being landlocked. That was a big reason for taking Crimea from those ingrate Ukrainians—*Bad as black men in Flint. Maybe related even*—to keep the Port of Sevastopol firmly in Russian control for the Black Sea Fleet.

But when the seas rose, Russia would be nice and cozy. For the imperialist western powers and the inscrutable Chinese? Disaster. Russia's great destiny, sought for centuries, would come to completion in the hands of Oleg Dernov.

Just a single warhead on a Trident II would be dozens of times more powerful than the Hiroshima bomb, and the Tridents with multiple warheads would most certainly drop the entire ice sheet into the ocean in seconds. So Oleg was understandably overjoyed to have someone, at last, to chat with about this triumph. An enthusiast, no less, much like himself.

"So let's do it," *Uno* wrote.

"Patience, patience," Oleg wrote back. Even if PP was correct that it was a greatly overrated virtue.

"Must target very carefully," Oleg typed. "Shave off portions of WAIS. Show them we're serious. Raise sea level a foot or two." Good-bye Miami, Amsterdam, good-bye parts of London, New York, Boston, and other cities too numerous to name.

Oleg knew, naturally, that you roll the dice when you bomb the ice because the awakened giant of WAIS, well, it could become chaos theory in action. Only this time it wouldn't be a butterfly flapping its wings in China, but a Trident II in Antarctica persuading those reluctant Arctic countries to leave the oil and gas fields on the top of the world.

They'd have to, anyway, because they'd all be in crisis.

But not Russia.

The strongest men in the Kremlin privately, quietly, had long ago given the go-ahead to certain Russian explorers to claim the entire Arctic for the motherland. The rest of the world laughed when Artur Chilingarov sailed a submersible to the floor of the Arctic Ocean, planted a titanium Russian flag in the seabed, and claimed all of the Arctic for the Russian Federation. To make his point even clearer, the intrepid Chilingarov rose from the ocean floor with words that were cheered by the country's true patriots: "The Arctic is Russian. We must prove the North Pole is an extension of the Russian landmass."

What the rest of the world didn't know was that with another wink and a blink, the same powerful men had also let it be known to an intrepid hacker named Oleg Dernov that his project was viewed most favorably from on high. Never a direct word—and wholly hands off—but Oleg's project had been blessed just as the minor efforts of lesser hackers had long been.

With the WAIS in the ocean—and massive emergencies all over the planet—who could possibly stop the Russians from exploiting the wealth that was properly theirs? They would sell the gas and oil to pathetic, broken countries, while having the technological capacity to suck carbon dioxide out of the atmosphere. Russia could raise and lower temperatures to reward friends and punish foes.

It wouldn't be the Russians' fault that history and destiny had seen to their safety and security. The rest of the world would be so preoccupied with simple survival that they'd scarcely have a moment to notice Russian extraction of gas and oil in the north.

"So when? When!" *Uno* asked.

"When I say. You have twenty-four hours to get ready. Go to work. Report back. Then you can launch the missile with the single warhead."

So Florida, get in your boats. Amsterdam, pull on your boots. Washington, break out your ditch bags.

And that would be just the beginning.

Oleg signed off with *Uno* but undertook some more direct hacking of his own. Nothing so challenging as trying to hack into the White House network. Now he was just tracking down Alexandra's deadbeat dad so he could put his fund-raising idea into action.

It didn't take Oleg long to find him, or to fill out the online form for a life insurance policy that would benefit the girl if something "unforeseen" should happen to her father. A really big policy with a special accident clause.

Oleg knew the little love of Galina's life needed the money. So the big love of her life would provide it.

"Always be generous to the women you love," PP had often said.

With a final click, Oleg prepared to follow his sage advice.

But there was something else PP had always said about girls. It was even more important, if Oleg remembered correctly. *That's it,* he recalled with a smile. PP had called it "the key to happiness." The old man had been dandling Oleg on his knee when he whispered these wise words into his ear for the first time: "The secret to a really happy life, firstborn son, is to always tip the really hot chicks."

It hadn't meant much to the six-year-old, but PP had repeated it every year on Oleg's birthday until finally, when he turned fourteen, PP's generosity found genuine meaning.

Before calling it a day, Oleg turned his attention back to *Uno*, finding that his protégé and his onboard help were maintaining command of the *Delphin's* Missile Control Center.

Oleg studied the scene in the Center of Submarine Control, COC, located in the upper level of the Operations Compartment. He couldn't help but admire the dazzling computer touch screens and the green, orange, and blue glow from the Attack Center, Ballast Control, and other displays reflecting on the faces of the sailors who stared so intently at them—the pure dynamism of America's weaponry. *Like Disneyland for death!* Or, as *Uno* had put it, "a very exciting video game."

Oleg knew that with all those dazzling technologies now under his command, there would be little to stop him from launching a direct hit on the WAIS. Massive fireworks would light up the Frozen Continent and unprecedented flooding would devour much of the world.

CHAPTER 7

LANA HAD SHED HER elegant heels to keep running from the National Cathedral, and now had the Prius in sight when one of Holmes's aides texted that the deputy director was calling an emergency session at NSA headquarters in an hour. She had assumed they'd be meeting tonight: a threat of unprecedented magnitude demanded immediate action.

When she'd received the message about the threat she should have turned right around and told Emma that she might bed down at Fort Meade tonight.

Too late for that now. Text her.

Lana slowed just enough to put her digits to work—"Working late. Don't want u home alone. Ask Tanesa to stay with u."

Holmes's aide sent another text with a detailed map of Antarctica and a color-coded view of the WAIS that highlighted the ice sheet's most vulnerable point. It lay just west of the Transantarctic Mountains, which ran roughly north and south like a fragile spine.

Even staring at the announced target, Lana could not help but experience a measure of comfort. At least the aim wasn't to vaporize Washington, New York, Paris, Berlin, London, or any other major city.

But that first flush of relief faded quickly. While she was glad to know that mass incineration of citizens wasn't on some terrorist agenda—if the hackers' communiqué about bombing Antarctica could actually be trusted—she also recalled that a slow-motion catastrophe, by thermonuclear standards, would be triggered if the WAIS were hit.

She wasn't an expert on Antarctica, but knew that scientists worldwide already considered it one of the major worries of climate change: if the whole ice sheet were cleaved from the continent by the warming, *or* a massive bomb, seas would rise by a staggering eleven feet, *in a matter of days.*

WAIS was such a looming topic for the U.S. Task Force on Climate Change that it was slated as *the* subject of next month's meeting in Annapolis, which now sounded like an academic exercise with the real threat of a nuclear missile strike—or *strikes*—on the planet's southernmost region.

Lana threw herself behind the wheel, wondering what an eleven-foot rise in the waters of Chesapeake Bay would mean. She was tempted to do the research then and there but weightier concerns saw her speeding out of the car park.

Not for long. She had to hit the brakes quickly, then fought traffic for blocks, noting the unworried faces of so many drivers and pedestrians, including the young couples, hand in hand, who were crossing at streetlights blissfully unaware of the impending peril.

If they only knew.

This was so unlike last year, when the whole country became aware of the attack with the speed of a blackout. That assault had come with no warning, taking down the grid and setting off a nationwide power outage on a balmy September morning. No couples had strolled hand in hand with traffic jams seizing virtually every intersection. Then train derailments began across the country, along with pipeline explosions and a vicious array of other cyberattacks, all of which were brutally visible, even if the cyberterrorists themselves had been wholly absent to the eye.

A nuclear attack on the WAIS, on the other hand, would be so far removed by comparison that most citizens of the U.S. and the rest of the world would feel little impact initially—but then the waters would begin to rise and all too quickly the horrifying ramifications would sink in.

It took Lana almost a half hour of grindingly slow city traffic to escape to the Beltway, which wasn't exactly the Indy 500, either. But at least the Prius was plodding along now.

Her thoughts quickly focused on the agents of the threatened apocalypse. She knew that word was far overused, but a sudden and radical rise in sea levels, with its consequent smothering of coastlines that had been stable for the last twelve thousand years, certainly did not make the term seem like a stretch. And all of it would happen in the geological equivalent of a blink.

Taking the HOV lane, she powered past miles of lone drivers on her right, feeling no compunction at all because she thought her car carried plenty—the weight of the world. Without the congestion, she felt free to think, but she still could not wrap her head around the idea that any country powerful enough to put this catastrophe into play would actually commit such a self-destructive act. Yet only a highly trained and immensely sophisticated cyberunit could have hacked the navy's communications and, with accomplices onboard, hijacked the *Delphin*. Those hackers now threatened to launch an attack that would change the very contours of the continents for millions of years to come.

Millions?

She could scarcely make sense of her own well-reasoned conclusions. Communicating this to the public would be unfathomably difficult. The attack last year had set off savage displays of panic; she could hardly grasp what would happen this time around—and didn't want to.

Lana had yet to hear back from Emma, so she tried again, adding "ASAP!" before hitting "send."

Respond, Em, come on.

The next instant she was back in professional mode, wondering when the cyberattackers—*Murderers, that's what they are*—were going to launch their lethal assault. The communiqué, which had been boldly sent to the White House and cc'd to Holmes, didn't reveal a countdown. Shrewd—from the unknown enemy's point of view. Whoever had decided on that strategy might have borrowed a page from last year's attackers who toyed with turning the grid on and off to keep everyone in a near panic. And then they turned it on with the vow to shut it down for good at any second, which had unleashed mass hysteria.

But what would Americans—and everyone else in the world—make of seas rising past shorelines and engulfing entire island nations and other vulnerable low-lying countries? Even in the developed world, whole cities and smaller communities would disappear under floods of Biblical proportions. Trillions of dollars' worth of water treatment plants and sewage facilities, hospitals—emergency services of all kinds—along with nuclear power plants, naval bases, and scores of defense installations, would disappear. So, of course, would hundreds of millions of people. Hiroshima and Nagasaki countless times over, but instead of fires raining from the sky, there would be relentless flooding by the seas.

She texted McGivern: "Is Besserman there?"

"Running late, but coming," she replied.

Excellent. Clarence Besserman was one of the government's top experts on climate change's impact on national security. He was also an ex officio member of the Joint Task Force.

Lana rolled up to Fort Meade's front gate, eyed closely by security personnel who waved her through. That had never happened before. But she was stopped seconds later by a band of marines from the service's Fort Meade detachment, one of whom tapped the passenger window and jumped into the seat a moment later.

"Ma'am, drive up to the door and deploy. I'm going to park your car. Your keys *will* catch up to you, along with the car's location."

Lana did as directed, pulling up to the biggest of the NSA buildings, the one with what appeared to be a white tray cake plopped on top. She popped the trunk and hopped out.

"Thank you, sir," she said to the young marine.

"Thank you, ma'am. Godspeed," he added.

She grabbed her computer case out of the trunk and rushed inside.

An NSA security guard was waiting to escort her swiftly to the SCIF, the secure conference room that was starting to feel more familiar than her own office at Meade.

She checked her watch: 10:30 p.m. Just before entering the electronically secured enclosure, she tried Emma again, apologizing to a pair of NSA guards waiting to clear her for entry to the room.

Lana tried texting Tanesa this time. No sooner sent than replied to: "Got Em at my house."

"Thx!" Lana answered before surrendering her devices and enduring the critical security protocol, which included signing off on the procedure. At least her daughter and Tanesa and children everywhere were peacefully ignorant of the threatened assault. But for how long?

That was the first question Holmes raised: "What's our countdown look like? Any ideas?" The deputy director looked every day of his seventy-eight years.

Admiral Wourzy, the chip counterfeiter, said he thought the enemy would strike in a matter of hours. "Or, more to the point, any time now."

"Why?" Holmes asked with unusual impatience.

"Now that they've announced their target," Wourzy replied, "they'll move quickly rather than risk shutdown. And once the attack has taken place, it gives them breathing room while chaos breaks out."

"Or it gives us a means of tracking the hackers to their lair," said the lean, bearded Tenon, once more speaking up early in a meeting, as if always fearful of being overlooked.

"In classic terrorism, that often holds true," Wourzy replied, "because the terrorist leaves behind physical evidence. But this has been engineered by hackers who are much harder to locate. To put it simply, this isn't like tracking an ISIL missile fired from the Iraqi desert. Plus, they've got to know we'll do everything we can to find and sink that sub, so I'd say the good money's on a fast launch."

"*Find the sub?*" Holmes asked. "What are you—"

"We've lost the *Delphin*," Admiral Deming answered. "They moved it into a deep trough and rigged for ultra quiet. The sub has the latest in sound-suppression technology. They've shut off all nonessential equipment, slowed down the fans, and reduced speed to less than ten knots. We've got two destroyers racing to the southern ocean now but they're going to have a helluva time finding the *Delphin*."

"How did we lose them?" Holmes sounded incredulous. "We had them literally in our sights before."

"That was when they used the buoy, and we saw them from the air," Deming replied.

"Believe me, I know how we saw them," Holmes fired back. "How long have you known this?"

"Minutes," Deming reported. "The admiral and I found out walking in the door here."

"What about the destroyers?" Holmes persisted.

"They were also too far away when the *Delphin* went to depth, and the hackers and their accomplices certainly appear to know their topography."

"And the sub's Operations Compartment," Wourzy added. "I'll give you odds-on that navigating the underwater canyons is the least of the challenges they've overcome. They've had plenty of practice of playing around with the navy's computers," he said with raised eyebrows.

An overt reference, Lana was certain, to a cyberincursion revealed by Snowden. As early as three years ago hackers had infiltrated a navy computer system. Iranians were suspected in that attack. A security upgrade—more layers, network segmentation, and enhanced monitoring—had been implemented, which made Lana doubtful that the Iranians had a part in the *Delphin's* takeover, largely because they always seemed too inept to avoid leaving their fingerprints on whatever havoc they caused.

The U.S., of course, had proved equally clumsy—the Iranians would say even more so—with its infamous Stuxnet attack on Iran's nuclear centrifuges. While renowned among experts for its almost flawless code, the U.S. was implicated when the worm escaped Iran's Natanz plant and made its way all around the world. But when a cyberattack was executed well, anonymity made responding quickly and forcefully almost impossible. There were plenty of potential culprits, but getting confirmation

of a single one was much tougher. And now Lana and her colleagues were up against an enemy unlikely to ever claim credit for
an environmental disaster that would devastate every continent
on earth.

Clarence Besserman arrived late, looking as if he'd stepped
from a World War II Defense Department photo, even though
the climate-change expert was in his early thirties. He sported
the wet-look haircut of a military attaché and a bow tie that could
have been filched from the collar of Winston Churchill himself.
Like the late British prime minister and war hero, Besserman was
chubby. In Lana's view, he fit the very definition of that word:
cheeks, arms, chest, legs, everywhere she looked he carried a few
extra pounds of padding. But not obese, not by any means.

Despite the starched bow tie and carefully oiled hair, he was
disheveled with his shirttail hanging out of his pants. It wasn't
simply that he'd been rousted late at night for a meeting, though,
because Besserman always looked like he slept in his clothes.
Only his computer looked crisply intact as he pulled it from its
case, likely because his screen wasn't yet visible. Lana would have
guessed his desktop might also need some ordering. But there
was no disputing Besserman's brilliance.

Holmes, she noticed, looked on the verge of saying, "Glad
you could make it, Clarence," but the younger man looked so
flustered that the deputy director might have spared him out of
charity alone.

"You have something for us, I gather," Holmes actually asked
him.

Did Besserman ever. He launched right into the geopoliti-
cal implications of a rapid rise in sea levels: "We just ran our
first climate-change war games last week. To prepare for the Task
Force presentation next month, we looked at who the actors might
be in a similar attack on the ice sheet. We weren't gaming with

a nuclear-armed submarine in mind because we didn't think the hacking and takeover of one was possible. A lack of imagination on our part, clearly. But we did decide after extensive analysis that hackers targeting the WAIS in any manner would have to be other than a state actor. No country with the ability to bomb the ice sheet into the ocean would ever have enough to gain to make it worth their while. But here was the quandary: No individual hacker would have the means to launch an ICBM in such a precise fashion. So before the *Delphin* was taken over, that was our conundrum and why we concluded such an attack was highly unlikely."

McGivern put up her index finger. Talk about looking war weary and ruffled. "I'm surprised to hear—"

"Except for Russia." Besserman had the presence of mind to let that bulletin settle in.

"But you just said," Tenon broke the silence, "that 'No state actor would have—'"

Besserman rode right over the analyst: "*Until* the *Delphin*. Taking over a submarine of that caliber by hackers working without the support of a state security apparatus is so unlikely that our latest calibrations rank it as a 1 in 1.9 billion possibility. It's not just the sub, it's all the onboard systems. And to launch the missiles, there are codes, required verifications, keys, and a number of manual procedures. We're looking at such extreme expertise needed in so many areas. U.S. submarine technology alone would demand teams of highly trained specialists, all of which would require unprecedented incursion skills, not to mention bringing all that to bear on the earth's Achilles' heel. It's so demonically inspired, it's mind-boggling."

"So nobody saw it coming," Wourzy said, "yet it was hiding in plain sight?"

"Yes," Besserman said. "It's the single most vulnerable climate-change catastrophe that could be set off immediately. We can watch Greenland melt, Arctic ice disappear, the Amazon burn—along with the American West—and the Sahara spread north into Mediterranean countries, but there's not much we could do to speed up any of that, other than what we're already doing inadvertently by continuing to accelerate the release of greenhouse gases. But as we all know now, the WAIS is the world's first big tipping point."

"So what changes if the ice sheet gets hit?" Holmes asked, urgency fueling his tone.

"What *doesn't* change is the question, if I may reframe what you've just asked, sir."

Holmes nodded.

"With an eleven-foot rise in sea level, every map of the world will have to be redrawn. It would shut down our country for months, at the very least, quite possibly years. Every port would flood, and many, if not most, would disappear. They would be underwater. Storm surges could be more than twice that eleven-foot rise. We're still assessing how many major military installations would be wiped out but I can tell you that we'd be looking at more than one hundred. Even if we were sure of how to respond to the attack on Antarctica, we'd still be severely handicapped by the absolute necessity of responding to what would be our overwhelming domestic crises. One hundred fifty million Americans, about half our population, would either be racing from the coastlines, with calamitous results, or those not immediately affected would be overrun by climate refugees. All imports and exports would cease right away, and not just on the Atlantic and Pacific coasts. The Great Lakes would rise, too. From the shores of Lake Superior to the St. Lawrence Seaway, cities would eventually flood. Chicago, Detroit, Buffalo, Milwaukee, Duluth, Syracuse, Rochester. Our most critical cities are on our shores. For all intents and purposes, they would come to a standstill at best, or float away at worst."

Besserman looked startled by his own words. His stunned gaze took in everyone at the conference table. Then he drew another breath and went on: "I've talked to every one of my colleagues at Defense, CIA, you name it. They all agree. This has got to be Russian in origin. The Russians are denying any role, but they've always done that and we know that's true because we've caught them red-handed at it, though nothing of this magnitude. And then they always blame it on 'patriotic citizens' hacking at their leisure. We've even discussed that in here. But this was not a casual incursion. This was planned for a long time and executed with precision."

"What's your sense of the likelihood of a launch?" Holmes asked him.

"*Strong* likelihood for one deceptively simple reason: The Russians will gain the international upper hand almost right away. They would not be spared entirely from the rise of the oceans, but given what their chief competitors would endure—meaning us, China, the NATO nations—the Russians would be mostly insulated from the worst impacts of the rise. The brutal truth is that in a matter of weeks they would become the dominant world power for decades to come."

"Not if we bomb them to rubble," Admiral Deming said.

"Of late, we've looked at that as well, Admiral," Besserman replied, "and that kind of response would be almost as dangerous as a bomb landing on the WAIS. We'd be cutting off our nose to spite our face because, first of all, we may never be able to conclusively prove their role. No smoking gun. And, even more painful to accept, maybe, is that we, along with the rest of the world, would become highly dependent on Russian aid.

Without it, billions would starve. Every year they have more arable land stretching up into Siberia because of the warming. Their vast agricultural base is expanding. And I'm sure you realize the radioactivity released from a massive bombing of Russia would soon sweep over the rest of the world, including America. And of course they'd respond in kind."

"So you're saying they're going to have us coming or going?" Lana asked, unable to keep the outrage from her voice.

Besserman nodded.

Lana didn't accept that pinning it on the Russians—if they were indeed the hackers—would be impossible. Identifying hackers was what she did for a living, but the other part, the radioactive blowback and depending on them for *aid*, well, that was truly "mind-boggling," to borrow Besserman's own words.

And humiliating.

"But the Russians are being ordered out of the Arctic, too," Tenon said.

"They're giving themselves cover," Besserman replied. "Nobody's actually leaving, are they? Which was the result the hackers no doubt expected. If and when the WAIS gets hit, Russia will probably pull out of the Arctic, too, but only for a little while. They'll argue that the gas and oil will be needed to help save the world. And the most galling fact is, they'll be right because with much of the fossil-fuel economy shut down everywhere else, Arctic resources will become very valuable. We certainly won't have the means to begin massive extraction up there. Every possible vessel and all our human resources will be dedicated to simple survival. That's going to be true for all the Arctic nations, and most of the rest of the world as well. Holland, for one, will disappear. If the Russians retreat from the Arctic at all, it will be purely a performance. They believe the Arctic belongs to them. They always have."

"Is it coincidence, then, that Professor Ahearn and his wife were murdered and his prototype likely stolen just before this happened?" Lana asked.

Besserman paused. "Outside my purview, okay? But I don't think it was a coincidence. If Ahearn had the breakthrough with AAC that we've come to believe, and the Russians took it, they'll have the means to use it on a wide scale while the rest of us are tripping over ourselves trying to recover from the collapse of that one very fragile part of the planet."

A messenger entered and handed Holmes a slip of paper. In the silence before the woman passed back through the door, Lana watched Holmes crumple the paper and drop it on the table.

He lifted his eyes to them. "They've announced the threat publicly. While we've been hoping they'd keep it secret for as long as possible, they were planning a worldwide communications takeover to say that at any moment a Trident II will strike the ice sheet."

Holmes, perhaps thinking better of himself, leaned forward and retrieved the balled-up paper and unfolded it. "They even wrote the headline."

Lana had no trouble reading it: "The Oceans Rise. Billions Die."

CHAPTER 8

AMERICA WOKE UP TO the momentous announcement. Montevideo, Oleg's favorite hippie city, woke up to it. Moscow went to sleep knowing about it. And everybody everywhere was shocked. The whole world was quaking to Oleg's threat. He sat watching reports on his big flat screen from all over the Big Blue Ball, which was about to get a lot bluer.

"A great flood is coming," a reporter with a gravelly voice announced over video of an endless sea on NBC TV in New York City. Then the same newsman intoned, "This clip from the movie *Noah* is what a huge flood might have looked like the first time."

Okay, Oleg got it now. The reporter who sounded like a three-pack-a-day smoker was mixing a little entertainment with the news by dragging that flick back off the shelf to make the most of the crisis. How purely American.

But the WAIS flood would be real, and people knew it. Boat prices were going through the roof. In fact, prices for anything that could float—rafts, dinghies, inner tubes, bathtubs—were getting priced right out of reach of most people. Bologna—the city, not the sausage—was putting up barriers to prevent coastal dwellers from the Adriatic *and* Ligurian Seas from overrunning its ancient streets.

There were boat people in Kiribati, the Maldives, Bangladesh, La Jolla. And in Florida, street gangs were "boatjacking" yachts, according to a reporter down there. The term caught on fast, but not as fast as the gangbangers in speedboats could catch up to cabin cruisers. Those banger boys were like cheetahs pouncing on lumbering wildebeests.

Oleg gawked at video of tattooed guys who looked like linebackers storming a sixty-foot boat. Two of the biggest grabbed a hefty woman in a muumuu by her ankles and wrists and swung her back and forth—"*Uno, dos, trés.*" He could read their lips—before they tossed her into the sea.

At least the *gringa* could float. Not all of them could.

He sat there stunned by what he was seeing. For reasons he could not fathom, "Itchycoo Park" started playing in his head. The worst earworm of all time.

PP's third wife used to sing it to Oleg when he was a teen: "It's all too beautiful, It's all too . . ."

He *hated* it, but loved the way her dangly earrings caught the sunlight. Finally, one day he grabbed both of them and jerked her close, head-butting the hippie. Fourteen years old and so sick of hearing "It's all too beautiful" bullshit that he couldn't stand another second of it. But he did like her earrings. He walked away with one in each hand.

Look, look at that! Big news. And it *was* beautiful. New York Stock Exchange—collapsed. NASDAQ—collapsed. Dow Jones—collapsed. The Nikkei—collapsed. London Stock Exchange—collapsed. Shanghai and Shenzhen exchanges—collapsed. The Moscow Stock Exchange—through the roof. Huge profit taking, and then even higher, like Trident IIs, up-up-up. Just like the Russian spirit when the President assured his people that their country would not leave the Arctic and succumb to a terrorist threat, saying, "Destiny is on our side." So was geography.

When the camera zoomed in on the Russian President, Oleg could almost glimpse another wink and a blink just for him. The President was a great man. He could ride race cars, race horses, racy women. All man.

Oleg clicked his remote, bringing in news from America. A white weather guy was talking to a black anchorwoman on a New York morning show. The weather guy was so funny. He actually said sinking the WAIS would be like raising the floor of a basketball court so that anyone could dunk.

Dunk? And they say Russians have a dark sense of humor.

Numero Uno called. Oleg muted the TV.

"Yes," he said in his most amused voice.

"Best bet for first Trident is the big ice shelves, like dams, near the Weddell or Ross Seas." The north or south part of the WAIS, close to the Transantarctic Mountains, which ran roughly north and south along the eastern edge of the massive ice sheet. "You choose, you can't lose, Oleg." The Ukrainian laughed.

"Help me," Oleg said gregariously. "North is closer to the U.S., right? Maybe get the gravitational shift going sooner." Which would raise the seas on both sides of America higher than in the rest of the world, but not the full 25 percent bonus that Oleg wanted most. That wouldn't come till the whole WAIS was bombed loose.

"Maybe not such a big gravity shift with just one ice shelf," *Uno* told him, "but oceans would get deeper. I can guarantee that. No telling how deep because this is chaos theory, like you say, Oleg."

Trying to butter me up. Another Americanism. Oleg knew he was watching too much American TV. But it was so much fun.

"Either one, north or south," *Uno* said, "will be like blowing up a big dam so lots of ice can slide into the ocean."

"Like a sleigh ride!" Oleg laughed.

"Sleigh ride? I don't think so," *Uno* replied soberly. "But very good chunk of ice. Hard to be so precise."

What? "You have their launch systems."

"Don't you worry. I'll take care of it."

"How are things on board? They still dead?" Oleg laughed again. He hadn't checked on the *Delphin* for a while. Didn't like micromanaging *Uno* or the men whom the Ukrainian was working with on the vessel, all under severe duress. Oleg had the same well-dressed crew that had seen to the Ahearns keeping a close eye on the families of the sailors assigned to the submarine's Operations Compartment, including the upper level where Control housed the ballast control panel, a navigation station, attack center, and more. In fact, photos of the Ahearns had even been shown to them. That was just in case they decided they didn't want to cooperate in keeping the vessel moving through the southern ocean, though watching the rest of the crew drop dead would have persuaded most anyone to put on an oxygen mask.

"Still dead," *Uno* replied.

"And Hector Gomez?"

"Don't see much of him but he's still kicking."

"Try to nail down what happens when you hit those ice dams," Oleg ordered before hanging up. "And I mean work on it," he texted *Uno* promptly. The hours were ticking by. He wanted to launch tomorrow. And *Uno* knew that. He should be ready now.

What? Do I have to do everything? Take out life insurance on deadbeat dad? Arrange his accident? Find way to hack into White House? And now Galina was texting him: "I *must* see u."

What's going on?

Made him a horndog to think of her so worked up.

Make-up sex, he thought right away, imagining her next to him, already quivering. *Are you really sorry? Super sorry?* He would whisper those words in her ears, lick the curly cartilage and watch her squirm with delight. Listen to her breath grow faster. *How sorry are you? Show me, bad girl, Galina.* Show *me.*

The "bad girl" business always got her. Made her crazy. Made her do things she swore she'd never done with deadbeat dad. And now she never would. Oleg was sure of that. Deadbeat dad would never do anything to anyone again, except provide a nice death benefit to little Alexandra.

He brought up the sound on his flat screen to hear the American President, who did not race cars. He did not race horses. But he had a very racy wife. So *hot.* Like horrible Henry Kissinger once said, "Power is the great aphrodisiac." *Only reason toadstool like him got laid.*

But the American President was starting to look like a woolly mammoth. Too tired for sex. He was getting grayer every day. All the American Presidents do. Fun to watch it happen. *Like Grecian Formula 44 in reverse.*

"My fellow Americans," he started. "We face an unparalleled challenge . . ."

Must have been reading a boilerplate response filed under "Nuclear Bomb Threat." But what Oleg listened for most closely was the finger-pointing. And there was lots of that. But—*Ho-ho-ho*—at everyone. Which meant no one. Everyone who's a terrorist, that is. Oleg wasn't a terrorist. Oleg was a Pirate of Diplomacy.

But now he needed to be sensitive for Galina, who texted that she was on the elevator: "I'm coming now. Now!"

He'd heard that many times before, under the most pleasing circumstances.

The elevator stopped and he opened the door, ready for some frisky fun.

But she was carrying Alexandra, arms under her knees and shoulders. The girl's head lolled back like a rag doll's. She looked shriveled, too, which did not arouse Oleg, who didn't appreciate

Galina bringing such sickness into his apartment. Penthouse, no less! That made Galina a very bad girl, but not a good bad girl. Just a bad girl. Nothing he would want to whisper into her ear. *What did she think the penthouse was? Kiddie cancer ward? Like book by Solzhenitsyn,* Cancer Ward. *Great story with magnificent hero named—what else?—Oleg.*

Galina rushed Alexandra to his couch and spread the girl's bunny blanket over her, the one that matched her bunny pajamas. The girl's eyes were slits. Such a pretty kid not so long ago. What happened? She needs to smile more. Cancer feeds on despair. Just read Solzhenitsyn. That was why they had an epidemic of cancer in America.

Galina turned to him. "What have you done?"

She sounded hurt, really upset. *Not* sexy.

"Done? What do you mean?"

"I've been busy." She moved her hands as though they were working an invisible keyboard, then pointed both index fingers at him. "*You* are doing this to the world. Do you know what could happen down there?"

"Down where?" He walked to his Sub-Zero Pro. "Do you want some fresh-squeezed orange juice? From Florida, the Sunshine State, but we better drink fast. I hear it's going to be Florida the Flood State pretty soon."

Smiling at her. *Making joke!* Brushing his dark bangs aside, giving her all the moves that made her moist.

She shook her head and advanced on him. She looked murderous.

"I worked hard on those AAC files. Did you think I couldn't figure out who developed it just because you tried to hide that from me?" She made her fingers dance on the invisible keyboard again, but Oleg noticed her eyes. On fire. "It was Professor Brian Ahearn, and *he was murdered!* So was his wife. They had two children, little girls even younger than Alexandra. And the prototype was stolen. Where is it? What did you do with it? And I want to see the rest of his files. You have everything, Oleg, because you took everything, or someone working for you did. I know you've got it. And don't try to tell me that the plan to bomb Antarctica isn't yours. It closes the circle, doesn't it?"

"Circle? What circle?" He poured her some juice. "Maybe her, too?" He looked at the cancer kid. "She looks like she could use some sunshine."

"Her? You mean Alexandra? Say her name. You haven't used it once since I told you about the leukemia. Show some guts, Oleg. Don't pull away because someone you love is sick."

Someone I love? Oleg found that most presumptuous.

He watched her glance at the TV. The woolly mammoth looked like he'd been eating ashes for hours, but he was still talking. All politicians can talk. But *his* words hadn't caught Galina's eye, and they didn't snag Oleg's for long, either. What held their attention was a simple declaration crawling continually across the bottom of the screen: "He lies! He lies!"

Oh, that's good. Definitely the work of *Uno*, who would get a bonus for his most creative thinking.

"I did not have the professor killed." Oleg walked over to the couch, where Galina had settled next to Alexandra, who was sleeping. He tried to hand Galina the orange juice. She shook her head.

"I don't want it. I want to know why the professor suddenly showed up dead. With his wife's finger chopped off."

"I think I know the answer," Oleg replied, putting the juice on an end table. "Maybe others tried to steal his secrets after we got them. Maybe they were a day late and a dollar short, so he had nothing to give up but his life."

"Hers, too."

"Could be. Very sad."

She looked like she believed him. He put that to a test by resting his hand on her knee, half covered by her summery skirt. Pale-yellow cotton. He loved her skirts, the delicious way they made secrets of her legs—and surprises of all her other wonders. With Alexandra asleep, they could scoot into the bedroom.

"No, I *don't* believe you," she blurted suddenly. "I don't believe in coincidence. Someone *else* tried to get secrets of the AAC just after your people got them? No. And that finger business? That sounds like KGB. Are you working with them? You must be."

He shook his head. "And it's not KGB. It's FSB now."

"Same thing, and you know it."

"I will talk to my people, find out the truth," Oleg vowed. He thought he sounded convincing. "I will ask if they did anything to hurt the smart professor and his wife. I will take care of them if they were bad. How about you, Galina girl? Are you bad?"

"Stop that 'bad' business. I'm not here for that. How are *you* going to take care of them? You're not even taking care of us." She looked at her daughter. "She needs the best medical care in the world and you still haven't paid me enough to get it for her. You owe me millions, and she needs help."

"I have paid you something. Everybody's getting paid everything in the end."

"That's what you said last time, after you came from your papa's."

And you looked so bad, he remembered. At least she had lipstick on now.

"So tell me, do I get paid before or after the killers? Afterward, I'm sure, because they would kill you otherwise."

"No killers, I promise. And you are first on my list."

"*What* list?" She sounded alarmed.

He knelt in front of her and began to rub her foot.

She jerked it away, showing her underpants for a second. Long enough. Flashing the green light. *Go-go-go.*

No, he realized a moment later. Just means *she* should go.

And take cancer kid with her.

But Galina wasn't done yet: "I was back at PP's last night because Dmitri was upset and your papa couldn't get him to stop his tantrums."

Oleg leaned closer to her, saying, "Yes?" But he said it in a new way, and she pressed her back into the couch as though she were scared of him. She'd never done that before. He'd never seen her fear. Only her anger, her accusations. Fear was better. Much better. "I told you I didn't want you going over there."

"They're my friends."

"Papa and Dmitri? Friends?" He leaned so close he could smell her lavender oil.

She stiffened, turning as still as Lenin in his tomb.

"Are you scared, Galina girl?" he asked softly, but not a whisper. A whisper wouldn't have been right. That would have sent the wrong signal. But he spoke those words directly into her ear, where they couldn't escape, where they would go straight to her soul. He repeated the question. Then he said, "*You* shouldn't be scared. But have you heard from deadbeat dad?"

She shook her head.

"You will," Oleg told her. "I'm making sure he pays you everything he owes you—and more!"

"What did you do to him?"

Oleg didn't reply. He placed both hands on her knees and then pointed *his* index fingers at her just as she had pointed to him only minutes ago, before making the most outrageous claims. Tit for tat. Then he curled them back so he could flick her hem high onto her thighs.

"Not now," she said.

But she was trying too hard to be firm. He heard the slightest quaver in her voice. He pushed his hands up under her skirt, watching the outline of his knuckles move under the yellowy fabric. Almost as soft as her skin. He started kneading her sweet soft flesh. Alexandra looked asleep. Her mother's legs were pressed together, unforgiving.

"Please. My baby's sick."

"She'll get better. I will take care of everything."

He let her push his hands away. Why not? He'd made his point.

She was shaking when she scooped up her daughter and hurried to the elevator. But she couldn't leave unless he unlocked the door.

Oleg strolled over, and from behind saw her bare shoulder. Alexandra's weight was pulling down on her mother's shirt. He wet his lips and kissed her warm skin, then her neck. He felt her shudder. Didn't mind. That was the nature of their relationship now: fear. He would make sure the insurance company spoke to her soon. He would also make sure the police had her identify the body. Even the rendering of deadbeat dad's face had been done with great care. Half of it remained just as it was when they made the cancer kid. It would be easy for her to say, "Yes, that's him."

Oleg inserted a red key and turned it, hailing the elevator. They listened to the soft hum as it rose, never saying a word. But he saw bumps on her arms, and said nothing to break the stark symphony of their silence.

He felt like a conductor again, waving his baton, leading the darkest orchestra of all.

The elevator doors opened. She stepped inside and turned around. He reached in and pushed the button for the garage. Then he ran his hand over Alexandra's brow. Galina stepped away.

"I'll see you soon," he said to her.

She was staring at where he'd just touched her child.

CHAPTER 9

LANA AWOKE AS IF she'd been catapulted from sleep in her small dormitory room at Fort Meade. The middle of the night, to judge by the darkness beyond the blinds—and the cosmic clock in her core. She wasn't far off: 3:05, according to a digital readout on the nightstand next to her bed.

She sat up and swung her legs over the side. Couldn't hear a sound, a silence so complete it felt eerie. She wondered if Emma was sleeping well at Tanesa's. She also wondered if her daughter would ever forgive her for all the times she'd had to leave her in the hands of nannies and babysitters. But Lana took comfort in knowing that the latest arrangement needed no apology, for Tanesa had proved the best caregiver of all.

It also occurred to her right then that although she had Tanesa's address in Anacostia, she had never, in fact, visited her home. *How safe is it there? Am I gambling with Emma's safety?*

When Emma was little, Lana wouldn't have even considered a childcare provider without carefully inspecting the premises. And now she'd sent her girl off to one of the toughest neighborhoods in the entire District?

Hold on, she told herself. *It was safe enough to raise a great kid like Tanesa. And safe enough for the wonderful family that raised that courageous young woman.*

Safe enough, she decided at once, for Emma, who had lived a life of relative privilege. Maybe it was time she saw how the other half lived.

Half? Try the other 99 percent.

Lana figured Tanesa's home was far safer and saner than letting her daughter spend much time with Doper Don, who was about to be released on parole after serving four years of his six-year sentence. Out early for "good behavior." Lord knows, she'd seen little of that when she'd been with him. And now he was saying that he wanted the company of his "long lost" daughter as much as possible.

He'd be getting out just in time for a catastrophe, Lana realized. *Maybe it'll get him.*

She forced herself to take a breath. Then, exerting more effort, she forced herself to say, "You don't mean that," as she headed to the bathroom to freshen up.

Minutes later, she left her room for the walk to her NSA office.

A marine greeted her as she exited the dormitory, as though he'd been waiting all night for the opportunity. Then he stepped to her side, clearly ordered to escort her on the short walk.

"Quiet tonight?" she asked him.

"Yes, ma'am."

"Did you get any sleep?"

"Yes, ma'am." Replies as crisp as the creases in his uniform.

She wouldn't pester him anymore. They were almost at the entrance. She spotted a scattering of office lights up above, including Holmes's. When she looked back down, her escort was turning her over to fellow marines. Two of them accompanied her up the elevator.

Lana stopped to look in on the deputy director. The pair of marines slipped away behind her. Odd to find Holmes without his loyal gatekeeper, Donna Warnes, who apparently got to sleep through the night.

"You too?" Holmes asked, when she poked her head in the door.

"I got three hours. I'm good to go," she replied. "How are our allies in NATO reacting?"

"There's some anger directed toward the President."

"Why?" He'd been working overtime to try to solve the crisis. She wasn't his biggest fan, but she would never begrudge his genuine efforts.

"There's a growing body of opinion overseas that we wouldn't be in this mess if the U.S. hadn't antagonized most of the world."

"That's the very definition of misplaced anger. Blaming a victim."

"Come in. Close the door and grab a seat." Holmes turned his screen aside, but remained at his desk.

She settled into a chair across from him. His eyes, always dark and clear, looked gray, as if they'd lost their luster.

"Imagine you live at 10 Downing Street and your city is about to be flooded, quite possibly right out of existence, because the U.S. and Russia, after the briefest détente imaginable, at least from a historical perspective, are back at each other's throats. How would you feel?"

Holmes didn't wait for a reply. "Or you're living in Rotterdam or The Hague, and you know for certain your country might cease to exist within days. That no matter what you and your fellow citizens do, you can't even begin to evacuate all your children, the elderly, all the infirm, even the healthiest young adults of your nation."

The deputy director fixed those graying eyes back on her. "We're not blameless, Lana. It may surprise you to hear that coming from me, but just look at how the rest of the world views our

Congress. Well, tonight I was ready to drown *them*. Those buffoons displayed the most deplorable behavior I have ever seen in the White House. And I've been around a long time, so that's saying a lot."

"I take it you mean during the meeting with the President?" He'd been scheduled to powwow with the Senate Majority Leader and the Speaker of the House, along with lesser-ranking members of both bodies.

"Yes, the wrecking crew. First, you have to understand that the President had just managed to get Canada, Norway, and Denmark to withdraw from the Arctic, along with us, of course.

"He was sticking his neck out politically, knowing the Russians would continue to refuse to withdraw, but he also knew that if the other Arctic nations pulled back, and only Russia remained, it would put their leaders in a very peculiar position if we're correct that the terrorists are Russian, or 'patriotic hackers' working for them. It would make it appear that they do, in fact, know something the rest of us don't. Well, whatever doubt I had about Russian culpability was all but crushed when a few minutes before the meeting, the Kremlin announced that they would never give in to the demands of terrorists, and that no nation with any courage or self-respect should ever take such a cowardly step."

"Their posturing is certainly taking a U-turn back to the bad old days," Lana said.

Holmes nodded. "It sure is, but I knew right then that the real audience for the Russians was the House and Senate leadership. As soon as the President explained the agreement he'd reached with the other three Arctic nations, the wrecking crew jumped up and started bellowing 'coward' right on cue. The speaker actually called him a 'quisling.' I'm sure he had to pull out his thesaurus for that one. Our dimmest bulbs played right into the hands of our greatest threat. The President's going to cave. And you know why? Because they're threatening to start impeachment proceedings if he pulls our two measly icebreakers out of the north."

"That's outrageous," Lana said. But not unexpected. The Senate and House leaders were a wholesale embarrassment. Not that the denizens of Capitol Hill cared what people outside their states or gerrymandered districts thought.

"I may be seventy-eight years old," Holmes went on, "but I had all I could do not to punch out those demagogues. At the very least, if we'd pulled back with the others, the Russians would have looked like the most belligerent of the Arctic nations, and that could have taken some of the international heat off us. Now *we're* going to be seen as having backed out of an agreement with our close allies that could have thwarted a nuclear attack. Damned if we do, damned if we don't."

"Were the House and Senate leaders briefed about where our investigation is pointing?"

"Absolutely." Holmes nodded heartily. "By *me*. They knew. But they don't care as long as they can make the next news cycle and drive down the President's numbers a little bit more. I'm sure the morning news shows are going to be full of leaks, so in a few hours the echo chamber will also be calling him a coward."

How do you rule the unruly? she asked herself.

"I've had some ideas about where to move with this," she said. "I should get on them."

"Anything you'd like to share right now?"

"Just something Jensen and I have been working on. You'll be the first to know. You always are. Try to get some sleep, sir." She glanced at his couch, on which he had spent many a night.

"After that tirade, I believe I'd better."

Lana settled at her computer and brought up the Ahearn murders. She reviewed all the forensic evidence, physical as well as the little they'd gleaned from Ahearn's computer. Her effort yielded nothing new, which didn't surprise her. But now it was time to apply the new data analysis techniques that she and Jensen had been working on and take another look at the metadata.

Metadata was data about data itself. It provided information about the *kind* of communication taking place—different from traditional intelligence gathering, which focused on the *content* of the information. Metadata would note that telephone calls had been made, but not what was actually said. But drill deeper into the metadata and you could well find patterns of phone calls that might prove damning. Patterns could also be found with email addresses, their times of communication, locations of users, along with ample technical detail about the nature of the data being distributed.

For this case, she and Jensen had been developing sophisticated link analysis tools for both structured and unstructured data, which could help establish larger patterns of communications. These rarefied data analysis techniques might also let them track individual devices, making it possible in some cases to determine the identities of users who were doing all they could to hide who they were.

She started by putting the new tools to work mapping out the geographical areas with the most data flows related to the Ahearn murders. More of a simple test of their model because that task was relatively easy and highly predictable. The greatest concentration centered on Massachusetts, Boston in particular, and for obvious reasons: outside of intelligence circles, no one had reason to connect Professor Ahearn and his wife to the threats against the WAIS.

Next, she applied their link analysis across all of North America. Beyond a two-hundred-mile radius of the crime scene, the interest in the Ahearn murders diminished notably. Where it did exist, it was confined mostly to academic institutions. The California Institute of Technology, for example, had a fair amount of metadata that appeared related to Ahearn. So did other institutions of that nature.

That also proved true of scientific journals based in major urban areas.

Comfortable that the link analysis was passing its initial challenges, Lana extended it across the Atlantic and Pacific Oceans.

Not surprisingly, China and Japan led the way, but Beijing's metadata flows far outstripped Tokyo's. In fact, Lana would have characterized China as having a consuming interest. It made her wonder what the Chinese, archrivals of Russia, knew or suspected. And it killed her to think the Chinese might already know more than the U.S. did.

Tokyo's lesser level of interest prevailed throughout Europe where metadata rose and fell largely along academic lines, with departments of physics, computer science, and, to a slightly lesser degree, math, displaying the most activity.

She saved Russia and its former republics for last. The latter yielded little, with the exception of Donetsk in eastern Ukraine, a hotbed of pro-Russian Ukrainian separatists. She would keep it in mind as she moved on to her major interest, Moscow.

Russia's capital was a veritable beehive with metadata levels linked to the Ahearn murders topping Beijing's. More notable to Lana was the *recent* intense interest, as in the last twelve hours.

She forced herself to remain steady, though, because dry wells with metadata were as common as the grimier efforts in the world's oil fields. *But you still have to drill,* she told herself.

Especially with billions of lives potentially on the line.

She began with Russia's energy sector, finding metadata way beyond the norm between Moscow and almost all of Russia's nuclear generating stations. Which made no immediate sense with most of the plants in no danger of flooding from an attack on WAIS. But it would make sense if a comment from Clarence Besserman after last night's meeting were about to bear fruit.

With his shirt fully untucked by that point, and even his bow tie drooping, Besserman had said that if *he* were looking for connections between the Ahearn murders and the threats to the WAIS—the issue Lana had brought up only minutes before—he would keep in mind that proponents of AAC advocated building those facilities near plants producing renewable energy. The reason was simple: until the AAC process was refined further, it would use a lot of energy to extract carbon dioxide from the atmosphere.

"See, there's no point," he'd added, "in pursuing AAC with dirty fuel. You'd end up pumping as much, if not more, CO_2 into the atmosphere than you'd take out."

Fingers flying, Lana now checked Russian hydropower, centered in Siberia and the eastern end of the country. Quantitative analysis of that metadata demonstrated even stronger linkage between Russia's foremost renewable energy sector and the Ahearn murders. Lana didn't need to make a similar check of wind and solar production in Russia because, for all intents and purposes, they didn't exist, providing less than 1 percent of the nation's energy needs. But hydro? A fat 16 percent.

Normally, she would have started diving into the metadata, unveiling the full content, but these were not normal times. She'd found connections, but not enough, not yet.

Pressing on, her link analysis also showed massive metadata flows from the country's largest hydroelectric plants and the Russian secret police, FSB, in Lubyanka Square, which had its own distinct flows to and from the Moscow Institute of Physics and Technology.

By comparison, she found only marginal levels of activity from, or directed to, the country's scores of fossil-fuel-fired plants. The significant metadata load emanated from those non-CO_2-producing facilities, which made sense, given the reality of AAC energy consumption.

Pushing herself even further, she worked the link analysis once again and watched a tangle of metadata take a neat and familiar shape right before her eyes.

Would you look at that? A nearly perfect equilateral triangle showed scores of unmistakable links between Russia's renewable energy sector, its secret police, and the Ahearn murders.

With the ice sheet added, the triangle morphed—even as she watched—into the four points of a square.

Focusing even more closely on Moscow, she saw a fierce flurry of activity based, of all places, in an apartment building in the city's downtown.

What the hell is going on in there?

She forced aside any considerations of that for now because what struck her most pointedly in the last few seconds was that the FSB was positively data-drunk with the WAIS.

Excavating deeper, she found no previous history of such metadata flows between those four points of interest.

Nice work, Jeff. She would call Jensen later to let him know their efforts appeared to be panning out.

But that would be the beginning and end of the good news. The metadata square made it appear that Russians were coordinating an effort that would have them bomb the WAIS, raise sea levels, take control of Arctic gas and oil reserves, *and* control the world's thermostat with AAC, which would be fueled by their ample reserves of hydro- and nuclear power.

Those reserves would be worth countless trillions of dollars once the means of extracting CO_2 from the atmosphere was in place. And with so many other oil-producing nations reeling from the shock of a sudden rise in sea levels, most of the planet would be forced, by necessity, to become Russia's customers simply to survive.

But what galled Lana almost as much as that scheme was the ongoing attempt by the perpetrators to create plausible deniability. Maybe that was the reason for all metadata arising from a Moscow apartment building.

She checked her watch. Three hours had flown by. But three very productive hours. She wanted to look into what the devil was going on with that apartment building but drilling deeper there would have to wait. Her head felt like it was about to explode. She needed to get away from her computer. Not only to clear her thoughts but to see her daughter. But not without a quick text to Jensen letting him know their work had paid off, and another one to Holmes saying they needed to talk as soon as he was vertical.

It was still early enough to beat rush-hour traffic, the millions who would be rising and driving, oblivious to the demons that were about to haunt their lives.

She found Tanesa's house quickly, a tidy single-story home across the Potomac. Tanesa's mother, Esme, met Lana at the door. She welcomed her like an old friend. They'd met ever so briefly at last night's choir performance at the National Cathedral. Lana apologized for arriving at such an early hour.

"You kidding? I'm on my second cup of coffee. You want some?"

"I'd love to but I am buried by work."

"I'll go get your girl."

Esme led Lana into the living room, then disappeared down a short hallway. Minutes later she emerged with Emma in tow.

Lana's daughter rushed up and hugged her tightly.

What a difference a year makes, Lana thought, hugging her back. Ninth grade had been a misery for Emma, and for her, too.

"Please thank Tanesa for me," Lana said to Esme. "And thank you, too, for having Emma."

"It was a pleasure, I assure you."

On the way home, Emma said, "It's bad this time, isn't it, Mom?"

"We'll see." Lana answered as vaguely as she could in good conscience, squeezing Emma's hand. Her daughter looked well rested. She was glad to see that, but certainly not about what her findings at Fort Meade portended.

As she drove toward Bethesda, her thoughts were drawn less to the metadata square she'd uncovered and more to that Moscow apartment building.

A lone wolf. A common intelligence term for a terrorist operating with strict independence. The words came to her as if on their own.

But in the heart of Moscow? Surrounded by all that interest in every aspect of this case?

That could not be a coincidence. But she had to allow that it was remotely possible. What she had not found was evidence indicating Russia's traditional use of "patriotic hackers." Indeed, the FSB appeared to not only be involved, but a vital link. And that strongly suggested official jurisdiction, even as the Russians denied every charge.

Which only made the possible lone wolf in that apartment more mystifying.

"Mom, you missed it!" Emma said.

"Missed what?" Lana thought of the Russians: what had she missed?

"Our turnoff."

"Oh, I'm sorry."

Lana had to get her mind back on the road. And then she had to get it back on that apartment building in Moscow as fast as possible.

What's going on in there? she asked herself again.

It was time to drill into the metadata. Time to see the content.

CHAPTER 10

GALINA THOUGHT SHE'D COLLAPSE from exhaustion by the time she carried Alexandra up the steps to their second-floor walkup. She wished she could have spared the six-year-old from being carted around all day, but she couldn't leave her with anyone. Alexandra was so anxious that she could not bear to be separated from her mother, even for a short time. Six, seven times a day, she asked, "Mommy, am I going to die?"

"No, you're not going to die. I promise. Mommy would never let that happen to you." Words spoken from the heart, yet so painfully empty of real meaning.

Now Alexandra asked again, clutching her bunny blanket close to her neck on the couch where Galina had just laid her down.

"No, I promise," Galina said, then checked her messages and heard the oncologist's receptionist confirming Alexandra for tomorrow morning. "Payment in full is expected before the appointment," the woman added at the end.

Why would she say that?

It was as though she knew Galina didn't have her money yet.

The pediatric oncologist was in such demand—with cancer rates sky-high in Russia—that he had his choice of patients, so he chose to take the ones wealthy enough to "augment" his income. That was how his assistant had put it, as though a fancy word would somehow make the payment less of a sleazy bribe.

Galina was prepared to pay under the table, happy to pay for the best medical care—and had certainly earned more than enough money to handle the extra bills that were never expressly invoiced—but Oleg had dribbled out only enough rubles for living expenses. He was controlling her—as he always had. And it infuriated her. He never would have dared to try it with the rest of his "team," those killers who worked for him in America, or the one who had basically hacked his way aboard the U.S.S. *Delphin.*

Galina had made headway tracking down the submarine hacker. Not who he was exactly, but his trail in cyberspace. She was now certain that he acted out of Donetsk in eastern Ukraine. She'd seen video of the dead American sailors, sickened by knowing that she was an unwitting player in a larger plot that linked her to the monster who'd killed them. What also weighed on her conscience was that she now understood without question that turning over the information about AAC to Oleg had led to two gruesome murders in the States.

Oleg had made the whole project sound like a great environmental dream—hack the AAC and save the planet. Save the children. Save all the animals.

But instead it was just kill, kill, kill.

When she did identify the sub hacker—and she thought she could—she knew precisely whom she would pass it on to. She'd have her choices because there would be plenty of buyers for that information. Two could play the game of betrayal, and she'd pit her skills against Oleg's.

And your life, she realized at once. *And Alexandra's.*

She sat back, recognizing the gravity of that step, and all the chess pieces that would have to be moved—if she were to forge ahead.

Think about it. Think hard.

Alexandra looked like she was settling down. Time to get back on the tail of the sub hacker. But first she ran to the bathroom and dampened a washcloth. Then she hurried back to Alexandra and placed it on the girl's brow, rubbing gently. Not to cool her off because of a fever or one of her pounding headaches, but to wipe away any trace of Oleg's touch. Galina's skin had almost crawled off her body when he reached into the elevator and rubbed her daughter's precious forehead. It was like he was cursing her.

Condemning her.

Fears that made her realize you didn't need to believe in the devil to understand evil.

"There," she whispered to Alexandra, who looked ready to rest. "Get to sleep, little love of my life."

Words that pierced her own heart. She used to call Oleg the "big love of her life" to distinguish between her man and child, the way her heart had gone out so fully to both. She needn't make that distinction anymore.

Twilight was peeking around the blinds as she sat on the couch next to Alexandra, still moving the cloth gently against her daughter's forehead. She kept the blinds drawn all the time now, worrying constantly about surveillance, the FSB breaking in and sending her to Siberia, then dumping Alexandra in a medical ward with the children of other parents who couldn't afford to "augment" their doctors' incomes.

Alexandra reached up, stilling her hand. "Is there something wrong, Mommy? Do I have a black spot from him?"

"No, don't be silly," Galina said as gaily as she could, but she knew she sounded grim as a grindstone. She laid the face cloth on her lap and kissed Alexandra's cheek. "Sleep, the big-big love of my life."

She started toward her home office as a series of knocks pounded the door, startling her and Alexandra, too, who now sat up, holding the bunny blanket so tightly her knuckles were white.

Galina hurried to the door and stared through the peephole. "Who is it?" she demanded, knowing the dire answer even as she spoke.

"Police. Open up."

Oh, God, what's he doing to us? Galina had no doubt that Oleg was behind the two policemen at the door, even if he wasn't in the hall.

She drew open the locks. A hulking man stared at her. He bore a neck tattoo of crossed axes that signified veterans who had been part of a secret military unit notorious for its atrocities in Chechnya. The other cop could have been a clerk in a supermarket. Tattoo spoke up: "You must come with us."

"Why? What have I done?"

"What have you done?" He leaned down. She barely came to his chest. "Did you *kill* him?"

"Kill who?" *What is he talking about?* "I've never killed anyone." As she said it, her deep-seated guilt about the Ahearns made her feel like a liar. She worried that she sounded like one, too.

He seized her arm. "You will identify a body first, and then we will see if you killed him."

"Wait. I can't. My daughter. She's sick."

The other policeman patted his burly colleague on the back, then looked at Galina. "You may bring your girl."

That only panicked Galina more. Adrenaline flooded through her. She wanted to run away with Alexandra—as far as she could.

The businesslike policeman smiled and shook his head. Almost kindly. But Galina knew better.

"She has leukemia," Galina said softly. "Can we do this tomorrow when I can get someone to stay with her?"

Tattoo shook his head and forced a smile, as if mimicking his partner. "We can get a special nurse to take care of her."

"You don't want a special nurse," the other policeman said. "You want to bring her."

Alexandra began to cry when Galina, more weary than ever from the burdens of her never-ending day, gathered her daughter into her arms once more. Galina would have wept, too, if she hadn't been more worried about the evidence on the computers in her apartment that could incriminate her in even more grievous crimes than the murder of some man.

Who? Oleg?

No, Oleg would never be the murdered. Oleg was the murderer.

Awkwardly, she locked up with Alexandra's arms around her neck, face nestled against her chest. For all the good the locks would do.

If they want in, they'll get in.

The two officers put her in the backseat of a black SUV with metal mesh separating her and Alexandra from the two of them.

Alexandra was weepy, so Galina kept telling her that everything would be fine. But Galina didn't believe a word of the comforts she tried so hard to give, and doubted her daughter did, either.

Tattoo looked back at her in the rearview mirror. "Why are you so sure everything is going to be all right?" He turned to stare at Alexandra. "She's not too young to know that life can be cruel."

No doubt he was an expert in that regard. Galina didn't reply.

Night was falling in full. Not a great time to go to the Moscow morgue, but that was where the two cops brought them, pulling up in front.

"Door to dead service," Tattoo said.

"Put your arms around Mommy's neck," Galina told Alexandra. "Can you do that?"

Her child, still weeping quietly, complied.

Tattoo opened her door and Galina slipped out of the car. The hem of her yellow skirt rose as she slid off the seat. The nice cop, who had come around to the curb, looked away. Tattoo stared so hard she thought he'd demand a replay.

They really are good cop, bad cop.

She followed them into the building, then walked down a marbled flight of stairs to the morgue proper. Galina thought of the thousands—no, tens of thousands—who had taken those same steps. But horrible as their journeys had been, they were the lucky ones. So many millions had disappeared into mass graves. Nobody had ever found them. Even the existence of their bodies—their locations and identities—were lost to history and the long blank stare of Stalin and his henchmen.

So she felt a dread that had been known to scores of others as a large room spread out before her downstairs, an open space bordered by offices on both sides. The reek of chemicals soured her every breath.

She had no inkling as to why they wanted her there, except that it had to be connected to Oleg. Everything in her world was now connected to him.

But a murder in Moscow?

Would they have a body waiting for her on a gurney, or in one of those drawers they pull out? Like in the movies where you're supposed to look at it and say, "That's him."

After placing Alexandra on a couch in the medical examiner's office, the two policemen led her out under bright fluorescent lights to a body bag laid out on a table. Tattoo unzipped it from the top of the dead man's head to his feet in a single flourish, as if he were a magician unveiling the final stage of an illusion.

But this was terribly real. Gritty beyond all measure, no matter how much Tattoo tried to make a performance out of it. The worst, though, was the reason she couldn't identify the body: The dead man's head was turned to the side—and missing all of its features. All she could see was bone and brain expressed through a gaped and cracked cranium, and the mashed inside of his torso—chest and stomach, liver, kidneys, intestines, squashed and mangled and scarcely recognizable. His legs had been flattened by a force so powerful that even the femur was less than a quarter inch thick.

"Somebody pushed him into a garbage truck," the nice policeman said. "We have a witness. I'm sorry, but you must look." He reached past Tattoo to turn the head aside. "This is a better angle."

And there was half of Viktor Vascov's face: one nostril, one eye, a mouth cleaved neatly—almost surgically—down the middle. Alexandra's father.

She'd had so few expectations of him, but never had she thought she'd end up down there identifying his crushed body on a gurney.

"Yes, I know him," Galina said, turning away as she spoke, her voice shaky.

"Who?" Tattoo demanded. "Who is this?"

She gave him the name.

"You are certain." Tattoo held up his hands flashing two peace signs. "V for Viktor," he waved his left hand, "V for Vascov," then his right.

She was still looking away, missing the show.

"Yes, Viktor Vascov. I know him." She looked at the open door of the medical examiner's office, making sure Alexandra was still on the couch. She didn't want her to come out and see this nightmare face that belonged to her father. "He is my daughter's father. Please, can we go? The smell."

"Not so good," Tattoo agreed, sniffing and smiling.

He zipped up Viktor's body with another dramatic sweep of his hand.

Galina thought she would be sick. She stumbled away. Good Cop wrapped his arm around her back for support, then guided her toward the stairs.

"Take her to my office," Tattoo ordered from behind them.

"Alexandra," she said.

"She'll be okay," said Tattoo.

Galina pushed past him and lifted her daughter off the medical examiner's couch. Each arm felt heavy as a ship's anchor as she carried her up the stairs. Good Cop led her into an office with a large portrait of Stalin on the wall. He was making a brilliant comeback, even in death.

"Sit," Tattoo said, apparently oblivious to the fact that she had already settled on a chair with Alexandra on her lap.

Tattoo swung his legs over his chair, macho style, and faced her, nodding to his left for Good Cop to sit.

"How did you kill this Viktor Vascov? You must tell me now," Tattoo said, a wry smile on his face. "You are so small, and he's so much bigger. You must be very good at it." He scratched his neck, right by the crossed axes.

"What?" she shouted, almost jumping out of her chair with Alexandra, whom she startled enough to look around, panic once more straining the girl's face. "It's okay," Galina whispered to her.

"What did you say?" Tattoo shouted. "There are no secrets in here. You must learn that quickly or it won't go well for you."

"I told her 'It's okay.' That's all. Because I didn't do what you say." She chose her words carefully, trying to spare Alexandra a reference to her father. "I would never do that. What does your witness say? I've been around people all day. I couldn't have done this."

"Last night you could have," Tattoo retorted. "That's when it happened. Our witness says a woman with dark hair, short, pushed him in."

"How? How could I push someone so big into a garbage truck? That's crazy."

"Not crazy," Tattoo said. "Because we are also following the money. Always follow the money," he repeated, as if enunciating a principle of investigation that had never been uttered before, much less one that had become a cop-honored cliché. "It wasn't like that in his time," Tattoo added with a respectful nod at Stalin.

Galina refrained from saying the reason Russian police hadn't needed to "follow the money" back then was that the Soviet state had been so impoverished there was no money to follow, though privileged Party members were often compensated richly in other ways. Often unspeakably so, even to this day.

"But now we have to follow the money," Tattoo repeated. "So let's do that. You just took out a life insurance policy on Viktor Vascov."

"What?"

"Don't play the innocent with me." He opened a file and peered at it. "Yesterday. What a coincidence. And within hours, Vascov is dead and you're supposed to get fifty million rubles. But my computer here found something else, a publicly registered document. It is Viktor Vascov's will. Such a careful man, making sure his estate was delivered directly into the hands of his daughter's mother. Isn't that something? The executor is someone named Oleg Dernov. He controls when you get the money to make sure you are 'responsible' with it. That is the very word Vascov used, 'responsible.' So tell me," Tattoo closed the file and leaned over the desk, "who is Oleg Dernov?"

As if you don't know. As if this whole thing isn't a show.

Good Cop eyed Tattoo: "Oleg Dernov is a son of—"

"A son of a what?" Tattoo asked.

"Of an oligarch. Petroleum and mining."

"I know what they are." Tattoo smiled, his every move as choreographed as a Kremlin dinner. "They're all sons-of-*bitches*. But that looks like your problem," he said to Galina. "My problem is your confession. We have a witness. We have followed the money. Everything leads to you. Would you like to make everything easy and confess?"

Only to stupidity, Galina thought. She wanted to kick herself for believing—if only for a moment—that Oleg would ever have done anything for anyone other than himself.

"Or do you think this Oleg Dernov killed your Viktor Vascov?" Tattoo asked, all his humor gone, his eyes as steely as the bars of a cage.

Good Cop shook his head almost imperceptibly, but Galina caught his eye and his meaning. Not that she needed the hint. She was sure Oleg had set this up, and it all came down to whether she would try to implicate him. If she did, she was dead. She was, in every sense, betting her life on her next few words:

"I can't imagine Oleg Dernov doing anything like this."

Tattoo's grimace softened. "Maybe we need to talk to our witness again." He waved her away. "Go. Take your sick kid and go home. You're a rich girl now. Or would you like me to give you a ride?" He winked at her. "I'm a very good driver."

She already had her phone out, dialing a cab. And Tattoo was already laughing again, closing a file as treacherous as his offer.

• • •

Oleg's ring tone went off—John Lennon's "Instant Karma." He had just downloaded it. With oceans sure to rise around America, it sounded so good: "Instant Karma's gonna get you . . ."

Lennon was the best Beatle. Ringo's an idiot.

But better to be lucky than smart, Oleg reminded himself in the next breath.

Reluctantly, he forced himself to mute the webcast of the Midget World Windsurfing Championships in Manila, men's competition. Dwarves in purple thongs were shredding tiny waves on tiny boards with tiny sails, using the surf to launch miniloops that took them twelve, thirteen feet in the air. Surreal. And these tykes were tough. Looked like little balls of muscles.

But the call had to be taken—from the medical examiner's office.

"She identified the body?" Oleg asked.

"Yes," the cop told him.

"And how did that go?"

"It set the mood."

"And when she heard about the life insurance and me?"

"She did not look so happy when your name came up."

Oleg cut the line.

Not happy? He'd raised fifty million rubles for her, made himself the executor so she wouldn't make foolish female money mistakes, like PP's many wives had done. *And she's not happy? Not grateful?*

Maybe he wouldn't give her any money now. But he knew he could never deny Galina, that his generosity would win out, after all. He would give her an advance on the life insurance. *Like a payday loan, like they have in America for all the unfortunates.* He would have to charge interest and special fees, of course, but if he gave her a little cash now under those conditions, he could afford to be generous to others, too, and use most of the money to pay off the operatives in the U.S.—before their impatience turned into something he'd rather not consider. Besides, they were on standby to pay special attention to the children of certain sailors, should their fathers fail to cooperate fully. After satisfying the operatives, he could then place an equal amount in a Channel Islands account for *Uno.*

His own benefactors were holding back until they saw a Trident II hit the WAIS. Then the first $2 billion would be released to him. A trifle, considering the long-term profits they would make, but enough for him to launch the construction of the AAC plants, which would be Oleg's real money mill.

He returned his attention back to the Midget World Windsurfing Championships where Mr. Universe, a muscled tiger of a man, was crowning the men's and women's winners. Both were sponsored by Neil Pryde, sailmaker to champions of all sizes, and both were built like fire hydrants with excellent glutes—*like bowling balls*—flossed so neatly by their matching thongs.

Please, drop trophy. Pick it up.

Oleg liked midgets. Maybe that was why he'd been so attracted to Galina. Not truly a midget, but pretty damn short.

He loved midget tossing even better than midget bowling. He once threw a midget more than a hundred feet. Won a big bet when, as he'd expected, a boaster in the hotel bar said nobody could throw a midget that far. Many thousands were bet against Oleg.

At gunpoint, Oleg marched the midget over to the elevator, and when they got up on the roof, he threw him off. Everybody paid up.

When you're right, you're right.

Maybe next year he would sponsor the championships right there in Russia. Extend a big Russian welcome to the little people of the world.

But those dreams would have to wait. He texted *Uno:* "So r u ready?"

"For prime time."

"EST, U.S." *Better be*, Oleg thought.

"Yes."

"Gives u 10 hrs."

"Gives me all I need."

Uno would have to get a bonus, even if it cut into Galina's share.

• • •

Galina fed Alexandra a bowl of her favorite cereal and tucked her into bed. Tomorrow, they would go to the oncologist, and Galina would beg.

For now, she returned to her keyboard. She logged on and typed in an elaborate code, planning to find the submarine hacker. After what she'd seen at the morgue, she'd made her decision. She couldn't trust Oleg *not* to kill her. Viktor, dead. For Oleg, that was more than just money. That was a message.

She sat back and watched the screen open to something she never expected and surely had not programmed:

WHO ARE YOU? in big block letters.

Galina froze, wondering *who* had left the message. But what shook her up the most was the timing: she had been asking herself the same question over and over the past few days.

Who am I? What have I turned into?

CHAPTER 11

EMMA HAD BEEN QUIET on the drive from Tanesa's. Lana had fought morning traffic, hoping she'd eke out enough time for her daughter to wash up, change, and head off to school. Or even talk, if she needed to. Emma's life had been a jumble of late with her mother gone so much. Lana also needed all the time she could squirrel away to brief Holmes about her findings, and certainly wasn't comfortable committing that information to the "hackisphere," as she'd started to think of it.

But one of the knotty challenges of raising a teen was they often didn't appear to want your attention—and were perfectly content to study their smartphones as if they were the Dead Sea Scrolls—until a light went off in their heads, instead of on their screens.

This would be one of those times.

After they arrived home, Lana toasted Emma frozen waffles, her favorite breakfast, and remembered that it was the same meal she'd fed her on the day the grid suddenly went down. Not so much coincidence as consistency, because left to her own devices Emma would have eaten frozen waffles with oodles of butter and warm syrup every day of her life. Nevertheless, she got to finish her meal this morning without the lights going dark. Success of sorts. And a smile. A teen fed and fueled and ready for the day with a load of simple carbohydrates to wreak havoc with her blood sugar levels.

"Dad gets out of the pen tomorrow," Emma said without preamble.

The pen? How much has she been talking to him? Argot already?

"Yes, I heard," Lana replied as neutrally as possible, which is to say that her jaw was so tight she could have ground her molars flat. Of course, Lana knew Doper Don was getting out of the . . . *pen* . . . tomorrow. As a matter of fact, she'd been waiting to see whether—more likely, *when*—the subject would rear its ugly head with Emma.

"Where'd you hear?" the girl asked.

"His parole officer."

"So do you know where he's going to live?" Emma asked.

"I presume somewhere close to a parole office." *So he may be remanded to the . . . pen . . . as soon as possible.*

"I do. It's a beach house near Annapolis. He's just rented it. He said he can't wait to walk along the shore and get his feet wet again."

Chesapeake Bay? Lana figured he was likely to get the whole of himself wet, given what she feared was on the horizon. Besides, a single man in a beach house? Donny boy wanted to get more than his feet wet. But Lana reined herself in. This was, after all, her daughter, so she posed a question instead:

"Does he follow the news at all, Em? There's a horrible cyberterrorist threat to the oceans. And the Union of Concerned Scientists says that the Annapolis area is already at huge risk from rising seas. After the last big hurricane up there, it cost the government

$120 million to fix things up. And that was *before* those cybernuts said they were going to blow up the West Antarctic Ice Sheet."

Emma offered a knowing shake of her head. "Dad says that Antarctica stuff is just a big conspiracy of bankers and real estate agents trying to drive up the price of homes that aren't on the shore because there's actually a whole bunch more houses behind them."

"Do you believe that?" *Please say you don't.*

"You've got to admit, it could be true."

Lana replied more calmly than she felt: "That's the nature of conspiracy theories. If they don't sound like they could possibly be true, nobody would believe them. Those are the same terrorists killing those sailors on the submarine."

"Dad says that's like the moon landing, easy to fake."

"What?" Lana was losing it. She looked at the clock. Emma was going to be late. "Let's save this for another time."

"You could be a little more open-minded, Mom, like you're always telling me to be. Anyway, he'd like me to spend the weekend there. Kind of a 'Welcome home, Dad' thing."

"A welcome home thing? You're not going anywhere near Chesapeake Bay right now."

"So do *you* know something about that thing on the news?"

"You mean the conspiracy?" Lana raised her eyebrows.

"Well, I'm not saying you're part of the conspiracy. Just tell me, is that what you've been working on?"

"You know I can't discuss my work ever."

"Look, Mom, if I can't go to Dad's new beach house, how about if he comes here for the weekend? He's getting out after only four years for good behavior. He should be with his family."

"He could have been with his family fourteen years ago, Emma. But he decided to be a pot pirate instead. And to do that he emptied out all our savings so he could fill a forty-four-foot sailboat with pot and punch his ticket to prison. We never heard from him again until last week. I think he should stay the hell out of our lives."

"I don't. He's my father and I want to see him, and I can't go stay at his place because you're worried about a little bit of water." With that, Emma stormed toward the front door.

"Stop, Em. I'm sorry. I'll give you a ride. He can come here," she added with such a false note of accommodation that her daughter rightfully rolled her eyes.

"Mom, you've been a big success. He's not. Show a little compassion."

That phrase stuck firmly in Lana's craw: more of her own words coming back boomerang style.

"You're running late, aren't you? First period's gym, right?"

"I hate it."

"I'll give you a note. Let me shower quickly and change."

"Maybe you'll actually like him."

It wasn't Emma's words but the sudden longing in her voice and eyes that stunned Lana. "Meaning?"

Emma shrugged. "Even you admitted he's good-looking."

"Not *that* good-looking, and he'll never be for me, so put that impossibility right out of your mind. He'll sleep in the basement on the pullout bed." *And I'll bring in a surveillance team so I can monitor his every breath.*

"Not even the guest room?"

Lana shook her head.

"I thought you might say that. If you're going to make the guest room off limits for *my* guest, then I'll sleep down there and he can have my room. It *is* my room. Why can't you show him a little respect?"

I'd rather show him the door—as soon as possible—so I don't want him getting comfortable.

But Lana stifled those words as she had so many others of late, figuring it was good practice for all that was likely to follow with Doper Don trying to wheedle his way back into their lives.

• • •

Within an hour Lana was back at NSA headquarters, feeling remarkably refreshed for the grudging amount of sleep she'd managed. But a shower and a smoothie—and a daunting array of supplements—had revitalized her enough to hurry down to Holmes's office.

Donna was back at her desk, waving Lana inside.

Holmes was on the phone, pacing and uttering a series of "Uh-huh . . . uh-huh . . . uh-huh . . ." that kept perfect rhythm with his steps.

He looked over to Lana and pointed to the screens on the wall, then brought up the sound just enough for her to hear the House Speaker on *The Today Show* lambasting the President, calling him a "coward." Certainly no surprise there. Neither was his skill at shoehorning the word into his next four sentences, which he spieled off in less than thirty seconds. He might not have two brain cells to rub together but he had earned a veritable PhD in sound bites.

Lana picked up the remote and switched to *Good Morning America,* where the Senate Majority Leader was performing a similar routine, using the same words as if he were literally an echo chamber and not merely a man who sounded like one.

The House Whip was working his dark magic over on CNN. And FOX had two members of the House and two senators who sounded like a geek chorus.

Holmes hung up and said, "It's been like this since they went on the air this morning."

"Hardly a bulletin."

"From your message, it must have gone well for you."

She briefed him about the four-pointed "square" between Russia's renewable energy sector, its secret police, the Ahearn murders, and the WAIS that she'd uncovered with her link analysis of the metadata last night. As she talked, she brought out her computer, summarized the "hops" through routers, gateways, and other systems, then focused Holmes on the unusually intense packet flows into and out of an apartment building in downtown Moscow.

"Here it is," she said, using Google Earth to show him the residence.

"I don't know what to make of that. It looks like a thousand other places around the world. Maybe that's the point. Keep it anonymous when you're going anomalous."

"I think it's feistier than that. I sent a message to the source of that transmission before signing off a few hours ago."

"You mean the person you suspect is in that building—if there really is an operative in there?"

"I think it is a person, unless, for some bizarre reason, Russian cyberagents have themselves set up in there as some kind of dodge. But I can't see why they would. Based on my trace-routing as well as activity trends and some behavioral analytics, I'm reasonably sure we do have an individual inside that building performing all these acrobatics. Not as efficiently as I am, because whoever it is lacks our resources, but they're doing a pretty decent job."

"A lone-wolf terrorist?"

"I don't think so. This is someone who's been actively trying to figure out who hacked into the *Delphin's* communications, so that means it's not the FSB or whoever might be spearheading this hacker group. They're not working for us, but given what they're doing, they might as well be. And in the recent past they were looking for links to the Ahearn murders and AAC. In short, Bob, whoever this is has been doing what *I've* been doing."

Holmes sat down on the couch, then stood right back up, as if he couldn't contain his energy. "I don't think it matters. If they know that much right there in the heart of Moscow, they're guilty. They're implicated. I wish we could send in a drone right now."

"But what if we're dealing with someone who, for whatever reason, has tapped into material that we don't have, but is not part of what the Russians are up to? Or even knows their plans?" She paused. "I put out a feeler."

"Meaning?"

"I let them know someone new was watching them. And I had the encrypted message sent through proxy servers that strip away the sender's personally identifiable information. Let's just say I don't care *who* they are, they'll never trace it back."

"But your subject can respond?"

"Absolutely."

"Okay, show me what you sent."

Lana turned the screen toward Holmes. "WHO ARE YOU?" appeared as he watched. "I kept it simple."

"In those block letters?" he asked.

She nodded. "It felt blunter that way."

Holmes scratched his head. She knew he was trying to figure out whether she'd been rash. She was ready for that. "Look, the Trident's missile launch system is very likely compromised, right?"

"Yes."

"They have control of a nuclear sub and they say they're moving ahead to send that missile somewhere, and we have no reason not to believe they'll detonate it right over Antarctica. Today, wouldn't you say?"

"That's why everyone with your level of clearance has been notified."

"So if this person is part of that plot—which I doubt because he or she would be working with the hacker, *not* trying to crack his codes—it won't make any difference. That missile is going to fly and we'll have a whole new world to contend with."

"And we'll lose all those scientists at the Amundsen-Scott research station."

"Oh, no. I thought we were set to get them out of there."

Holmes shook his head. "You know how bad the weather can be down there. We couldn't get them out. Go on."

She paused respectfully for a moment. "Anyway, if this hacker's connected to those killers, let's see what kind of reaction we get. Maybe he'll panic. Maybe it's a she. If whoever it is tries to figure out that I'm onto them, they'll never get through our computer security defenses."

"I wish you had cleared that with me."

"I've done this before. We move when we have to. You've always given me that latitude."

"The stakes are extraordinarily high," Holmes said.

"I know. We're talking about the geologic clock speeding up so fast we could see billions die in the days and weeks ahead."

"And then be left with Russia in control."

"Of everything," she added.

Holmes walked over to his desk and sat down before going on: "You don't think you're getting played, do you?"

"No, not at all. And you'll be the first to know, either way. What's going on at the White House? From the 'Uh-huhs,' it sounded like the Oval Office."

"It was the President's chief of staff. His boss, *our* boss, met with the Russian ambassador early this morning. It was deny, deny, deny."

"We didn't really expect anything different, did we?"

"No. I'll tell you something we expected even less. The Chinese ambassador is in the Oval Office right now offering his country's considerable assistance."

"What?" That floored Lana. The U.S. wanted to prosecute Chinese military officials for hacking U.S. corporations and government secrets.

"I know, it's hard to believe," Holmes replied, "but China has four of the world's top fifteen cities that would be hit hardest by a sudden rise in sea levels, more than any other country. And the total numbers for China are sobering to the extreme. They're looking at twenty-two million people *directly* threatened with just a half-meter rise, and we're looking at a lot more than that. And about $7.5 trillion in losses. Their economy would be shredded and the internal disruptions would be monumental and pretty much impossible to contain."

"Those are extraordinary numbers. The brink of disaster for them, too, then."

"So they have very sound reasons to help. Russia, by the way, doesn't even make the list. We're next, after China, with two cities, the New York-Newark region and Miami. The Russians aren't just targeting us. They're also targeting another old rival."

"What about their economic ties, the gas and oil deals?"

"I think worldwide domination trumps that from the Russian standpoint. Besides, they'll still be selling all the fossil fuels they want, along with a tax, I'm betting, to cover the AAC fees that will be in every contract the Russians sign after this."

"So we're going to accept China's help?"

"Not officially. You can imagine what the Speaker and Majority Leader would do with that." They both glanced at the muted TV screens. "Unofficially, we wouldn't say no to anyone who walked in the door and said, 'Here are your hackers.' So good work on that apartment in Moscow," Holmes said, nodding at her screen, "and good luck. I'll let you get back to work."

"Thanks for the update. That was stunning news."

As Lana went to shut her laptop, Holmes pointed to her screen and said, "What's that?"

She turned it toward her and said, "That's called a response."

"From the hacker?"

"Yes!" She held it up to him: **WHO ARE <u>YOU</u>?**

It wasn't much, but this wasn't a hit-and-run posting. The hacker had signaled a desire for a conversation.

The very first step across the cyberminefield.

CHAPTER 12

GALINA COULDN'T SLEEP. THE night had turned into a long dark voyage that would not end. Each time she felt herself drifting off, she'd be seized by fears about Alexandra. Not her daughter's cancer so much as whether she would be abducted in the middle of the night. Galina's weak hold on her own fate made her even more wary of Alexandra's.

Finally, after checking on her repeatedly, Galina climbed into bed with Alexandra and held her close. "No one's going to take you. I promise," she whispered. *Not God, not cancer.* Nor any of the devils who had been haunting their lives.

She watched with weary eyes as first light painted the familiar features of Alexandra's room, the porcelain dolls on her shelf that had been Galina's playthings little more than twenty years ago, and a pair of ballet slippers in their special place at the center of the top shelf. They looked so new, for Galina had given them to Alexandra only two days before the leukemia first left her too weak to dance.

A clown-face clock showed the time, 5:25, its eyes fixed on a stuffed bunny as big as Alexandra herself, won by her father at a carnival last year. Galina could not think of Viktor as a "deadbeat dad" anymore. He was Alexandra's father, and every once in a while he had been wonderful to her. At the carnival, Viktor had accepted the barker's dare with a smile and insisted that Alexandra stand by his side as he confidently sank ten free throws in a row to win the grand prize. Till then, Galina had not known that Viktor had lived, eaten, and slept basketball for most of his childhood.

There must have been so much more about him that she hadn't known. And now, she realized, she'd never be able to give his daughter a full understanding of his life. She hadn't loved Viktor in the end—and had been enormously frustrated by him much of the time—but she missed him on Alexandra's behalf. Another fatherless child in Russia.

Oleg had killed him or had him killed. As soon as Galina had heard about the terms of Viktor's so-called will, she'd known its true author. And when Tattoo had tried to get her to blame the murder on Oleg, she'd also known the deadly trap Oleg had tried to set. Galina would never let him near her again—or Alexandra. It still filled her with revulsion to think of him touching her daughter's forehead in the elevator.

But what could stop him from killing her? Or Alexandra? Those questions ate at Galina as dawn opened up the sky. The lone answer, though, could have darkened the noonday sun, for nothing, *nothing* could stop Oleg from yet another murder. He'd seen to the merciless slaying of the Ahearns, Viktor, and the sailors on that submarine. And now news reports were saying the scientists in Antarctica would likely die from radiation poisoning if the missile landed on the continent because none of them could be evacuated.

Galina, still sleepless, propped herself on her elbow and looked around Alexandra's room, forcing herself to take deep breaths to try to relax. She saw her daughter's two favorite picture books open on the floor. One featured a little girl as the captain of a pirate ship that sailed the seas in search of the most wonderful treasure of all: love. And the other showed the stars twinkling on a snowy night, lantern light soft on a city's white street.

She'd read those books—and so many others—to Alexandra dozens of times, and remembered her daughter's pure joy as she was ushered into those richly imagined worlds.

Galina smiled and dearly hoped she would read so many more to the "little love of her life." And she believed she would— if Galina could just get her the cancer care she so desperately needed.

The next time Galina glanced at the clown clock, an hour had passed and she understood that she'd finally snoozed.

She sprang from the bed and bolted to the bathroom, showering and washing her hair. She wanted to make herself look as presentable—and as affluent—as possible, donning one of her most tasteful dresses.

Galina planned to plead with the older woman who ran the oncologist's office. She had a voice like a man's and was as burly as those testosterone-laden female Russian weightlifters who, along with their East German counterparts, had dominated their Olympic events for so long. Her father had laughed heartily as they'd watched a documentary during her childhood about those "great Russian female athletes," as the narrator had described the masculine-looking medalists on the podium.

Her poor papa. In truth, he had laughed very little, making that occasion in front of the TV so memorable. She wished he were alive so she could flee to him, have his help, but at fifty-nine he had died the slow-motion suicide of a functional alcoholic and chain-smoker.

Galina's mother had died even younger from a botched gall bladder surgery.

With Alexandra's room fully lit, she woke her daughter and fed her the same cereal for breakfast that she'd eaten last night. "When they are this sick," a nurse at a pediatric clinic had told her, "give them whatever they'll eat that's reasonable."

Galina didn't know if cereal that was supposed to taste like mini chocolate donuts was reasonable, but the milk had protein and healthy fats, and Alexandra let her mother spoon it into her mouth. Galina felt like a mama bird feeding her frail offspring.

They arrived at the doctor's office right at eight thirty, when the staff unlocked the door. The doctor's hours started at nine.

The office manager's steely gray hair was pulled back so tightly it looked like the pressure would pop the roots right out of her hairline.

"I don't know if you remember, but I'm Galina Bortnik," she said quietly. "I was in last week to make the appointment, and then I called yesterday. We talked about the money."

"Do you have what you need to see the doctor?" the woman replied obliquely.

Galina lifted Alexandra up so the office manager could see her over the counter. "I have my daughter. She has leukemia. I know your doctor can do miracles."

"We do not do miracles for everyone. Do you have what you need?" she asked again, less patiently.

"Money, yes, I know. I have so much coming in. That's not even an issue. I just inherited fifty million rubles."

"And I am Czar Nicholas. Go." She waved Galina away. More women with sick children were lining up behind them. "And don't come back," the manager warned. "You waste my time and are disturbing everyone."

With tears streaming down her cheeks—and Alexandra asking, "Why won't they help me, Mama?"—Galina carried her daughter outside, still bundled like a baby in her bunny blanket.

Every day her daughter got lighter, even as Galina herself felt weakened by the horror of what was happening to her child.

She sat with Alexandra on a bench by the parking lot in back of the building. She'd seen photographs online of the doctor smiling at charity events for "cancer kids." She would curbside him. That was a term she'd read on American websites. There was no Russian equivalent that she knew.

At precisely nine o'clock a black Mercedes coupe with smoked windows pulled into the parking spot reserved for Dr. Kublakov. It was closest to the rear entrance. His Benz was shiny black with sparkling chrome. Perfect. Not a speck of dust on it. She wondered how many "cancer kids" had made that purchase possible.

Galina lifted Alexandra and stood as the driver's door opened. But the handsome doctor did not get out. Instead, a stocky man with a shaved head and dark sunglasses stood and scanned their surroundings, as if for assassins, then buttoned his black suit jacket and walked around to open the passenger door. That was when she saw the revered doctor for the first time, the man the media called a "miracle maker."

"Doctor Kublakov," she called to him. "My daughter needs your help so much."

She carried Alexandra toward the two men. As she neared them, the bodyguard placed his ample bulk in front of the oncologist, who was hurrying toward the door.

When Galina tried to reach past the bodyguard, he karate-chopped her arm. His hand felt like steel. It hurt so badly she almost dropped Alexandra.

Kublakov disappeared through the doorway.

"Go away," the bodyguard told her. "Do not be here when I come back."

Galina, forearm throbbing, retreated to the bench and sat back down. She watched with blurry eyes as the bodyguard paused to glare at her one more time before following his boss into the building.

She rocked Alexandra, forcing herself to stop crying, then climbed to her feet and trudged to her car. She made Alexandra comfortable in the backseat, checking her messages quickly. Just one, from Oleg: "Where are you?"

The question chilled her, and she was glad she'd found and disabled the customized app locator he'd put on her phone. She certainly didn't reply. She turned out of the lot, knowing she had only one possible course of action.

The drive home, through the thick of Moscow morning traffic, took longer than she expected. Alexandra, so startled at the clinic, now looked sullen, without hope. Galina wished she could say something to cheer her up, but what would that be?

She hoped the answer would come soon. After carrying her daughter to the couch, where she'd been spending most of her days, and tempting her with berry juice and crackers—overjoyed at seeing her eating anything on her own—she rushed to her computers, moving every vital file from her desktop to her laptop. Then she burrowed a trail deep into the "cloud," where she secured backups of her most important files. She also logged on to Internet Relay Chat, IRC, where the first anonymous message had appeared, sitting back in surprise when she saw the simple response: "I am someone who can help you and your sick daughter."

Oleg, she thought at once. He was setting her up. Now that Tattoo had failed, he was testing her.

She called PP, asking if she could see him for just a few minutes.

"Yes," the old man's familiar voice said. "But I won't be back until later this afternoon. Come join us for dinner. I was going to call you. Something's come up with Dmitri. He's very upset. Maybe you could talk to him. He's saying your name."

"Yes, of course." The "Gull, Gull" that passed for it, she presumed. "One thing," she said to PP. "I hate to ask this of you, but *please* don't tell Oleg I'm coming over."

"Don't worry," PP said so soothingly that it scared her, though she couldn't be sure exactly why.

Galina spent an anxious day packing up her daughter's belongings and medications. She also took a few changes of clothes for Alexandra and their toiletries. *Not too much,* she advised herself. *If they come, you don't want them to know right away.*

Who were "they?" She was sure only of Oleg but she also knew that he had a team that killed for him. And a cop—or two—who might be part of it.

As late afternoon turned orange and golden, she fired up her computer one more time and found yet another message: "I am not who you think I am." Again, she thought only of Oleg. But then she wondered.

She shut off her laptop and placed it in a well-padded carrying case. Driving out of Moscow, checking her rearview constantly. She didn't know what to expect, but more trouble of the kind she'd experienced at the morgue seemed likely.

Galina heard Alexandra singing to herself in the backseat. She appeared so much better now that she'd napped and put the experience at the clinic behind her.

The electric eye opened the gate to PP's country palace, as it had for her many times before. She figured her old Renault was the most humble vehicle to ever roll through the entrance.

In seconds, she turned into the car elevator, which lifted her to the second floor, rotated, and left her facing one of the visitor spots.

Carrying Alexandra—the poor child seemed to have no strength left for walking—Galina entered a hallway that ringed the main floor of PP's huge residence. She peered at a door that opened only by iris recognition.

PP welcomed her with a gentle hug, encircling both mother and child in his strong arms. He led them into the high-ceilinged kitchen. His cook, a Eurasian woman in a pale-blue muslin dress with a crisp white apron and matching cap, was tossing cilantro into a Thai stew. Steam rose to a copper vent, fragrant scents to Galina's nose. Her stomach rumbled; she realized she had eaten very little all day.

PP had set a place for them, and timed the meal well. Even Alexandra ate spoonfuls of broth, noodles, scallions, and a shrimp. Dmitri, oddly, was not present.

"And papaya juice?" PP asked Alexandra. "It came all the way from Hawaii just for you."

The girl, wide-eyed at PP's attention, nodded.

And she did drink the juice—eagerly. Galina thought that if Alexandra could live like this and see Dr. Kublakov, she might survive the leukemia.

PP used a napkin to dab his lips, the cotton so crisply ironed that it unfolded like a deck of cards.

"Now that we have eaten," he said, "tell me what is wrong, Galina. Did Oleg hurt you?"

How should she respond? In the pause she took trying to answer her own question, PP nodded and spoke again. "I am not certain of what he is up to, but it is not good."

Again she did not respond quickly enough.

"What did he do to you?" he asked more sternly.

"I can't say, PP. I'm so sorry. But he did not hit me, nothing like that. Did you want me to talk to Dmitri? I thought he would be here."

PP shook his head. She didn't know if that was in response to her refusal to say what Oleg had done, or to the concerns about his younger son. He called out the fifteen-year-old's name in a voice both commanding and consoling. "Come, Galina is here to see you. Gull has come."

Dmitri shuffled into the dining area, looking warily at his father and Galina.

"This is the first time he's left his room since last night," PP said.

"What happened last night?" she asked.

"He took a photograph of Oleg that was hanging in the upstairs hallway with other family pictures. His fine motor skills are not so good anymore, so to get it out of the frame he broke the glass. Maybe that explains the gash in Oleg's face in the picture," PP added dubiously as he held up the torn photo. "Maybe not. Here he is. Have a seat, my son."

The fifteen-year-old, bigger than most men, settled next to Galina and took her hand. She squeezed his gently. Two children, one on her lap and the other to her side. Both holding on to her.

"Do you remember how he would walk toward the door to the dungeon, then hurry away from it?" PP asked.

She nodded.

"He does that with Oleg, too, always approaching him then turning away. Then last night, after taking the photo of Oleg, he made horrible sounds, like he had a pain deep in his belly. He was bent over, one arm cupped around his stomach, the other holding out the picture of Oleg. It was like he was holding it as far from himself as possible, and then he started for the dungeon door again, but this time he pounded on it as if someone down there would open it for him. So I did."

Galina looked at Dmitri, who was staring at her hand, still holding it, but she thought he was also listening very carefully to his father, who went on:

"He looked down the stairs, so I turned on the light. By then poor Dmitri was crying. 'Go,' I told him. 'Papa will come with you.'"

"He'd never been down there?" she asked.

"Only the one time that I know of, and that was with Oleg."

That's right. She remembered now.

"But I'm wondering about that now," PP added quickly.

He held her gaze. Neither the old man nor young woman spoke for a moment. Then he continued: "We went down the stairs all the way to the museum."

PP's word for the dungeon with its macabre collection of medieval torture devices. Galina had been down there only once, and had not been able to leave fast enough.

"Then he started with the back-and-forth business," PP said. "This time by the skull crusher."

A metal skullcap attached to the end of a heavy-duty screw that was turned from above by a wooden crank. Just thinking about it tightened Galina's belly. A gruesome instrument.

"That was when he said your name," PP told her. "Every time he turned from the skull crusher, 'Gull, Gull.' I wonder why?"

Galina felt accused. Nothing PP said exactly, but still . . .

"Would you see if he'll go downstairs with you? He tries so hard to talk to you. I think it's important we try this."

Galina cleared her throat. "May I put Alexandra to bed?" She didn't want her daughter out of her arms, but she wanted her down in that dungeon with those devices even less.

At PP's assent, she took Alexandra away and settled her in one of the many lavishly appointed guest rooms, promising that she would be right back.

Please, dear God, let that be true.

Alexandra looked sleepy, perhaps from eating, and hardly seemed to notice her mother leaving.

Galina held Dmitri's hand, now sweaty, and led him down the stairs. But once they reached the concrete floor, she had to coax him to move. PP stayed up by the door. She guessed that he might have thought Dmitri would be more forthcoming if just the two of them were alone. At least she hoped that was the reason.

Dmitri, indeed, proved more willing—but not with words. They walked past the rack, from which Dmitri pulled away, and armaments, including a spiked ball and serrated swords, mace and maul, halberd and war hammer. Galina had to avert her eyes, but curiously, Dmitri stared at the medieval weapons in what she would have called wonder. Maybe that was why he was so surprised when he realized they'd come upon the skull crusher.

The young man bellowed, as if hacked by the halberd, which had held his gaze seconds ago, then wrapped his arms around his abdomen. That was when Galina spotted the photo of Oleg crumpled in his hand. PP must have given it back to him when she was putting Alexandra to bed.

Then, with another shout—pure emotion, no attempt at a word—Dmitri lunged at the skull crusher and slapped the balled-up photo on the metal plate where a victim's head would lie. He began to crank the wooden arm.

It creaked horribly, as if in protest, a sound almost overwhelmed by Dmitri's own cries. It seemed each creak of the crusher were coming alive under his skin.

When he finished turning the crank, the crumpled photo sat under the cap like a pea in a shell game. But there was no longer any mystery for Galina about what the skullcap was hiding: the unvarnished truth.

She embraced Dmitri and let the young man with the broken mind of a little boy sob loudly in her arms.

"I'm so sorry," she said softly to him. "Nobody should ever have to go through something like that."

She guessed she would have to tell PP what he had not witnessed. She hoped he would believe her. She still felt uneasy in his presence tonight and couldn't fathom why, which compounded her anxiousness.

Galina led Dmitri upstairs. She glimpsed PP standing feet away from the landing. The rage on his face was unmistakable. She wanted to shrink from him, but didn't dare.

"I have to tell you something," she managed, wishing she sounded less apologetic, but she felt bad for the boy; he had carried such a brutal burden for so long.

"You don't have to tell me anything," PP said, smashing his fist against the brocade wallpaper in the short hallway.

He turned to a built-in walnut cabinet, throwing open the door. Inside was a screen and recording device. He punched a button and video appeared of what had just transpired.

"I put cameras in after Dmitri's 'fall.' The moment the light switch goes on, it triggers the digital recorder. I know what he showed you. I've waited years to find out what happened."

"It's so sad."

Her cheeks were wet. Dmitri destroyed, his father now broken by the ugly truth about his only healthy son.

"I want to thank you for what you've done. It's not easy to be the bearer of bad news—of the worst news," he added with a shake of his head. "You don't have to tell me what Oleg did to you because you have just told me what he did to my baby boy. He is capable of anything. Here."

He handed her one of his finely spun cotton handkerchiefs. She felt hollowed out by what they had just learned. And yet she wasn't surprised, just horrified. There was such a vast and disturbing difference.

"What do you need?" PP asked her. "I know you need something."

"A loan. I'm so sorry to have to ask."

"Whatever you need. You are the rose. If I were fifty years younger . . ." He shook his head. He looked like he might have been ruing the fleet passage of the last half century—only to arrive at the torturous revelations of this moment.

"Go get Alexandra. Meet me in the kitchen."

When she walked back downstairs with her daughter, PP handed her a thick envelope. "That will take care of you wherever you're going. I can help again, if you need it. Do not hesitate to ask. This is nothing to me." He indicated the money. "He is everything to me, though." He looked at Dmitri, slumped on a chair. Then he peered into Galina's eyes. "But you and I must have an agreement."

"Yes, of course. What is it?"

"Never to speak to anyone about what you learned here. And I shall never ask you to go through anything like this again."

She nodded, as solemn a vow as she had ever made.

"You need to get away from Oleg. You should not take your car," PP warned her. "They will be searching for it."

"They?" she asked, remembering that she'd asked herself exactly the same question at home.

"Whoever Oleg has hired to do his dirty work. Thugs. Take my Macan." He handed her the key fob for a new Porsche SUV Turbo. "The papers are all in the glove box, if you need them."

"Thank you."

As she left the house, she saw PP staring at the dungeon door. He looked aggrieved, as sad as any man she'd ever known.

Galina carried Alexandra to the silver Porsche, nestling her daughter in the backseat.

The car elevator lowered them to the ground floor and she drove out the front gate into the velvet blackness of the rural Russian night.

A car appeared almost immediately in her rearview mirror, out of nowhere it seemed. She reached to put the envelope stuffed with cash into the glove box—and discovered a small gun.

With another look in the rearview, her foot found the adrenaline-pumping power of the Porsche's gas pedal.

CHAPTER 13

LANA WAS GATHERED WITH the rest of Deputy Director Holmes's closest advisors and aides in his office. They had received one more communication from the submarine hacker, announcing the launch of the Trident II for one a.m. Greenwich Mean Time, which would be nine p.m. Eastern Standard Time. Prime time, they all recognized at once, in the nation's most populous time zone.

Other than noting the carefully calculated schedule, there had been little talk, either from Teresa McGivern or Joshua Tenon or Clarence Besserman. Few comments even from General Sprouse, Commander of the U.S. Cyber Command, or Chief of Naval Operations Admiral Deming. Admiral Wourzy also appeared subdued, as if his arrest for chip counterfeiting had taken place only seconds ago. All seemed stunned into silence, including Lana, by the imminent prospect of the launch.

Now, with fewer than thirty seconds remaining, never had a deadline held a more lethal or precisely defined threat.

With eight screens on, Holmes's office looked like a network control room. They were monitoring the major news outlets, all of which had interrupted "normally scheduled programming." Plus, Holmes had had a satellite feed from above Antarctica brought in, along with a screen devoted to the radar that would track the launch. Lana could still scarcely believe it would actually come to pass.

The digital readout on a clock solely devoted to this unprecedented catastrophe wound down to eight seconds. Lana trained her eyes on the numbers, as if will alone could undo this act of mass murder: ". . . 3, 2, 1."

The Trident II launched. Though she did not see it on any screen—a mere speck on the radar tracker—she had no difficulty imagining the light-colored missile rising from the sea in a blaze of solid-rocket fuel turning the blackness orange and red, and white hot in the center of its wake.

Within seconds, the latest advances in the Aegis Missile Defense System flew into action. Aegis had begun in the mid-eighties, and had many successful test knockdowns to its credit. But nothing was foolproof.

Aegis had its own radar, of course, but the military's high-resolution defense system was also tracking the Trident with its single missile head. In its infancy, the weapon had been a hedge against war, a key component of MAD, Mutually Assured Destruction. Now in minutes it could rain down from the heavens onto the frozen continent with heat unimaginable to most nonscientists—but there would be nothing mutual about its destruction, with worldwide catastrophe striking many, but not all, nations.

An aide wearing headphones and peering at a computer said the Trident was, indeed, heading toward Antarctica.

The speck on the radar screen indicated nothing of the ICBM's lethality. But would the technical wizardry noted by the Pentagon briefer actually work? All she'd ever known of missile shields and interceptors made them sound more mythical than real, no more likely to actually shoot down an ICBM than a lightning bolt from Zeus or—more appropriately, perhaps—a strike by Neptune with his primitive trident, for which the missile had been named.

It would be brutally ironic, Lana realized, if the U.S. could not save itself from one of its own creations. And a single Trident II rising from the sea could claim much of the whole world if it exploded on the WAIS.

"Time?" Holmes asked.

The aide with the earphones nodded at the digital readout, where another countdown had begun. Eight minutes turning to seven in the frightening increments, red diodes spelling out the time remaining in the color of blood.

Lana caught Holmes's eye, then glanced at the door. He nodded. She had to call Emma. She was all but certain that her daughter was watching coverage of the missile launch somewhere. And if Lana could offer her any comfort, she wanted to, but quickly.

Once in the hallway, she reached Emma on the first ring.

"Why, Mom?" Emma asked as soon as she answered.

"Where are you?"

"Tanesa's."

Thank God. "I'm glad you're not alone."

"No, Esme's here. And so is Dad," she added hesitantly.

Lana didn't want her daughter feeling torn between her parents, especially at a time like this. "I'm happy for you, if he can be of any help."

"Not exactly, Mom," Emma said impatiently. "I'm going in the other room," she said to the others.

"What is it, hon?" Lana asked.

"He and Esme got into an argument. She didn't appreciate him saying this whole missile thing was nothing but a big conspiracy, like the moon shot."

"No, I can't imagine she did."

First, through Emma, Lana had learned that Esme did not suffer fools gladly. Second, through research, Lana had found out that Esme's brother was an astrophysicist who had played a key role in the success of the Apollo 11 moon landing. In fact, he'd counted Neil Armstrong among his closest friends. Lana asked if Tanesa's mom had mentioned any of that.

"All of it."

"And your dad said?"

"That lots of people got duped by the moon landing and he figured lots of people would get duped by this, too."

"Emma, this is very, very real. I am so sorry to have to say that."

"I know that, Mom." Emma started to cry.

"Go ahead, tell me," Lana said, checking her watch, knowing she had to get back in that room *soon.*

"It's just so, I don't know, embarrassing to have him say crap like that. I mean, it's one thing sitting around and talking about stuff, but Esme must think we're all idiots, and I really respect her, Mom."

"I promise you that Esme doesn't think *you* are an idiot." Lana left the rest of what she could have said remain unspoken.

"Where are you? I wish you were here," Emma said.

"I'm at work. I wish I were with you, too."

"Will I see you tomorrow, Mom?"

"Yes, you will. You're going to stay there tonight, right?"

"I'm not staying with him," Emma said angrily.

"I understand."

"I doubt *he* will," her daughter said.

"Don't worry about that. I love you."

"You, too, Mom."

Lana took a deep breath and cleared her own eyes, recognizing that she'd nimbly sidestepped Emma's first question: *Why, Mom?*

That would have taken more time than the moment allowed—and more horrors than she wanted to visit upon her daughter at a time like this.

• • •

Down to less than thirty seconds again in Holmes's office. As Lana walked back into the room, the Aegis missile interceptor plunged into the sea more than two hundred miles from the Trident II. They knew immediately that it failed because tracking devices showed it vanish from the screen. But the Trident II was very much aloft, charted every moment by the military's high-resolution defense system.

"What happened?" Holmes asked, sounding numb.

Admiral Deming looked up from his computer. "It looks like the hackers were ready for Aegis because a geostationary satellite that we needed to pinpoint the Trident II was hit with a denial-of-service attack."

The final seconds were approaching fast.

Lana took her seat, feeling as numb as Holmes had sounded. She imagined what it would be like at the Amundsen-Scott research station right now, or one of Antarctica's other facilities. Prayer vigils were reportedly being held at many of them, certainly at Amundsen-Scott, which only mirrored what was also taking place in churches, mosques, synagogues, and temples all around the world.

She wondered if the vigils in Antarctica were well attended. The scientists she knew were the least likely to find hope or solace in prayer. But she understood the impulse. While she was unlikely to ever pray to some omnipotent power—about whom she had the gravest doubts—to save her own life, she'd learned the hard way that when Emma was in danger, she'd crawl across miles of broken glass to try to curry the favor of a creator.

It hit her right then: Emma's life might well be on the line.

Lana squeezed her eyes shut and offered prayer, drawn from the distant annals of childhood.

The digital readout slipped from 1 to 0.

The countdown ended.

The nightmare began.

PART II

CHAPTER 14

GALINA REACHED 160 KILOMETERS per hour so quickly that the speed scared her, but not as much as the car tailing her, keeping pace like a panther after its prey. She picked up her pace to 180, about 110 miles per hour. The beast still clung to her trail three car lengths back, an extremely short distance at these speeds.

She had no faith that he would ever give up. He was too tenacious. Had to be a cop, but he hadn't put on his flashers. She had PP's money, a lot of it. *Does he know that?* If he searched the car, he'd find out fast enough—and steal it. *Cash in an envelope?* It would be her word against his, and she didn't figure hers would be worth much with the powers-that-be these days. Namely, Oleg. And if it weren't a police officer behind her? That could be even worse. A hired thug answerable to no one but Oleg.

But she had that small gun in her right hand. She glanced at it gleaming in the reflected light from the dashboard. Blue steel dark as midnight. Murky as murder. Bleak as the soul who would use it.

She couldn't kill. She was for peace. She'd been a regional director for Greenpeace, for Christ's sakes. Peace on earth. Peace *with* the earth. She couldn't use a gun.

Galina rested it on the passenger seat.

"Mommy, why are we going so fast?"

She's awake.

"We're not going so fast, Alexandra. It's a different car, that's all. It's newer so it seems faster. Go back to sleep."

The car was inching closer, only one length back. He had his brights on. They filled up the rearview mirror, like the blazing eyes of a nightmare. Up ahead was a four-lane highway. She had no training for taking the long curving on-ramp at high speed, but she feared slowing down at all.

She glanced back, remembering that her daughter was lying down. *Not strapped in.*

"Alexandra, sit up and put your seatbelt on right now."

"Mommy, I'm too tired."

"Do it, Alexandra. It's very important, please." Her foot pressed down even harder: 255 kilometers per hour.

Alexandra fiddled with the belt. Galina heard Alexandra's seatbelt click shut. "Good girl."

They raced by the sign for the turnoff: "1km." If she'd blinked, she would have missed it.

But then she hit the turn so soon—in such a flash of highway markers—that she felt the Porsche slipping, sliding. Little wonder: she'd slowed only to 130 in a 70-kilometer-per-hour zone.

The unknown vehicle hung on her bumper as g-forces jammed Galina's shoulder against the door.

Jesus, don't roll it.

And then she slowed just enough that the Macan seemed to take ownership of the curve. Galina realized PP had given her the right car, at least for this. The small SUV had a racer's heart. Her tires squealed, but the radials held the road.

She peeled onto the four-lane highway and pressed harder on the gas, bolting right back up to 255 kilometers per hour. Like the

Autobahn, but better. Not a car in sight, not at this hour. She no longer felt fearful of the car's performance.

That was when the police lights came on, ending the mystery. Not a bubble top. She would have seen that in profile. The flashing lights were hidden in the grill. She thought it might be the Federal Security Service. But who knew anymore? And just that quickly the mystery deepened. It could even be private security.

Galina slowed, watching the speedometer needle recede to the left. She looked for a place to pull over. No challenge there— paved shoulder as far as she could see. No excuse for any further delay.

When the speedometer dipped to under sixty, she let the Macan roll to a stop. Still no other cars in sight. Her mama used to say the Russian night was "quiet and dark as the inside of an oyster, where the pearls come to life."

Galina had lots of doubts about pearls right then.

Put away the gun. It was still on the seat next to her, but she thought it would look suspicious if she leaned over to slip it into the glove box, like she was actually pulling out a gun. Instead, she tucked the small pistol under her right thigh.

The papers. PP said they were in the glove box. She could get them out. That would be legitimate. Have them ready. She reached into the glove box and felt around. There was the envelope with the cash, a comb, pen, the owner's manual, and the registration sealed neatly in a clear plastic pouch.

She sat back with it, ready to hand it over. But they would want more than papers. Whoever they were, they hadn't been sitting in the shadows waiting to check the registration. *Don't kid yourself.* Then she realized she could have put away the gun when she was digging around in there. She didn't dare now. It would look supremely suspicious if she started going through the glove box again.

She glanced back at Alexandra. There was no fooling her daughter. She looked petrified; oddly, that made Alexandra seem more alert, more *alive* than she'd been in weeks.

In the rearview, she saw the man get out of his car. The vehicle looked American, like a wide-bodied Chrysler, but that seemed unlikely. The big sellers, at least in Moscow, were the German, Japanese, and Korean makes.

And then she gripped both sides of her seat. Not the Federal Security Service. Not unless *they* were hiring the worst breed of thugs, because the man approaching the Macan was Tattoo.

He tapped on her window, surprisingly gentle, then waved his hand in small circles for her to roll it down. She feared he'd grab her neck as soon as she did and choke the life right out of her.

Cooperate. Don't piss him off.

She pressed the window control. It rolled down. A low hum. Cool air. The window disappeared. Tattoo bent over, resting his meaty arms on the door, his face no more than eight inches from hers. He hadn't shaved in at least a couple of days. She tried to hand him the registration. He shook his head, as if to say, "Don't bother."

"Galina Bortnik. And Alexandra." He smiled at her daughter. "See, I never forget a pretty girl's name."

It appalled Galina that he'd remembered. She studied Alexandra's reaction in the rearview. No reaction at all. Flat affect with her eyes frozen on her mother.

"What are you doing driving like a maniac in the middle of the night, Galina? You must be high on drugs. Is your mommy using drugs, Alexandra?" He sucked on an imaginary pipe.

Apparently, he thought that was funny. He prodded Galina's shoulder and said, "Laugh."

She did not laugh.

"What kind of drugs did you take to make you drive so fast, Galina Bortnik? You should tell me. Whatever I find, it won't go well for you. And I will conduct a very careful search of your car. And you. Or maybe you're one of those drug users who has her little girl hide the drugs. I can search her, too. Did she do that to you?" he asked Alexandra. "Use you like a drug mule? Bad mommy."

"I've never used drugs. Ever."

"Yes," he patted her shoulder. "You look like such a good mother." He left his hand on her. The weight unnerved Galina. A shudder passed through her. "But we all know that even good mothers make mistakes. And I think you have made some very big mistakes lately. What do you think, Galina?"

He squeezed her shoulder. His hand felt big as an oven mitt. As hot, too. He started kneading her flesh. The tips of his long fat fingers reached the top of her breast.

"Please stop."

"I don't think you want me to stop, Galina, because if I stop I'm going to have to do other things. But since you asked, I guess it's time to get started. Unlock your door."

When she hesitated, afraid he'd grab her breast if she turned toward him, he reached in, unlocked the door, and swung it open.

She didn't move, not even her eyes. They were still on him. His gaze was on her chest, the breast he'd been touching. Then his gaze drifted to her legs. She pulled her modest skirt over her knees, as though he might not notice if she did it casually. But almost all women know better. So did Galina. Men like Tattoo *always* noticed. He smiled and crouched down. She thought of the way his car had trailed her like a panther. He seemed like a huge predator now, ready to spring at her.

"I told you, didn't I? One thing leads to another."

With that he put his hand on her thigh. "I heard you have such soft skin. Yes, you do . . ."

"Please stop that." She tried to push him away.

He seized her hand, his grip so hard it felt like he could crush her fingers if he chose to. In another quick movement, he reached across her and unsnapped her seatbelt. Then he swept her skirt up onto her legs, exposing her underpants. When she tried to push the hem back down, he grabbed her hand again and shook his head. "One thing does what, Galina Bortnik?" When she shook her head, he answered for her. "Leads to another. That's right."

He sniffed the air loudly, closing his eyes for just a second, as if he were savoring a scent he couldn't possibly smell.

He tormented her with another whiskery smile. "I have to search the car for contraband. I'm going to have to search you, too. It's standard police protocol when we have such a reckless driver. I'm also going to have to search Alexandra. You were endangering such a nice girl."

The fine hairs rose on Galina's neck. A paused followed in which he said nothing. Galina could hardly breathe.

Then he seized her leg like it was an axe handle and pulled it so hard he swung her halfway around in her seat. He held her leg out the door.

Instinctively, she drew the other one to it—and felt the pistol exposed by her side.

Her hand fell to it. She gripped it, but kept it down. It looked as though she were bolstering herself because of the awkward angle he'd put her in. And she was bolstering herself, but not because of that. She pointed the pistol in his face.

Now *he* froze.

"Get your hands off me and back away slowly."

"Galina, you're making this very bad. This won't turn out good for you now."

"It was never going to turn out good for me so quit saying that."

His hand dropped away from her leg. She pulled her skirt down. "I said to back up."

He did, but remained hunched over, as though he were still leaning on the door—or getting ready to attack her.

Shoot him. Just do it.

Still, she couldn't pull the trigger—until he lunged for her gun hand. She fired into his broad belly and watched him sink to his knees. Fearing he would pitch forward, she pulled her legs back toward the car.

He did come forward—with unbridled fury. He grabbed the waistband of her skirt. She fired again, and that was when she learned the small gun was a single-shot derringer. Just enough ammo to make him a madman.

He dragged himself toward her, ripping off her skirt. She leaned back into the car but he had her by the legs.

She sat forward and bashed him in the face with the butt of the small pistol, drawing blood from his cheek. Alexandra screamed.

"She's next," Tattoo swore.

Galina hit him again. He grabbed her hand and started crawling up her body, using her limbs like a ladder.

She couldn't pull away. He gripped her shoulders next. Galina threw herself back toward the passenger door, breaking his hold, but the weight of him still pressed against her legs. They felt like they'd been sunk in cement.

She stretched out her upper body, but his hands slid over her bra and clamped back on her shoulders. He dragged his bloody stomach over her underwear. Then he grabbed her neck, enveloping it with one hand, and began to crush it with his thick powerful fingers. Alexandra jumped out of her seat and hit him, screaming, "Go away! Leave Mommy alone."

Galina tried to tell her to stop but couldn't talk. Couldn't breathe. He was strangling her.

He pushed himself up and backhanded Alexandra so hard

the frail girl slammed into the backseat, shocked so deeply that her wail didn't come for seconds. But she'd bought Galina a few quick breaths.

"You little bitch." He grabbed for Alexandra. She ducked. *Thank God.* But then he lunged partway over the seat for the girl.

Though pinned by his other hand, Galina reached for the glove box, fingers scrabbling to get inside, then grabbed the pen. She jammed it into the bullet hole as far as she could, jerked it back and forth and thrust it deeper still.

Tattoo howled. His eyes widened, and he grabbed her hand, pushing it away. She let him—and left the pen in his gut.

He pressed her hand against the passenger door and held it there, panting and creating the macabre appearance of a man having sex in a car.

Blood spilled copiously from his wound now. She must have hit an artery.

His grip on her hand weakened.

Die! Die!

He let go of her. She tried to push him away. He groaned loudly. She realized he'd been groaning since she'd stabbed the bullet wound. And then he clamped his hand back on her neck. A final seizure of murderous violence, as if he were determined to take her with him.

She tried to turn away, but he outweighed her by at least two hundred pounds.

He pushed down, cutting off the last of her air. But he began to shake and she heard a croaky sound rise from his throat. Then he shook so hard he rolled over, jamming himself between the seat and dash. He stopped moving.

Galina opened the passenger door and pulled her legs out from under him, falling onto the paved shoulder in her haste to get out.

She hurried to his car and shut off the lights. She didn't want anyone stopping. His radio wasn't on. He might have been off the clock. *Of course, freelancing.* She looked for his gun. A quick search didn't turn it up, but she found his Taser and took it. She wanted to make sure he was dead, and sure didn't want to check his pulse.

Alexandra came up beside her. Galina was about to tell her girl to get back in the car, then thought better of it.

"Wait here, okay?"

Alexandra nodded.

Galina returned to the passenger side of the Porsche. One of Tattoo's hands was draped limply over the edge of the seat. She thought it was the one he'd used to choke her.

She tased it. No reaction.

Galina dragged and pushed and finally hauled him onto the shoulder of the road, swearing at him silently.

The Macan's black leather seats were smeared with his blood. So were her legs and belly.

She wiped it off herself with her torn skirt, and used the sullied fabric to clean up the seats as much as she could. She took a fresh skirt from her suitcase and slipped it on, moving feverishly, frightened almost senseless that a car could come along and stop. One had raced by on the other side of the highway when he was attacking her. Others might have as well. Someone could have called the police. Two cars by the side of the road in the middle of the night? Suspicious, especially to a citizenry trained to be wary.

"Let's go," she said to Alexandra, who wanted to sit next to her.

Of course, her daughter was terrified, shaking. She wanted to be near her mother.

Galina pulled a dress from her suitcase and draped it over the passenger seat. She didn't want Alexandra to get a trace of that animal's blood on her.

They drove away. Only then did Galina understand that she'd been wheezing and hadn't taken a full breath in minutes. Her throat hurt, but as they gained speed—and distance from Tattoo's body—she began to relax enough that she stopped sounding asthmatic.

Alexandra's eyes were closed. She looked like she was sleeping. Galina put on the radio, keeping the volume low. She wanted to know about Antarctica. Was it still there? Who really knew what a nuclear missile would to do the ice continent?

The explosion had taken place, as threatened, on the West Antarctic Ice Sheet. The radio announcer's voice was grave. For good reason: more than three thousand scientists and support staff from around the world had died, swept to their death by powerful blast waves. Now, nuclear snow was said to be falling on parts of the southern ocean.

"And the seas are rising," the announcer reported.

Not over centuries, Galina thought, as so many of those men and women on Antarctica had predicted, *but with the speed of terrorism itself.* And that was very fast, indeed.

She shut off the radio and kept driving, grieving as first light creased the eastern sky. She wasn't sure where they would go. Only that there was no turning back.

CHAPTER 15

THE SILENCE IN LANA'S NSA office belied the tragedies on several split-screen monitors she kept tuned to government and commercial news feeds. she'd muted the sound, needing to hear nothing more of drowning victims, environmental devastation, and the open panic of the world's population. The massacre of all the scientists and support personnel in Antarctica was so shocking that she still had difficulty comprehending the loss, made personal when she learned that her college roommate, a renowned paleoclimatologist, had been among the murdered.

The Trident II had hit the continent just north of the Thwaites Glacier at an altitude of about two miles to exert maximum damage from the air. Not a direct strike but close enough to immediately calve glacial chunks the size of Rhode Island into the southern ocean—and incinerate billions of tons of ice now forming massive blizzards that were sweeping across the seas.

Scientists had long considered Thwaites crucial for holding so much of the region's ice in place, but the blast had widened the glacier's mouth. And it most certainly had compromised its grounding line, the border of the land that supported the ice and the body of water that would receive it. Glaciologists were certain the explosion would speed up the glacier's path to the sea, which had been expected to take hundreds of years. The potential for a death toll in the billions from the missile strike would turn into a fast-forward reality if all the ice backed up behind Thwaites were shaken loose, as so many experts now feared.

None of the experts working for, or consulted by, the Defense Department were predicting anything but the most dire ramifications from the explosion.

"Expect sea level rise for a period of weeks, maybe months," had been the bulletin from DOD. "Expect severe radiation poisoning as polar easterlies carry toxic plutonium from the continent. Expect disturbances both domestic and foreign among threatened populations."

The parched language of panic.

Already, scientific consensus held that the world was heading for an absolute minimum rise of a meter—if the planet were exceedingly lucky and all of the WAIS didn't crash into the ocean, a catastrophe that would lift sea levels the full eleven feet. But a meter still constituted a century's worth of warming in the geological equivalent of a blink.

Trampling had become the leading cause of death in lowlying countries, such as Bangladesh, as populations crowded along coastlines raced away from rising waters. The number of victims already numbered in the hundreds of thousands. The Maldives, Kiribati, Tuvalu, Samoa, Nauru, and other nations throughout Oceania were losing territory—and lives—by the minute.

But the biggest numbers of victims might yet hail from the biggest names in cities: New Orleans, which looked as if Hurricane Katrina had returned on steroids; New York, where subway trains had been caught in flooded tunnels, killing more than one thousand passengers; Los Angeles, where famed beach communities had been obliterated; Tokyo, where trampling killed hundreds; and Amsterdam, where even centuries of living below sea level could scarcely prepare the populace for such a swift onslaught of the ocean. The compounding tragedies also included Mumbai, Shanghai, Singapore, Jakarta, and Dhaka. Water treatment plants were flooded; basic sanitation had washed away with the floods; diseases, such as dysentery, were predicted to become epidemic; and widespread starvation was expected within days.

In the U.S., Miami was a worst-case scenario all on its own—possibly in a literal sense: Southeast Florida was among the most imperiled places on the planet, and if the waters kept rising, Miami would be cut off from mainland America within two weeks. It was not hard to imagine that in the next century its famed high-rises would form coral reefs as dead as so many of nature's had already become.

Traffic on I-95 and I-75, heading north out of Florida, was choked by vehicles that had run out of fuel. Truck stops had shut down, only to be looted by motorists, including armed families, desperate for food and water and nonexistent gasoline. Shopping centers throughout the Sunshine State were ablaze, a fast-moving phenomenon not confined to Florida cities. It was as if arsonists were trying to fight floods with fire.

The mayhem was almost incomprehensible, and yet it made perfect sense to Lana. The world as people had known it all their lives was ending.

Meetings of every conceivable government agency remotely related to climate change, emergency services, and the nation's security were underway, but as Holmes had confided to his closest aides only hours ago, "It mostly comes down to what we can do to stop these madmen." Tellingly, his eyes had landed on Lana.

What her eyes could not avoid taking in now was the video once more feeding from the *Delphin*. The ghostly interior of the submarine, strewn with dead bodies, now looked like a preview of what the hackers had planned for the rest of the world.

This is how we got started, she imagined one of them saying, *but soon this will be everywhere.*

She told herself to look, really look at that sub. Hacking it, hijacking a nuclear missile, had been almost inconceivable—until it happened. Just as it had been difficult to comprehend the atomic bomb before Hiroshima, or the most virulent hate before the Holocaust. Or any number of other mass deaths.

She also kept the sound muted for the sub. *Just look,* she told herself again. She didn't want to be distracted by the white noise coming from a submarine that had become a submerged crypt.

The only person she saw alive was First Class Petty Officer Hector Gomez, who had moved back into frame.

What are the odds, she wondered, *that the man in charge of the Missile Control Center had survived?* The very officer who knew the intricacies of launching the missiles.

Yes, she was aware he'd been vetted thoroughly since the hijacking, but she called Jensen anyway and told her CyberFortress VP to join her at NSA. She'd always made sure he was available full-time to run the show at her security firm, but if they didn't stop this madness quickly, there would be no CF or much else of value to save.

He arrived looking graver than she'd ever seen him, and that was saying quite a lot about her Mormon right-hand man with his rock solid beliefs in a family-filled afterlife.

She pointed to the screen.

"Poor guy," the navy veteran said. "Can you imagine being down there, still alive?"

"That's why I want you to check out Gomez every which way from Sunday. I know DOD did that, but I'd like you to do it one more time. Come in cold. Don't take any of the routes DOD did.

Treat Gomez like a blank slate in that regard, the tabula rasa of cyberspace."

"You sure you want me to take time for that now?"

Jensen had been helping Lana with the link analysis and network profiling to figure out just what was going on in that apartment building in Moscow.

"Yes, this is your priority."

He looked dubious, and she could hardly blame him. But she was in a "fire all guns" mode, and that included questioning even the putative heroics of a sailor like Gomez.

Besides, she'd begun to worry the hacker she'd been communicating with anonymously had detected Jeff's fingerprints analyzing the metadata from the apartment building, light to invisible though she believed them to be.

She returned to that data bulge on her own, keeping a satellite feed of the Moscow building in the corner of one of her screens. She wasn't sure why. She'd had the impulse so she'd put it there. A reminder of the hacker's essential humanity, perhaps? His or her habitat? Sometimes her instincts paid off, so she left it there.

In the next hour she came across emails to an Oleg Dernov. Those provided the first concrete information beyond the large-scale communication patterns. It was so easily unearthed that Lana was suspicious. More so when she found Dernov was a graduate of the Moscow Institute of Physics and Technology, and the son of one of Russia's wealthiest plutocrats.

"I've been handed this," Lana said aloud to herself. *Set up?* she wondered. Disinformation had long been the coin of the realm for so much of the spy trade. Why would it be any different in cyberspace?

Or?

The hacker, for whatever reason, wanted to give Dernov to her.

Hmmm. Lana stared at the IRC page on her screen that she shared with the hacker in that building, glancing at the satellite feed once more. At least she hoped it was shared only by the two of them. She typed a message:

"I've found a man's name. Prominent. Did you give that to me?"

She wondered how long she'd have to wait for an answer, imagining the seas rising a foot or two before the hacker deigned to respond.

Not much more than a second, as it turned out: "Yes."

"Why?"

"You are too intelligent not to know."

Or I'm too stupid not to see that I'm getting set up here. Worked, as it were, by a twenty-first-century barker in a cyber-sideshow who likely wanted to lure away her attention and keep her busy with worthless distractions.

She decided to hold off on a response, searching the metadata for more easily accessed emails. She found the hacker had all but put a welcome mat down for her, starting with several emails to a pediatric oncologist named Dr. Kublakov. That was when she learned that the hacker whom she'd been communicating with might be an individual named Galina Bortnik. Also—*possibly*—that she had a six-year-old daughter named Alexandra with leukemia.

Personal facts, now, served on a platter?

More to the point, what does she want from me?

Could this be the hacker's version of the classic honey trap, but instead of seducing with sex the hacker preyed upon the vulnerable emotions of a mother with a daughter?

Lana's skin suddenly went cold.

Could she know that *as well?*

Don't be stupid, Lana chided herself at once. Of course she could. Or *they* could, if the hacker were part of a group, as she'd originally presumed. Lana's cover had been revealed after last year's attack and her counterattack. Her identity in the real world was clearly known. The question, though, was did "Galina" have the technological wherewithal to have determined that Lana Elkins was the person she was speaking to in cyberspace? If the answer was yes, Lana realized that she might have met her match. The very thought produced a deeply uncomfortable and wholly unfamiliar feeling.

"Let's come clean with each other," Lana now wrote back.

"How do I know it is you?"

This gets convoluted, Lana thought, because the answer to that question depended on who the hacker thought "you" was. Lana could hardly answer without knowing that.

"We need to talk."

"On a phone."

"Yes," Lana replied, excited, wary, heart pounding, yet bone weary from so little sleep for so many nights.

"Good."

Here we go, Lana thought, sensing a riptide of events about to sweep her far from familiar shores. "Do you want me to call you?"

"No. Give me a secure line to call. If it is not secure, I will know and you will never hear from me again. That would be a great loss to the world."

Now the hacker was trying too hard to lure her. *Or perhaps too earnest for her own good?*

Already accepting the female pronoun.

Lana thought about giving her the number for her secure NSA office landline phone, then shook her head. If she's really good, I'll never hear from her. So instead she gave up her cell number, which was as secure as the President's. The hacker left the message board an instant later.

Given the pace of their back-and-forth messaging, Lana thought it likely that her phone would ring posthaste. The world had come to expect everything *now*. She was no exception, especially at this moment.

It didn't ring. She looked at her phone. "Come on, damn it."

"What was that?" Jensen asked, hurrying into her office.

Almost two and a half hours had passed since she'd redeployed him.

"Nothing," she replied. "What do you have?"

"Almost eighteen months ago Gomez—whose real name is Grisha Lisko, and is no more Mexican American than I am—became a member in good standing of the U.S. Navy, with goodness knows how-much help from his friends just across the Russian border. I say that because he's Ukrainian by birth."

"So he's a sleeper agent."

"That's right, and he's finally awake."

"Lucky us." Lana shook her head. "What do we get out of letting him know that we're onto him? Or taking it straight to the Russians? He's got to be working for them. I agree with you. No Ukrainian on his own, I don't care how bright, gets the high-level training to be some hacker's weapons expert on a nuclear sub."

"It certainly gives us a better idea of how these terrorists could have overcome all the safeguards on that sub. I know DOD has been studying those scenarios but they couldn't figure out how it could possibly be done without Gomez, I mean Lisko, being part of the attack. Somebody trained him well."

"Somebody Russian," Lana said, wishing she could vaporize the Kremlin.

"This would certainly appear to confirm that."

"Let's go see Holmes."

The deputy director was in his office with two Chinese officials, according to Donna Warnes, who raised her thin eyebrows the slightest bit when she imparted that information. "I'll let him know you're here."

Holmes's assistant nodded toward the couch. Though sleep deprived, Lana couldn't bring herself to sit. They had two substantial leads: a woman with a sick cancer-ridden child and the wherewithal to make herself known to one person only—Lana. And Jensen's identification of Grisha Lisko, a.k.a. Hector Gomez, whose swarthy looks and penchant for ethnic typecasting had let him flourish on a nuclear sub that he now, in effect, commanded.

Holmes ducked out of his inner sanctum to confer with them. Jensen nodded as Lana revealed the news about Lisko. She then briefed the deputy director about the individual going by the name Galina Bortnik.

"This woman, if that's what she is, hasn't called you yet?"

"No," Lana answered. "She has not."

"If she does, record it."

"I plan to."

"We'll want to run it through voice analysis."

"What if she wants to meet me?" Lana always tried to anticipate the next step.

Holmes shook his head slowly. She had known him long enough to recognize the gesture not as a negative response but a stalling pattern.

"What have we got to lose?" she asked him. "They're launching nuclear warheads."

"You," he said simply. "We could lose you. You could be the prize in their response to this whole Internet forum gambit."

His last word resonated for Lana, for it made her realize she hadn't thought once about gambling since the real world stakes had escalated, much as last year she'd escaped any desire for poker by trying to stop the assault on the grid. Even the worst news, she realized, had a flip side.

Lana returned to her office, telling Jensen to get everything he could on Lisko and Dernov. She briefed him about the latter, adding, "I know it's not much."

"It's a start."

"Or a dead end. That's what worries me more than them going after me—that they're burning up our time so they can burn down Antarctica."

But in the next thirty minutes she found emails between a clinic and Dr. Kublakov about six-year old Alexandra, with all of the girl's medical records attached to the last message. If this were a sting—and Lana still couldn't rule that out—it was certainly growing more elaborate all the time. *But that's how stings work,* she cautioned herself.

She also found passport photos of the mother and daughter, smiling when she saw that they really looked like two peas from a very cute pod. But what heightened Lana's interest was learning that Galina had been a regional director for Greenpeace. She confirmed it was the same woman with the organization's staff photos from two years ago. The confirmation didn't rule out a sting, but it made the likelihood at least marginally smaller.

Lana's phone rang. She took a steadying breath, then saw it was Emma. "Mom, how could they do that to the world? Why?" She was crying. "All those scientists are dead. People are freaking out. They've got another bomb all ready to go. Are you going to stop them? This is crazy."

"Everybody is trying very hard," Lana answered obliquely, as always.

"Mom, you have to stop them." Emma, as always, ignored her mother's attempt to distance herself from any intelligence work. "Did you hear about Miami? And that subway in New York? That was so horrible. Can you imagine being in one of those cars when that happened?" Emma was crying so hard that she had trouble talking.

"Do you have your keys, and are you with Esme?" Lana knew that Emma was staying with Tanesa. She wanted to get her and Tanesa's family out of Anacostia before it succumbed to flooding.

"Yes on both counts," Emma said.

"Please let me speak to her."

"Sure, but I need to talk to you about—"

"I'm so sorry to interrupt, Emma, but this is urgent."

Tanesa's mom got on the phone. "Emma said you needed to speak to me."

"Yes, thank you. Anacostia is going to flood. I'd like your family and Emma to relocate to our house. I know that's asking a lot, but I have access to projected flooding in the District, and you'll be in the middle of it."

"Wow, that's a lot to take in. I was worried about that. You're sure?"

"Absolutely."

"I have my sister and her family two blocks over."

"Our house is big, too big. Have her come, too."

"She has four kids."

"Good, we'll have plenty of company," Lana said without pause. "We're all in this together."

"We'll bring all the food we've got."

"Good idea. But traffic is going to be horrible. Is your gas tank full?"

"Topped off two days ago, and I haven't done anything but food shop since."

"Great, but you must hurry, Esme." Lana glanced at her watch. "May I say good-bye to Emma?"

"She's right here. And I want to thank you, Lana."

"Are you kidding, the thanks are all mine." Lana couldn't begin to express the gratitude she felt toward Tanesa and her mom. Emma had grown up so wonderfully in their presence, which only made Lana feel, once again, inept as a parent.

"Mom, it was better last year when the grid went down." Emma was no longer crying. "At least I was doing something."

"And you did it with incredible courage."

"Now I can't stop anything. I feel like an idiot crying."

"Emma Elkins, you are *not* an idiot. Is your dad there?" *Speaking of . . .* Lana let that thought trail off unfinished.

"Him?" Emma said indignantly. "He's all upset because his new rental is flooded and he's not sure he'll get his deposit back. I just want him to go home."

"Emma, all of you—and that's going to have to include him— are going to head to our house. Right—"

Lana had another call coming in. *The* call, she thought. "Em, I *have* to go."

"Mom! *I* have to talk to you."

"If you want me to try to stop this, I have to take another call. I love you."

"Bye." Her daughter hung up.

Lana brought up the call. "Hello?"

No voice greeted her. Thirty seconds passed. Lana watched them go by on her watch. It felt like the longest silence she'd ever experienced on a phone. It was as if the caller were still debating whether to speak to her. Finally, Lana said, "I have a daughter, too."

She heard a breath and then a woman said, "I know. That is why I am talking to you."

CHAPTER 16

OLEG KNEW HE SHOULD have been celebrating. *Numero Uno* hacker had scored a hit on Antarctica. The whole world was in chaos. And Russia was doing very well. He could tell the Russian President was doing all he could not to gloat. Like he was winking at Oleg right through the TV when he said the greatest country in the world had long been prepared for the worst. "The weaker nations," the President didn't specify, "did not take proper precautions." The President had shaken his head wearily and added, "Very sad."

Uno, of all people, was complaining, saying he'd wanted to knock out the biggest glacier and send all of it sliding into the sea. But then it would have been game over. You needed to leave something on the table in any negotiation. If the Arctic nations didn't capitulate now, Oleg could use a second Trident II. "It can't always be instant gratification," he'd told *Uno.*

Definitely not instant gratification for Oleg. Police Sergeant Sergey Volkov was dead. *Not possible,* had been his first thought. Sergey was a police thug, covered in tattoos of snakes and barbed wire and guns. Sergey was a killer. He definitely wasn't supposed to die. Oleg dispatched him to "dispose" of Galina and whatever else he found in her car—whiny kid, toys, everything. *Get rid of it all. Like used tissue—or nasty feminine product.* But she had disappeared and left Sergey dumped by the side of the road like refuse. Bullet in his belly. And Oleg was left at his workstation in his penthouse, staring at his monitor and phone and wondering where Galina was. She was number one, too. *Number one suspect,* he thought.

What kind of person does that to man of the law, Galina?

Oleg would have bet a casino full of cash that PP, his despicable money-grubbing father, had given her millions of rubles because why else would she have gone to him and then—*poof*—vanished?

Why?

Oleg knew. Because she needed that money. She'd been badgering him for it, whining all the time: *Give me money, Oleg. Give me money.* But she'd never said it was so she could leave.

She and PP and his lame-brained brother—never had that term held greater meaning—had been up to *murder.*

Galina girl—*No, Galina bitch*—hadn't even had the basic human decency to answer his texts. Calls? Didn't even pick up.

I give her pretty dresses, fancy underpants, special videos to make her moist, and crazy guy sex, and she can't even stay in touch? What are friends for?

Worse—yes, *worse*—she had shut off an app he'd secreted onto her device that had recorded her geolocation, which had then uploaded to an Internet server that sent him the data.

Where's the trust? Not even for the people closest to you?

Very sad, like the President said.

He could not abide this kind of betrayal because surely she must be in cahoots—how he loved that uniquely American word—with some coldhearted people to kill with a gut shot and a *ballpoint pen?*

A police officer—nobody Oleg knew—had found Sergey's body on the shoulder of a highway. Minutes later, Oleg had a medical examiner on the case. Body not even cool. The ME reported the bullet missed the splenic artery, but a Bic pen tore it up like a wood router.

"How do you know it was a Bic?" Oleg had demanded. *Very good forensics,* he figured.

"It said so right on the side," the ME replied, "where you click it. The pen was still stuck up in there."

So absurd. So Russian.

And so very bad of Galina to bring some guy along to do her dirty work.

Oleg stewed in front of his screens. He wanted to kill Dr. Kublakov. If the oncologist had agreed to care for Alexandra, no way would Galina have left. She would have been in her apartment, not going to PP's for help. And Volkov would have been able to visit her in the comfort of her own home. In fact, if Kublakov weren't caring for the spawn of high-ranking government officials, Oleg would have had him dropped into the Baltic from thirty thousand feet this very day.

Instead, Oleg had to go see PP to try to find out what was really going on with Galina.

He took the elevator to the lobby, brushing past the wheel beast and his crippled girlfriend. *Stalkers!*

The girlfriend called him a *gandon*—condom—and said, "We're getting you evicted."

He stopped and stared at the two of them, lined up like they were ready for a race. "You think so. How about I really do buy the building and throw *you* out? You think I'm kidding? I'll make sure you live in a box on the street."

He used the stairs to rush down to the garage. He definitely felt better, glad to have gotten that off his chest. Honesty is the best policy. Good for his health, too. Blood pressure got too high if he didn't express his innermost feelings. Hadn't Galina always said, "Oleg, you have to let me know how you feel. It's a better way to live."

Look what that touchy-feely shit got him. She left without a word. No good-bye kiss. No good-bye *sex*.

What had happened at PP's? That was the mystery.

He called the old bastard as he scurried to his Maserati. "I'm coming over," he announced when the ex-husband of six women picked up. "We need to have a talk." Oleg thought he sounded impressively sinister.

"We do," PP replied simply, which unnerved Oleg *slightly.*

Not much, really, he assured himself.

What a terrible father PP was. Oleg vowed to be a much better dad. He would sire only sons and bring them up strong. *And no dumb beasts like Dmitri.*

Can you imagine raising one of them? He shuddered at the thought.

Oleg motored out of Moscow, keeping to the speed limits until he made it past the city's outer ring of suburbs. Then he raced past the poor peasants in the countryside. He could almost smell them. Not like Galina's lavender scent, that was for sure. *Stink bombs.*

The gate to PP's mansion opened and Oleg gunned his engine, racing down the long driveway, narrowly missing a calico cat that always gave him the evil eye. One day he'd squash that creature, crush him right under his wheels. He'd been trying for at least a year. *Quick little devil feet.*

No parking elevator for him today. He pulled up by the front door. Would have left the Maserati running, too, if PP hadn't freaked out last month and threatened to slash the tires if Oleg ever did that again. "It's patriotic," Oleg had tried to reason with the old man. "Burn gas, oil, and don't worry. The planet will be fine for your grandchildren."

PP was always saying that we had to think about the rug rats. Not those words exactly, but the thrust of his thinking ran in that direction. No wonder Galina liked him.

Actually, it was Oleg taking care of the future, quietly contracting with Russia's biggest construction firms on secret projects to build AAC plants near nuclear generating stations and hydropower plants. Everything hush-hush, from commissioning designs to wiring money. Scores of AAC plants would rise soon, the pride of Russia, the country that would save the world—what was left of it, anyway.

PP opened the door himself.

"What happened?" Oleg demanded. "She was here. She left. I know that. Now I can't reach her."

"Come in, my son. I have long wondered about that question, too. What happened?" PP shook his head. In sorrow? That was what Oleg thought. *Well, get over it old man.*

But it wasn't sorrow at all.

• • •

Galina headed to Sochi. So many tourists went there, even now, thanks to the Olympics, that she believed she could get lost in all the fresh faces. But she would have to spend the night in Voronezh. She found photos on Airbnb of a seventeenth-century monastery that provided a few rooms for "sincere guests."

She was plenty sincere in wanting to stay there, thinking that nobody would ever look for her in a monastery.

Galina and Alexandra arrived just before dawn. The monastery appeared to have been carved out of solid rock.

She led her daughter, bleary from sleep and sickness, to the entrance, and knocked on a thick wooden door. No one answered.

"It's early," she explained to Alexandra.

She leaned her shoulder against the heavy door and pushed it open. They started down a wide walkway. Statues of religious figures, saints, Galina presumed, perched on stone shelves built into the walls. A reliquary with bones and scraps of clothing appeared behind a small square window.

They heard the murmur of chants as a woman in a nun's habit walked toward them. She asked if they needed help.

"I wonder if we could take a room for the morning. We are weary travelers," Galina said, falling into a strange speech pattern for reasons she could not explain, except for the stone walls and floor and ceiling. They seemed to demand obeisance to another era. She was too tired to resist.

The nun studied her, then looked at Alexandra. "You are both troubled in your own ways, aren't you?" she said. Galina had to choke down tears. Again, she didn't know why. She nodded.

"Will two small beds suffice?" the nun asked.

"Yes, thank you."

The nun asked for a modest sum, slipping the rubles into a compact leather pouch that hung next to a rosary with a large silver cross. The transaction completed, she led them to the cloister.

Their room was at the end of a narrow hallway. The nun lit a candle on a corner table. It was the only light but for the sun slowly graying the sky.

The sister bid them adieu, backing out of the room with a genial smile.

"Mommy, are we going to eat?" Alexandra asked. "I'm hungry."

Galina thought her daughter would want to sleep, but it had been a long night with no stops.

"I'll go ask them for food," Galina said.

Alexandra tugged her sleeve and pointed to a Bakelite phone, black as the blankets that covered the two small beds.

The woman who answered said she would bring them bread and cheese and butter.

In fewer than five minutes the humble provisions arrived, along with hard-boiled eggs and cold water in a gray ceramic pitcher that might have been as old as the monastery.

Galina thanked the initiate who had brought them the platter.

"How much do we owe you?" she asked the young woman, who shook her head and left quickly.

The chanting increased in volume. Galina realized they must be close to the chapel.

Alexandra picked up a crust of bread. She dropped it on the table. It was so stale it bounced. But she snatched it up at once and broke off the end, chewing it with difficulty. She had lost most of her baby teeth and had the whitest niblets coming in. But perhaps they weren't quite up to the task of tackling stale chunks of bread.

"The cheese might be easier," Galina advised. "Or you could dip the bread in water."

"That's okay, Mom. It's really good bread."

It *was* good. They ate slowly, deliberately, with no distractions, only the mesmerizing chanting. Amid such peace, Galina found it difficult to comprehend that the world had been plunged into such extreme turmoil. It was even harder for her to believe that Oleg had masterminded the devastation.

When she'd met him at the Moscow Institute of Physics and Technology seven years ago, she'd taken him for just another handsome, bright young man. And when he'd recruited her to track down the AAC technology—"For the betterment of all humankind," he'd claimed—she'd been thrilled to take such a daring step to help clean up the atmosphere. She'd hacked scores of emails and articles by scientists before she'd found the startling revelations in a math professor's computer files at MIT.

Now, she felt her own soul needed saving for the role she'd played. Turning over the math professor's data to Oleg had led him to Professor Ahearn, and that had resulted in his murder, along with the shooting death of his tortured wife. Their children were now orphans. She looked at Alexandra and could have wept. The notion of penance came to her at almost the same moment she thought of the brief conversation she'd had with a woman who also said she had a daughter. They'd both been circumspect on the phone.

And look at where you've ended up, Galina said to herself. She had a strong suspicion the woman was an operative, and almost certainly American. They had great pediatric hospitals there. But that step could get Galina killed or imprisoned for life.

Still, she had the woman's number. And they had agreed to talk again.

When they finished eating, Alexandra took her mother's hand. "Come with me. We should go and see them."

They walked down a stone corridor toward the sound of the chanting. It grew louder, but never harsh.

Entering the rear of the chapel, they saw two dozen nuns seated in hand-carved pews that probably hadn't been moved in centuries. The women's voices affected Galina. She filled with emotion as she and Alexandra sat in the last pew, kneeling moments later when the nuns shifted forward.

Galina prayed for her daughter. A new chant insinuated itself into her consciousness, and she joined in. So did Alexandra.

Morning light began to filter through stained glass windows above a rudimentary altar.

Galina saw that Alexandra's eyes were fixed on a crude wooden cross that was catching the reds and blues and yellows from the windows. The crossbeams were bound with thick rope.

The girl's eyes soon pooled but she didn't sob. Tears spilled down her cheeks soundlessly. Galina wiped them away. Alexandra still had her gaze fixed on the cross.

Galina bent close to her. "What is it, my dearest?"

"Mommy, I'm going to die and go to heaven."

"No, you're not going to die. I promise."

"And you are, too," Alexandra said. "That's what's so sad. You're not even sick."

• • •

PP turned from the video of Dmitri and Galina in the museum. "What do you make of that, Oleg? Second-born son crumples up your picture like it was your head and puts it in the skull crusher. Tell me, what does that mean?"

Oleg looked around. He hadn't seen Dmitri tonight. The scaredy-cat kid the size of an NHL enforcer was hiding somewhere. Dmitri could make the cruelest charges—with Galina's help, of course. She probably encouraged him to put the photo in the crusher—and Oleg couldn't even face his accuser. It was like American Gitmo justice. Disgraceful.

"I think she put him up to it, PP. She has taken off. She's *running away.* She's guilty. The guilty always run like rats."

"You say that about Galina?"

PP looked ready to shoot Oleg, firstborn son, *maybe.* Oleg was outraged that he had to fear his own father. Oleg had a gun, but it was in the Maserati. *What was I thinking?* He'd been in too much of a rush arriving. Special people in Russia got to carry concealed weapons. Oleg was special. But so was PP.

"Tell me where she went," he shouted at PP, unwilling to back down from the plutocrat. A man had to maintain his dignity, his self-possession.

"She didn't tell me. She just left."

"Did you help her? Did you give her—"

"What if I did?"

"That would be a mistake, giving money to someone like her. She needs my help, not your money."

"She doesn't think so. She's afraid of you."

"Of me? That's ridiculous." Though, in truth, Oleg was flattered to hear that. To instill fear was to instill respect. "She must have said something," he insisted.

"She said she was very sorry."

"See, what did I tell you?"

"Sorry that poor Dmitri had to go through that horrible experience in the museum."

That again? "Can't you leave that alone? That's garbage. He's brain damaged. Stupid beyond repair. But not because of me. Because of those stupid stairs. I'm leaving."

Oleg thought he'd better. PP had a certain look about him, and the only time Oleg had seen it before was when he was moving carnivorously against a doomed business competitor.

His father grabbed his arm. Old but strong. It felt like a metal band around his bicep. "No, I don't want you to leave. I want you to stay. I'm enjoying our little talk. Let's bring Dmitri into the discussion."

"Mr. Mumbles? Into the discussion? You're crazy. You're both crazy. I'm the only sane one here."

He jerked his arm free and backed away, scarcely believing he had to worry about his father shooting him in the back.

What has happened to this family?

Oleg made it to the door and stepped outside. Never had the air of the Russian countryside smelled so good.

He hurried to the Maserati and roared toward the gate, worried PP would lock it, then hunt him down.

What has happened to this family? he asked himself again. *A firstborn son,* maybe, *should never have such sorrow. There's a sickness here. Sick, sick, sick.*

The gate opened, thank Christ, and Oleg raced out to the road. He opened the window, sucking in the untainted air, definitely in pursuit of Galina. Already calling Police Sergeant Sergey Volkov's superior to put out an alert for Galina Bortnik. He gave him the make, model, and year of her shitty car. How far did she really think he'd let her run after taking so many secrets? Secrets about Antarctica and AAC. Secrets about a dead professor and his wife.

Secrets like little tiles that Galina could turn into a very dangerous mosaic.

CHAPTER 17

CNN KEPT REPLAYING VIDEO of the mushroom cloud taken by a satellite over the South Pole. The repetition was stomach churning, like the coverage given to the attacks on the Twin Towers. Yet Lana could hardly bear to look away, and she was not alone. Tanesa and her family, including her Aunt Eve and her four children, were all sitting around Lana's living room paying rapt attention to the screen. Doper Don was there, too. Thankfully, he'd kept whatever conspiracy theories he still harbored to himself. Perhaps Esme's reaction to his rants last night kept his lip buttoned.

Walking in and seeing him in the house with the others had given Lana a start, even though she knew he'd be there. It was the seeming normalcy of his presence, after so many years of absence, that she found most unnerving. It was as if somehow he'd never been away. That puzzled her almost as much as the fact that he looked none the worse for wear. She thought prison was supposed to age people—fast. Of course, he'd done his time in a federal facility with tennis courts and a kidney-shaped swimming pool.

Don wasn't the only one keeping his peace. None of the others had piped up, either. Under normal circumstances—if they were even imaginable tonight—Lana would have suggested the younger children go to the den and watch a movie, but that felt wrong this evening. Aunt Eve's youngest two—a three-year-old girl and a six-year-old boy—clung to her fearfully. Children, Lana reminded herself, absorbed much by osmosis, but perhaps nothing so quickly as fear.

News reports said the hackers had detonated the Trident II with its single missile as close as possible to Thwaites Glacier, without actually striking it directly, because that caused what a navy spokesperson called "maximum break impact" on the ice.

That also provided the powerful visual impact of the towering mushroom cloud, which an explosion under the ice, easily delivered by a submarine, would not have accomplished. But an undersea attack might have delivered even more damage. Scientists were openly discussing whether the hackers had favored powerful optics over a possibly more crippling explosion, even as a second missile was ready for blastoff. As it was, the Trident II was plenty terrifying—one thousand times more powerful than the Hiroshima atomic bomb, which had killed upwards of 135,000 people.

The direct death count on Antarctica, at about thirty-three hundred, was a fraction of Hiroshima's—and a fraction of those who were likely to die in the coming days and weeks as sea levels swallowed entire islands, along with cities and towns built during less apocalyptic times. More would die from radiation poisoning as nuclear winds carried the plutonium to the far corners of the globe.

Emma had been shaking her head slowly for minutes, as though in disbelief. Now tears spilled down her cheeks. Lana gently massaged her daughter's neck. The girl didn't look at her mom. She appeared completely unnerved.

When CNN returned to its newsroom for a series of predictable reports about domestic turmoil—flooding, rioting, looting—Lana asked if everyone had eaten.

"We kept it simple," Tanesa's mom, Esme, said. "There's potato salad in the fridge and cold cuts. Even had a nice green salad that Eve made, and we saved some of that for you, too. I just hope we don't have a blackout because we could lose a lot of food. I don't think you could fit a pickle in there at this point."

"We'll be okay," Lana replied, "even if there's a—"

"We've had plenty of blackouts in Anacostia," Esme said.

Lana nodded. "I have a generator built in to my electrical system."

"Ah," Esme nodded. "Well, that's one less thing to worry about."

Lana was starving and battle weary. Her break from combat, as it were, would be brief. Holmes had asked her to call the "Internet forum woman" as soon as it was six a.m. Moscow time.

"It's our only play right now," he told Lana. "But don't let that cloud your judgment because I still think it may be a means of sucking you into action just to waste your time or, worse, get you in a position for a grab." Abduction.

"Nobody's going to grab me," Lana had told him, "because I won't be moving anywhere without your approval." And without the backup support he would undoubtedly insist upon.

Actually, nobody was without government approval. The only commercial flights permitted were those essential to evacuating people from low-lying areas. Otherwise, any airborne planes belonged to DOD, and those fighter jets and troop transport planes were very active, indeed, on both domestic and foreign fronts, from what Lana had learned.

She headed quietly into the kitchen and filled a plate with cold dinner. Every cubic inch of the fridge was packed, just as Esme had indicated, and at least a dozen bags of groceries were sitting on the kitchen counters, nonperishables, she saw with a quick survey. Esme hadn't exaggerated when she'd said they'd been stocking up. Still, Lana wondered whether she should ask Tanesa's mom to come up with a ration plan. With coastal cities flooding and in widespread disarray—violent chaos, in many cases—the vast number of tankers and container ships couldn't off-load. Many had fled harbors for open ocean where they wouldn't be subject to the havoc of unusually powerful tidal surges set off by the sudden rise in sea level.

Even the interior of the country was slowing down as fuel supplies dwindled rapidly. The President had mandated gas and diesel rationing, with special consideration granted only to shipments of food, medicines, emergency medical supplies, and military hardware.

But as bad as that was—and the death toll already had surpassed more than fifty thousand—the U.S. was infinitely better suited to deal with the crises than its neighbors to the south, while Canada, like Russia, was weathering the unprecedented challenges in *relatively* good shape. The Canadians, with the world's largest supply of fresh water, were diverting substantial reserves to hard-hit California, which had been enduring drought-induced shortages long before its frightened citizenry had started hoarding water in all forms—bottles, huge plastic containers, bathtubs, and backyard swimming pools. The irony of water shortages on that scale, amid such widespread flooding, was so obvious that all but the dimmest TV commentators—and there were more than a few—even bothered to comment on it.

The West Coast's biggest ports—Seattle-Tacoma, Oakland, and

Los Angeles-Long Beach—were turning away ships packed with vital supplies—along with countless tons of plastic crap from China—so dock workers and engineers could make desperate attempts to shore up the wharves that were indispensable to the rest of the U.S.

The crisis—and the word seemed wholly inadequate to Lana—had sent the stock market into free fall, while banks across the country were taking an emergency "holiday" mandated by the federal government.

As Lana forked up the last of her potato salad and sliced turkey, Emma sidled up to her.

"You don't look so great, Mom."

"And you are an honest child," Lana said, cupping Emma's cheek for the first time in ages. "You're right, though. I'm tired."

"Are you going to get some sleep now?"

"Not just yet." She finished her last bite and put aside her plate. "I'm going to duck into my office for a while, and I'll probably be gone before you wake up in the morning. Everybody getting along okay?"

"Oh, sure. Even Dad's keeping his mouth shut. I think he knows it's real—*finally*. Besides, Esme wouldn't take any more of his BS, even if he still thought it was all one big lying conspiracy. But he doesn't. He even said that if he ever got his hands on the people who did this, he'd break them into pieces."

At last, something Don and I can agree on, Lana thought. "Where's he sleeping?" she asked Emma.

"A cot in the upstairs hallway. He's the only guy. Well, the only big guy, so he doesn't get a room. You want to know the other arrangements?"

"Not if you guys have it covered."

"You're still in your room, but Tanesa and I will be using the sofa bed in there."

"Fair enough."

"Mom?"

"Yes, Em." She watched her daughter swallow, expecting more tears. Emma surprised her:

"I'm really worried about you. The last time it got really bad you took off and almost got yourself killed. Promise me you're not going to do anything like that this time, that you'll just sit at your computer and that's it."

"I promise," Lana said. Perhaps too blithely.

"I mean it, Mom."

"I'm not going anywhere." *Right now.*

Emma returned to the living room. Lana headed to her office, locking the door and pulling out her phone. She wondered how long service would continue. Could last for a while, she realized. It was hard to flood communication towers on mountains and hilltops, and satellites were safely removed from earthly insanity.

Before calling Galina Bortnik, she checked with her colleagues to see if there were any leads on the *Delphin*'s location. At this point, knowing what they did about Hector Gomez, a.k.a. Grisha Lisko, the navy was gunning for its own vessel. But finding it was the challenge. DOD announced that the service had pinpointed the launch in the Southern Ocean near the fortieth latitude, a region known as the "Roaring Forties" for its fierce westerlies, but it could easily take days to get ships there, giving the rogue sub ample time to leave quietly. And at ten knots or less, the *Delphin* would be all but impossible to find. Its stealth capacities were phenomenal, and the only real limit to how long it could stay out there to launch all two dozen of its missiles was food. And Grisha Lisko and whatever help he had could not eat all the provisions in two years of bombing and feasting.

Nobody believed the sub would actually go undiscovered for a year or two. It could actually fire off those missiles with no more than fifteen minutes of preparation, a sobering reality that appeared to elude the House Speaker and Majority Leader, both of whom had said the U.S. should never retreat from the Arctic because of terrorist threats. *Threats? They'd just nuked Antarctica.* Lana still could not believe those two cretins would make such an ignorant statement. But the President, according to Holmes, felt hemmed in by the demagoguery on Capitol Hill.

"Who cares?" Lana had replied, sitting across from Holmes in his office just hours ago.

"Everyone running in the midterm elections," he'd replied.

"What midterm elections? There won't be any if this keeps up. Can't they just put that crap aside for this?" she exclaimed. *If they can't, how can the country ever survive?* she wondered, but only to herself.

"No, they can't put it aside," the deputy director said.

It would appear the House and Senate leadership, like the sub, could outlast any stalling strategy by the White House. According to Holmes, Admiral Wourzy had advised the President's chief of staff that the sub could also go very deep.

"How deep?" Lana had asked Holmes, who had shaken his head. That was his muted manner of saying the information was classified.

Wourzy had also said the sub could make the most of the ocean's salinity gradients to enhance its cover. All of which would make locating the *Delphin* harder than trying to find the missing Malaysian passenger jet a few years back, and that aircraft had been equipped with a pinger to make location and recovery possible. Plus, the crash itself had undoubtedly left an oil spill on the ocean surface. Wourzy had also noted that in stealth mode the *Delphin* would slow down all its fans and shut off any major equipment that wasn't absolutely essential to the sub's operation. "With its speed reduced, it'll cover fifty miles in five hours. I know that doesn't sound like much but that that'll vastly increase the search radius compared to it holding steady," the admiral had added in his briefing to the chief of staff, to which Holmes had been privy.

Which was why Holmes had begun to place special emphasis on Lana's Russian contact. He'd wanted at least five of their colleagues to listen in, even prompt Lana if necessary, but she'd scotched the idea, pointing out that Bortnik had already demonstrated superb hacking skills. They could not risk any discovery that would undermine whatever trust Lana had developed with her so far.

She checked her watch. Almost 6:05 a.m. Moscow time. It felt much later than nine-plus Eastern.

Lana heard the children getting ready for bed. None of the exuberance that she recalled from when Emma had had sleepovers. The kids really were absorbing the fear on the faces of their parents.

She dialed Bortnik, who answered on the third ring. This time the woman didn't wait to speak.

"I know your name," she said to Lana.

"And I believe I know yours."

Neither actually used the names; Lana considered that savvy on Bortnik's part. "But there's a problem," Lana said.

"Go ahead."

"How do I know that you are who you say you are?"

"You have video capability, of course. You can—"

"Yes, but that isn't foolproof. I've already accessed photographs of you and your daughter. I need much more," Lana said.

"Fingerprint and iris recognition? Would that help?"

"Yes," Lana answered. "That would certainly be much better, but I want to see you, too. When you talk, videoconference with me."

"Okay, but I will also send you instructions on how to access secret files about me so you'll have all of that at your disposal."

Though Bortnik hadn't specified, she had to be referring to FSB records, which Lana was glad she was volunteering. "But I want something in return," Bortnik said.

Lana had a good idea what that would be, but asked anyway.

"I want the same from you," the Russian replied.

"That will make my bosses uneasy."

"And what I'm doing could get me killed. My daughter, too."

"But you want to come here, don't you?"

"Possibly."

"Don't play games with me. Do you or don't you?"

"Yes, I want to come."

"You know what we could guarantee you and your little girl, don't you?"

"I do."

"And, I repeat, you came to us."

"Not 'us,'" Bortnik corrected. "To *you*. I will give you what you want."

Lana thought she sounded nervous. *Who could blame her? Who knows who's listening?* "And your daughter. I want to see you both in our videoconference. Have her on your lap."

A pause now greeted Lana, even longer than the one that came during their first call.

Bortnik broke the silence: "Yes, my daughter, too. But there are critical time restraints. You have to get us out of here. I have traveled close to a coastline. That is all I will say for now, except that I can't cross a border checkpoint. People are looking for me. You *must* come for us very fast. Not just for us. It's in your interest, too."

"And what will you do for us, if we get you out?"'

"I can give you many pieces of the puzzle," Galina said, speaking rapidly, as if she feared she'd be silenced—by her own timidity or the harshness of others—if she didn't say everything at once. "But I am dead, and so is my daughter, if you don't come right away. I mean *you*, Lana."

Using her name for the first time. Not her surname, but still a gamble. "Why me?" Lana asked.

"Because I want to know the person I'm betting my little girl's life on is betting hers as well. Simple *quid pro quo*. But there's something else you must bring—all your expertise and computers. We will have to go to work immediately to stop this madness. These men are crazy. They think they are playing games. They won't stop with one missile."

"Why are they waiting now?"

"To make everyone cower. They think they're in total control."

They are, thought Lana reluctantly.

"Every minute is precious, Lana. Do you understand?"

"All too well. Let me see what I can do. I'll look for that information you mentioned. We must start with that, and the means of verification must be foolproof."

"Then let's begin." Bortnik hung up.

Lana imagined the woman's fear, fleeing Moscow with her only child. Near a coastline, either in the north or south of her country. Which wasn't giving away much, either to her or those searching for Bortnik.

But Lana also imagined a setup. How could she not? Bortnik, or whoever was posing as her, had put tremendous pressure on Lana to take personal action to exfiltrate her and her daughter from Russia. No mean gamble, especially at a time like this.

Plus, Emma had been right: Lana had almost been killed the last time she got involved in kinetic action against hackers. Physical derring-do wasn't her strong suit. And she'd promised her daughter that she wasn't going anywhere.

But at each stage of Emma's development, Lana had tried to protect her from the bleakest, most age-inappropriate truths.

She'd edited fairy tales, for instance, when she'd felt her daughter wasn't ready for the unexpurgated Brothers Grimm. Now Lana felt that Emma, even at fifteen, hadn't grown beyond the simple comforts of her mother's deceptions. So she wouldn't tell her if she were deployed overseas. Lana would just go, if it came to that, and trust that she'd return in one piece—and quickly.

There were always myths a famous mother couldn't control, though. After last year's violent cybersiege, Lana wished Emma had not accepted that her mother could overcome the grimmest possibilities and most excruciating penalties.

Lana had tried to tell Emma that what actually had happened in Yemen was much more complicated than the torrent of news stories would have had the world—and her own daughter—believe. Truth be told, Lana felt she'd been more lucky than brave during that climactic struggle—and that whatever had passed for her courage then was about to be cruelly tested again.

Fearing that she'd fail herself, her daughter, and her country, she glanced at the phone and shut off the light.

Sleep did not come easily.

CHAPTER 18

GALINA AWOKE JUST BEFORE noon, her sense of displacement so great that she did not recognize the monastery room for several seconds. It looked so small it could have been a prison cell—but for the sleeping beauty in the bed across from her.

Alexandra lay with her eyes closed and mouth slack, looking blissfully happy, but five hours was all the sleep Galina would get. Even so, it represented the longest uninterrupted rest since she'd first spoken to the woman whom she now knew was Lana Elkins, owner of a cybersecurity firm and a former NSA star. Elkins, Galina had learned, was a troubleshooter for that agency and had survived a brutal firefight that ended the cyberattack on the U.S. grid. All of which told Galina that Lana Elkins had the clout to provide her with what she most wanted: safety for her daughter and herself from men who would kill them on sight. That had certainly been Tattoo's goal, and she doubted Oleg would stop simply because the first thug he'd sent after her had failed.

She hoped Alexandra's slumber would continue a while longer. With a belly stuffed with bread and cheese—and a body fully exhausted from all the stress they'd endured since thug number

one had shown up—Galina thought it likely her daughter would
sleep right through her mother's next contact with Elkins, this
time directly via satellite; the monastery did not have Wi-Fi but
a satellite dish nested on a nearby building, so she would poach
its digital video broadcast signals to get to the Internet posthaste.

She started hacking her way back into FSB's cybercenter, following the invisible trails she had blazed long before to Russia's
darkest secrets. Next, she created a file to provide virtual paths for
Lana Elkins that would lead the U.S. spy to everything FSB had on
her *and* on Galina herself. She had read the Elkins files as soon as
she'd managed to identify her. That was why she had been so comfortable moving forward with her: Elkins was formidable enough to
have warranted lots of FSB interest. A credit to her, in Galina's book.

But before executing the final keystroke to her own files, she
froze at the sight of a surprise video greeting from Oleg. It was
as if he were standing in the room staring at her, his eyes boring
holes into her own.

It can't be in real time, Galina thought. *He must have placed it
here, setting it up to be triggered by me.* And she might have been
right, but his message was much more menacing than even his
shocking appearance could herald:

"Galina girl, you have come back to nest in the FSB files. I
wonder why you are doing that. I wonder if you are betraying
your own country now. But of course you are. Do you know that
by betraying Mother Russia you are betting your own blood, and
your daughter's, on an act so terrible it can only fail? I wonder,
most of all, if you know the price of betraying me? I will have you
again. That is the price. Yes, in the midst of so many responsibili-
ties, of so many great historic achievements—of literally changing the face of the earth—I am also on your trail. Why? Because
you must and will be stopped. I could be outside your door right
now. That would not even be a small achievement for a man who

has accomplished what I have in the past few days. Why don't you take a look? I really might be there."

Galina paused the video and looked up. She couldn't help herself. It was as if she suddenly believed in ghosts, or the idea that a bloodthirsty killer could be hiding under her bed. *Or outside your door,* she thought. After all, the rational side of her knew what Oleg was suggesting—that he was actually doing all this in real time only feet away—was supremely unlikely, but *not* impossible. That was what made her so uneasy.

She stared at the door, genuinely frightened that it would swing open and he'd storm in. *No,* she told herself. *If he wanted you, he'd have grabbed you by now.* So that made no sense. But neither did this:

"That's right, Galina. I know you so well. You are wondering where I am, and if I can get you. The answer is yes, but how am I going to do it?" He smiled, so genuinely that it raised the hairs on the back of her neck. "That's a secret you can't hack. You'll know that's true when I put my hands on you and Alexandra. There can be only one reason you have disappeared: you betrayed me."

He raised a big knife. It looked like a blade a hunter would use to slay a boar. He ran the shiny tip across his cheek to just below his eye, pressing the flat side against the very bottom of the socket. So close to his eyeball that she flinched.

"You are blind to what you are doing, Galina. You'll never get across a border. A short, twenty-six-year-old woman with a sick, six-year-old daughter? Good luck. I'd like to see you *hack* your way through that." He turned the blade till it reflected the light.

"And when you are caught, guess who you'll be delivered to? Me, because you are my responsibility, just like Alexandra is yours. You will see that you have betrayed your little girl's trust. Everyone who means anything to you in the coming days will also suffer. Good friends. Your former colleagues at Greenpeace.

We'll get them all. That has been made clear to me, so it is only fair that I make that clear to you."

He waved good-bye with the knife, letting it catch the light again. She wondered how long ago he'd posted the video. She worked for several minutes trying to determine the answer before deciding she had bigger priorities.

She also wondered what the posted video would mean to Lana Elkins. Would she believe her now, if she actually saw it? Or would she consider it an elaborate orchestration?

Galina still wanted to hack her files for Elkins, but when she finally worked her way past Oleg's video, she found they were missing. Completely removed. After all that, she had nothing to offer Elkins. Why would the NSA star ever believe her now?

● ● ●

Oleg was not outside her door, but he was nearby—on a hilltop overlooking Voronezh. He wasn't certain Galina was in the city that spread out before him, but Police Sergeant Sergey Volkov had been murdered on the main highway heading south—and so ruthlessly that Oleg was appalled, even offended, that a man working for him had been treated with such cruelty. *A bullet and a Bic pen?* He still could hardly believe it.

He thought Galina *might* have braced herself to backtrack through Moscow, when she most wanted to leave that city—*and for good reason,* he chuckled to himself—but he doubted she'd have the stomach for that. Which would mean that if she were heading south she would have to pass through the city before him.

Pass through? Maybe not.

She might have been so tired, so stressed-out by the time she arrived with her cancer kid that she would have been eager to rest. Made sense. That was when an almost feral presentiment told him that if he were to just look, really look around Voronezh, he'd find her.

He gazed, once again, at the city. His eyes roved left to right.

Then again, he thought: intuition was one thing, Google was another.

"Places of interest." He found a literary museum built in the eighteenth century. *How quaint.* Named after a poet Oleg had never heard of. A house bearing the name of an agronomist. A city square. A monastery.

None of it aroused his instincts, so he googled "Places to stay."

An art hotel. He groaned. Holiday Inn. He gave his phone the finger. A hostel. Possibly, even likely before Galina became a mom, but not with a sick child. And the monastery again.

It had come up twice, like a slot machine with two cherries. Galina could be the third. The thought first amused, then intrigued him.

From where he stood on the hill, he should be able to see the monastery; according to what he read online, it had been carved from a mountain so it would always be prominent to the faithful. He certainly considered himself faithful to the mission of finding—and *killing*—Galina.

He was trying like hell to pick out the monastery when *Numero Uno* texted him.

Until now, he had always welcomed hearing from *Uno.* But the Ukrainian hacker had been badgering him for the go-ahead for the second Trident II, reminding Oleg that the missile was ready for launch.

"I am going to bury it in the ice sheet this time before it explodes," he added. "That will melt even more ice and send a tsunami all the way to Asia."

"Not yet. No means no," he texted *Uno* back. It was like dealing with a two-year-old.

Oleg had his own people to answer to, and they thought there was plenty of flooding in the world right now, with terrific results: Canada, Norway, Denmark, and, of course, Russia, were pulling their ships out of the Arctic region. The only stubborn nation was the U.S., which was ruled by idiots. They were like bad poker players trying to raise the ante with the worst possible cards. The Russian President was known to be laughing at his pathetic rival in Washington.

So there was no need to launch the twenty-three missiles that were left. *How much radiation do we really want,* Uno?

But he could see that *Uno* was intoxicated with the power of being the man with his finger on the button. And Oleg understood that: with the coordinates fixed on the Smith Glacier, just south of Thwaites, Oleg felt twitches of envy over *Uno's* chance to play nuclear plenipotentiary.

"Not now," Oleg insisted in a postscript. "Wait as I have instructed you."

"I don't want to wait. Waiting is a mistake," *Uno* replied with unmitigated gall. "Waiting makes us look weak and fearful."

What was *Uno* really saying? Oleg wished he'd actually met the Ukrainian in person at some point. You can be in nearly constant contact with someone for three years, as he and *Uno* had been, but that was still not *knowing* him.

While *Uno* had done exemplary work with Grisha Lisko, the only reason the pair had actually been able to pull off the hijacking of the *Delphin* was the tomes of research by Russia's own cadre of hardcore FSB hackers who had made countless incursions into the U.S. Navy's command center for the Atlantic fleet in Norfolk, Virginia.

So *Uno's* success was built on a platform designed and built by many others, although *Uno* knew only what he needed to know.

"Do not lecture me," Oleg warned him. "And do not launch the second missile."

"I will wait," *Uno* replied.

Of course you will.

Oleg wished he could be as sure of Galina's moves. The monastery intrigued him because she'd been brought up in the faith. Like so many others, though, she'd abandoned it. But Oleg had heard that people often found it again when they had a child with a terminal disease. They might not ever think of praying for themselves, but for a sunken-cheeked cancer kid? And Alexandra was Galina's whole life.

There it is. He'd finally picked out a cross and building that had been carved out of a mountain a couple miles away. They'd been revealed in stone the way a sculptor will uncover a face with his chisel and hammer.

Why not take a closer look? There wasn't much else between Voronezh and Sochi. Just small burgs. And Sochi itself had turned into a $50 billion ghost town since the Olympics.

He walked back down a short trail to his Maserati.

• • •

After watching Oleg on-screen, and finding her own files missing, Galina couldn't rouse Alexandra and leave the monastery fast enough.

"We've got to keep moving," she told her daughter. She couldn't be as terse with the nun who had checked them in and wanted to know why a mother with an obviously ill child would be hurrying out the door in the middle of the day.

"I need to get home. My mother is not feeling well. Maybe dying."

"What about your daughter? She looks like she needs rest. And you look like you need to pray."

"She will sleep in the car," Galina responded.

"And will you pray when you drive?"

"I'll try."

The nun appeared unimpressed with Galina's sincerity. Galina felt the woman's eyes on her back all the way out to the Macan.

Galina drove down the narrow streets of old Voronezh, eyes on the rearview mirror as much as the road ahead.

The bright sun, high in the sky, filled the narrow streets with harsh light that felt brutal and made her fear they had no place to hide.

But he doesn't know you have PP's new car.

No, she corrected herself immediately. *You don't know what he knows—or where he is.*

But he felt as present as the sun, and as threatening as the shadows that darkened with every passing minute.

• • •

Oleg pulled up to the monastery and strode to the door. He knocked as if he owned the place, reminding himself that he probably could if he wanted to.

A nun greeted him with a curious glance, but no words. Beside her, head bowed, stood a younger woman not in a habit. A novitiate, Oleg presumed. An apprentice in the discipline of denial—of self, sex, and all the keen excesses that made life worth living.

The information center for Voronezh had noted that the nuns were "self-sufficient." This one looked at him as if she not only owned the monastery, but his soul, too. Oleg loathed that kind of arrogance. *Who does she think she is?*

"How may I help you?" the nun asked in the manner of one who wishes to provide no help at all.

"I understand you have rooms for 'sincere visitors.' Is that true?"

She nodded. He thought he might have detected the slightest softening in her demeanor. Once again, he prided himself on knowing how to instinctively strike the right note with these bitches.

"And you are 'sincere'?" she asked.

"Very much so." Oleg managed not to smirk or offer even a hint of a smile. "May I stay here?" The monastery had three rooms for visitors, according to the city's website.

The nun appeared obliging, but showed him only two of the rooms. The novitiate trailed silently behind them.

"Isn't there a third room?" he asked.

"It is not clean. It was just used."

He shrugged as though it didn't matter to him, but then said, "I'd like to see it anyway. If I like it, I'll be patient while you clean it for me."

The nun peered at him. He thought about what he'd just said. What could possibly be off-putting about saying you'd be patient?

She shook her head. "It's not ready."

"Is that it?" He nodded at a door across the hall, the only one in the small cloister that he had not entered.

She did not respond, at least not quickly enough to suit Oleg. He walked across and opened it, finding Galina. Not her person, but her scent. The lavender he loved so much on her skin, which rose so seductively to his nose when she began to sweat. Unmistakable amid the old wood and stone and tiles.

"Dark hair. This tall." He held out his hand. "With a little girl, right?" He spoke with none of the patience he had just professed to have.

The nun glanced at him, saying nothing. But the novitiate raised her face to Oleg for the first time. Such a sweet-looking creature, perhaps seventeen, eighteen, just coming into bloom, which even her shapeless black frock couldn't hide. Neither could her face, frozen with alarm, deny the truth of what he'd just stated.

Oleg knew, and the novitiate knew he knew. He thought to calm her. "Do not worry. She is a dear friend. Which way did she go?"

The novitiate looked at the nun, who replied for her: "We don't know who you are talking about."

"You are lying," he said as he approached the old woman. "Have you had a bad experience with a man?" She was ugly, with big pores on her nose. How he loathed them. But the novitiate looked sweet, pure, unadorned and untouched. *But not for long.* Any guy worth his manhood could see that immediately. Oleg made a point of letting his eyes settle on the nun's charge, who averted her beautiful green gaze.

"You must leave. Call the police," the nun said to the younger woman.

"No need," Oleg replied, smiling and grabbing the novitiate's wrist. "I am the police. So, I ask you again: Which way?"

"I don't know," the nun said. She had the audacity to even offer a shrug. And she, a religious woman. What kind of example was she setting for the novitiate?

Liar.

"It's too bad that you don't know." Oleg still held the young woman's wrist. "What car was she driving?"

"Car? I didn't look," the nun said. "Now let go of her."

Oleg shook his head. Then he pushed them both into the room with the lavender scent that he'd always found so arousing, and closed the door behind him. It had an old lock that he snapped into place. He turned back to them, smiling.

● ● ●

Where is everybody? It's empty. What was I thinking?

There had been so few cars on the road to Sochi. Galina had seen five to be exact; two were police SUVs. How was that possible? Billions had watched the Olympics, and now nothing? Millions had visited Sochi, and now nothing?

Worse than nothing. There were potholes; curbs breaking away from traffic circles; and apartment buildings that looked empty, eerie with the same two chairs and table on every balcony.

How could they ever get lost among the faces of tourists if no one was even there?

Galina realized she'd been living in her own world, such an insular life in Moscow, so focused on Alexandra and AAC and fighting global warming that she'd become oblivious to other events in her own country.

They found a restaurant in the southernmost part of the city. Galina donned a scarf and told Alexandra to stay in the car. With dark glasses, despite the setting sun, she walked inside and ordered potato latkes.

When she came out, her daughter said she had to go to the bathroom. Galina drove her to a park they'd passed; it had been built for the Olympics. Now the grass was overgrown and the concrete paths cracked. But they found a bathroom. When Galina flushed the commode for Alexandra, it roared and raised a brown geyser that made them run like refugees under fire.

Still breathing heavily, they hurled themselves into the Macan. The night was darkening. It was the only cover Galina could find for them.

Gratefully, she started driving, but after twenty minutes realized she was lost. She didn't dare go online to check maps, haunted, as always, by Oleg's desire to track her down.

She found a car park and shut off her engine, thankful for the anonymity of darkness, but haunted by every pair of passing headlights.

CHAPTER 19

LANA WAS READY TO leave for Fort Meade after less than five hours of sleep, yet she wasn't tired. Fatigue had been overwhelmed by urgency. Just one more thing to do, but she was certain it would be the hardest task of the day: She had to say good-bye to Emma, even if the girl was asleep, because Lana was all but certain she would soon be deployed to a coastline somewhere in Russia. Regardless of the reservations that she and Holmes and the White House itself had about letting an "asset" as valuable as she enter Russian territory at a time like this, she expected to be airborne in a matter of hours. Holmes as much as said so in a message only minutes ago: "You're our best bet."

Our only bet, Lana had almost volleyed, which she considered less an egotistical comment on her skills than the dearth of leads available to the intelligence services.

She left her travel mug of coffee on the kitchen island and hurried upstairs to where Emma lay next to Tanesa on the foldout futon in Lana's large bedroom. Her daughter's eyes were closed, her breath scarcely a whisper. She had her arm draped over Tanesa's side. They looked like they'd known each other all their lives.

In a way, they have, Lana thought, if the most important measure of a full life with someone came only *after* surviving a near-death experience with them. Those two had certainly endured that—and more—together.

At least Emma and Tanesa weren't in direct peril this time. But another mother and daughter were: Galina and Alexandra Bortnik. Six thousand miles away, or thereabouts, Lana guessed. Who knew where they really were? *Near a coastline.* That was all Galina had revealed to her.

While it was true that Russia did not have the world's most significant coastal cities threatened by rising seas, Galina's hint could mean that she and her daughter were in any one of hundreds of small towns, cities, and ports from Russia's northern seas to the Baltic and Black Seas in the west and the Caspian Sea in the south. Just thinking of the thousands of miles of shoreline—and all those radiating possibilities—made Lana realize she could be gone for a while.

No, Lana corrected herself: *You could be gone for good.* If she'd learned one truth since the attack on the grid, it was that there were no guarantees you'd return. God knows, so many hadn't back then.

She kissed Emma's forehead, thinking she'd slip away without waking her. Daylight was only now easing past the blinds. But Emma gripped her mother's hand even before her eyes blinked open.

"You're leaving?" she asked.

"Yes, I'm going to Meade."

"No, I mean you're leaving the country. I know you are. You're going *somewhere.*"

Lana felt caught in the crosshairs of her own conscience. Had she been too blithe last night in assuring Emma that she wasn't leaving? Too quick to reassure her one more time? Had Emma detected the same cosseting tone that she'd heard her whole life whenever her mother had sought to soften the toughest stories for her?

"*Mom?*" Emma said, demanding an answer.

"I'll let you know if I *have* to go."

Lana expected a volley of furious complaints, a temper tantrum even, though Emma hadn't thrown one of those in a long time. Instead, her daughter shocked her: "Be safe, Mom. I want you back. And don't lie to me anymore. I know what you do, and I know why. Someday I'm going to do it, too."

Lana kissed her again, choking down a flood of emotion, some of it pride. Most of it, though, was barely repressed grief at the fear of dying and never seeing her daughter again, just when her deadbeat dad came back into her life. The irony would be almost piercing.

"How will I know if you're gone?" Emma asked.

If I don't come back, Lana thought. But she promised to let her daughter know, "no matter what."

"For real this time?" Emma asked.

"For real."

Lana made excellent time driving out of Bethesda. Commuter traffic had thinned considerably as social chaos affected work schedules as much as shipments of goods and the delivery of vital services.

As she drove, she received a message from Galina explaining that Oleg Dernov had left a threatening video—and pillaged Galina's FSB files. Then, just as Lana wondered who the devil Dernov was—and whether she'd missed a message from Galina—the woman dropped a bombshell: Dernov was the superhacker who'd been "running" Galina and the entire operation.

Galina added that Dernov was not officially FSB—a contention Lana would have Jeff Jensen chase down—and attached a copy of Dernov's threatening video.

Lana turned it on as she merged easily onto the Beltway, glancing at her laptop on the passenger seat just long enough to catch Dernov's smirk. She knew that she, along with many others in the nation's intelligence services, would need to study the video closely, but she wanted to hear the gist of his message as soon as possible.

In a word, it was creepy. Dernov's standard-issue charge that Galina had betrayed her country was one thing, but what snagged Lana's attention much more was when he said, "I wonder, most of all, if you know the price of betraying me?" Making it personal in a way that was the very antithesis of cyberwar with its calculating, almost clinically cold cunning. His threats then went further: "I could be outside your door right now . . . Why don't you take a look? I really might be there."

Megalomaniacal, too, by claiming that tracking her down would be a "small achievement for a man who has accomplished what I have . . . literally changing the face of the earth." Lana had met many men and women with ample egos in the cyberfield, but Dernov appeared to be in a class of his own, which she guessed he'd relish hearing.

His efforts to intimidate Galina included a hint at real violence when he unveiled a large, gleaming knife. Even though all Lana could do was glance at the screen while she drove, she still squirmed when he pressed the shiny tip of that blade just below his eye and told Galina that she was "blind" to what she was doing.

But what Lana took personally was Dernov's vow that Galina and her daughter would never get out of Russia.

We'll see about that.

Lana hurried directly to Holmes's office. He looked up as she entered and, before he could ask, she lifted her laptop, as though in victory. "I've got it right here."

He watched the video in silence. When it ended with Dernov's threats to Galina's erstwhile Greenpeace colleagues, Holmes shook his head: "Amazing that he's the face of the enemy."

"Almost too bizarre, but cyberspace has always had a disproportionate share of brilliant crazies."

"When are you going to video link with her? Soon, I hope."

Lana checked her watch. "In less than thirty minutes."

"We want you to do it in your office. Keep it as normal as possible, plus there's no telling whether she's already seen your office."

An allusion to remote activation of computer cameras, though Lana had as much security protecting her system as anyone up to and including the President.

"I doubt she's seen my office, but I'd prefer to do it there for the reason you first stated, keeping it nice and normal. With your flowers in the background," she added. Delivery of the deputy director's weekly bouquet had not been stopped by the crisis.

"We'll have our voice analysts and psychiatrist present. I want to keep the group small, though. Everybody will have a chance to go over the recordings of both Bortnik and Dernov later."

"I don't see how the Russians can play innocent after this," Lana said. "The video was embedded in FSB files, for God's sakes."

"They'll say he's a great hacker and messed with their files, and then they'll make a big deal of *saying* they'll arrest him as soon as possible. But that won't happen until they finish whatever business they have planned with those missiles. That's what they want," Holmes added matter-of-factly, "to sit on top of the world, no matter how damaged, as long as they're number one."

Lana agreed. It was as if many powerful Russians shared dreams of empire and would sooner take possession of the planet, no matter how damaged, than squat further down the food chain in a healthier world.

She reminded herself that past performance was often the best predictor of future behavior. And past performance with the Russians now included a nuclear missile strike and dangerously rising seas.

"The Chinese ambassador contacted me this morning to say he's received approval to send over more than a hundred of their top cyberspies."

"Does anyone outside this office know we're going to be working with them?"

"The President, of course, his chief of staff, the secretary of state, the joint chiefs, and the heads of the various intelligence agencies along with their chief deputies. Only people with the highest security clearances. Absolutely nobody on the Hill. Not even the chairs of the intelligence committees. They'll be screaming."

"Let them," Lana said, unable to hide her contempt.

"Even so, there's always a risk it'll leak."

"The Chinese might even find a leak in their interest," Lana noted.

"McGivern says they're much more intent on stopping the damage to their principal ports and cities." McGivern was NSA's chief China expert. Holmes went on: "We may not know the meaning of bipartisanship in Congress, but we do with one of our chief economic and military rivals. Go figure."

"That would take much more time than we have," Lana replied.

Holmes nodded. "You should probably get ready."

Lana checked her watch. Indeed.

As she headed to her office, she wished she'd had the time to actually study Dernov's video before linking to Galina. Lana's takeaway, based mostly on hearing him—and a few glances at his imperious facial expressions while she was driving—was that he was a control freak, perhaps to his own detriment. Going after

Galina right now, with all that he had in motion, did not appear to make sense, unless Galina was truly in a position to torpedo—perhaps in the most literal sense—his whole operation. In any event, Lana was anxious to catch the psychiatrist's take on Dernov.

She'd already performed cursory research on the Russian mastermind. He was a son of a plutocrat: Dernov *père* was an oil, gas, and minerals magnate. She'd found nothing in a quick search on Dernov senior to indicate that he was anything more than a moneymaking machine who had achieved prominence, along with so many Russian plutocrats, by plundering state-owned companies after the fall of the Soviet Union. Still, that was more than she was able to unearth about Galina in FSB files, just as the woman had warned. She'd done no better trying to dig any deeper about the younger Dernov.

She messaged Jeff Jensen and added Galina and Dernov's father to his research tasks.

After studying the Dernov video, she saw that she had about sixty seconds before she was scheduled to link to Galina and her six-year-old. She was beginning to wonder whether Holmes and his team were going to show up on time, when they strode into her office.

At precisely the scheduled moment, an exhausted-looking woman with a hollow-cheeked child appeared on a large monitor mounted on Lana's wall. It was almost shocking to see the girl, who appeared so genuinely ill that Lana regretted asking Galina to put her through this. The child also had a dark bruise on her face.

Emma had been a lean girl by that point in her life, but strong. Alexandra was curled up on her mother's lap like a three-year-old.

Galina herself had stylishly cut black hair that came to her chin. Clearly, a woman who had taken care with her appearance—until she'd gone on the run. Now her hair hung limply. Some of it stuck to her round cheeks, as though she hadn't had time for a shower and shampoo in days. And her eyes, large and round, had dark circles under them that were only accentuated by the lousy lighting of video sessions.

Lana would have bet her career then and there that mother and daughter were not poseurs.

"Did you see his video?" Galina asked.

"I did," Lana replied.

"He's not as crazy as he seems in that. Don't underestimate him and think he's just nuts. He's not."

"Were you intimately involved with him?"

"Yes," Galina answered without pause. "Until recently. He is not Alexandra's father. Her father died recently." She said it in such a way that Lana knew Alexandra's father had not died of natural causes—and that Galina wanted to shield her daughter from that news. "I was asked a lot of questions about his passing," Galina added.

"I understand that you and your daughter might have been accosted as you drove south from Moscow."

For a blink, Galina looked worried that Lana had mentioned the direction; she hadn't reacted to "accosted." Then Galina recovered and nodded: "It was terrible. She witnessed it."

More than witnessed it, Lana thought with another glance at Alexandra's face.

"Was this, in your view, an assassination attempt?" No way to dance around that question. Lana simply hoped the English word meant nothing to the Russian child, who gave no indication that it did.

Galina nodded again. "It failed because Oleg's father gave me a small but powerful gift."

"And you were able to use it?"

"I had no choice. A man was going to—" Galina stopped herself from adding any details, though surely the child had sensed the threat to her own life as well as her mother's when Galina had used the "powerful gift." But the child also looked fragile as an ancient ceramic doll.

"You must see that there is very little time for me. They have reason to arrest me now. They will give reasons for doing more than that." She looked purposely at the back of Alexandra's head, as much as to say, "and to her, too."

"You know the means we've used in the past to communicate?" Lana asked.

"Yes, I do."

"We will return to that now," Lana said. Holmes was nodding. Nobody in the room seemed to need to go longer—and they all knew there was a risk of interception. The signal could even be traced. Better to keep it to minutes.

"I will contact you soon."

"Immediately," Galina said, raw panic in her voice for the first time. "The second missile, us. Everything is on the line."

"We know," Lana said.

The link ended. No one said a word for a full beat. Holmes spoke first: "We must get her out of there. I believe her. What about you?" He looked at the two voice analysts.

"She's either the very best liar we've ever encountered, or she's for real," the senior of the two said. The woman next to him nodded.

So did the psychiatrist. "Very difficult to assess much at this remove and with such brief exposure to the subject."

All the caveats Lana had come to expect from the psych corps, but she still wanted to hear his thoughts, which made his preamble all the more frustrating.

"But I would say she's genuinely frightened. Did you see the way she held her daughter? Both arms around her, like the camera itself were a weapon."

"Which it could be if we fail her trust," Lana said. "There's no telling for sure if she's just been exposed."

"But you have no doubts about Bortnik herself?" Holmes asked her.

"I always have doubts," Lana replied, "but very few about her."

"Find out which coastline she's near," Holmes said. "We may be able to pin it down with the signal, but then again, that's not always bankable. It's going to be difficult to exfiltrate them. We are stretched beyond the limit here."

"But we will, right?" Lana said.

"Yes, we will," Holmes agreed assertively. "Somehow. But a big military operation, like the way we got you out of Saudi Arabia last year, is going to be terribly hard to pull off. We're all dealing with sea-level rise, while Russian security services are on full alert from the New Siberian Islands to Tartus." The latter was on Syria's Mediterranean coast. It contained a small Russian naval base, the country's southernmost, and the only one outside Russia proper.

Before her colleagues even filed out of her office, Lana was back on the IRC: "We're committed to getting you and your daughter. You must tell me where you are."

In seconds, as promised, Galina fired back. "I'm hiding in Sochi. I want to get out of here. I've been seeing water getting higher and boats leaving. Should I find a place to charter one?"

"We'll need to coordinate that. Please don't make any arrangements yet. Just find a safe place for the night, but a place where we can be in touch. Okay?"

"Yes. I'll try."

She sounded nervous, Lana thought. *Who can blame her?*

Lana ran the chartering business by Holmes right away.

"I was thinking of something like that," the deputy director said. "A very low-key effort that would take advantage of the challenges that every seaport is having. Boats are heading out to sea everywhere to try to avoid the destruction that will come with being moored on a coastline. But we'll have one of our people handle the charter. For security reasons, Bortnik can't be risking that kind of move."

"So send in the navy? I could talk to Jensen." Reminding Holmes that her number two at CyberFortress had been a navy cryptographer.

Holmes was shaking his head. "If we send a military unit in there and they get caught taking them out, the Russians might claim it was an invasion. I don't want to even think about what that could mean. And let's not forget, the way this is playing out the Russians are likely to be the world's preeminent power." He looked out his window. "If they aren't already."

"But *I* have to go."

"That's right, and you will go precisely because you're not military. Let's face it, Lana, if you get caught, they'll love you to death just like they loved Snowden, in hope that you'll eventually turn the world over to them. But your expertise is not in exfiltrating operatives and smuggling them into our arms on the high seas. We've got to find a private citizen, preferably a shady character, who knows how to operate below the radar screen, in every sense, in the middle of chaos and vast surveillance."

"A drug smuggler?" *Oh, my God,* she thought. *He's been leading me there all along.* "Donald Fedder?"

"What do you think?" Holmes asked her.

"My ex?" She was so flabbergasted she had to confirm that she and Holmes were talking about the same person.

"Yes, that Donald Fedder."

"He's a flake."

"Not as much as you might think. I'll get to that in a minute. Just tell me what you think of him, other than he's a flake. Then I'll tell you what we think of him."

"Well, he's a great sailor. There's no questioning his seamanship. He could sail without electronics. Hell, he could sail without a rudder. But I think there's plenty to question about his character. He just got out of prison, you know."

"I do, but he spent a great deal less time behind bars than you think."

"What are you talking about?"

"He's been working with the DEA since his arrest. But he had to go through the courts and get sentenced and do *some* time to establish his bona fides. All the time you thought he was incommunicado in prison, though, we had him back down in Colombia moving drugs with FARC. The drugs ended up in the ocean but the intelligence he gave us on FARC was remarkable. It's a key reason some of FARC's top guerilla leaders have died in targeted strikes."

"You are—" Lana almost blurted "shitting me." But what Holmes had just said would explain why Doper Don looked like he'd spent his four years in a country club: he'd been cruising the Caribbean.

She had to sit down. "That guy never breathed a word of this to me."

"There's a reason he was recently paroled, Lana."

"Does he have any training with guns, that sort of thing?"

"Quantico. The full course."

"To be honest, Bob, till this moment I just considered him a ne'er-do-well."

"All the better. Has he said anything notable about what's going on?"

"Yes, at first he told our daughter that it was nothing but a conspiracy theory of the military-industrial complex."

Holmes laughed. "Oh, boy, was he ever jerking your chain. Anything else?"

"Yes, last night he sang a different tune to Emma. He said that if he ever got his hands on the people who did this, he'd break them into pieces."

"He's playing it all to script, except now you need to know."

"So you're planning to have Donald Fedder, with me aboard, smuggle Galina and her kid out of Russia?" It sounded so improbable to Lana that she could hardly form those words into a sentence.

"It's not ideal, but given exigencies here and our resources, we don't have a lot of options. Fedder has been thoroughly tested. He's pulled off tougher coups than this."

"Will there be any backup?"

"Yes, but they can't sail away with Galina and her daughter. You can. So can Doper Don."

"That's *my* nickname for him."

"I know. He told us. Lana, it's everybody's nickname for him now, except we use it ironically. I suspect you will, too. Right now, you two need to talk privately. Your daughter cannot know any of this until you and Don bring the Bortniks back here safely."

"I'll go home and talk to him now."

"No, I'd suggest you go down the hall to the SCIF. That's where he's waiting. We'll leave you two alone to sort things out."

"He's *here*, in a SCIF?"

"Correct."

"Who's in charge?" Lana asked.

"You're in charge of the operation," Holmes said. "But he'll be the captain of the ship."

"That leaves room for conflict."

Holmes shook his head. "There's no room for conflict, only success. You know the stakes."

"Does *he*?"

"Yes. He's not the man who left you, Lana. He's the man who wants, more than anything, to come back."

"To me?" That was news to her.

"To you, his daughter, and his country."

Lana stood, feeling numbed by the news, and started down the hall. Each step made her feel like she was boarding a pirate clipper, about to ship out with Blackbeard himself.

She went through security and found Don sitting alone at an empty conference table in the windowless room. Despite her every instinct, she smiled when he looked up.

CHAPTER 20

FROM THE REST AREA in Sochi, Galina found an apartment building's satellite dish and intercepted its signals, which had made it possible to comply with Lana Elkins's request for a video link. But it was dangerous to spend so much time in one place and she desperately needed to head north to get out of the city.

Before leaving the rest area, though, she dug through an overnight bag, searching for Tylenol. Poor Alexandra's joints and bones were hurting so bad. Six tablets so far today, and it was still only late afternoon. Galina shook her head because what Alexandra really needed was a doctor who could prescribe serious painkillers for her leukemia.

She found the Tylenol and a bottle of pineapple juice. Alexandra took two more tablets.

Galina hoped her daughter could hold them down. Her stomach was souring on acetaminophen; she'd vomited within minutes of her last dose two hours ago.

Looking left and right, Galina pulled onto a highway, feeling as obvious in the Macan as a goldfish in a bowl. She hoped to find a fishing village where boats were coming and going and chaos reigned because of sea-level rise, a crowded frenetic place where she and Alexandra could get lost among the panicky faces. That way if Lana Elkins failed her—and Galina would give her twenty-four hours, period, to exfiltrate them—she could use PP's money to charter a boat and get Alexandra help in a country where the child was not the subject of a police search.

That was what outraged Galina the most: the authorities had announced—on television, radio, and the Internet, including social media—that both mother *and* daughter were wanted for the "brutal murder of Police Sergeant Sergey Volkov," who was described as a "decorated war hero."

Hero? Not how Galina thought of him. Beast was more like it. Probably had been a beast in Chechnya, too. So many were.

But it wasn't about Sergey the Beast, anyway. It was about Oleg and his operation.

The late-model cars breezing by—cabriolets and six-figure coupes—worried Galina. She needed peasants, poor people who were not wired into the news of the day. She wondered if even among the impoverished there were people who fit that description anymore. And what did she know of the peasantry? She knew plenty about the sophisticated airs of Moscow's *nouveau riche* who patronized the city's finest restaurants and clubs—and also gobbled up whatever absurdities the Kremlin dished out. But she'd sooner trust her fate to a man riding a donkey than a celebrant of the capital's splashy soirees.

She whizzed past Dendrariy, a picturesque part of greater Sochi, which stretched up and down the coast. The region's renowned funicular caught Alexandra's attention, as it undoubtedly had captured the eyes of millions of children before her.

"What is that, Mama?"

She told her, explaining, "It's like a car on a cable. It goes all the way up the mountain. There's a beautiful arboretum up there."

"What's that?"

Galina was encouraged that her daughter was energetic enough to ask questions. "It's a pretty yellow-and-white building surrounded by the most colorful flowers and plants."

"Can we go on the funicular and see the flowers . . . someday?"

Galina could have cried when Alexandra added "someday" so tentatively, as though she already knew how hopeless it would be to ask to stop now for anything resembling fun or beauty. They were on the run, that was clear even to a leukemia-stricken six-year-old.

Still, Galina said, "Yes, someday we'll go. I promise," knowing full well that if they ever escaped Russia, they would *never* come back.

But America had funiculars, too. She thought they called them trams, and America would welcome them and give them a home if Lana Elkins, to whom Galina had entrusted their lives, could actually find them safe passage out of the country.

In searching for a rural seaport, Galina was forging a backup plan, a redundancy, like you'd find in any sound computer software. Nobody with a conscience would bet the life of their child entirely on a stranger.

She soon spotted moorages, but they catered to cabin cruisers and large sailboats, whose hulls had risen with the sea and now shadowed the docks from heights she'd never seen before. Despite that, most of the slips were still occupied; the affluent boat owners were less concerned, perhaps, about their weekend pleasures than a fisherman who depended on his vessel for his livelihood.

She was surprised to see bearded men—Muslims, if she were not mistaken—walking alongside the road. More of them as she drove farther north, one with prayer beads in his hand. Headscarves on some women, too.

Galina checked her odometer—about fifty kilometers away from the heart of Sochi. She felt like a rube. How could she not know that Muslims lived in this region? She would have checked online right then but she planned to keep her phone power off unless she absolutely needed it.

Dimly, from a source she could not readily place, she recalled that there was, indeed, a sizable Muslim population up there.

Yes, that's right, she thought. During the Olympics it was a reason given—not in the most overt terms—for heightened security.

That could be good, she realized. There might be people among them who despaired of the official Russian propaganda line, who might not even avail themselves of it. People who could sympathize with a woman who had killed a "hero" of the Chechnya war in which so many Muslims were ruthlessly tortured and murdered, including scores of children.

Galina took stock of her other resources. She had a bundle of cash and a gun. No bullets, but a gun. As a last resort, brandishing an unloaded derringer might be better than having no weapon at all, especially in the hands of such a notorious hero-slayer. Her reputation might not only precede her, but clear a path for them as well.

She glanced in the rearview mirror to see what such a murderer looked like.

Tired, she decided at once. *Very tired.*

The sun was going down across the sea. She didn't dare look for an established hotel or inn. She passed billboards for a number of them with their locations and distances noted, but ignored them.

She had not seen the frantic small seaport she'd been hoping for, but the more Muslims she spotted, the more she considered a much different plan.

Farther north of Sochi she spotted a village from the road. She had to make a decision soon or she might find herself driving aimlessly through the night, when she would be able to see little.

Galina exited onto a freshly paved but extremely narrow road. Not hard to imagine that it had been resurfaced with macadam to

accommodate vehicles other than carts pulled by beasts of burden—
not all of them animals in the annals of Russia's often brutal past.

When she found herself driving too directly toward the town,
she turned onto a winding forest two-track through lush decidu-
ous trees, still leafy in the subtropical climes of the coast.

She came to a place where the trees to her left thinned enough
to provide a vantage point for the village. Alexandra, after her
brief burst of energy, had slumped in her seat and gone to sleep.

Easing her door open and closed, Galina walked past the
branches until she could see the small harbor in all its simple
splendor. She counted twelve fishing trawlers, their nets off-
loaded, apparently replaced by boxes and bikes and suitcases
glowing golden in the day's dying light.

Three sailboats sat moored a few hundred feet away in what
appeared to be a protected inlet. Beautiful vessels. The two sloops
and ketch ranged in size from about ten to twenty meters. Peering closely, she saw a small gathering on the ketch, the largest
of the three. She thought fishermen, desperate to flee with their
families, might be more likely to help her than yacht owners who
appeared to be riding out the crisis in party mode.

The water here also had risen almost to the docks, making
them look unusually low next to the boats.

As she looked at the sun setting across the dark waters of the
Black Sea, she realized that not too many years ago she could have
sailed straight out from the Russian coastline to escape the country's territorial waters. Not now, not since Russia had annexed
Crimea, laying even greater claim to the Sevastopol naval base.
Now Russian territorial waters had many zigs and zags, which
complicated navigation to international waters.

After checking on Alexandra, she hurried back to surveil the
town and port, pleased with her viewpoint. Ten minutes passed
before there was any sign of life below. Then four men walked out

of a small building, not much bigger than a shed. She caught only a glimpse of small rugs inside, but enough to realize they'd been offering their sunset prayer. The sight elated her and gave her hope.

She watched them keenly as they checked their boats, each studying the height of their hulls. A man raised two fingers. She thought he was flashing the peace sign until he called to the others: "Two days. And then we have to leave." He shrugged and shook his head.

Two days, that's a long time to sit and wait with a sick girl. Too long, Galina decided at once. But she might persuade one of them to leave sooner. In the morning, when the men had their morning coffee and rolls in their bellies, she would find out just what PP's money could buy. She would don her big dark glasses and a headscarf, but if she were recognized, she might also find out if it were true that the enemy of your enemy could be your friend.

• • •

Oleg had enjoyed his respite in Voronezh. Once he closed and locked the door to the room in the monastery and pushed the young woman onto the bed, the women's tongues started wagging, if not the way he would have preferred with the novitiate, certainly in a manner that made him comfortable with the progress of their tête-à-tête.

He determined very quickly, for instance, that Galina and cancer kid had stayed at the monastery, now occupied by nuns. He thought the monks of old would turn over in their dusty graves if they knew all those menstrual cycles were churning within their once-sacred stone walls. Who could blame them? It made Oleg shudder, and he knew he was a man of the world, not of cloistered celibate living.

But he hadn't been able to confirm the car Galina had been

driving until he'd taken special measures. They'd balked, naturally, when he asked, even when he cupped his hand around the novitiate's soft neck and shook her like the proverbial rag doll. And when she still wouldn't say, he'd squeezed harder and lifted her hem to the horror of that dried-up old nun, who started saying, "Peugeot, Mercedes, Toyota" in such a frightened voice that he knew she would have said anything that might have stopped him from throttling the young woman. But why would he want to stop? How silly. Her flesh was so soft, so yielding, and he could feel her neck cords tightening—just like his pants.

"You really don't know, do you?" he asked the nun.

"No, no. I'm so sorry."

"So you lied to me. '*Peugeot, Mercedes, Toyota.*'" He pushed the novitiate's face into a pillow, as though to smother her, but then released her, saying, "Don't move or I'll kill you."

"You," he turned to the nun, "I have a special treat for."

He pulled out his knife and used it like an index finger across his own lips to indicate his sincere desire for silence. He even said "please" without making a sound, mouthing the request, modeling the behavior he was demanding of them in his most persuasive manner.

Then he pressed the blade against the nun's lips, surprisingly succulent up close, puffy enough to part deliciously with just a tiny bit of pressure. The thinnest line of blood swelled appreciatively, exciting him immensely. The line became drips and dribbles that spilled down her chin, leaving a nice fat track.

He spoke, keeping the blade in place. But he wasn't a cruel man; he refrained from slicing through to her gum. Instead, he just wiggled it slightly when she tried to back away. But there's always a wall. "Don't you know that?" he said to her. Of course, she had no idea what he was thinking. She just shook her head. But that stopped very quickly with the red blade back in place.

"Are you absolutely sure you could not see her car, even though you still have *eyes?*"

He knew she'd seen it, felt it in his very fiber. She might not know the make of the car but she'd seen it. He saw the truth in her eyes. He'd cut them out if he had to.

"Silver," she gulped. "Like those cars for camping."

Remembering all that fear now as he drove to Sochi made him laugh because only a nun wouldn't have known enough to call it an SUV.

But that still made no sense. What would Galina be doing with—

Oleg shook his head in wonder. What was it, a month or two ago when he'd heard PP talking to Dmitri as if moron boy were actually intelligent enough to make sense of anything more complicated than his shoelaces? PP had been telling Oleg's hulking younger brother about a new car Porsche was making.

As Oleg drove swiftly away from the monastery, he called a Moscow-area Porsche dealership. Yes, the Macan was available in silver.

He speed-dialed PP, who did not deign to pick up, so Oleg spoke slowly into the answering machine: "You bought that Porsche SUV, didn't you, PP? And then you loaned it to Galina, didn't you, PP? *Silver.* Isn't it, PP? And that means you are aiding and abetting a known terrorist, aren't you—"

PP picked up as Oleg presumed he would.

"What are you talking about?" PP demanded.

"You know exactly what I'm talking about. You loaned Galina a new car and told no one, even though you knew she and her kid are wanted for murder. You didn't even tell *me*, and I was there."

"You would have found nothing here."

"I would not have found your new Porsche, that's for sure. I *will* turn you in, PP. I'm much more important now. I have influence. You don't." It felt immensely satisfying to state the obvious, force it right into the old bastard's face.

PP didn't respond. Oleg relished the silence, the *power* of a father cowed by the strength of his son.

"Tongue-tied, PP?"

"I know nothing of what you think she's done. Nothing. I doubt she's even done it, whatever you think it is."

"She murdered a war hero and police sergeant. It's on the news. You know what she did. The medical examiner says he was murdered. The police say by her. Don't try to pretend that you don't know what she did. And do not try to protect her. You have many enemies, PP, none so powerful or important as I. So simply tell me yes or no about the car and give me the plate number."

Another long pause followed, but this time PP spoke up: "Yes." Then he hung up.

Oleg figured PP was trying to preserve his dignity by not providing the number. Old men don't have dignity; he also knew that to be true. They have only memory, and memory is a slippery whore like Galina. He had ample proof of that. He drove into Sochi at sunset, the town that had been cursed by the Olympics. It used to be packed with tourists enjoying the sunshine in a country mostly cloaked by clouds. But since the Olympics, even the Russians had stopped coming. Right now, that was good, though: so few people would make it easier for him to flush Galina and cancer kid from whatever hive they'd found.

He drove to the local police headquarters and met with the superintendent. Oleg dropped names and made promises of promotion. Then he provided photographs of Galina, *all* of them taken secretly as she enjoyed the pleasures of his body.

"You can see she's not just a killer, she's a dangerous whore," he said.

"The most devious traitors are like that. Killers, too," the superintendent said.

After raising a smile on the man's face—and likely another part of his anatomy as well—Oleg knew he had the complete cooperation of the department.

"I should also tell you that she is not above trying to trade her body for freedom when she's caught. You might want to know that. She's very, very good."

The superintendent assured him the search for Galina Bortnik would be thorough, indeed.

In less than a half hour, a motorcycle officer learned that a woman in a fancy silver SUV had bought takeout latkes.

"But she is not staying in Sochi," the superintendent told him twenty minutes later. "Every hotel and inn has been checked. I took the liberty of providing the most identifying photos—of *her*, of course."

He and Oleg shared a smile.

"Where would you go, if you were her?" Oleg asked.

"To bed," the superintendent said, "with me."

They laughed. Oleg considered him a fool, but listened closely when the man turned serious and said, "Not south. She'd run right into passport control in Abkhazia."

Both men shook their heads at the brutal prospect of spending any time in a country so ruined by strife.

"But up north, you know what the criminals say?" the superintendent asked him.

"No, what do they say?" Oleg dutifully played the straight man.

"That both the trees and boats are thick but only the boats can save you. And I can see," the superintendent stared at a particularly graphic photo of Galina, "that losing her would be a crime."

"Thank you. You are a smart man. I will commend you to the Minister for Internal Affairs."

Oleg left him smiling. But the hours of the day were not so kind to him: he would accomplish very little at night in the municipalities that lay before him. So he took a room in Sochi and checked the financial news online.

The ruble was reigning supreme among the world's currencies. He had bought many millions of them weeks ago. In the United States they would have called that insider trading, and they *might* have prosecuted you for it—depending on your station in life. In Russia they would have called it the same thing, but if you were Oleg or others like him, they would only congratulate you for your sharp business acumen.

With that profitable business aside, he contacted *Numero Uno,* who started whining again.

"Just tell me," Oleg interrupted, "how is Grisha Lisko?"

"Grisha is very good. Grisha is busy. Grisha is *ready.* The question is, are you?"

"Not yet, but you must be ready at any moment."

To die, Oleg thought, for having the audacity to question him.

• • •

Under the cover of darkest night, Galina received an urgent message from Lana Elkins. They met on the IRC in seconds.

"I've been tracking Dernov's data. He's in Sochi. Is that close to you?"

Galina's groin tightened. "You tell me," she replied, wanting to shut off all her electronic devices immediately. Though surrounded by trees, she'd found another satellite dish in the small fishing village. But if she could do that, Oleg might be able to track her.

"I will tell you that we're coming to get you," Lana said.

"I think," Galina typed slowly, feeling the night air close in around her, "that you are not the only one."

CHAPTER 21

LANA HAD BARELY GOTTEN over the shock of see-
ing Don's persuasive smile—and settling across from him knowing they'd been impressed into service together on the high seas
under high stress—when she'd been yanked from the secure conference room by an urgent message from Jeff Jensen.

In the seclusion of her office, he'd shown her Dernov's metadata stream, which placed him in Sochi. She'd contacted Galina
in the next few seconds. The woman's reaction had left little
doubt that she was not far from the Olympic city, either—and
the monster who stalked her.

Lana now rushed back to the SCIF, knowing it was time to
compartmentalize—and quickly—by putting Oleg aside to deal
with Doper Don.

On her second go-round with Doper Don she refused to be
taken in by his grin. Instead, she bored right into his recent past:
"You worked for the DEA?"

"Do we have time for this?" he replied.

"Yes, you do," Holmes asserted as he entered the conference room on Lana's heels. "I want you two sorting out whatever

needs sorting out right here, right now. If you need a couples counselor—"

"We're not a couple," they both exclaimed in unison, Lana furious at what Holmes—or Don, for that matter—might perceive as the cute synchrony of their response.

"Be that as it may," Holmes went on, "we have a mediator on hand to make sure whatever issues plague you two get put aside."

"I don't think we'll need anyone," Lana said.

"As long as you *both* leave here knowing there's no room for personal animosity. And you'll do it in the next fifteen minutes because there's a flight waiting for you. Have I made myself clear?" Holmes stared at Don, which Lana took as a pledge of good faith in her own professionalism.

"What else is up?" she asked Holmes. She didn't believe for a moment he'd come into a highly secure room to urge them to get along. She was right:

"We're having difficulty communicating with our contact on the Black Sea coast." His gaze was back on Don. "Do you have a charter you could pull out of a hat there?"

"Maybe," Don replied.

"Come with me," Holmes said.

When Don returned ten minutes later with Holmes, the deputy director said their flight could be delayed "a bit." Then with a smile, he added, "Go to it."

As he left the SCIF, Lana had only to raise her eyebrows to finally get Don's answer about the DEA.

"Yes, I worked for them. I didn't have much choice. Do you know how much they caught me with?"

She did, but wasn't about to let on to him that she'd been interested enough in his criminal proceedings to read the court record, so she gave him her most censorious look and asked, "Are you going to brag?"

"No, of course not. But it *was* more than four thousand pounds. A lot of bud. I had to make a deal."

"Four thousand pounds? Wasn't that a bit much for a forty-two-foot sloop?" recognizing, as she referred to the *B. Marley*, that she might just have given away her close examination of his case.

"A little," he admitted, "but my plan was never to try to outrun anyone in a freaking sailboat. I was trying to blend in. Look, Lana, when they offered me a deal, I had to take it. And now they're offering to expunge my record if I get that woman and her kid out of Russia. They need people like me, obviously."

"Drug smugglers?"

"No! People who know high-end sailing and navigation. I'm talking about when all your electronics go down and all you have left are the stars, and you have to sail in the black of night through hostile territorial waters with channel markers and buoys disappearing, and crowded with all kinds of boats trying to stay clear of land with the oceans rising. Not to mention the Russian Navy."

She could buy the need for criminals like him, but not the more startling Doper Don news of late: "Did you actually tell the deputy director of the National Security Agency that you're looking to get back together with Emma and me? I can accept that they gave you a great deal. I can even accept that there's an ounce of patriotism in you that might just possibly outweigh the tons of drugs that have passed through your greedy hands, but I can't accept that a man who abandoned his two-year-old daughter and wife to play a stoned version of *Pirates of the Caribbean* really gives a damn about his family."

"Quite a speech." He stared at her. "Do I get to respond?"

"Sure. Be my guest."

"I made a huge mistake. I'm looking to make amends. I've risked my life to take down some real savages in Colombia who would have delighted in torturing me slowly to death. I was a shitty husband and father. I was irresponsible. I'm the opposite of all that now. And, believe it or not, I'm the right person for the job."

"Give me a break, Don. It's a big country. There are thousands of qualified sailors. Not all of them with a nickname that pays homage to illicit drugs."

"By the way, I would appreciate it if you'd stop referring to me that way in front of my daughter."

"I've *never* called you that in front of her."

He seemed delighted. "Well, thank you."

"I fight fair."

"As for those thousands of sailors you just mentioned, they're really busy right now. I could clear a couple grand a day, if I were a free man."'

Undeniably true. In the past few days, the nautical world had been turned upside down. Yacht owners were desperate for their captains—any captains—to save their floating palaces, but the captains generally worked for several boat owners at once; few ocean gentry had them on the clock twenty-four seven. Plus, the feds, under emergency provisions, had forced the recruitment of thousands of seamen who had served in various government capacities—merchant marine, Coast Guard, and so forth—just as they had impressed them in past centuries. They needed them to keep harbors from getting obstructed by boats breaking loose from their moorings—or by their wealthy owners scuttling them to make a quick insurance claim in a time of crisis, which had happened with such abandon after the 2008 financial collapse.

In short, skilled sailors were in unprecedented demand by the public and private sector—and making more money than ever. Except for Don:

"Instead," he went on, "I'm still earning twenty-three cents an hour. That's my prison wage and will be for the foreseeable future."

"You're saying you're a bargain?"

"A great one."

"Just answer one question for me. Answer it honestly, and we can tell Holmes we're good to go and get moving: Why are you doing this? For real now, Don."

"Because somebody set off a nuclear missile. Because in addition to the flooding, radiation is sweeping all over the earth. Because I have a daughter I *love*. And, goddamn it, I have an ex-wife who does incredibly important work for a country I want to serve. And nobody will take better care of you, Lana, than I will. I will get you in there, and I will get you out."

He was so fierce, so impassioned, he almost convinced her. She suspected a residue of doubt would always remain.

"You realize, Don, that if we get caught, we'll be leaving Emma an orphan."

"You're that sure they'll kill us?"

"I'm that sure they'll kill you and never let me go."

He nodded somberly.

"So did you really find a charter over there for us?" she asked.

"Better than the Passport 44 the DEA was talking about," he said with dedicated disregard. "Too beamy," he explained, or thought he had: now Lana looked puzzled. "Too wide," he explained. "Great for cargo—"

"You would certainly know about that."

"But *slow*. I contacted an old boat broker of mine with, let's say, a demanding clientele. He's got a Dehler 38 waiting for us."

"Tell me we're picking it up somewhere close to the subject."

"We are, in Pitsunda, Abkhazia."

"What? We might as well be going to Moscow." Abkhazia had broken away from Georgia, with Moscow's wholehearted approval. Predictably, Russia was among the few countries that did recognize the teensy country, which was sandwiched between the two antagonists.

"Not really. Pitsunda's a little bit beaten and a little bit lawless. But from what I've been told it's really close to where we're supposed to get that woman and her kid."

"The Russian shadow falls all over Abkhazia."

"It wasn't my call. I just got the boat."

"Tell me about it."

"It's not a race boat but it's very quick and nimble. *Cruising World's* best cruiser in its class. It'll also have the right look for us. Affluent, but not so pricey that it would be out of line for a sport sailor trying to save his prize from the clutter of rising harbors. It won't attract too much attention."

One of Holmes's runners rushed in: "The deputy director says it's time to move. He wants you both in his office."

Holmes stood as they entered. "We double-checked your boat broker," he said to Don. "He's solid."

"I know."

"We didn't," Holmes retorted. "You better be solid, too. I know you've done some fine work for the DEA but what you're getting into now is more important than all the dope deals and FARC intelligence put together. Do not lose Lana, and get that woman and her child out of Russia. Then point that boat west and move out as fast as you can. We can't help you for the first two hundred miles, and those territorial waters are a bit of a maze. You wouldn't be the first captain to find himself towed into Russian territory because they found it convenient to do so."

"Pitsunda, right?" Lana asked. "*That's* where we're getting the boat?"

Holmes nodded, as though he could appreciate her skeptical tone. "I know, it's dicey, but the Abkhazians are intent on keeping up the façade of being independent of Moscow. It's a little scary there, but let's face it, so are some of the people we'll have in place to keep an eye on you two. They can't do anything for you once you enter Russian waters, but in Pitsunda and its surrounds, it shouldn't be too bad."

Famous last words, Lana couldn't help but think.

"We've got a Sikorsky to fly you out to Andrews. You'll board a Gulfstream 650. That's for the first leg. The second will get more interesting. Get some sleep while you can. Once you're on that boat, you'll be all eyes all the time."

"What do you mean, about the second leg getting 'more interesting?'" she asked.

"It's all 'know as you go.' Sorry," Holmes said.

• • •

Packs of sailing clothing and supplies were waiting onboard the bird. They lifted up over Fort Meade, air space reserved for very few. It was all clear for the two of them and their young pilot.

Don looked green. Only then did Lana remember his uneasiness in the air.

"You going to lose it?" He had on American Airlines on their honeymoon flight to Saint Martin. Repeatedly. Ah, romance.

He shook his head. "I'm okay."

She handed him an airsickness bag—just in case.

He buried his head in it—then most of his stomach—seconds later.

Lana turned from the revolting display, remembering—with a wrenching roll of her own stomach—how contagious regurgitation could get.

The flight to Andrews at dusk took them over the flooding Potomac. Water had reached the National Mall, and the reflecting pool at the Washington Memorial had disappeared into the larger vat of the rising ocean. Anacostia looked particularly hard-hit. She was glad Tanesa's family had found refuge with them—for so many reasons.

Andrews, thankfully, was dry. They boarded the Gulfstream, an especially swift jet that should deliver them to their destination in less than eight hours. The pilot and his second would not tell them where they were going, though.

"More 'know as you go'?" she asked the woman.

A quick nod and the pair disappeared into the cockpit.

Two hours later, unable to sleep, Lana peered into the darkest night knowing the sea was shifting radically thousands of feet below. In the complete blackness that now enveloped them, the watery world could have been reaching to swallow them and the stars.

They landed at a remote airstrip, but not in Abkhazia, or anywhere near Pitsunda. In Turkey, the pilot informed them, saying no more.

She and Don were taken to a hangar where a pair of F-15 fighter jets were waiting: his and hers, as it turned out.

"Why?" Don asked uneasily.

"We're taking you to the U.S.S. *William Jefferson Clinton.*"

"An aircraft carrier? We're landing on an aircraft carrier at night in rising seas?"

"That about nails it," the new flight commander said.

Don hurled again, sans sickness bag. But at least he wasn't in the fighter jet . . . yet.

Now he was. Lana waved good-bye. He was off. She was belted in by experienced hands.

At least Emma won't be orphaned on this leg of the journey, she thought, because what were the odds of both pilots missing the heaving deck of an aircraft carrier and crashing?

Actually, higher than she realized, given the wildly unsettled sea.

The lights on the carrier appeared in the distance as a pinprick on a vast black screen.

That's it? Lana thought. *That's all?*

As they raced nearer, she saw raging whitecaps smashing into the side of the *Clinton*, sending spray across the deck, storm conditions that had to be on the very margin of safety. *Or death,* she thought at once.

She squeezed her hands into fists, sweating heavily.

Lana wondered if Don had made it safely aboard. Right then she saw his fighter jet approaching the carrier for a landing.

The wings of the F-15 tilted back and forth, as though the pilot were trying to mirror the wobble of the landing platform itself. Then, at the last moment, the jet's engines flared brightly and the F-15 aborted the landing, blasting back up to the black sky, presumably for a second chance.

Her pilot said nothing. She imagined his eyes glued to the deck. She squeezed hers shut. The seconds hung with the weight of eternity.

Think about them, she told herself sternly: Galina and Alexandra Bortnik. *They're the ones in real danger.*

But she had a hard time believing that because when she peeked out of the cockpit, all she saw was the carrier rolling like a barroom brawler on the waves below.

CHAPTER 22

LANA KNEW VERY LITTLE about landing an F-15 on an aircraft carrier, but she was certain each fighter jet had a hook on its tail that needed to catch on a steel wire stretched across the deck. More than one wire, if she recalled correctly.

She had no time left to worry: the F-15 hit the heaving platform, nose slightly elevated—*That's good, right? So it can catch?*—and raced like a dragster down the tilting surface.

Catch, damn it.

The pilot gave his engines full throttle.

She swore, thinking they'd also missed the wires and needed to blast off to avoid ending up in the sea.

But no: turned out it was standard operating procedure *in case* the pilot missed one of the steel wires. He caught the hook and they came to a stop—incredibly—in less than two seconds.

If Don doesn't lose the rest of his lunch, I'll be amazed.

In what seemed like a blink, she was helped out of the cockpit and rushed off the deck.

She heard the jet with Don approaching, and realized how

terribly torn she was between watching his landing and contacting Galina ASAP.

Then she saw seamen unfurling a huge net barricade across the deck.

"What's that for?" she asked the taciturn pilot who had flown her to the carrier, which was pitching noticeably beneath her feet.

"He lost the nose wheel on his first attempt so he's got to crash-land it."

Crash-land it? With Don?

She swore again, but softly this time. Not enough, however, to escape the captain's attention: "You can say that again," he muttered.

Lana looked at the netting. She looked at the jets parked, wings up, along the side of the carrier. Tough to imagine the netting stopping a sailboat, much less a fighter jet traveling in excess of two hundred miles per hour.

Before she realized it, she was whisked off the deck to an observation window safely removed from the looming accident, because any way she looked at it, an accident was about to take place.

When Don's jet hit the deck seconds later, the nose cone scraped across the surface, as if to plow it up. Then it hit the net and stopped almost as quickly as hers had.

A team of sailors carrying ladders and fire-suppression gear descended on the F-15, pulling Don and the pilot out of the cockpit.

"Always a chance of a fuel fire or explosion," an officer who had just appeared by her side explained nonchalantly.

Don was stumbling, helped by two sailors, one on each arm. *He made it. We're okay.*

"I need the communications room," she said to the officer.

"We can give you that for ten minutes," he said, leading her through a doorway to a room filled with communication cubicles.

She realized at once that it was no accident that he was standing next to her. "But you'll be getting onto a boat a lot smaller and faster to get you to your destination."

"In these seas?" she asked. He nodded. "How far?"

"A little more than fifty nautical miles."

Nautical miles? It took her a second to remember that they were almost a thousand feet longer than a regular mile. And they had "a little more than fifty" of them to cross? *In these seas?* she repeated to herself.

"You've got to go under the radar," the officer went on. "There's no guarantee that will happen, but there's less of a chance you'll be noticed in a much smaller boat, especially with all the traffic on coastal waters these days."

"What about this thing?" She looked about the *Clinton.*

"We're in a narrow sliver of international waters to get you this close. Plus, the Abkhazians don't exactly have much of a navy."

Lana rushed a message to Galina: "Where are you?" Cutting to the chase.

Galina must have been on edge waiting to hear from her because she fired right back: "I need to get out of here before daybreak."

"Stay put. We're coming to get you."

"How soon? Oleg is very close."

"Do you think he's close or know that he is?" Lana asked, worried that he would get his hands on her. Just hours ago, Jensen had tracked Dernov's data to Sochi, where he presumably had spent the night.

"You and I both know he's close," Galina replied. "I need to leave before daylight. Where are you?"

"I can't say." She looked at the officer. "How long till daylight?"

He checked his watch. "An hour fifty."

"We won't be there by daylight," she texted Galina, seeing no point in mincing words.

"How long?" Galina asked. Lana could almost hear her impatience. "You must have an idea of how far away I am."

She pulled up Jensen, who had been the second person she'd planned to contact once aboard the *Clinton*, and asked him if he had any notion of where Galina was.

"She's been very quiet," he reported. "No data streams, but if I had to guess, I'd say she's north of Sochi, but not too far."

I could have guessed that.

"What's the problem?" the officer asked.

She told him.

A young woman's head popped up from behind a partition. "Whoever you're communicating with is 110 kilometers north of Sochi in what appears to be a small seaport town. I can't get a name for it. It might not have one, at least on any map we have."

"Thank you." Though it concerned Lana that Galina's position had been sniffed out so quickly; at least it was by friendly forces.

She turned to Don: "From Pitsunda, how long will it take us to get up there?"

"We'll be moving fast in these conditions. A half-day's sail at worst. What's the latest weather?" he asked the room at large, perhaps hoping for another head to pop up. One did:

"Strong winds, near gale force, till tonight," a male sailor said, looking up from his computer.

"She won't wait a half day," Lana told Don. "She sounds like she expects us to be there in the next ninety minutes."

"What choice does she have?" he asked.

Lana, more diplomatically, asked Galina that question.

"Can't say, but I can't wait," she replied.

Lana relayed that reply to Don.

"It seems to me she's got one good option, and that's to go to sea and head south. She's already said something about chartering, right?"

Lana nodded.

"I can give her captain coordinates for a rendezvous at sea," said Don.

"That could look very suspicious," said the officer who'd been by Lana's side. "A busy Russian navy might miss that, but satellites are hardly going to."

"I don't see any option but to take the risk," Lana replied. "You said yourself there are lots of boats out there." She messaged Galina with Don's suggestion of a rendezvous.

No response came from her.

"Galina? Did you get that message?"

Still nothing.

"Galina? I need to know if you're okay."

• • •

Good question, Galina thought, shutting down her connection with Lana Elkins. She was worried sick that Oleg might have located her, though the only activity she spied from her perch above the village was the house lights flicking on.

She considered rushing down to the dock just long enough to make contact with a boat captain, but could not bring herself to leave her daughter alone. Neither could she bear waking the sleeping child to another day of leukemia and pain.

Instead, she drove the expensive Porsche SUV into the village of perhaps a dozen run-down homes and a handful of cars and pickups older than she herself was.

Galina parked near the dock and stuffed PP's cash into her shoulder bag, then shoved the derringer into her pocket so she could grab the gun easily if she had to.

Donning a headscarf out of respect—and dark glasses out of fear—she stepped from the car as a man jumped to the dock off a trawler. She wondered if he'd slept on it. But when she approached him in the dim light, his eyes looked bright, as if they were reflecting the last of the night's starlight.

He didn't appear at all surprised by her appearance, asking gruffly who she was, as he might have demanded of anyone else at any other time of day. He sounded like a man who did not suffer distractions easily.

"I need to charter a boat."

"A fishing boat?" He shook his head, maybe in disbelief, then peered closely at her. "Take off your glasses." When she hesitated, he removed them so swiftly she had no time to react. "I know you," he said. "You are the 'Porn Star Spy.' I've seen naked pictures of you on TV." He shook his head again, this time in obvious disapproval.

Porn Star Spy. That's what they're calling me? Oleg, that son of a bitch. He'd made a mockery of her. She knew it was easy to do: Russians loved their "news" tawdry and tabloid, just like the Brits and Americans.

"Please, listen to me," she begged. "He was someone I loved. I didn't know he took those pictures. I never would have done that. He's horrible."

She sounded desperate. She was. But even then she knew she'd rather deal with a Muslim man's indignation—and from what she'd observed yesterday afternoon, this was a Muslim village—than Oleg's murderous revenge. That the captain had taken offense only over the sex photos, not the spy allegations, had not escaped her notice, so she went on: "But it's true, I'm a spy trying to stop this Russian criminal from bombing Antarctica. That's what's making the oceans rise."

She glanced at the hull of his trawler; the bottom was now pressed against the top of the dock. The water had risen at least half a foot since last night. Soon there would be no dock.

"Who do you say is doing this to you?" he asked. His gruffness had not eased.

Now she saw that she would have to take the biggest risk of all: "A very rich Russian man. He's bought influence with the Russian police. He's doing this to me. He's afraid of what I can do to him."

The captain stared at her. He said nothing.

She played her last card—cash—pulling out a fistful of rubles. "If I don't get out of here, they will kill me and my little girl. She's in the car. You are a man of faith. I saw you coming from your prayer yesterday. You know what the Russians did to your brothers and sisters in Chechnya. They will do that to me, too. And *then* they will kill me. Help me, please."

He eyed the money. "How far?" he asked.

"Out of Russian waters. A rendezvous at sea south of here. I can get the coordinates."

"Your daughter, they say she's sick. They say she needs help. That you're a bad mother."

"She is sick. She does need help. But not their help." Galina stared into his eyes. "She needs yours."

• • •

Oleg woke early in his luxurious suite in Sochi. He splashed water on his face and headed down to the kitchen, finding the lazy cooks sitting around a television and smoking.

"Not open till seven," a swarthy man in chef's whites said. He sounded surly as a hangover.

Oleg flashed his FSB identification, conveniently provided for this foray to the coast. "You're open now. Eggs, potatoes, bread. Coffee. Spit in it and I'll have you arrested and beaten senseless."

He took no chances. Often threats weren't enough. They could, in fact, instigate recklessness, so he watched them prepare his food to ensure they didn't do to him what he would have done to them, if the circumstances had been reversed.

He glanced at the small screen and saw a magnificent video of water. "Water everywhere, and not a drop to drink . . ." A westerner's words, but who cares. It was he, a Russian, who had made those words blaze with truth: Water flooding the capitals of the United States, Britain, the major ports of Europe and Asia. And all of it saltwater from the rising seas. Nothing good for drinking, but plenty good for drowning.

And, yes, some small problems in his homeland. But the Russian President was on TV right now, looking supremely confident. And who had made that possible? The right people knew the answer.

He ate quickly. In thirty minutes he was driving up the coast. He wished he could have called in a helicopter or two, but there were limits, given the small-scale crises facing the defenders of the Russian shoreline. But he had placed calls to every rural police agency up to Tuapse in the north, telling them he was tracking down the Porn Star Spy in their jurisdictions, news that had excited every one of them—until he informed them in his gravest voice that if she escaped from any of their areas of responsibility, they would answer to Russia's top cop, the minister of Internal Affairs. Those interrogations were not known for their concessions to sentiment.

The officers were already calling him from hamlets all along the Russian Riviera, and from seaports used by the owners of magnificent pleasure craft, men mostly long accustomed to soaking up the sun in the company of whores and paramours.

Nobody had seen PP's Macan. All had seen boats heading out to sea. Of course they were: rivers were reversing their flow, flooding and breaking up homes that had withstood hundred-year floods. But with docks disappearing and homes ripping apart and floating away, this was a force much greater. This was a once-in-a-millennium flood caused by a millennial man. No human in the annals of recorded history had ever accomplished what he had done. Jesus might have turned water into wine, but only Oleg Dernov had turned water into the world's most powerful weapon.

Thanks to him, Russia had flipped the hegemony of the west on its head in a matter of days. So drown the river rats down there. Sink their shitty little homes. He imagined he could even hear them cracking apart from up on the highway. These people should be grateful to him. Most would live, unlike so many others. The great nation would have the resources to let them adapt to the new world forming all around them.

Would the Dutch be able to do that for their citizens? The Americans? The British? The French? The Chinese? He smiled at the very thought of those Asian pretenders. The "Beijing Miracle"? The great growth monster was turning into a joke. They were no longer a rival. Russia had no rivals left. All were drowning, first and foremost in their own regrets.

Water, water everywhere . . .

His phone started ringing. Police officers with nothing to report. No sightings. But the fourth call came from an officer looking down from the highway to a village so small it had no name. Not officially, but the officer, who sounded as if he'd been running, said the village had a nickname: "Raghead City."

Oleg smiled.

"And there are boats getting ready to leave," the officer added.

"Of course there are boats leaving." *What an idiot.* "Have you gone down to look for her?"

"The Porn Star Spy?" He sounded even breathier using her nickname.

"Yes," Oleg shouted. "The naked one on TV. In a silver SUV. Porsche. Go!"

He ended the call, furious over the timidity of these rural officers.

When the phone rang seconds later, though, he was furious over another man's temerity: *Numero Uno* was demanding that Oleg approve the second missile launch *now*: "If you don't make that decision, I will," he threatened. "You can't stop me."

"Can you give me a little time?" Oleg asked, sounding so timid himself that he wanted to spit—in *Uno's* eye. But he could do better than that, much better.

"How long?" *Uno* asked.

"Just give me till tomorrow, six p.m. I promise the answer will be worth the wait."

"There is only one answer," *Uno* replied.

"Six, tomorrow?" Oleg asked again, grinding his teeth.

"Yes, I will give you till then."

Oleg hung up, relaxing his jaw. *All the time in the world.*

● ● ●

Galina had gone dark. *Who can blame her?* Lana thought.

She and Don were in a small, powerful boat skipping over the waves. It looked like a seagoing version of an AFV, armored fighting vehicle. She felt them go airborne at times, but always under control. To her surprise, Don didn't appear to relish the experience, calling the swift vessel a "stinkpot," which she understood to mean a fossil-fuel-powered watercraft.

The half dozen SEALs accompanying Don and her gave off the same vibe she'd felt last year when their cohorts had saved her life in Saudi Arabia. A little different now: they were putting Don and her *in* danger, while offering some short-term protection that would pass as soon as they sailed that boat into Russian waters.

The wind that had buffeted the *Clinton* still howled, as the sailor had predicted, which did brighten Don's mood:

"Almost as good as it gets for what we've got to do," he announced. "We'll be on a broad reach heading into Russian waters. If the Dehler does the job as well as advertised, we'll be carrying twelve to fifteen knots. That's quick. You'll love it."

"Love it?" He sounded as though they were about to embark on a day of sport racing.

"Why not? *Carpe diem*," he bellowed to the wind.

She saw light creasing the dark sky ahead. Despite the *whump-whump-whump* of the hull hitting swells and cutting through whitecaps, she tried reaching Galina. She had signals. She lacked only Galina.

Briefly, Lana wondered if she'd been set up by Russian intelligence. But she immediately worried that Galina and her seriously ill daughter were the ones fixed most firmly in those crosshairs.

• • •

These concerns were not far off the mark.

Galina's persuasiveness, or cash—she wasn't sure which—had convinced the captain that she was worthy of his assistance. He'd let her know that he himself had scarcely escaped death in fleeing Iran.

He had just started his big diesel engine, black puffs rising into the gray sky, when a Lada with a cherry top drove down to the dock. The officer behind the wheel parked next to the Macan. The contrast was remarkable, but Galina didn't notice, so concerned was she that Alexandra keep her head down.

"You are under arrest," the hefty officer said, squeezing out of the small car in such a rush that he didn't have his handgun fully drawn.

Before she was consciously aware of it, Galina had her derringer aimed at his chest, rushing him as though fearless.

"Don't try anything," she warned him. "I've already killed Sergey the Beast. I will kill you, too, so keep your gun down."

He complied.

She kept moving forward. "Back up." As he obeyed, she had him drop his weapon, a Glock. The Lada might have been ancient but his pistol was impressive. She snapped the slide back, chambering a bullet, and slipped her empty derringer back inside her pocket.

"Take his handcuffs," she ordered the captain, "and put them on him, hands behind his back." As she spoke, she pointed the Glock at the ship captain just long enough to offer an unspoken threat to him. For her savior's sake, she didn't want him to appear to be collaborating with her. "So now I have two prisoners," she told the officer.

The Muslim captain appeared to catch on, cuffing the officer, but apologizing for what he was being forced to do.

Galina saw more lights coming on in the houses. People were watching. She hoped there were no "Heroes of Russia" hiding behind those curtains. She doubted many Muslims had been so honored.

"Are you going to kill me, too?" the officer asked.

"We will see. Search him for other weapons," she told the captain, who quickly found a knife sheathed inside his boot.

"Throw it in the water."

The captain gave it a good toss, perhaps too enthusiastic, she thought.

"Now get him in the boat and get some rope ready. I want him tied down, and if any of your neighbors come out, tell them to go inside and close their eyes."

The captain raised both hands and waved at the homes. Lights went out. It seemed they'd all had plenty of practice in not seeing.

Alexandra exited the Macan and walked toward her mother, dragging her blanket. She looked pale in the wan light. Galina was glad to see her. She hadn't wanted to leave the captain and cop to retrieve Alexandra. The most convincing words can unlock the heaviest chains, though the feckless officer hardly appeared a likely mouthpiece for effective personal propaganda.

"We're getting on the boat," she told Alexandra. "You two first," she ordered the captain and officer.

Once on board, she checked the cabin. A hard bench with a couple of stained cushions. Fish blood, she guessed. "Tie him to that." She pointed to the bench.

She watched the captain carefully.

"Now take us to sea," she ordered him. "We'll see if he ever comes back."

"Please don't—"

"Shut up!" she yelled, cutting off the cop's words.

She bundled Alexandra in her blanket and placed her on a bunk toward the bow.

The captain cast off. She stuck the Glock's muzzle in the officer's face.

"Where's Oleg Dernov?" she demanded.

"He's coming up the coast." The officer shook as he spoke. "Maybe thirty kilometers away."

Fifteen minutes at most.

"Move faster," she told the captain. "Don't worry about your wake," she added, with a glance at the other docked trawlers.

He shoved the throttle forward. The big engine answered. They moved away from the disappearing dock at a rapidly increasing rate.

"Do you have a wife and children?" she asked the captain.

"Not yet."

She was happy to hear that: no one to cry behind curtains for him—or cooperate with Oleg.

As they neared the opening to the harbor, Oleg's Maserati barreled into the village. She watched with the captain's binoculars. As soon as the vehicle rolled to the dock, all the lights in the homes went out.

"Nobody ever sees anything," the captain whispered to her.

But he does, Galina thought, glassing the dock as Oleg raised his own binoculars. For a second they peered at each other. Then she waved.

She hoped good-bye.

CHAPTER 23

OLEG DIDN'T BUDGE FROM the dock, and he held those binoculars on Galina as if he were aiming a weapon. She begged the captain to go faster. He toyed with the throttle. She *might* have sensed a bit more speed, but not enough to discourage Oleg, of that she was certain. Short of teleporting across the globe, she knew nothing was likely to stop his murderous pursuit of her.

Oleg simply had too much at stake not to kill her. Galina had worked with him long enough to have strong ideas about how to crush his assault on Antarctica and, by extension, the entire planet. But to do that she had to stop running long enough to work on her computer, preferably with the American, Lana Elkins, by her side. Elkins had already displayed daunting skills in tracking down Galina. Now the Russian hacker hoped her American counterpart would prove just as effective in exfiltrating her so the two of them could team up to bring Oleg down—before the deadly flooding and radiation got even worse.

Oleg bolted down the dock toward the nearest house. His sprint caught the captain's eye, too. "I'm going faster here than I've ever gone," he said before Galina could beg him again for more speed. "But I must be careful. There are old moorings in the water. You can see them at low tide. Maybe not now, when low tide is like high tide. I don't want to hit them."

"The last thing we need," she had to agree.

"That's him?" the captain asked. "The man who took those pictures of you?"

She nodded.

"Let me see him."

She handed over the binoculars. He stared at Oleg, who was nearing the door of the house. Galina expected he'd be rooting out one of the captains in the next minute or two to chase them down.

"He's ruthless, a killer," she said.

"I understand," the captain said to her. "I had to do ruthless things to get out of Iran. And those people," he pointed to the house, "can be ruthless as well. They won't open their doors."

"I'm afraid they'll have to," Galina replied.

As if to prove her point, Oleg kicked it in. A woman in a headscarf shrank from him as a man marched out of the interior shadows. Oleg held up his ID—and his gun.

Galina refocused the binoculars as the man of the house slowed down and put up his hands. Oleg's mouth moved and the man eased past the woman and edged out the door. He headed toward the dock, waving for Oleg to come with him. He reminded Galina of a mother bird faking a broken wing to try to lead a predator away from her nestlings.

Oleg followed the man, gun trained on him, to a trawler that looked similar to the captain's.

"Is his faster than yours?" she asked him.

"About the same. These are not speedboats. But last winter he rebuilt his engine. I'm going to do that this December."

"So what does that mean, rebuilt his engine?"

"Not much, I hope. Maybe more reliable. But mine's a good boat," the captain said, slapping the wheel.

Already black puffs of diesel smoke were belching from the other trawler's stacks.

Oleg and his captive captain were underway.

• • •

Lana thought landing at Pitsunda was like hitting the beach at Normandy. A huge exaggeration, which she recognized, but the captain of the armored boat gunned the engine loudly as they raced down ten-foot waves, surfing them at times, until he ran the nimble vessel right up onto the sand.

Fortunately, they were not met by gunfire. Instead, she heard the staccato command of "Get out-get out-get out" from the SEAL leader, a red-haired man with the unlikely name of Johnny Walker; he'd already been the subject of obvious jibes in Lana's presence.

But the SEALs took their commander's words seriously; they moved rapidly onto the sand with their weapons drawn, scanning the beach with their night goggles. Lana, on the other hand, had her eyes on the rough shore break wondering where the Dehler 38 was moored.

The same thought must have occurred to Don because words to that effect passed his lips seconds later.

"The other side of this dune," replied Johnny Walker Red, as he was known to his men. "That's where the marina is, and where they'll be waiting."

The dune rose about two hundred feet on a steep slope that was crowned with short trees; Lana guessed scrub pine. It looked like a perfect place for a machine gunner to open up on them.

The slog up the dune proved exasperating: two steps up, one

step down as the fine white grains gave away quickly under their weight.

Three SEALs were deployed in front of Lana and Don. Two moved on their flanks. One followed. She felt as protected as she could under the circumstances—until she received a text. She pulled out her phone thinking it was from Galina, worrying that Oleg had spotted his prey. It wasn't from the Russian, though it was heartbreaking news: Tanesa's mother, Esme, said Tanesa and Emma had been lost in a flood in Anacostia.

What? Lana looked up, as if an answer to her horror might be written in the night sky. She recalled seeing the rising waters in Anacostia as they flew in the chopper to Andrews, but she'd had no idea Tanesa and Emma were down there.

She returned immediately to the text, reading as she trudged up the dune that "Unknown to me," Esme wrote, "the girls had volunteered to fill sandbags in Anacostia." They'd been working on a headwall when the sea broke through. Tanesa's mother wanted to know if Lana had any contacts who could help search for the girls.

Damn it! It was just like Emma—*and* Tanesa—to jump into the fray. Emma had been feeling so useless during the crisis, and had said as much, compared to the heroics that she and Tanesa had displayed last year. And what was fighting a flood, the two must have thought, compared to going up against men with a backpack nuclear bomb?

Lana did the only thing she could under the circumstances: she forwarded the entire text to Holmes. She didn't need to add a single syllable. Her own desperation was so great *it* could have been etched in the sky—and would be immediately apparent to the deputy director. Then she sent a quick message to Esme saying that she'd alerted federal authorities who might be able to help.

What Lana did not do was tell Don, struggling up the dune

to her right. She didn't believe a dope dealer, of all people, could do anything to help Emma right now.

All the SEALs were looking side to side, which did little to protect them when floodlights poured down the dune and a man's deep voice bellowed in accented English for them to stop.

"Halt," Red ordered a split second later.

What choice do we have?

All Lana could spy behind the floodlights were shadows blending into one another. She wondered how those men had known they were hitting the beach. Or had they been using the bluff to watch both sides? "Is this how your guy does business?" she asked her ex.

"That's not him. My guy has a squeaky voice. He got kicked in the throat by a horse."

From Red's cautious manner, he already knew they'd been met by the wrong party.

For a moment, Lana thought maybe they'd been intercepted by a routine patrol.

Maybe, maybe, maybe. It felt like a million maybes might flood through her mind in the next few seconds—along with a few well-placed bullets.

"We're here to meet Nikita Mikov," Red called out.

"Mikov? Mikov's not feeling so good right now," the commanding voice responded. "He said you should talk to us instead."

"Maybe I will," Red answered. "Depends."

"On what?"

"On who I'm talking to. How much are my words going to cost me?" Red asked.

"So you are prepared to pay for the privilege of conversation?"

"I'm an agreeable man."

"Then put down your guns. I find they reduce the desire for honest negotiation."

"What are we negotiating for?" Red replied, still holding his weapon by his side, as were his men.

"What you were always negotiating for. A boat."

"Dehler 38," Don muttered.

Red nodded. "The Dehler 38," he called out.

"Yes, a fine boat. One of our best."

"And I think I know what's going on here," Don said softly to Red. "This guy must have taken control of the marina."

"I hear you," Red whispered back.

"It's happening all over Europe," Don added.

Not just in Europe. Lana recalled the gangbangers in Miami seizing boats and gleefully giving the owners the old heave-ho right into the harbor.

"We can't drop our weapons," Red yelled up the dune. "But we can promise you that we came to complete a deal."

"American dollars?" the man asked.

"Good as gold."

"Used to be. Rubles are better."

"We've got them, too," Red said.

We do?

"Whatever you want," the SEAL went on.

"Then by all means point your weapons down and we'll walk down there to you. But if one of your men makes a move, a grenade is going to land right on your heads. Let's do it peaceably."

And they did. A squat man walked out of the shadows with gunmen on either side of him who also kept their weapons low.

The leader pulled out his phone and showed them photos of the Dehler and quite a few other available boats.

"The Dehler," Don insisted.

"*Storm Season,*" said the squat man, pointing to the name. "One million rubles for five days."

"Hold on," Red said. "That's $22,000."

"Yes, it is. That's the price to charter," said Squat, who looked even shorter up close.

"Mikov said $10,000."

Squat looked around theatrically. "Do you see Mikov? I don't see Mikov. He can't protect your interests. To be honest, Mikov can't even protect his own anymore."

Red looked at Lana, who nodded quickly. *Let's just get the deal done.*

"Five days, one million rubles," the SEAL agreed.

Lana noticed Squat hadn't demanded a deposit for the boat itself. Further proof, Lana thought, that he and his men had hijacked Mikov's boat-chartering business and wouldn't be sharing the profits with the boat owners themselves. Squat would be indifferent to the boat's return if he and his hoods planned to be gone by the time she and Don got back.

And where would Emma and Tanesa be by then? She had a horrible image of them both drowned.

After strolling down a wide dock, the thugs lit up *Storm Season,* a handsome, sleek-looking sloop.

Don hurried to check the furled sails, nodding as he announced, "Carbon fiber, just like Mikov said."

Squat nodded as if he knew why Don was elated.

"And fully battened," Don added. "She should move." He put out his hand to help Lana on board.

The cabin had a raked-back racy look with long, angled windows. The helm had electric winches for the halyard and sheets—the lines that raised and trimmed the sails. They made it possible for one person to sail the Dehler, which was good because Lana didn't expect to be much help when it came to the actual voyage. And right now she needed to provide the rendezvous coordinates as soon as possible to Galina.

"We'll wait till you're under way," Red said to her and Don.

The mood dockside turned amiable with the transfer of funds. Squat offered vodka to the SEALs. Lana was pleased to see that none accepted.

"Duty calls," Red explained.

"Me, too," Squat replied. "And my duty is to give praise where praise is due. To Stoli Gold." He raised the distinctive bottle high.

"To Stoli Gold," his men amen'ed.

Squat glugged down the clear alcohol for several rewarding seconds, to judge from his sigh when he stopped.

Don activated the depth finder and started the engine to motor out of the marina. The fuel tanks were full. He asked Lana to check the seventy-nine-gallon freshwater tank under the companionway. Topped off as well. Evidently, Mikov had been around long enough to attend to the details.

Lana also checked her messages, thinking she might have missed the telltale vibration. Nothing from Holmes, Esme, or Galina.

The vodka drinkers on the dock gave no indication of knowing anything more about sailboats than how to squeeze money out of a hijacked charter service.

But Lana thought the drinkers could have been more alert to the vagaries of their trade. With *Storm Season* under way and a couple hundred feet from the dock, Red and his men quickly disarmed the band and took back more than 500,000 rubles.

"Big mistake!" Squat bellowed.

"Don't threaten us," Red replied as loudly. "We've got your guns." He looked at the weapons. "Not worth a damn," he pronounced, ordering his men to throw them into the harbor. Lana watched them vanish into the dark water.

"Much harder to get than boats." Squat was still shouting.

"Not where I come from," Red replied evenly.

Don kept looking back from the helm. "He shouldn't have

done that. Bad blood over some rubles that aren't even ours. Doesn't make sense."

"Sure it does," Lana said. "It was all a lead-up to disarming them. Makes a lot of sense."

But she worried that Don was right. Those trees on top of the sand dune still looked ominous to her, even after passing through them to get to the marina. Squat's men had used only one flood-light to cast a narrow beam when they'd led them through the dense forest. Just looking up there made her imagine countless eyes peering down on the SEALs, who were already climbing back up the dune to get to the beach and their boat.

Lana opened the sail bag that had been packed for her at Meade. "A gun in there?" Don asked.

"AR-15," she answered, snapping the barrel and stock together and cramming in a clip. "A Sig Sauer, too." She preferred it over larger pistols.

Don put *Storm Season* on autopilot as they motored out of the harbor, then plundered his own bag. "I'm outfitted the same way."

The marina was dark, the sea ahead alive with a smattering of distant lights. Likely boats whose owners were hoping to ride out the storm of rising seas. She wasn't worried about their lights. She was worried about huge gaps of darkness out there large enough to hide a navy. And she was even more frantic about Emma and Tanesa.

Don pointed the bow into the wind and took off the cover of the mainsail, raising it seconds later with the electronic winch. In the same manner, he unfurled the jib. Both luffed and filled as he turned the boat and cut the engine. Far from shore, he turned on the touch screen electronic charts at the helm.

Lana resisted contacting Holmes about her daughter's plight. He was a man whose time was sacred in a crisis. And with nothing to tell Esme, she sent no update. But Lana did message Galina, succeeding in rapid fashion. Galina asked right away for the coordinates.

Don had the answer ready for Lana. "Technically, that puts us out of Russian waters for the rendezvous," he added.

"Technically?" Lana asked.

"It's so close they could claim anything but it's about the halfway point. Ask how much speed they have."

"Twelve knots," Lana replied a moment later.

"We've got fourteen. That's good. Ours will vary with the wind."

A boat engine came to life from the point of the short peninsula that separated the beach from the marina. She and Don both looked back. Lana hoped it was the armored boat heading toward them.

As the engine noise grew louder, Galina messaged that Oleg was gaining on them.

"He's chasing you?" Why hadn't she said so? Not that she and Don—or the SEALs, for that matter—could do a damn thing to help her from this distance.

"Not close enough to shoot," Galina replied.

"What do you have?"

"I'd rather not say," Galina said.

Lana realized the Russian was worried Oleg was intercepting her communications. In any case, she doubted Galina had a combat rifle.

From *Storm Season*'s port side the boat drew closer. Red flashed a light to let them know who they were. Lana was glad; she'd been about to pick up her AR-15.

The SEALs moved up alongside them as Don started heading north, sailing away from land on a broad reach, as he'd foreseen.

Lana yelled to Red that Dernov was chasing Bortnik.

The commander nodded as a gunshot blew out *Storm Season*'s starboard cabin window.

Lana ducked and looked right. Just the big black gap until the next muzzle flash, which quickly turned into a fusillade that riddled the Dehler. The shooting stopped almost as quickly with her and Don huddled on the floor of the cockpit.

The SEALs raced ahead of them, speeding around the bow toward the source of the firepower. Lana kneeled, peering over the gunwale on the starboard side. She followed them by sound. She could see very little. The armored boat didn't have powerful lights, or else Red had chosen not to use them.

But the gunmen who'd opened up on them had no such reservations. They turned on a beam that lit up the whitecaps and made the SEAL boat blindingly bright. She couldn't make out the size of their assailant's craft, but using the light allowed their position to be pinpointed. That seemed crazy to Lana. And at first it appeared she was right because the SEALs responded by shooting at the light. But just before their volley shattered it, Lana saw a rocket-propelled grenade launcher rise up in the other vessel. An instant later she followed the rocket's red trail all the way to the armored boat.

The explosion ripped off the stern and sent SEALs—some immediately dismembered—into the air, eerily lit by flames flashing red on streams of blood.

We're next.

But huddled on the floor of the Dehler, Lana received a text from Holmes that scared her far more: "Knew about girls. Have not found them. Bad here and getting worse. Stop them!"

So Emma and Tanesa had been missing long enough for a search to have failed. Lana's whole body stiffened with fear. The desperation in the deputy director's text didn't help.

She scarcely looked up from the screen when a SEAL started screaming. His pain sounded unearthly.

And then Lana heard the horrifying whine of another rocket.

CHAPTER 24

EMMA AND TANESA WERE in a van on their way to the Capitol Baptist Church in Anacostia to fill and stack sandbags. The flooding Potomac River was threatening the historic building. Emma was fierce with the simple desire to help out, and Tanesa had told her that the spirit of Jesus filled her every time she came to the aid of others. The church desperately needed volunteers, according to Shawn.

The lean young man was at the wheel, a very different position compared to last year when his leg was broken as he and other choir members tried to hold back traffic to save motorists fleeing horrific explosions in the first minutes of the cyberattack on DC. Lana was among those saved before a driver ran over Shawn.

After reading his text at Emma's house, Tanesa had said, "We've got to go."

"What's your mother going to say?" Emma had asked, glancing at the door to her own mom's bedroom, where, in Lana's absence, she and Tanesa were sharing a king-size bed.

"Well, if it were some other kid going to pitch in, my mother would say, 'That child's so amazing, so selfless.' But with me it would be, 'What's *wrong* with you, girl? You got curly gel for brains? That could kill you.' So let's just sneak out. I'll tell Shawn to pick us up at the 7-Eleven down on River Road." Which was more a point of reference than an actual convenience store, since it had been looted and burned to the ground by nicely groomed suburban kids.

"Could going there really kill us?" Emma had asked next. She knew her own mother would freak if she found out Emma was sneaking away in the midst of this crisis to go fight an unprecedented flood.

"Look, I'm going, and I don't even know how to swim. And I'm guessing you've been swimming since you were a tadpole."

True enough.

They'd snuck out the window and found their way into Shawn's old Jeep Cherokee within twenty minutes, progress that slowed as they drove closer to DC. Shawn said he knew how to avoid the worst of the flooding, but that didn't prove to be a state secret: so did every other driver, apparently.

Traffic wasn't as bad once they finally approached Anacostia by late afternoon. Days were still long, so Emma figured they could pack sandbags for the church for at least a couple of hours. She figured if they got home by eight o'clock there was even a good chance they wouldn't have been missed. And if they were, it was still early so Esme couldn't be too pissed, right?

"Don't bet on that," Tanesa warned.

Emma tried not to feel uneasy as Shawn drove past groups of young black men who glared at the van. She felt it would be racist to make any judgments, and she knew that if white guys had been staring at them like that she'd be plenty paranoid about their intentions, too. She sure hadn't gone anywhere near the burning of the convenience market. But a glare was a glare, no matter what the color of the skin.

"How close are we to the church?" she asked Shawn. Emma

had been there many times for choir practice, but to avoid the flooding, Shawn had taken a circuitous route.

"Few more minutes."

Emma could see how tight his jaw was. The tension in the van felt combustible.

They sure skirted a lot of flooding. The river now covered some of the new parks built in recent years along the waterfront, and had risen halfway up the stairs of some of the pedestrian bridges.

"Man, that's high," Tanesa said, sounding daunted.

Volunteers were sandbagging the lower banks of the river, which sloped every few hundred yards. But Emma couldn't see how they could hold back the Potomac, if the sea kept rising. She could actually make out the river flowing backward. It looked bizarre. Emma pointed it out to Shawn and Tanesa up front.

"That's never happened in all of human history," she said.

"That is surreal," Shawn replied.

As they neared the church they saw a wall of sandbags only partially completed near the back of the building. The choir and church members looked like they'd abandoned it to take the fight right to the river's edge. They were all working feverishly down there, filling bags and raising them higher.

"Can those sandbags hold back that much water?"

"They've got to," Tanesa replied. "Those bags go, there goes the church."

"We're looking for a miracle, I guess," Shawn said.

But they spared little of themselves packing bags and lugging them to the wall.

Shawn, tall as he was, teamed with another guy to stack them as high as they could, sweating buckets in the hot September sun.

Nobody took a break. But what Emma had feared came true: the rising water pushed back a bag that Shawn had just helped heave into place.

In less than thirty seconds, water swept aside adjoining bags. Heavy as they were, the sandbags could not hold off the rising river.

The choir members and church volunteers tried frantically to push sandbags back into place. Emma and Tanesa did their best to help them, but even when they managed to wedge a bag into the wall, others broke loose.

Emma started backing up as sandbags tumbled away and the rush of water became a flood, washing over her feet, rising up her shins.

Tanesa was retreating as well. Both watched Shawn press his shoulder against the wall. Tanesa yelled for him to come. He either didn't hear her or really believed a miracle would save him and the others and the church.

The sandbag wall collapsed around Shawn and consumed him in its dark gushing maw.

Volunteers were running up the slight slope to the church. *It's hopeless,* Emma thought. She braced herself for the wall of water, spotting a group of young men—definitely not part of the choir—watching from a nearby riverfront trail. They were on higher ground about a hundred feet away.

Tanesa ran to Emma, panic frozen on her face. Emma grabbed her hand, no longer thinking about saving a church.

Only her friend and herself.

• • •

The rocket that Lana heard coming right at them ripped through *Storm Season*'s jib and kept on going, leaving a burning ring two feet wide in the gray carbon-fiber fabric.

Holy shit.

She looked starboard, expecting to see the attacker retargeting, but only darkness filled her gaze.

Don was already up, grabbing an extinguisher to put out the blazing sail. Lana couldn't have been more grateful; the fire had put a bull's-eye on the only target in the sea.

In less than sixty seconds, Don snuffed the fire. The man had serious *cojones*, Lana had to admit. The whole time he put out the flames in the bow, he was the only visible human target.

Lana raised her eyes above the gunwale again. She still saw nothing but darkness. No lights. No muzzle flashes. A strange silence had ensued. The SEAL who'd been screaming most likely had died, along with others, she guessed, based on what she had just seen of the explosion.

Then she heard the wind rushing through the hole in the jib, and Don yelling at her from twenty-five feet away: "We'll use the genny. We'll be okay."

His words had barely registered when Red, balancing in the sinking bow of the armored boat, fired a rocket from a grenade launcher.

A heat seeker, she figured, when it ran a wickedly fast course across the rolling sea and blew apart the small vessel that had just fired on them.

When she looked back for Red, he and the bow of his boat had disappeared into the blackness.

Don jumped down into the Dehler's cockpit, thrusting aside the extinguisher and grabbing the wheel.

He shoved a boxy lantern into her hands. "Up to the bow. We've got to rescue them if they're still alive."

She scrambled past the cables that helped hold up the mast, then grasped the railing all the way to the front of the boat. As she threw the switch on the lantern, she hoped like hell Red had taken out all the attackers because otherwise she was about to replace Don as the only target on the sea.

She immediately spotted three SEALs, including Red, trying to hold on to the other men, none of whom could possibly have been alive, their wounds gaping and deadly at a glance.

"Slow down, they're to port," she yelled to Don, pointing left.

He dropped the sails with the electric winches and started the engine to give them maneuverability.

Then he brought the stern in tight to Red and dropped *Storm Season's* swimming platform, which fell to the water line. With the sea rising and falling, and the wind howling, Don did a superb job of holding the boat in position. Lana dragged the SEALs' rocket-blasted bodies aboard, sickened by their wounds. Arms and legs were missing, faces blown away, and a chest had been ripped open. But she and the SEALs worked hard to claim what they could because those remains would mean much to their loved ones.

Only two of the dead still had intact life jackets. The other bodies were hauled to *Storm Season* by Red and Veal—another SEAL with a nickname, she presumed—and Kurt, who was bleeding from his shoulder. Struggling, he had to use that arm to push the dead onto the platform.

Finished loading, Red and his two compatriots climbed aboard. The SEAL commander told Don to head toward the wreckage of the enemy's boat. He grabbed the lantern and joined Veal on the forward deck. Both had armed themselves with the boat's AR-15s. Their own weapons were soaked and not firing.

Kurt settled on a cockpit bench and asked for a first aid kit. Lana brought it to him but he refused her offer to help.

She pulled out her semiautomatic handgun, as had Don, and joined the watch from the stern as he piloted them through the debris.

"No survivors. Seven dead," Red announced after scanning the sea with the lantern.

"Was it them?" Lana asked, glancing back at the peninsula.

"No," Red said, shaking his head.

Though Lana had no regrets over the deaths of these men, she averted her eyes, knowing how cruelly steadfast her memory could be. She'd already seen too much of the night's carnage.

Red scrambled back to the helm and asked Don to slow the ship so he could check the bodies of his victims more closely. After relieving them of numerous weapons, including grenades, automatic rifles and pistols, and an RPG, he looked at various flag tattoos on three of the dead. "They're Russians, and proud of it. Help me get them aboard."

His compatriots pulled the bodies over the transom. Then Red said they'd also keep the wet armaments, "in case we have to argue about who violated international waters first."

"What do you mean?" Lana asked.

"We can't go back to Pitsunda," Red said. "We can only go toward Russian waters, and this is far from over. They're the ones who all but declared war. They fired two rockets at us and sank a U.S. navy vessel *before* we returned fire. So we're going to take the battle to them. We don't have any choice."

Lana felt a chill deep in her core, like an icicle twisting in her gut. She knew it wasn't from the mangled dead in the boat or the corpses floating limbless in the sea. It was from knowing that Red was right: none of them had any choice, and this really was just the beginning.

She also had no idea if the Russians the SEAL had just killed were on Squat's payroll as enforcers, or coordinating their attack with Oleg and others farther north who might be targeting Galina at that very moment.

She checked for messages from Holmes or Esme, hoping for some good news about Emma and Tanesa.

Nothing.

Then she sent a message to Galina.

• • •

The wall of water hit Emma and Tanesa like a powerful wave, tumbling them and twisting them apart. Tanesa's hand was torn from hers. Emma tried to swim to the surface, but for those first few moments she had no idea if she were upside down or right side up. As the fierce current swept her along she was terrified of smashing into the stone church or a concrete bench. She felt like a sock in the rinse cycle of a washing machine, lungs compressing for lack of air.

She broke through the surface gasping, only to see more water before it washed over her. The current was sending her rushing toward a sapling, which was good because when she hit it, the skinny tree bent and absorbed most of the impact. She held on, grateful it didn't snap.

In the dusky light, she screamed for Tanesa, certain her closest friend was drowning. Then she spotted her about a hundred feet away getting hauled up onto a riverfront trail by one of those rough-looking guys who'd glared at them earlier.

Maybe they're okay.

Tanesa was shaking badly, but Emma didn't see any blood or obvious signs of broken bones. It took minutes for the swirling waters to settle before she even considered swimming to Tanesa. In the distance, she saw choir members dragging themselves from the water, but not Shawn. She yelled, asking if anyone had seen him. The only response came from a young girl who shook her head. The others looked shocked and battered by the flood.

Then she heard a guy say, "Hey, girl, lemme help you."

A man about twenty with faux hawk hair pulled up alongside her in a kayak. It had an open deck, which would make it easy to board. She wasn't sure she wanted to, though, because a closer look showed he was another one of the younger men who'd given them the stink eye. But now his eyes had softened—on her.

"Get on," he said more firmly.

Her wet clothes clung to her as she boarded the kayak. She felt like an unwitting participant in a wet T-shirt contest.

She looked for Tanesa, but couldn't see her now.

"Where's my friend? I saw her getting pulled out of the water."

"Yeah, that's right, we saved her ass. Yours, too, now."

He paddled like it was a Sunday afternoon lark in the park.

"There she is." He pointed. "Now get off," he added in a sharp voice, pushing her into hip-deep water.

Emma trudged across the grassy bottom as a huge guy, at least six foot six and two hundred fifty pounds, extended his great mitt of a hand.

She took it. That was when she saw the abject fright on Tanesa's face and knew they had not found the comfort of strangers.

"How you doing?" the big man said. He looked like a boxer or kung fu fighter. Late twenties, shaved head, close-cropped beard, lots of muscle.

"Fine," Emma muttered, back to eyeing Tanesa. "You okay?" she asked.

Tanesa shrugged.

"You're not going to say 'Thank you for saving my life'?" The big man glared and clapped his hands together so loudly they made Emma jump. "Show some gratitude. We look like the Coast Guard? We didn't need to do that shit."

Emma took Tanesa's hand. "Come on, we've got to go find Shawn."

"You aren't looking for nobody," the man said, dropping his hand on Emma's shoulder. "Know why? 'Cause I've been looking at you two real close, and even with your hair all wet and funky, and looking like a couple of drowned rats, I know who you are. You're those hero girls from last year. So do you know what that makes us?"

Emma was barely listening. What had mostly registered was that his grip on her shoulder was increasing its pressure.

"I asked you two a question, and I asked it nice. You better start learning some manners or we're going to have to teach you some respect."

"No, I don't know what the hell that makes you," Emma said, trying to shrug off his hand. It didn't work.

"Your knights in shining armor. And I'd say you two give us some serious bargaining power."

"Bargaining for what?" Emma demanded.

Before she got an answer she and Tanesa were surrounded and pushed toward a parking lot where a long black Hummer with darkened windows was parked.

"Get in the back with my friends," the big man said.

Emma balked. "Bargaining for what?"

"Couple of hero girls like you haven't figured that out?" he replied. "Your *lives*. What else? Now get the fuck in there."

He pushed Emma so hard he sent her sprawling across the backseat.

• • •

Galina had barely slept after responding to Lana's message. She'd worried that an attack on Lana's boat could mean there would be an attack on hers. But so far the morning hours had passed peacefully under a brilliant sun whose heat had been lessened by a firm breeze.

She'd been keeping a keen eye on Oleg's trawler, though, which rose and disappeared with the large swells. So did the boat she was on, captained by Abdul Majid Younes, as he had formally introduced himself yesterday.

"Does the other ship have any weapons on board?"

"A nine millimeter maybe, for shooting sharks. That's all. Maybe a rifle."

"What do you have?"

Captain Younes raised his eyebrows. "I have a few things lying around."

The way he said that made Galina hope he had an arsenal aboard. He had fled Iran, after all. "If they take my daughter and me, they'll kill us both," she whispered; Alexandra was asleep on her lap.

"I protect women and children on my boat. It's a matter of honor. You may not know it yet, but you picked the right man."

Galina studied him openly. Could she really have been so fortunate as to have found a veritable prince in that tiny seaport? He'd betrayed no nerves thus far, sailing on course with hardly a glance back, casually drinking the powerful coffee he'd politely asked her to fix for him.

The cop he'd tied to the bench in the cabin was slumped over, evidently sleeping.

Captain Younes asked Galina to warm up cans of soup for all of them. She took on the duty of helping the officer, who brightened when he realized that she'd come to feed him, not fire a bullet into his brain.

"Just do what I say," Galina told him as she spooned more broth and leeks into his mouth. "The cop I killed was a beast. He was trying to rape me. Don't try to escape or hurt anyone and I won't hurt you."

When she returned to the helm, Oleg's boat had neither gained nor lost distance on them.

"He doesn't want to catch up," Captain Younes said. "I've tested them, slowing down and speeding up. Always the same with them. I think he wants to know where you're going and why."

"I think he already knows all that. He's a master hacker."

It made sense that Oleg would stay back so he could try to capture both her and whoever she was meeting. Or simply kill them, for that matter. What he would fear most, she figured, was having them work together against him. Otherwise, Galina was certain he would have tried to grab her as soon as he could.

She sent Lana a message about Oleg's careful stalking of her boat. Most of her morning had been spent trying to hack into the U.S.S. *Delphin,* fearful that at any second the crazy man Oleg had in that sub would launch another Trident II. But she hadn't been able to penetrate the sub's cybersecurity. What she had found was deeply curious, though: A tremendous amount of data was flowing from Moscow to the submarine, which was now deep in the South Atlantic. That location was also the best guess of the U.S. Office of Naval Intelligence, which had released that information to the news media.

The data flow surprised her. It was as if her fellow Russians no longer saw any reason to hide their involvement in the hijacking of the sub or the bombing of Antarctica. Which was crazy. Any evidence linking them to either could be a *casus belli* for nuclear retaliation. It made no sense to her. But there was no denying the data.

Twice Oleg left her messages. In one he'd had the gall to say that if she came back to him now she could still be his "good bad girl again." She shook her head in amazement. Didn't he realize that she'd shoot him if she had the chance?

She stroked Alexandra's head and prayed they'd both survive the rendezvous and whatever Lana had planned for it.

"Up ahead," Captain Younes said, pointing. He was looking through his binoculars. "I see a sailboat. It looks the right size."

She stood to take a look, glassing the sea, but catching only a glimpse of gray sail in the distance.

Galina turned around to look at Oleg's boat. It had started to close the gap.

"He's closer," she said to Younes.

"I have been looking," the captain said calmly. "I saw him speeding up before you did. But I'm afraid my friend is pushing his engine as hard as he can, and he's a little faster than I thought."

Galina told Alexandra to go back to her bunk and stay bundled up. The child must have sensed the urgency and danger because she scampered down the companionway, past the prisoner, and into the forward bunk.

Her mother raised the Glock and racked the slide to ensure a bullet was in the chamber.

Captain Younes nodded approvingly. "Take the wheel," he told her.

He opened a locker in the cockpit and pulled out a shotgun and a hunting rifle. Pointing to the former, he said, "That's for if they get close. The other one is to make sure they never do."

"Are you good with those?" she asked.

"Good enough not to get caught in the middle," he replied, "because that's how you get crushed."

Ten minutes later, with *Storm Season* in sight, a bullet ricocheted off a winch drum that operated the towing booms for the nets.

Calmly, Captain Younes put the trawler on autopilot, then picked up the hunting rifle, searching for Oleg with his scope.

The next shot struck Younes directly in the head. The captain dropped to the deck, dead, looking as if an axe had hacked open his skull.

Galina dropped below the level of the gunwales, shaking uncontrollably. Alexandra raced to the cabin doorway.

"No! Go back!" Galina screamed. "Now!"

The six-year-old darted to her bunk, but Galina knew that her little girl had seen Younes's fatal wound and the copious blood washing across the deck.

She looked up at the wheel wondering how she could possibly steer the boat *and* try to keep Oleg at bay.

You don't have to steer, she reminded herself: Younes had put it on autopilot.

"I can help," the cop yelled from inside the cabin.

Galina ignored him, picking up the rifle. Staying as low as she could, she peered through the scope.

In an eerie replay of what she'd seen as they'd sailed from the inlet, she spotted Oleg staring back at her through an eyepiece of his own. Only this time it had a rifle attached.

He fired again.

CHAPTER 25

OLEG'S SHOT MISSED GALINA'S head by less than six inches, but tore through the cabin walls with enough force to leave a bullet burn on the cop's chin. An inch closer and the man would have lost his face.

Galina took no notice of this, worried far more that Oleg's ammo would rip through the length of the trawler and kill Alexandra in the bunk at the front of the cabin. She wished she could hide her daughter behind one of the nets' heavy winch drums, but she didn't dare try to move her now.

She poked the hunting rifle over the gunwale and eyed Oleg again, firing as soon as she saw him.

The rifle kicked back into her shoulder with enough force to surprise her, but not enough to keep her from seeing that she'd made Oleg duck.

Still smiling?

Galina then shot out a window in the pilothouse of his ship. The glass shattered completely. She saw the captain duck away from the wheel.

As she scanned the trawler for Oleg, another bullet ripped into the stern a foot below her. A second shot followed quickly, nicking the railing inches from her head.

She ducked again, hoping they were getting closer to Lana's boat. Galina needed help.

She crawled forward and peered over the port side, exposing herself as little as possible. She started to raise the binoculars when Lana's sailboat rose easily into view on a swell. It was still more than a mile away, but in minutes their paths would cross if Younes's trawler kept trudging along.

But a glance backward showed Oleg's ship still catching up. It seemed to be gaining speed as it moved closer.

Oddly, though, he had stopped shooting, which made her uneasy. His boat was still disappearing when it moved down a swell, granting her only glimpses to shoot at him. She had little faith in her ability to do more than make him take cover.

But the swells also gave Galina breathing room when he couldn't shoot her. She used that time to message Lana that Oleg had shot and killed the captain of her boat. She tried to communicate quickly, but her boat still rose and fell several times on the rolling sea before she turned her attention back to Oleg's trawler, freezing when she saw the vessel only half a soccer field length away.

She stared through the riflescope for him, tense as one of the trawler's steel cables.

The cop must have seen her burgeoning panic: "I can help," he yelled from the cabin. "Cut me loose."

Don't be a fool, she warned herself. *He works for them.* Galina realized she must look scared and desperate. *But I'm not stupid.*

As Oleg's ship rose back into view, she tried again to pick him out with the scope. Still no luck, but she fired anyway, hoping to give Oleg the impression that she'd sighted him. What else could she do with the ship sailing ever closer?

Captain Younes's VHF radio crackled. Someone was trying to reach them, but the voice kept breaking up. She couldn't tell if it was Oleg, or possibly Lana or someone else on her boat. Or maybe another boat entirely.

Each time her ship rose on a swell, Galina looked over the stern, then both sides, ready to shoot. Oleg, she realized, could be anywhere. The radio crackled again.

She crawled forward, still holding the hunting rifle, and reached up, grabbing the VHF mouthpiece from next to the wheel. Clicking it, she thought she heard Oleg's voice, when she wanted more than anything to hear Lana's again.

"Drop dead!" she shouted.

"I think that was the other captain trying to reach you," the cop yelled from the bench in the cabin.

Galina froze. Was the cop trying to confuse her? But if that were the other captain on the VHF, where was Oleg? A haunting question.

The answer came, but not on radio waves.

As Younes's trawler rode up another swell, Oleg appeared right beside her ship in a Zodiac with an electric outboard.

For the briefest moment, she thought he would fall away and she could rush the railing and shoot him at will. But in the same instant he hurled himself over the gunwale with his pistol in hand and lunged toward her.

She tried to raise the long hunting rifle, but it was cumbersome in such close quarters. He grabbed the barrel, pushing it down as she fired, and jerked the weapon from her hands.

He tossed it aside and pointed his nine millimeter at her face as he walked toward her. His smile returned. Cocky as ever, he shoved the pistol into the back of his pants, as though daring her to fight him with her hands.

She threw herself at him, knowing Alexandra's life was at stake, too.

He swatted her arms away easily, seized her neck, and, *still* smiling, started choking her.

• • •

Lana hung up *Storm Season*'s VHF radio in frustration. There was a lot of co-channel interference, probably from the unknown numbers of unseen boats plying the waters in an attempt to escape the hazards of staying moored or docked in rising seas. Even so, Lana was pretty sure she'd heard Galina say, "Drop dead," although it could have been from another boater frustrated by the radio interference.

"That crap happens," Don said to Lana. "I'm guessing the troposphere is lit up with signals about now."

"That's not the kind of interference we should be worrying about," Red shouted, studying Galina's trawler with his binoculars. "Dernov's going aboard. Oh, shit, he's grabbing her. He's strangling her!"

"What?" Lana asked, grabbing the binoculars when he set them aside and started tearing off his pants and shirt.

Veal quickly followed his commander's lead. Kurt joined the rapid disrobing.

"No," Red said to the wounded man, without slowing down his own efforts. "Not with your shoulder. It'd be like trolling for sharks."

"You're swimming over there?" Lana said as Red and Veal pulled on dark skullcaps and goggles that fit as snuggly as their shirts and briefs. Each hitched on what looked like tool belts with knives, lights, flares, and handguns.

"Why do you think they call us SEALs?" Red said, pulling on flippers. "I want you two to stay right on course until you risk a serious chance of getting shot, then just sail away."

The pair climbed over the starboard side, out of view of Galina's boat, and disappeared instantly into the sea.

Oleg and Galina were no longer in sight, either; Lana guessed they were struggling on the deck. *If she's still alive.*

Don kept checking the water for the SEALs' reappearance, but neither man had surfaced after two minutes. "They've got to be on a different set of swells by now."

Lana nodded, still glassing the trawler with Galina. "I can't see them."

"Did you see the guns on their belts?" Don said. "German. Heckler & Koch. They shoot steel darts. They're made for the water, but they can do a lot of damage in the air, too."

Lana listened, but kept moving the binoculars over Galina's trawler. Oleg and his prey still hadn't reappeared. It was hard not to imagine her dead on the deck. At least the son of a bitch wouldn't get away.

Before she looked back at Don, he spun the wheel, veering from the trawler they'd been heading toward since early morning. "I hope that doesn't give away too much," he said, "but we're in gunshot range now."

As Don jibed, she checked messages. Maybe Galina had overpowered Oleg somehow. Or there was news from Holmes or Esme.

Only Holmes had left a message: "We're looking for the kids. Church members said they were driven away by the Fourth Street Kings gang." But what perplexed Lana was Holmes's order: "Tell Don."

She followed Holmes's directive.

Don listened, studying the sea with the binoculars Lana had set down. Still no sign of Red or Veal. He had her repeat the message before responding: "Tell your boss to set up communications directly between me and Michael Prince. He's their leader."

"Why, Don? I can't just tell Holmes to do that."

"Yes, you can because Prince and I have some history. That's why he told you to tell me. Now do it, and then you can tell me why you never said a word about *our* daughter going missing."

Lana messaged Holmes. Looking up, she remembered all too vividly the reason she'd never told Don about Emma: she'd figured a convicted drug dealer would be useless in this situation.

"You're right," she said to him. "I should have told you. I'm sorry."

Don held the binoculars on Galina's trawler. Without lowering them, he responded to Lana: "Goddamn right you should have told me. I know that crew. They run a lot of drugs in DC. They're fully integrated vertically, from the Colombian producers down to street dealing. You do *not* fuck with them. But guess what?" He lowered the binoculars and stared at his ex-wife. "You do *not* fuck with our daughter."

At any other time in their lives, Lana would have considered Don's words mere bluster. But she didn't now. Maybe it was nothing more than hope on her part, but she'd been seeing a different side of him since the shades had been lifted on his secret life. It was a scary side, to be sure, but she was deeply grateful to discover it. They needed someone who might spark fear in the men who'd taken Emma. Maybe he could do the same to Oleg Dernov—or just kill him.

There was still no sign of him or Galina.

● ● ●

Emma and Tanesa had been squashed into the Hummer's backseat between two "soldiers." That was what the big guy called the young men next to each of them. The pair called him Prince. Both had semiautomatic pistols pressed into Emma's and Tanesa's sides.

"They know to shoot if you try any shit. You hear?" Prince said from the front passenger seat. A guy almost as large was behind the wheel.

"Yes," Emma said. Whatever defiance she'd felt at the edge of the flood had been overwhelmed as surely as the sandbag wall.

"They don't need any permission," Prince went on, "because they've got all they need."

The big beast of an SUV plowed right through the flooded streets of southeast DC, one of the most violent neighborhoods in the U.S. They came to a warehouse district, where the flood had receded to less than six inches. Other than the water, the area was empty.

The driver gunned the engine, racing up a concrete ramp toward the loading dock behind a windowless brick building. There were five doors, each large enough to accommodate a Freightliner.

The driver clicked a remote on the sun visor. The door in the center rose so swiftly the Hummer never had to stop moving. As soon as they rolled into the darkness inside, the door closed behind them.

Then the driver hit another button on the remote, which switched on ceiling lights that illuminated rows of long wooden crates stacked three high.

"Now get out," Prince said. "But if you try any hide-and-seek with us, we'll make you wish you drowned back there."

Emma believed him. She didn't sense a single bit of bluff in his words or manner.

"On the other hand, do what you're told and you might live," he added with an unpleasant grin.

Emma and Tanesa piled out of the backseat.

"What's all this stuff?" Tanesa asked, staring at the long narrow crates.

"You can't tell by the shape? You're too white for a black girl. Kids around here, they don't need to look twice. Show them, Ship."

The driver, his thick arms only a little tensed by the weight of the nearest crate, lowered it to the floor.

He unsnapped metal buckles that Emma hadn't noticed till then and opened the top. A gleaming mahogany casket, corners padded with custom-fitted Styrofoam cushions, appeared.

"Someone I know well gave me the keys to this place," Prince told them. "Maybe 'cause I'm so good for business, you hear? Open that up. Girl should see where she's bedding down for the next day or two."

"What!" Tanesa exclaimed. "Don't do that to me. I'm scared to death of tight spaces. That's my nightmare."

Emma put her arm around Tanesa's back. "Hold on," she whispered.

"That's cute," Prince bellowed. "White girl getting close with her black girlfriend. Makes me all warm inside. Maybe we should squeeze them both inside that thing. Yeah, that's what we should do."

"No!" Tanesa screamed.

Prince strolled over to them. He pushed Emma aside and glared at Tanesa. "You look at me, girl. You're going to get your black ass in that coffin or I'm going to cut your heart out and put you in there for good."

Just that fast he pulled out a switchblade and clicked it open.

"Oh, Jesus, oh, Jesus, help me," Tanesa said, as Prince shoved her into the casket.

While the others laughed, Emma looked around. She thought if it had been a movie she would have seen something to save them, but she saw nothing but stacks and stacks of crates. A lot of coffins. It sickened her to know that sooner or later they'd all be filled from the flooding. *And other kinds of death.*

She looked back at Tanesa, who had curled into a fetal position.

Prince was leaning over her. "Get on your back and put your hands across your pretty chest," he snapped at her. "And keep your big browns open."

Tanesa, tears streaming down her cheeks, obeyed.

"Get another one over here for ivory," Prince ordered. "Line it up, and get our cameraman," he told one of the soldiers. "We need the video."

Emma lay down in a matching coffin, wondering if they'd actually close them up and how long they'd keep them locked inside.

Prince ordered the cameraman, a short skinny man with big glasses, to take video of them lying side by side. He raised his camera and went to work.

Nobody spoke until Prince walked over and stared at Tanesa. "We'll bury you alive," he told her. "I've done it before, and I'll do it to you. That's why they call me 'The Undertaker.' You'll be in there all by yourself, six feet under, and there'll be no chance in hell anyone will ever hear you."

Prince slowly lowered the lid on Tanesa's unearthly screams and her hopeless attempt to keep him from closing the coffin. Locking it muffled her anguish so effectively it might not have been heard five feet away.

Then he closed Emma's casket. She was terrified, too, but mostly that they'd load her onto a vehicle because that could mean burial. She couldn't bear to let herself even think about that. Instead, she prayed as best she could, which she realized might never be good enough.

And she hoped—oh, God how she hoped—that she wouldn't run out of air because they might not have thought of that.

• • •

Oleg and Galina were fighting furiously, rolling across the trawler's deck. Early in their struggle, she had kicked him hard enough to break his stranglehold and back him into a bulkhead-mounted grappling hook. When he'd reached down, as if to grab the knife-wielding hand of an attacker, she'd twisted her head away, squirming and punching. Gasping for air, she'd fought madly to get away from him.

He swung wildly at her now, striking her mouth and drawing blood from her lips. She stumbled backward, looking for any help she could find on the deck. Her fear of dying at his hands was great, but nothing compared to her dread for Alexandra once she was gone.

As he moved toward her, she remembered he'd slipped his gun into the back of his pants, cocky enough—or so vengeful— that he wanted to make her murder as personal as possible. But when she tried to circle around him to reach for his weapon, he seized her hand.

"I know you want the gun, and you'll get it."

Galina tried to pull away, but his other hand latched on. Before she could fight back, he forced her onto her knees, his hands like steel clamps around her neck once more.

"Stupid girl. You could have had the whole world with me."

Galina tried to speak, a futile effort with him draining the last of her air. But he must have wanted to hear her because he eased up just enough for her to cough and say, "I had nothing with you but lies. Better dead than with you."

He pressed his thumbs back into her neck and snapped her head around. "I will strangle your cancer kid next. I promise."

His eyes bulged with anger, and his hands squeezed harder. She couldn't break his grip. She looked around frantically once more. Anything.

There.

The cop was frantically trying to work his hands free from the bench where he'd been tied up. All she had was hope, spurred by his offer of help only minutes ago.

Get his gun, she thought at the cop. *The gun.*

Galina fought for every extra second of life now, pounding Oleg's hands, but to no avail. She began to black out. The cop had loosened the rope, but was still entangled in it.

Galina threw a desperate punch, trying to pound Oleg's scrotum. She missed, but alarm filled his face, and she guessed she must have come close. She tried again. He caught her fist this time.

He was still choking her, but with only one hand. She was grabbing half breaths, telling herself she just needed a few seconds more.

His gun. Grab it. Staring at the cop again, hoping he really was on her side. Black splotches appeared before her eyes. The cop rose to his feet.

The gun, she pleaded silently one last time.

But the cop would never get it because Oleg reached back right then and grabbed his nine millimeter. He shoved the barrel into Galina's mouth.

She choked.

He laughed. "What does this remind you of, bad girl?"

Then he froze: The cop had the muzzle of Galina's hunting rifle pressed against the back of Oleg's head. The only part of him moving now was his mouth:

"You will be tortured and killed unless you put that down now."

"No. It's not what I will do," the cop replied. "It's what you will do. Take the gun out of her mouth or you're a dead man."

"No, he's not," a voice called from the stern.

Galina could just make out a red-haired guy with swim goggles propped on his forehead. He was pointing a bulky handgun at Oleg, who was now targeted from two positions.

"I'm Lieutenant John Walker," the man said. "U.S. Navy. We don't want him dead. So, Oleg, if you put down your weapon, we can do business. Otherwise, we'll have to let him shoot you."

"Put it down," the cop yelled, jamming the barrel into Oleg's head hard enough to draw blood.

Oleg kept the gun in Galina's mouth, but he'd eased the pressure until she was no longer choking.

"I want to go to Moscow," Oleg yelled at Walker.

"We want you to go back there, too," the lieutenant replied. "That's the honest-to-God truth. We don't want anything messy happening out here."

The Russian cop smacked the side of Oleg's head with the barrel. "I will shoot this son of a bitch, no matter what he says, if he doesn't get that gun out of her mouth."

Oleg slowly withdrew it.

"Put the gun on the deck," Lieutenant Walker said. "In front of you."

"Moscow?" Oleg said.

"Moscow," Walker echoed.

What choice does he have? Galina wondered. *They've got him both ways.*

The SEAL walked up and grabbed the nine millimeter. "You're a Russian policeman, right?" he said to the cop, who nodded. "I'd like you to stand down."

"I want asylum in the U.S. I can't go back. Did you hear what he said? They'll torture and kill me."

"You've got asylum," Walker replied quickly.

"A guy in flippers," the cop looked Walker over, "can do that."

"This guy can," Walker said, removing the cumbersome fins.

The cop lowered the rifle.

It disgusted Galina that Oleg was going to get away. He had his eyes on the navy guy, his hands off her, so she tried again with her uppercut, this time smashing his ballsack so hard Oleg doubled over and fell facedown on the deck.

She fell back herself, sitting heavily on her rear. The navy lieutenant gave her a thumbs-up. The cop was smiling.

"Are you a SEAL?" the cop asked Walker.

"I've been called worse," Walker replied. He grabbed the back of Oleg's shirt and pulled him into a sitting position. "Sit up so I can watch you."

Oleg looked green. Galina edged away, almost tripping over Captain Younes's body. She hurried to check on Alexandra. Another SEAL appeared near the bow.

"You two had it covered," the cop said to Walker.

"We try. You made it a helluva lot easier than it would have been. Saved her, too. Nice job."

"I was going to kill him."

"We couldn't let you do that."

"You going to trade him for that NSA guy, something like that?" the cop asked.

"*Something* like that," Walker answered.

"I've got a better idea," Oleg gasped to Walker. "I'll stop those missiles. Just give me my computer and you won't even have to take me back to Moscow. My own people will come get me."

"Who the hell do you think you're dealing with here?" the lieutenant replied. "SpongeBob? You'll never get your hands on another computer. And I never said *we* were taking you back there. Veal, get his wrists and ankles."

The SEAL slapped plastic cuffs top and bottom on Oleg.

For a moment, Oleg looked worried. Then he lifted his head and his most imperious expression appeared.

With Oleg shackled, Galina carried Alexandra into the cabin. She watched Veal and the cop board the trawler's own Zodiac.

"He's going to take him over to the sailboat and get Lana Elkins," Red told her.

Right then Galina pointed to the trawler Oleg had hijacked. It had stopped moving. "His computer," she said. "It's probably over there." She spotted the captain through the window she'd shot out, relieved he was still alive.

"Friend or foe?" Red asked her.

"He was hijacked."

Walker rushed to the stern. "Search the trawler for his electronics, computer, phone, anything he left there," he called to Veal. "The captain should be okay." Then the lieutenant used the ship's radio to talk to Lana. "Tell NSA we're set for Stage Two. Veal's coming over to get you. Galina's waiting."

"What's Stage Two?" Oleg demanded as soon as Walker put down the mouthpiece.

"Your flight out of here."

• • •

Ten precious minutes passed, mostly in silence, then Lana Elkins climbed aboard with Veal. She carried a large computer case and Oleg's laptop.

"So you're Lana Elkins," Oleg said.

"She's a big reason you're sitting on the deck of this boat all ready to be shipped back to Moscow," Walker said.

Lana said nothing to Oleg. She walked up to Galina and introduced herself, then glanced into the cabin where Galina's laptop sat on a table. "I see you have yours ready. I've got mine, too, and his, but first *he* has to be thoroughly searched."

"Keep her away from me," Oleg said, staring at Galina.

"Stand back," Red said to her.

"What did you do to him?" Lana asked Galina.

The Russian motioned upward with her fist, then pointed to his crotch.

"What goes around comes around, right?"

Galina glared at Oleg. "Let's hope so."

Red and Veal found a pair of camera memory cards and three thumb drives in Oleg's pockets.

"Awfully casual about your data," Lana said to him. His pants were down around his bound ankles.

"Bend over," Red told him.

When Oleg refused, the lieutenant grabbed Oleg's privates. He bent over.

"It's nothing," Oleg said about the memory cards, and grimacing from Red's rude intrusion. "Tourist shit."

If so, it had been a grim detour, Lana saw after inserting one of the cards into her camera. It revealed photos of a dead nun and a terrified expression on the face of a naked young woman backed into a corner. The second card focused less on the murder and more on violent sex. Oleg had taken a ton of pictures.

"Did you kill her, too?" Lana asked Oleg, pointing to the younger woman.

"I have diplomatic immunity," he replied.

"In your own country?" Lana shook her head, then used a virtual machine to reveal the contents of the first thumb drive; she would never have stuck a stick with unknown data into her own computer. Rows and rows of code appeared. She scrolled down.

"What is it?" she asked, expecting no answer. She didn't get one, either, not from him.

"I might know," Galina said.

The other two thumb drives contained the same kind of material. Lana handed them over to Galina, who hurried into the cabin and went to work. Lana turned her attention back to Oleg: "Give me the codes you used on the *Delphin,* and I'll make sure you live." More than anything, she feared a second Trident

II launch—or a whole series of launches; the submarine, after all, still had twenty-three missiles in its arsenal.

"Don't they tell you anything?" Oleg replied. "I'm going back to Moscow."

"Look at me," Lana said. "I've just been authorized to tell you that there are men in Moscow who are going to kill you as soon as you arrive. That's all I can say, unless you cooperate. If you cooperate, we'll take you back to the U.S. and tell the Russians and some others to go to hell. We're willing to break some very critical deals we've been making lately if you're willing to cooperate. But don't fuck with us. If you come and don't play ball, we'll make every remaining second of your life a misery."

"Yes, you Americans are good at torture now. I'll never go with you. You say they'll kill me in Moscow? No, you are the one who should worry about dying, you stupid bitch. I know who you are. Big hero last time. Not such a hero now."

Red squatted in front of him. "Oleg, you're in handcuffs. Think about that. She's giving you the best offer you'll ever get."

"Come live in America," Oleg singsonged. "You think you can always play that trump card: 'Come live in America.' I'd rather die on this stinking fishing boat than go live in your country. And I'm not giving you any codes."

"I think we've got them," Galina called from the cabin.

"You realize that right now Galina's sharing everything she ever learned from you with the NSA via satellite," Lana said. "Nothing's going to end the way you wanted."

"Yes, it is. There's one more surprise you have coming, I assure you," he told her.

Lana wanted to swear, but kept an impassive expression. "Listen to me, you're going to die if you go back. We've been intercepting communications between your President and his staff, and they're making one thing abundantly clear: you're expendable.

There's a chopper coming for you. If you don't cooperate, you'll be getting on it and you'll die."

"What, are they going to fly way up into the sky and throw me out like you Americans do?"

Lana grabbed his face and made him look into her eyes. "It'll be worse than that."

"You can't scare me. And I don't believe you because if I were in your shoes, I'd be saying the same thing and it would all be lies."

"But I'm not you, you're not in my shoes, and I'm not lying." Oleg shook his head.

Disbelief is denial's first ally, Lana thought.

A helicopter flew toward them. Oleg smiled at her. "Fuck you. I'll be eating caviar at the Kremlin before the sun goes down."

"You stupid son of a bitch," she said.

"It's his call at this point," Walker said. "We'll be keeping the deals we made."

"I know all about deals," Oleg said to them. "Russians take care of their own."

"Yes, you do have a long history of that," Walker said, smiling when a man was lowered from the helicopter on a steel cable with a double seat.

"Who's that?" Oleg demanded when he saw that his rescuer was Chinese. "See, we take care of people who help us, too," Red told him. "And since you've decided your future is short, I'll let you in on something. Our Chinese friends call themselves *Magic Dragon*, and they were instrumental in blocking radio signals on the high seas, when others might have warned you that we were coming to take you. They also provided a terrific amount of cyberexpertise tracking down your tight network. Now they're going to use you to pay *their* debt to someone you know very well."

Veal and the Chinese man seized Oleg and strapped him into a seat.

"What is this shit?" Oleg said. He sounded unsettled for the first time. "What's going on?"

"Come with us," Lana said.

"It's too late," Red said softly, barely above the sound of the chopper.

"But I'm going to Moscow . . ." Oleg's voice trailed off as he and his escort were lifted up into the helicopter's cabin.

• • •

The first thing Oleg noticed was that the bird was being flown by a Russian crew. But the cabin itself held four other Chinese men.

"What are *they* doing here?" Oleg yelled at the pilot, who ignored him. With his headset on, the man might not have heard Oleg.

"Do any of you speak English or Russian?" he asked the Chinese men.

"I do," replied the man who'd brought him aboard.

"Who do you work for?" Oleg asked.

The man smiled. "An oil and gas company."

"That asshole. PP's saving me?"

"PP? No, we call him Mr. Dernov. He is a partner of our country. Saving you?" The Chinese man shrugged and smiled even more broadly.

A horrible flood of anxiety swept through Oleg. He remembered the video PP had played for him of Dmitri and Galina down in that goddamned museum with its medieval . . . devices, and how fortunate he'd felt when he raced his Maserati away from his father's estate.

This wasn't a rescue. This was retribution.

CHAPTER 26

LANA SAT IN THE trawler's cabin holding Oleg's computer on her lap with all the care she would have given to a Fabergé egg. Galina was perched by her side, working on her own device, but she nodded at Oleg's.

"It's all going to be in there," she said. "And on these." Galina held up the thumb drives. "He was a control freak. He wouldn't have surrendered the freedom to launch to anyone else, no matter what he might have told them."

Lana's own laptop lay on a small navigation table feet away. Red was piloting the ship. With the boat pitching from stern to bow in the unsettled sea, Lana was finding it awkward to work her keyboard. She noticed that Galina was facing the same challenge.

Less than ideal work conditions, but with stubby black antennas protruding from all three computers, they did have vital satellite links to the NSA—and that meant stateside support from Jeff Jensen. Even so, Lana was running into one computer security defense after another: "I can't even get into Oleg's trash," she growled.

Lana was frustrated, but still grateful the cyberbeast hadn't tossed his laptop overboard. She figured he was too arrogant to have believed there would ever be any call for such an extreme action. But for all the progress Lana was making hacking the device, it might as well have been jettisoned.

She had just resorted to dumpster diving, a hacker term that held the same meaning for them as it did for the hungry homeless: plundering someone else's trash. But again she'd failed to penetrate Oleg's access controls.

"I put a keystroke logger on him two weeks ago," Galina informed her, "when I first started to worry about what he was doing. If it worked, we should have a record of everything he's done since then. But we need deciphering software to read out the results superfast."

"I have that," Lana said, leaning forward so her fingers could fly over her own keyboard on the navigation table. "But he could have used a virtual keyboard to prevent the capture of his keys, or even changed his character encoding."

They hadn't kept Oleg on board to try to coerce his cooperation because Lana knew he could have led them right into a cyber self-destruct payload, which, as the name suggested, could wipe out the data they wanted.

Complicating matters more was a message that had just come in from Jensen that he'd found data streams from Donetsk in eastern Ukraine that he thought might prove fruitful. The data had been submitted to the Black Sea—most likely to Oleg—and the southern Atlantic Ocean, most likely Lisko.

Did the data to Lisko contain an alert about Oleg's capture? That was what worried Lana most.

The data streams all but confirmed that Oleg had been working with more than one far-flung conspirator. If one or both of those men didn't already know he'd been taken into custody, she wondered how soon they'd find out their mastermind had been forcibly removed from their attack plan. What contingency had they planned in that case? Plus, Oleg might even have buried a heartbeat signal deep in his software to launch the missile—or all twenty-three of them—if he went incommunicado for a specified period of time.

"I'm in!" Galina announced. The deciphering software had worked and she'd penetrated a flash drive. "Here," she copied lines of code onto Lana's computer.

"Why do you think this will work?" Lana asked. It looked like thousands of letters and numbers.

"The sequencing. Pattern recognition. I have a good eye for it. It's similar to data he gave me that helped me access Professor Ahearn's computer before I found out about the murders. Just try it."

Lana did, this time landing smack into Oleg's trash bin— only to find he'd cyber-incinerated everything.

Wanting to tear out her hair, she realized he—or an accomplice aboard—might have installed a rootkit, an intrusion into the submarine's computers that would remain almost undetectable. *What a frickin' nightmare.* It was malware that allowed a hacker remote entry, but also hid its own tracks even as it provided openings for polymorphic malware—attack software that could not only spread quickly from one system to another, but also change its file hashes, persistence mechanisms, access codes, and locations in memory *every* time it duplicated itself.

If she could track down the rootkit, she could start roaming the submarine's computers, too—or send in her own worms to disable the *Delphin's* entire system. Shutting down power and lights would certainly hamper the manual efforts necessary to launch the missiles.

But any keystroke could also set off a virtual trip wire that would launch them. Lana watched Galina typing away frantically, breaking only to sweep her fingers across the screen to move data. As calmly as she could, she voiced her worry.

"I'm working strictly with his own code right now, and I'm

not altering anything." Then she stared at Lana. "What choice do we have?"

She's right. They had no choice. That was when it also occurred to Lana that a conspirator—in the eastern Ukraine or on the *Delphin?*—might at that very moment also be trying to penetrate Oleg's defenses, but with a different goal: to empty the sub's arsenal so all of the WAIS would shatter into the sea and drive ocean levels up the full eleven feet.

She felt like they were in a race with a phantom that was already haunting Oleg's systems. In the next few seconds she learned she was right: Oleg's screen burst alive with Grisha Lisko smiling at Lana as he stood in the Missile Control Center. He exhibited no surprise at her presence. The dead bodies of sailors lay in the background. Lana figured he was sending his signal through the submerged submarine's radio buoy.

"I know what you're doing, but you're too late." Lisko held up the captain's key. "We're ready to fire. You can watch, but that's all you can do."

Galina gripped Lana's arm, whispering, "*That* man is crazy."

"You know him?" Lana asked.

"No, but look at him."

Lisko was joined by two other sailors on the screen for the first time, though Lana knew the previously unseen collaborators had to have been present when Antarctica was bombed.

Lisko turned around and slipped the captain's key into the console. He smiled as he grabbed a microphone. "Ready the Tactical Firing Trigger." Then he cranked the key he'd just inserted. Lana knew the officer to whom he'd just spoken must be using a second key in another part of the sub so they could unleash the lethal madness once again. Two keys in separate locations—in combination with other security precautions—had once been thought sufficient to stop an unauthorized missile attack. But that had been in the era before cyberwar.

One more missile on Antarctica and even Noah's mythical flood would look like a kitchen spill. Twenty-three more would mean death to billions.

"How much time?" Galina asked.

"Thirty seconds," Lana replied. "Maybe."

• • •

Emma lay in the blackness of the coffin trying to control her growing panic. Unlike Tanesa, Emma's intense fear didn't stem directly from a lack of space, but a distinct lack of air. Her worst fears of using up the oxygen in the tight confines were coming true, sending her anxiety levels rocketing upwards. She was terrified of an asthma attack, and knew that her fear alone could trigger one.

Don't panic! But she was screaming that warning to herself.

She attempted every trick she'd ever used to try to calm down but they all involved breathing, so they didn't work when breathing brought so little relief. A big gulp of air led only to the next big gulp . . . and the next.

In biology last year they'd studied expiration and learned that as carbon dioxide became more concentrated, it made you drowsy. And if you didn't get oxygen at that point, it would put you in a coma and kill you.

With the last of her strength, Emma tried to beat on the lid, but even to her ears, just inches from the impact, the sound was muffled, weak, not enough to raise the nearly dead.

• • •

"He's got to have used a Trojan to get in there," Lana said, her mind racing wildly for a way to stop Lisko as he sat in the Missile Control Center. Trojans were malware that were supposed to look like regular programs, but were designed to take out specific targets, including cyberdefenses. In her less frenetic moments, Lana thought of them as a cyberwarrior's smart bombs. But if she or Galina could possibly find a Trojan that Oleg had inserted into his computer as a defense mechanism—and Galina was still working at a furious pace—they could activate its destructive potential, perhaps on a key part of the sub's system.

Galina was down to her last thumb drive. She must have read a thousand lines of code in the last minute because she'd been scrolling without stopping. "Maybe this," Galina said, highlighting a line and shooting it over to Lana.

Lana used it, knowing at this point she was relying completely on code Galina had culled from countless lines under enormous pressure.

But she got you into his computer that way.

In moments, Lana entered the line onto Oleg's screen and activated the code. It felt like a shot in the dark. Then they waited to see if they'd collaborated successfully. What else could they do if the code didn't work?

The answer came to Lana in a flash: a *kinetic* attack. She messaged Holmes about the thick data stream the hacker had established with the submarine. If the NSA could detect it—and with extraordinary speed—they might stop the launch in time.

As Lisko began to speak into the microphone again, the lights on the submarine went out. Blackness filled Oleg's screen where Lisko's head had been visible a blink before.

"What does that mean?" Galina sounded as surprised as Lana felt. Had the sub's missile launched? Or was the *vessel* dead in the water?

• • •

Prince's phone vibrated in his pocket. He figured he finally had Lana Elkins on the line. *Bitch better be ready to do some business, use her clout to get his soldiers out of the federal pen down in Middleburg, Virginia.*

But it wasn't Lana Elkins. It was freaking Don Fedder. *What the fuck?* Talk about prison . . . Prince hadn't heard from him in years. "I can't talk to you, man. I'm waiting for an important call, so *adios amigo.*" Last time he saw Fedder they'd shared a few *cervezas* down on a beach in Colombia as white as the coke Prince sold by the truckload. Fedder hadn't been a competitor; he'd moved pot—*tons* of it.

"No," Don shouted. "I am that call. That girl you've got, the one named Emma Elkins, she's mine. *My* kid!"

Kid? Since when did Don ever have a kid? "You're fuckin' with me, right?" But hearing Fedder's words worried Prince because Don was a lot of things, but never a bullshitter.

"Listen to me carefully, Prince. We all make a mistake once in a while. It's part of the game." The "game," what he and Fedder had called the drug trade back then. They'd never been super close, more like colleagues from different companies in the same industry. They'd only come to know each other as fellow expatriates down in South America. But Prince had liked Don. The guy'd known how to survive—till he got busted on his boat.

That old familiar voice was growing more and more serious in his ear: "And you made a big mistake grabbing those two girls. That young black woman is Emma's best friend."

Oh, shit. Prince saw where this was going. He shook his head.

"You don't believe me," Don went on, "you ask Emma who her dad is."

"Okay, I got it," Prince replied, still shaking his head, already imagining the fury on the faces of his men down in Middleburg.

"Remember the deal I made with you six years ago? You got to keep your garden . . ." Prince's coca plantation about a hundred miles from Cali. "And the road in and out of there . . ." His smuggling route. "And you gave me those addresses." FARC *jefes.* "Remember?"

"I hear you," Prince replied noncommittally, not knowing who the fuck was listening in, but appreciating Don's discretion on the line.

"I'm glad you remember," Fedder said, "because you've got to get Emma home. And I hope to hell you don't have her in one of your coffins."

Don knew about them because Prince once told him they served three purposes: the first was to smuggle coke in the hollow walls, bottoms, and lids; the second was to imprison informants and scare them to death; and the third was to bury them, when necessary.

Prince was already opening Emma's lid and nodding at Ship to free her friend.

"They're out, even as we speak, Don."

"Let me talk to Emma."

"Here she is."

Prince stepped back while the girl, who sounded a little breathy to him, talked to her father. The sister looked shaky.

"Shit, girl," he said to Tanesa. "I'm sorry. I had no idea you all were tight with big Don Fedder."

Tanesa looked puzzled at Don's name coming out of Prince's mouth.

Emma handed Prince's phone back to him. Prince studied her face.

She kind of looks like him. The shit you don't know about people.

"Like I say, Don, I didn't know. She doesn't have your name."

"Yeah, well, blame that one on her mom. One more thing, Prince."

"Yeah, you got it."

"You still have that bulletproof Hummer?"

"Newer model."

"Armed guards."

"More than ever."

"Use all that to get those two back to my daughter's house safely in Bethesda. You do that and I'll help you with the feds, if you ever need it."

"You're saying I've got a chit I can cash."

"Yeah, that's what I'm saying."

"Good, but I was going to do it anyway, Don. I'd never leave them hanging around this hood."

"Thanks."

"Back atcha."

Prince put away his phone and looked at Emma and Tanesa. "Hey, you two, I'm sorry. Sometimes a man makes a mistake, so I'm going to take you home. Thing is, to seal the deal, you got to forget any of this happened. This place, all of it. You cool with that?"

"My dad already told me, and I told her. We're cool."

Tanesa was nodding beside Emma.

A minute later they were back in the Hummer, just them and Prince and the rising waters of the Potomac parting for his beastly SUV.

• • •

Lana waved Red into the cabin. He put the wheel on autopilot and hurried to the doorway. "It's over," she told him. "The *Delphin* was taken out by a P-8." The navy jets had been airborne over the southern ocean since the news of the hijacking broke. "The sub-killer nailed it with a torpedo after locking onto the data stream."

"Nice work," Red said.

"The submarine? Sunk?" Galina asked.

"Yes," Lana replied. "It's gone," she added, as she messaged the news to Don.

Red shook his head. "Man, the damage those sons of bitches did."

Lana nodded. "The next thing we're going to hear, you watch, is the Russians saying Dernov was just another one of their rogue hackers working all on his own for patriotic purposes. They'll be covering their crimes by providing some data after the damage was done, and the net result is we lose 150 or more sailors, a nuclear-armed sub, and the whole world is flooded. But fuck if they'll get away with it," Lana cursed. "We've got his computer. We'll do the forensics. We got into it, and now we'll track down his links to whoever he was working with, wherever they are."

But even as she spoke, Lana had her doubts. Shaking her head, she wondered how much cyberscrubbing was going on as she and Galina were working with tiny antennas and three laptops on the high seas.

Red looked up from a handheld device. "Here's a report that Ukrainian separatists have abducted a hacker who goes by the handle *Numero Uno* across the border into Russia. I'm guessing he's about to meet his new bosses."

Lana felt even more dejected. She had hoped to follow those data streams to Oleg's other conspirator.

She looked at Oleg's black screen. There was nothing there, nothing for all the families of the men and women who'd died so miserably—and so publicly—on the *Delphin*. There would never be any body retrieval for any of them. She hoped Oleg was dying a death equal to all their pain. *And then some.*

A message from Holmes brightened her mood immeasurably: Emma and Tanesa had just arrived back home. Lana shared it immediately with her companions on the trawler, then with Don on *Storm Season,* adding, "Thanks for whatever you did."

"You're welcome," Don texted back. "I'm just glad that nightmare is over. I know it's been horrible for you. It's been horrible for me."

She wanted to hug him. It scared her to realize that. Really hold him and let the swell rock them together.

What are you thinking? she scolded herself.

Red checked the autopilot and ducked back into the cabin. "Your ex must have some kind of clout with one of the heaviest hands in the DC drug trade."

Lana nodded. Mostly, she wondered if Don was starting to have that kind of clout with her heart. It was as if he'd slipped a rootkit into it. Information security specialists feared the damage rootkits could do once they were loose in a system. Lana worried Don's own version was already breaking down the access controls surrounding her heart.

No, she barked at herself. *Don't go confusing gratitude with . . . With what?* she asked herself earnestly. *With love? Lust? With wanting to have your family back together again?*

She sat in the cabin trembling, hoping neither Galina nor Red noticed.

Look, she finally told herself in exasperation, *he saved their lives. You're hugely relieved. That's all it is. Get a grip.*

That was her story, and for a few seconds—certainly no more—she stuck to it.

Then she slipped past Red and stood near the stern, waiting. In seconds, *Storm Season* rose with the sea. She saw Don and waved, knowing she'd be on that swell soon enough.

EPILOGUE

LANA SAT WITH GALINA and Jeff Jensen at a large oval table in a secure conference room at CyberFortress, where they'd been working together since the seas stopped rising three weeks earlier. World leaders said earth was now in a "Post-Flood Era," though "flood" felt inaccurate to Lana and most other scientists because it suggested the water that had surged across so many coastlines and overtaken so many cities would eventually recede. That was not going to happen in anything short of geologic time.

The six glaciers of the West Antarctic Ice Sheet had been ruthlessly unsettled by the nuclear strike and might well have reached a tipping point that could lead to the loss of the entire WAIS and the eleven-foot rise in sea level. There was no question that the missile strike directly on Thwaites Glacier had sent it moving in fits and starts to the sea. Four feet of sea-level rise had been recorded so far, even more than scientists had feared. But Thwaites appeared to have stabilized, which was to say that it was still moving toward the Amundsen Sea but at a reduced rate. "Appeared to" was the language of uncertainty that kept scientists, political leaders, and informed citizens on tenterhooks.

The death toll in the U.S. was estimated at 230,000, mostly from widespread drowning, though thousands had died of thirst and starvation in the ensuing mayhem. More would likely die from dysentery and other rapidly spreading diseases. Then there was the long-term impact of poisonous radiation spreading across the globe.

At least the number of fatalities could be estimated. The damage to the country's infrastructure was incalculable. Many trillions of dollars, at least. The damage was so extensive—and still getting surveyed—that nobody could estimate it more accurately so soon after the catastrophe.

The Eastern Seaboard and West Coast had taken the hardest hits as the added weight to the oceans from the massive release of ice affected earth's rotation, forcing its gravitational field northward. The subsidence of so much land along the Eastern Seaboard, which had been exacerbated by the drought-driven pumping of groundwater in recent years, compounded the damage from rising seas. More than ten million Americans had been forced from their homes in that part of the country alone. The central and southern California coast was also flooded, displacing six million and drowning at least twenty thousand. Rescue workers were still dredging for bodies along both of America's coastlines.

Lower Manhattan appeared lost forever, its poorest residents now crowded into shelters; their wealthier counterparts had fled to their second or third homes in dryer locales. While the value of the U.S. dollar was fluctuating wildly—measured against the Russian ruble, now the currency of choice worldwide—it could still buy a lot, but not luxurious apartments in a city in which absolutely none were available.

There was even talk of moving the nation's capital. Giant sump pumps had yet to drain most of the water from the National

Mall. Many government offices, including the President's, had already moved to more secure enclaves inland.

More than $400 billion worth of Miami real estate, including the city's iconic waterfront high-rises, had become complete write-offs with the flooding undermining the structural integrity of the buildings to such an extent that one had already toppled into the sea. Others were leaning at Pisa-like angles.

Bad as conditions were in the U.S., Asia faced far greater crises. Four of the hardest-hit cities were in China: Shanghai, Guangzhou, Tianjin, and Ningbo had suffered more than a million deaths. Fifteen million residents of those cities now found themselves homeless, starving, and dying by the thousands every day. Those tragedies were trumped only by the twin catastrophes of Dhaka, Bangladesh and Kolkata, India, where accurate body counts—certainly of many millions—might never be known, for the flooding that had claimed those low-lying cites also swept innumerable dead out to sea.

South America and Europe were still reeling, too. The latter was besieged not only by internally displaced citizens but also by a massive number of refugees from Africa. Most European countries had tried to close their borders, if they still had them. Hardest hit, of course, was the Netherlands, with more than 60 percent of the country now underwater, where all those fields and towns and cities were destined to remain. Even the nation's sophisticated system of dikes, dams, floodgates, and pumping stations had not withstood the towering tidal surges that came with the four-foot rise in sea levels.

Neither had the Thames Barrier in London, where raging currents had rushed down the city's historic streets, drowning thousands.

Down Under was no different. Following storm surges the distinctive roof of Sydney's famed opera house now rose from the flooded harbor like the dorsal fins of giant sharks, as if those carnivorous beasts had grown large on the feeding grounds of that dying city.

It was difficult to point to any place on earth that remained unaffected, though Russia had escaped relatively unscathed. Which had led to a wholly different form of finger-pointing. Furious leaders from across the globe had been charging for weeks that Russia had nurtured the cyberterrorist who had turned the earth into a charnel house. Russia leaders, including its outspoken President, had just as vehemently denied the accusations, allowing only that "a terribly misguided rogue patriot might have wreaked such havoc."

Lana and her team had not found a smoking gun to prove otherwise; the trail in Oleg's computer had turned cold. Even worse, they realized the files for the technology that over time would have sucked carbon dioxide from the atmosphere—and stopped the deadly thawing—had been deleted by a virtual trip wire in the mastermind's laptop.

"It was his final 'fuck you' to the world," Galina said, sitting back.

"Would he really have done *that*?" Lana could hardly believe anyone would have taken such world-changing—world-*saving*—knowledge to the grave.

"Control freak, in everything," Galina replied, repeating words Lana had heard from her before.

Despite the outcry and opposition, Russia had emerged as the world's preeminent power. The U.S. still had the largest arsenal of nuclear weapons, but was so consumed with delivering emergency relief to its citizens, while trying to maintain the integrity of its vastly shifting borders, that it could hardly mount a challenge to Russia's overnight hegemony.

Most of the U.S. Army had been deployed to try to maintain order. Breakdowns of every type were threatening the lives and livelihoods of almost all Americans. And with interstate and local highways underwater, the Air Force was making food drops all along the nation's coastlines, which had led to wild gunfights over the scarce provisions.

Lana had hoped for a breather after the *Delphin's* sinking and Dernov's death, which had been by the most medieval means possible. A video of his demise in a skull crusher had been posted on YouTube. But she and others in the intelligence community were witnessing a great unsettling spread across the world. Populations were on the move, hundreds of thousands in boats seeking homes wherever they could. Despite its problems, America remained the preferred destination for millions—and the target of terrorists whose hatred of the U.S. had only been whetted by the country's sudden vulnerabilities.

Only this morning Deputy Director Holmes had tasked Lana and her team with tracking the chatter of radical Islamists. Holmes had informed them the NSA had intercepted communications that made their violent intentions known, but not their precise targets or tools. "They did it in the most oblique language," he'd explained. "It'll make sense when you read the briefing paper I've had prepared for you."

The paper noted several jihadist references to a "new" weapon for suicide bombers, which now had Lana, Galina, and Jeff researching what could possibly constitute the latest development in suicide bombs. In just the past year and a half, jihadists had gone so far as to stuff a nuclear weapon into a backpack.

Could it actually get worse than that?

Lana had her doubts. And jihadists weren't above using disinformation against their enemies. They'd become savvy enough to provide it in heavily encrypted communications, with the understanding that the harder the threat was to decipher, the more it might be valued.

But she and her colleagues could take no threat lightly, not after witnessing worldwide devastation from the lethal combination of cyberattacks and kinetic warfare.

• • •

Personally, Lana felt fortunate. Her family had not only survived, it had thrived. Don was living with Emma and her, along with Esme, Tanesa, and Esme's sister and her four children. Esme and her sister's homes in Anacostia had been destroyed in the flood, and even when their insurance money arrived, which was slow in coming for claimants everywhere, the women would be hard-pressed to find affordable housing. But they didn't need to: Lana wouldn't hear of their displacement. Her large house finally felt fully used, and her guests were welcome as long as they needed shelter.

So was Don, she recognized more every day. Last weekend he'd taken her for a cruise on Chesapeake Bay. At first Lana refused to entertain the idea of pleasure boating. But Don told her they'd combine work and fun because he'd contracted with the navy to inspect smaller harbors on Maryland's central shore for newly submerged pilings that could scuttle watercraft.

Don and Lana had motored out on a thirty-four-foot, aluminum hull boat that the navy had stripped of its .50 caliber and 7.62 machine guns, along with the forty-millimeter grenade launchers.

"Too bad," Lana had joked when he'd told her the military had figured he could do without the heavy weaponry.

The day was brilliantly sunny and unusually warm for mid-November. After Don checked on three harbors, they stood gazing at a sailboat in the distance.

"You envious?" she asked.

"Not at all. I'm with you." He slipped his arm around her back. "I'm never going to let you go," he added softly.

"It's not me I'm worried about," she replied. "It's Emma. She's growing closer to you. She needs you. I never would have believed that before you came back, but she does."

"Me either. And it kills me that I missed so much of her growing up. I was a fool. Believe me, I could never leave you guys again."

She slipped out of his grip, but turned to look him in the eye. "You vowed never to leave me once before."

"I'm a different man now. I hope you can see that."

And he was different, it was true. He was brave and loving, but most of all he was with her and the child they had borne.

She took his face in her hands and kissed him.

Three hours passed before they noticed the sun dipping below the western shoreline.

"We better get back," Don said.

"I think we've already started," Lana replied, smiling.

ACKNOWLEDGMENTS

I'd like to thank my literary agent, Howard Morhaim, who represents me well and provides valuable feedback on my writing. Thanks also to his assistant, Kim-Mei Kirtland, who ensures that no detail is overlooked.

I wish to also thank Jason Kirk at 47North for his enthusiasm for my work and helpful editing of my manuscript. I would also like to thank the rest of the 47North team, particularly Britt Rogers and Ben Smith.

Most of all, I thank my readers for their encouragement and their word-of-mouth support.

A number of people were particularly helpful to me in researching and writing this novel. For details on technology and cybersecurity, I thank Andrew J. Cordiner, Jr., Supervisory Special Agent, FBI Cyber Division, Cyberterrorism Unit (CTU); Corey E. Thomas, President and CEO of Rapid7; Benjamin Johnson, Chief Security Strategist at the software and network security services company Bit9 + Carbon Black; and Roger A. Grimes, author, speaker, and a twenty-five-year computer security consultant.

For insights into naval affairs, I thank Admiral William A. Owens, U.S. Navy (retired) and former Vice Chairman of the Joint Chiefs of Staff; Vice Admiral N.R. Thunman, U.S. Navy (retired); and Shawn P. Kelly, submarine officer, U.S. Navy (retired) and CEO of Active Grid Technology.

Any factual mistakes in this novel are mine.

ABOUT THE AUTHOR

Thomas Waite is a best-selling author of cyberthrillers. His debut novel, *Terminal Value*, was critically praised and reached #1 at Amazon. His best-selling second novel, *Lethal Code*, was also widely acclaimed.

Waite is the board director of, and an advisor to, a number of technology companies. His nonfiction work has been published in such publications as *The New York Times* and *Harvard Business Review*.

Waite received his bachelor's degree in English from the University of Wisconsin—Madison and was selected by the English Department to participate in an international study program at the University of Oxford.

Trident Code is Waite's second Lana Elkins Thriller.